JOHNSON'S BIRD

JOHNSON'S BIRD

Alexander Fullerton

MACMILLAN
LONDON

First published in 1989 by
MACMILLAN LONDON LIMITED
4 Little Essex Street London WC2R 3LF
and Basingstoke

Associated companies in Auckland, Delhi, Dublin, Gaborone,
Hamburg, Harare, Hong Kong, Johannesburg, Kuala Lumpur,
Lagos, Manzini, Melbourne, Mexico City, Nairobi, New York,
Singapore and Tokyo

British Library Cataloguing in Publication Data
Fullerton, Alexander, 1924–
    Johnson's bird
    I. Title
    823'.914 [F]

    ISBN 0-333-48902-0

Typeset by Wyvern Typesetting Ltd, Bristol

Printed in Hong Kong

1

I'd been flat out on my bunk; now I was maybe fifty per cent
awake, groping bare-chested and bug-eyed up into the saloon
where the telephone's shrill bleating was wrecking the night's
peace. A telephone in a yacht, heaven's sake . . . Not that you
could call this sleek conveyance a yacht, in any true sense of the
word: it was a rich man's toy, the kind conventionally referred
to as a 'gin-palace', and my connection with it was strictly
temporary and professional – to take it from this present
location – Southampton, England – and deliver it in Cassis on
the French Mediterranean coast.

I make part of my living from delivery jobs, shifting boats of
one kind or another around the world. My own boat is based
in the Mediterranean: she's my home and business too, and
she – the *Bird of Dawning* – truly *is* a yacht.

Will Wyllie, blundering aft from the forward cabin, beat me
to the telephone by a long arm's length.

'Yeah?'

Like a snarl. Even at his best, he's not exactly jolly.

I subsided on to a cushioned bench seat. The interior of this
craft, and its furnishings, smelt more like a new motorcar than
a boat. Will turned – tall, stooping under the low deckhead –
and held the phone out towards me: I was thinking it might be
a girl called Lucy, calling to say goodbye. Lucy did keep

7

'unsocial' hours, and I couldn't think who else this might be. Then I woke up a bit more – to the fact this was Sunday night – Monday morning, rather – so it wasn't likely to be her: and Will growled, 'Some half-pissed sod called Fountain?'

I put the phone to my ear, said something like, 'It's a quarter past two, Tommy, in case you didn't know.'

'Sorry, Matt, *sorry* . . . But – listen – leaving tomorrow, are you?'

The words were rushed more than slurred; Will might have been right, but I'd have put it down to stress more than to alcohol. Anyway the voice was wrong, he sounded like a man under stress. I thought, *Here comes bad news* – and I'd never been more right, although at that moment I'd no idea *how* bad . . . I told him yes, we were shoving off at first light.

'Would you have room for me?'

I hesitated. Looking round to where Will had been hovering but was no longer, having sensibly departed to put his head back down . . . I said into the phone, 'Room, yes. But *time* – that's something else. You'd need to get your skates on, we really are starting at first light, I can't hang about . . . What's up, though?'

I could guess at the basics, from what he'd told me a couple of nights ago in London. Now he was suddenly brighter – a load off his mind – and grateful, thanking me so profusely that from a friend of such long standing it seemed excessive. I cut in with, 'We're in a ritzy set-up called Ocean Village Marina. Quite new, a section of the old Southampton docks. You'll find it easily enough.'

'Right. And I'll explain when I see you. Over the phone it's—'

'Yeah. Boat's name is *Lady Be Good*. Looks like some sort of spacecraft, you couldn't miss her.' I gave him the berth number in the marina. Then hung up, guessing he must have had some monumental bust-up with his wife, and hearing Will Wyllie calling from up forward, 'What was that about?'

I went through, to the luxurious cabin with its own shower and heads. For 'cabin', in fact, you might read 'stateroom' – I'm sure the owner would. Will was flat on his back on the double berth with a blanket over him and his eyes shut. He had his own boat too; in fact we'd come in his to Marseilles, and

8

we'd be picking it up there after depositing this glamour-barge in Cassis. He'd come along because he'd had no charters on hand and he'd wanted to come over, to see his wife and/or children, and I'd needed someone to give me a hand in the passage of the French locks.

I told him, 'Tommy Fountain's a good bloke. We were in the Marines together. Lloyd's underwriter, now.'

'Work all night, does he?'

'He's got wife trouble. May be why he wants to come with us – which is what he was asking. I told him if he's here by dawn, why not?'

'What about the clearance?'

'Yeah. I know.' I'd already cleared through Customs, and obviously there'd been no mention of any passenger. 'Can't be helped, in the circumstances, can it?'

'Well. You're the skipper, Matt.'

Meaning I, not Will, would stand to get rapped over the knuckles for it. As a professional, I didn't like it, it wasn't in my best interests to ignore the rules: but there it was, too bad. Any delay – like hanging around to make another call at Customs – would mean missing the tide up-river from Le Havre.

Getting back into my bunk, I was hoping that this might turn out to be a good thing for all of us. It would be great to have Tommy along – if he could get back to being his old self – and some extra muscle when we were dragging this mobile hotel suite in and out of the locks on the French canals might come in handy. But as much as anything, that 'old self' bit – a break might be just what he needed.

He certainly needed *some* kind of help.

The first I'd known of his problems – wife problems basically, but as he worked for the girl's father there were job complications too (in fact one might debate which had come first, the chicken or the egg) – had been a few nights earlier when he and I had met in London; it was the first time we'd seen each other in years, and I'd been looking forward to it.

But at first sight of him I'd had a shock. He'd looked – the best word for it's *seedy*. I don't mean poor – he was a City slicker now, something to do with Lloyd's of London, and cash-flow was no problem. I mean that he was nothing like the guy I'd served with in the Royal Marines, or known later when we'd both been brand-new civilians. Tommy, like me, had been in the SBS, and if you can hack it over *that* terrain you've no business looking as he was looking that night – like a man running scared or desperate. In your thirties, that's *no* way to look.

(He's four years younger than I am; and last year, when these events were taking place, I was forty-one.)

We met in the Special Forces Club, of which we're both still members. I guessed he'd had a few drinks before he got there, and the first one in the club's bar went down so fast he could hardly have known what was in the glass. I and the third member of the party – a man called Harry Loder, who runs a chandlery and yacht agency in the City and had just started acting as my agent for charters, and who'd joined us because this was the only evening he'd had spare – had barely touched ours before Tommy was ordering the next round; and it went on like this, in the dining-room as well.

None of it did him any good. Or did us any, either. He hardly spoke, and had a tendency to stare glassily while obviously not listening, anyway not hearing. Wrapped up in his own problems: at which, at that stage, one could only guess. For me it was frankly embarrassing: Loder hadn't met him before, and earlier I'd been singing my old chum's praises – and now, this . . . It wasn't surprising that soon after the meal Loder made a show of noticing the time and being surprised by it, having to rush away; I didn't blame him in the least. I took him down and saw him out of the club: apologizing in the hall, 'Sorry I let you in for that.'

'Well – reunions are often disappointing, aren't they . . . But listen, Matt – the minute I get you a few more paying customers, I'll cable. Turkish waters for preference – right?'

'Accent on *paying* customers. Waters immaterial. But – yeah, given the choice, definitely.'

We'd been talking about it, upstairs. Southern Turkey *is* my current preference for charter cruises: the harbours and anchorages are still comparatively uncrowded, the coastline's beautiful as well as smothered in ancient ruins, I like the Turks and find them easy to get along with, their food's good and not expensive, drinks ditto, and – well, the customers are always happy, and what more could a charter skipper want?

Well – short answer is I'd have liked a few more bookings. Loder knew this: he said in parting, 'Don't worry, I've several good prospects for you, and you've got these Lawrie people for a start . . . I'll cable new developments to Lorenzo's – right?'

Lorenzo's is a bar–restaurant in Menorca, owned by a Scottish couple who are friends of mine, and it's my communications base when I'm on that island. I told him, 'I'll be there in about three weeks. Then say a week to get *The Bird* smartened up, and I'll be in the Lazzaretto marina a day or two before the clients arrive.'

A Mr and Mrs Lawrie, whom he'd booked for a Turkish cruise. The only charter he'd lined up for me this summer, so far. It was why I'd had him along this evening. I wasn't by any means the only Med skipper on his books, and maybe the business was going elsewhere, so I'd thought it might be as well to work on the personal relationship. That had been the intention, anyway: and Tommy hadn't noticeably assisted with it.

Although he *had* come alive when Loder and I had been talking about Turkey. Tommy knew the country quite well, still corresponded with Turkish friends acquired during a NATO staff appointment at the Ankara HQ, years ago. He'd reminisced about them, and about local leaves he'd taken on the south coast – where in those days there'd been virtually no tourism at all, hardly a visiting yacht to be seen. He'd muttered, 'God, I'd *love* to be going with you, Matt,' and I'd said, 'Any time – just let me know.'

Then I'd hoped to God I hadn't now committed myself to having him *and* that wife of his on board. When I said just now that I hadn't known he had any problems, I mean that I'd thought he'd somehow made a go of the marriage, contrary to all his friends' earlier expectations. None of us who'd known the girl he'd been marrying had thought he was being anything but a prize idiot, at the time of the wedding. Seven years ago: then, I wouldn't have given it seven months. And now that it was ending on the rocks my guess was that only his dogged perseverance had held it together anything like this long.

I'd said to him, when I got back upstairs after seeing Loder on his way, 'All right, Tommy, let's hear it.'

'Uh?'

Then, God help us, we had to go through it from the start. He'd had that much to drink, it was stored up, ready to flow. But in a nutshell – young heiress, Penny, daughter of City magnate Hugh Benedict, marries dashing young Royal Marine officer, special-force expert with way-out experiences behind him – intriguing background, in fact – who's unwisely fallen madly in love with her . . . Which now, he surely was *not*. He'd caught on to the fact – or pulled his head out of the sand and made himself face up to it – that she was playing around, and being himself dead straight, it had really thrown him: faithlessness, duplicity belonged in some other world, not his. He told me, 'Biggest turn-off you can imagine. For me, anyway. I'd never have believed *anything* could've turned me off her, but – well, Christ, when I was finally sure . . .'

So then it would be *his* fault. As she'd see it, she'd have justification . . . And meanwhile he'd have shed the glamour, the action-man image; in that City world, financial circles, he'd be an also-ran – a basking shark, you might say, in waters cruised by Great Whites as well as whole schools of barracuda.

She'd go for the Great Whites, I guessed. Just as she'd gone for the SBS captain, the SBS reputation for ruthless action. Her interest would be in winners, in the guys with killers' instincts, the sudden swirl of water staining red . . .

Except, in this analogy, for blood read money.

And the bottom line to Tommy's situation was simply that his marriage was a busted flush: so call it a day, get out, was my advice to him.

He'd more or less agreed. But gone on to explain that he'd then be faced with a different kind of problem. Penny's father not only ran that insurance syndicate, he had wide influence in the City. Once Tommy ceased to be Penny's husband, he'd be out in the cold. He hadn't ever really found his feet, and nobody was going to fall over himself to hire a guy who'd only had *that* job through nepotism, and noticeably failed to shine in it.

'What other way do I know of making a living?' He'd picked up his empty glass, peered into it, put it down again . . . 'Only left the Corps because she and the old man convinced me the City'd be my fucking oyster!'

It grated. So much so that my inclination was to say

12

goodnight, let him get on with it. But I controlled the irritation, told him this wasn't *him* talking, that he was no wimp although he was doing his best to sound like one.

Seven years had been too long. They'd worn him down.

And the bar had been closing: just as well, he'd been sinking doubles even faster since Loder had taken off, and it was really showing, he was having to articulate with slow, slurry imprecision. Also, as it happened, I'd had a late date, too; Lucy, who was a dancer, currently performing in a Lloyd Webber show, would be putting her clothes on by now. Tommy had mumbled, 'Been good of you, listening my troubles. Had your own – my God, didn't you . . .'

'Oh.' I shrugged. 'Lot of water under the bridge since then.' (Implying that I was over it by this time. Which was a lie.)

'Didn't come weep on *my* shoulder. Or anyone else's, eh? Compared how I'm acting now, how *you*—'

'The circumstances were completely different, Tommy. There's *no* comparison.'

A car smash on the M3, late at night and in foul weather. My wife, and our toddling-stage daughter. It it hadn't been for me – my own delinquency, which Tommy didn't know about and I wouldn't have *wanted* him to know about, incidentally – she wouldn't have been on that road, driving too fast for the prevailing conditions, and – I guess – somewhat incautiously. Meaning wildly . . . The memory of the smash was visual and horrific – mostly imagined, because I of course wasn't there and nobody'd been able to tell me much about it, but indelible in my imagination, like some horror video re-run each time I was reminded of it. Like now, for instance.

It was the reason I was on my own, have been since that night. The reason my nearest and dearest now is a Swan 48 called *The Bird of Dawning*.

Tommy mumbled to me on our way down to the street, 'Way things've turned out, you're awfully lucky bastard, Matt . . . Can't tell you how much – envy you.'

Meaning – apart from his own clearly *un*enviable situation – that he envied me my freedom, the fact I'm about as independent as a man could be. It was a fact, and still is, I do have this terrific self-sufficiency, and it *is* – to coin a phrase – bloody marvellous. As far as it goes . . . Others had said the same thing, of course, you didn't have to be in Tommy Fountain's unhappy situation to see it. As long as the charterers roll up, and the delivery commissions come in, thus enabling one to pay the bills, maintain the boat, eat and drink . . . But there are snags, of course, and by no means everyone who tries it makes a go of it: what's more, ninety-nine per cent of the people who express envy as Tommy had just done wouldn't ever take the chance themselves. Usually for the best of reasons, of course, reasons like dependants, jobs, responsibilities – whereas in my case the whole thing had been made inevitable by that smash.

At the time, I'd been a farmer. I'd resigned from the Marines two years earlier, ironically enough as the result of a decision to opt for family life. I'd decided – without any prompting from Alison – that either a Service career or family had to come first, if one was to make any real success of either, and that was the choice I'd made. Then it happened, and to have stayed there without her – without *them* – wasn't thinkable. I sold up, took off, and eventually found the *Bird*. I can't say it was ever a planned course of action, it was simply how things had worked out.

Will and I were up and about before dawn that morning. Stars were beginning to fade, the sky clear after yesterday's rain showers; improvement had been expected but probably wouldn't last. We were more or less ready for departure, but there are always a few last-minute jobs, and I was checking the boat's draft when Tommy arrived – on the jetty, shining a torch down at *Lady Be Good*'s glistening white forefoot, when I heard him call my name, then his long strides approaching. It was a relief that he'd already parked his car, hadn't brought so much gear that he'd have needed to drop it off here and then go and park. There'd have been space enough in this millionaire's plaything, but when we transferred to Will's ketch there wouldn't be.

I was checking the draft because we'd trimmed her down – with fully topped-up fuel and fresh-water tanks, etcetera – so as to reduce her above-water height as much as possible. The intention was to top up again with fuel at Le Havre, and tonight when we moored in the Seine we'd be unshipping the twin radio masts and the assembly of radar gear abaft the flying bridge. I'd checked that these were easily removable, and that we had the tools we'd need. The reason for this was that there are height limits in the French inland waterways, bridges to get under, and although from Le Havre to Paris you can get away with nearly six metres, south from Paris it came down to only 3.38. Fortunately – or maybe by design, with this passage in view – *Lady Be Good* had an unusually low profile, in comparison with other motor-cruisers of her type and displacement. Many of them – the larger Princesses, for instance – couldn't have made it.

I swung the torchbeam on to Tommy as he reached us. 'Hi there, Thomas . . .'

He was in a sweater, jeans and anorak, and carrying a sausage-shaped hold-all. I pointed my torch at the gangplank, simultaneously illuminating Will, who was stowing gear in a cockpit locker. 'Step aboard. That's Will Wyllie. We'll be transferring to his boat in Marseilles for the trip out to Menorca – if you elect to stay with us that long . . . Will – Tommy Fountain.'

'Hi.' From the deck, Will extended a long arm for the bag. 'Welcome aboard.'

'Thanks. You're – very kind . . .'

Tommy's voice was thin, and I'd been shocked by what I'd seen in that flare of torchlight. He looked sick, really awful.

Decision time, I thought. He'd walked out on her . . . I checked the draft at *Lady Be Good*'s blunt end and went on board. Will told me gruffly, 'I've put him in the forward cabin. You and I can share, he'll be better up there.' He added something to the effect that I'd told him nothing but the truth, Tommy was no tiddler; but I guessed he'd seen what I had, realized the guy needed rest, peace and quiet.

Or a bed in a hospital.

Will said, 'I'll take the springs off, OK?'

There wasn't all that much hurry. He was being tactful, leaving us to talk. He added, 'And run the blower a while, before we switch on the donks?'

Donks – short for donkeys – engines. They were Volvos, twin 235-horsepower turbocharged diesels. Capable of planing to Le Havre – if we'd been in that much of a rush – at more than 25 knots. The blower would waft potentially explosive fumes out of the bilges; diesel fumes aren't all that combustible, and it mightn't have been necessary – I didn't know any more about it than Will did, neither of us being into powerboats, but we'd embarked fuel only the day before and I agreed, better safe than sorry.

Tommy appeared then, stooping into the saloon's bright light, having dumped his bag and shed the anorak. He said, 'This is a very luxurious barge, isn't it . . . And what have I got, the royal suite?'

Trying to seem casual: and not getting anywhere near it.

'What can I offer you? Tea, coffee – Scotch?'

'Brandy?'

'Sure.' I moved to the bar – forward end, port side, opposite the steps that led up to the internal steering position. 'How d'you want it – soda?'

'As it comes, Matt.'

'Right . . . How did you get the telephone number here?'

'Huh?'

I repeated the question. He said, 'Oh – your agent. Loder. I rang him – woke him up . . . Been up all bloody night, you see.'

'Now you can sleep all day. Except you'll want breakfast. After we clear the Solent, OK?'

'Thanks, but no, I'm not hungry, I'll just—'

'Here.' I'd poured him a stiff tot. 'All right, we'll leave you to it . . . I suppose you've finally bust up with Penny.'

He'd taken a gulp, shut his eyes as the spirit burnt down. Hands shaking so much it was a miracle he'd got it there. Then: 'What did you ask me?'

'This pierhead jump – why, Tommy?'

'It's – oh, God – long story . . . Tell you the truth, I can't seem to – well . . .' Tongue-tied, looking around as if he'd forgotten where he was, or why— 'Christ, it's – *nightmare* . . . I don't think – here and now, I doubt I'd make sense of it.'

'Don't bother, then. Sleep on it.'

'Yeah.' He half smiled: an attempt at a smile, rather. 'You're a pal, Matt. Always were.' He took another swallow. Then: 'Look . . . You said just now that if I wanted I could travel to Menorca with you. But – how about Turkey? Would that be too much – I mean, could I work my passage?'

16

'I don't see why not.'

'D'you *mean* it?'

'Only thing is, you said "work your passage", but I expect you'd have to stay with us, leave with us. Not just take passage and stay there, I mean.'

'Oh?' He was looking at me curiously. 'Why?' He went on, the words spouting in a rush, 'I'd thought I'd park myself on that guy – Turks I was telling you about, they have this hotel now—'

I cut in, stemming the flow – 'Local regulations say it, Tommy, not me. Crew lists have to be the same on departure as when you enter. Same in Greece, actually.'

'And they check, do they?'

I shrugged. 'In the season, they couldn't, not as routine. Too many boats coming and going all the time. But you could stay with your friends, then I'd pick you up again?'

'Right. Right . . .'

The prospect of a Turkish cruise seemed to do him a lot of instant good. And maybe the brandy . . . But I was thinking, thirty or forty minutes later when we cast off our lines and motored slowly out of the marina, taking care not to make too much wash with those powerful, deep-throated engines, that a good long sleep and then a few days' fresh air might be all he needed.

Ignorance – as has been said before, a few times – is bliss. And there could hardly have been a prettier fool's paradise. It was a really lovely morning, the sort of day on which it's a waste *not* to be up to see the sun rise; and the best place to see it is surely on the water. I remembered what Tommy had said to me a few days earlier – how lucky he thought I was, etcetera – and I remarked to Will, 'You know, we're probably among the most fortunate guys on earth?'

He glanced at me over his shoulder. A hunch to the shoulders, and long legs, long nose – he has the look of a somewhat lugubrious heron. We were on the *Lady Be Good*'s flying bridge, the upper steering position, with the new day's glitter on the water, a layer of sea mist floating, sky still milky but with a hint of colour in it too, a pastel tinge that would be hardening into brilliance soon after we'd left the Nab astern. Will took a long breath of the clean, salt air, muttered grudgingly as he turned away, 'Could be right . . .'

There's nothing special to record about the cross-Channel passage. The boat gave us no problems; averaging 18 knots, well within her engines' capacity – settling down to that, admittedly, after an early burst of speed just to see what it felt like – we had Cap de la Hève abeam to port in just over six hours, and I was reckoning on a night's mooring well up beyond Rouen – as far as we could get, making the best of a flood tide and of the Seine's speed limit of eight knots. That's the maximum for craft displacing up to 20 tons; big ships are allowed to plough along at thirteen and a half. But we'd get well up-river to some quiet mooring, and have time to dismantle the topside clutter before dark.

We'd left Tommy to sleep, and as far as I know he'd been flat out all the way. Since he'd told me he wasn't interested in food, we didn't disturb him when we had breakfast soon after clearing Spithead, or later when I made sandwiches for lunch. I left a couple of sandwiches in the fridge though, so that if he woke up hungry he'd find them there, where the beer was too.

Lady Be Good was creaming into the Seine estuary, following the buoyed route and with the intention of turning in to the fuelling quay presently, when a French police launch which had come out on an interception course slid into close company on our quarter and a guy with a loud-hailer requested us to stop engines. My only reaction – apart from complying – was to hope that whatever this was in aid of, it wouldn't take long. We'd nothing to hide, and the boat's papers were in order; I guessed it would be some kind of spot check, for smugglers or drug-runners.

Except these were fuzz, not Customs . . .

We lay wallowing, the launch ran alongside – Will chucking out some of the extra fenders we'd embarked for use in the canal locks – and three Frogs scrambled on board. One was in plain-clothes, the other two uniformed. Will took their line and secured it, and I heard him trying out his French and not getting much response. Then they were crowding into the saloon – under my feet – and he trailed in after them, complaining, 'Look, if you'd tell me what you *want* . . .'

18

Rude awakening imminent for Tommy, I thought. I also wondered whether this boat had some kind of history. I wouldn't have thought she'd been in the water long enough for that. But the owner might be bent, of course – previous or new owner, whichever ... I'd never met either party; nor had Harry Loder, who'd fixed up the delivery contract for me.

There were no other craft near enough to be any danger, and no navigational hazards, and anyway the Frog crew were there alongside and presumably wouldn't let anything run us down, so in the hope of getting this over quickly I went down into the open stern cockpit and ducked into the saloon. Warning myself to be cooperative – knowing I've a tendency to over-react when faced with high-handed officialdom.

Will told me over his shoulder, 'Looking for a Monsieur Fontaine, he says.'

Fontaine ...

I wondered what they might want with Tommy. By this time they'd inspected the smaller cabin – mine – and were trooping forward between the open galley and the door of the heads and shower. Checking in there too ... I called, 'Can I help you?' – mainly as a warning to Tommy, so at least he'd have his eyes open before they burst in ... But just then Will turned in the cabin doorway, looking puzzled: he'd been peering into that fore cabin over the Frenchmen's shoulders. Taking another peek now: *just* like an old heron. But as I closed up behind him he swung round and muttered what sounded to me like 'Not there ...'

I edged in past him; and the group opened up – Will and the nearer cop letting me squeeze by, and the other uniformed one moving further into the cabin so that I and their boss were now face to face. He was about my own age – burly, with sideburns and dark hair with a shine of oil on it. Flat, dark eyes: focussing over my shoulder now, telling the guy out there to check in the engine space.

'You are Monsieur –' he had a notebook open in one hand, and glanced down at it, then back up '– Monsieur Johnson?'

Behind him, the double bunk had nobody in it or on it. There were these two Frenchmen in the cabin, and me, and no one else.

I nodded. 'Right.'

19

'Your passports, if you please, and your English clearance paper.'

I didn't have far to go to fetch them. He told me as he took them from me, 'I search a Monsieur Fontaine.' He'd pronounced it as a French name, and corrected, 'Fountain?'

Frowning, finding no such name listed. Then flipping through both passports: and apparently hanging on to them . . . Glancing round to where a green hold-all gaped open, unzipped. Will Wyllie's, not the one Tommy had brought with him. That one wasn't in sight – and I had just enough sense not to look around for it. Obviously Will hadn't moved his stuff out before Tommy had turned in.

At this moment I wasn't sure how to play it. Not knowing whether they'd know for sure he *had* been here . . .

The detective asked me, 'You have acquaintance with Monsieur Fountain?'

I nodded. 'Why, what is all this, what's—'

'Where did you put him on shore?'

'Put him – ashore?' I frowned: turned to glance at Will – committing myself and him, now, telling the Frenchman, 'I really don't know what you're talking about.'

It was a risk that had had to be taken: coming off the fence, assuming not only that Tommy wasn't on board but also that he'd left no traces. The fact that his bag had vanished with him seemed to justify the gamble. Whatever this was, it couldn't be in Tommy's interests to tell them more than one had to. In any case, one didn't *know* . . .

Thank God this guy hadn't asked me – or asked Will, when he'd first climbed on board – the straight question.

Now he gestured towards the hold-all.

'This is yours?'

'Mine.' Will's voice, behind me. *Lady Be Good* rocking in the wash of some passing ship, and the other policeman was back – in the doorway displacing Will – telling his boss that the engine-room contained only machinery. That hostile stare was on me again now, as if he was trying to force his way into my thoughts. It was as well he couldn't, because – to my shame – they weren't pleasant, at that moment. I was remembering how Tommy had sounded on the telephone in the middle of the night, and the state he'd been in when he'd arrived on board, and what he'd told me in London about his marital affairs. The scenario to which all this contributed was by any standards highly *un*pleasant: but you can't help this or that coming into your mind, not if you're cursed with an imagination, and I was already confused with the riddle of where and how he could have left us.

Which led to another supposition – morbid enough to fit neatly with the first one – that Tommy might not be alive now, might have gone over the side.

Well – the stern. He *could* have done, without us seeing it happen, somewhere out in mid-Channel maybe.

No need to look for motive. Remembering the state he'd been in, one might have guessed – even anticipated . . .

But then another question: whatever their reason for wanting to talk to him – or to arrest him, whatever – how had they known he might have been with us?

I told the Frenchman, 'I'll be on deck.' Will was out there somewhere, but this expensive contraption was still my responsibility. The delivery contract said I had to park it in the harbour at Cassis in good order, and I have a professional reputation to maintain. The Frog said, behind me, 'The explanation, Monsieur, is simple.' Glancing back, I saw him poking at Will's hold-all – turning the label with a forefinger, pretending he was just fiddling . . . He said, 'It is that I have instructions to detain you. A *request*, I should say, from London . . . If there has been some error, therefore, it is not ours – you understand?'

'You said – *detain* us?'

'Until the arrival of your police from England.'

Will, returning, had heard this . . . 'How long we going to be stuck here, then?'

'Per'aps not so very long time, Monsieur . . .'

'Meaning all bloody afternoon – right?'

Bang went hopes of that nice, quiet mooring above Rouen . . . I was beginning to think that maybe I should have told them the truth because they'd probably end up getting to it anyway.

Except I didn't know what the truth *was*.

'If you will be so good, Messieurs'– as we arrived out in the open, in the stern cockpit, our appearance triggered activity in

21

the launch alongside – 'please to follow, to where you can tie up?'

It was more than five hours before a French police car brought Inspector Harrison of the CID to the wharf where we'd been obliged to sit and wait. They'd allowed us to refuel – staying with us and watching every move – but since then we'd been stuck here. Two uniformed men had been left with us, and Customs had paid us a visit – which was something; we wouldn't need to visit *them* now – afternoon was growing into evening, and when Harrison finally arrived Will and I weren't in any mood to greet him with sunny smiles.

He introduced himself, showed us his warrant card, and said he was from the Chelsea nick. This figured, since Chelsea is where Tommy and Penny Fountain live.

Or lived.

I told him, 'We'd planned to be the other side of Rouen by now. So if you'd just tell us what we're being held here for—'

'Not exactly *held*, sir. More a case of assuming you'd want to help us with our inquiries.'

'That's quite an assumption. Considering no one's told us what the inquiries are about.'

'Well, you've a point there, I suppose.' He was still out of breath. A thickset, pale man, seemingly none too fit. He'd climbed awkwardly down the vertical iron ladder from the quay, and he was looking back at it now with resentment, as if he thought that had been a lot to ask of him. His attention came back to me: 'No question, they should've told you. Language problems, I suppose – always tricky . . . Anyway – thanks for being so patient.'

The Frog detective was on the quayside, I saw. I pointed, and told Harrison, '*He* said he was looking for Tommy Fountain. But Fountain's not with us – as he saw for himself bloody hours ago – and I'm not feeling the least bit patient.'

'I know . . . That's to say, I can – guess . . .' He nodded to Will. 'Mr Wyllie, isn't it?' Will nodded, but didn't speak, and the policeman asked me, 'Can we sit, somewhere?'

I pushed the sliding door back and led him into the saloon: we'd shut the doors to keep out some of the shoreside industrial and biological smells. I said as we distributed ourselves around the small, rectangular space, 'If you wouldn't mind making it quick, Inspector, we might still get some way up-river before sunset.'

'Sure.' He opened a notebook on the table in front of him, poised a ballpoint. 'Sure. And – apologies for the inconvenience . . . But believe me, it was unavoidable. Primarily because – as you know – we need to put a few questions to Captain Fountain—'

'Yeah – what about?'

'—and we've had reason to believe he left Southampton in this – er – vessel . . . Now you've said he did *not* join you there. For the record – *my* record – would you confirm this?'

'If he had, he'd have been on board, wouldn't he? We didn't touch land anywhere – or have contact with any other boat—'

'Might he have swum ashore, somewhere or other?'

'If he'd been on board in the first place, I suppose he might. But God knows where or why.'

'Ah, well, there *is* a small point there . . . Since Captain Fountain was – like you, sir – in the Special Boat Squadron of the Royal Marines, one could assume he must be – again, like you – an unusually strong swimmer?'

'As it happens, yes. But *why* would he—'

'You're positive he didn't join you at Southampton?' Harrison glanced at Will: 'You'd corroborate this, Mr Wyllie?'

'Sure.' Will scowled. 'Why would you think he'd lie to you?'

The ballpoint completed another note, and Harrison turned to me again without having answered that question.

'When did you last speak with Captain Fountain, Mr Johnson?'

I wondered why he kept calling me 'Mr' while referring to Tommy as 'captain'. The 'mister' was right, in fact; I'd left the Marines and left my rank behind me too, but the same applied to Tommy, and you'd have thought he'd have been more consistent. Maybe Penny had liked the 'captain' bit, and hung on to it . . . But something more immediate had just registered: I'd been about to answer Harrison's question with 'Four nights ago, in London,' when I'd suddenly caught on to the way he'd phrased it – *speak with* . . . Then I'd seen how he was watching me – like a hunter waiting beside a trap, or a copper thinking he was being bloody smart.

23

I said, 'If you mean face to face, about four nights ago. But actually he telephoned me last night – between two and three in the morning.'

I saw a flicker of – well, it might have been disappointment. I felt sure he'd known about that call.

'Mind telling me why he was ringing at that time of night, sir?'

'No, I don't mind. Although it's bound to stir up the suspicions you seem to have already ... He rang to ask whether we'd have room for him, take him with us. It wasn't exactly a bombshell of an idea, he'd said in London how he'd have loved to have been coming along, so—' I shrugged. 'OK, it was an odd time to telephone, but we were on the point of leaving, and he knew it – so if he'd just made up his mind ... Well, there you are.'

'In the event, he did *not* join you?'

I nodded. 'As I've mentioned, several times.'

'But you didn't think of mentioning that he'd had the intention of doing so?'

'No, I didn't.'

'Did you tell him he could join you?'

'If he could make it by first light, yeah. But we weren't waiting, we had a schedule to keep to.' I nodded to the policeman. 'Which is now shot to hell, incidentally ... And he didn't show up, so we left without him – as I'd warned him we would.'

'He's an old friend of yours, and – well, former comrade in arms, clearly rather a special friend, would I be right in saying?'

'Yes.'

'Such a close chum, *very* keen on making the trip with you – keen enough to have phoned in the middle of the night – and you'd have enjoyed his company, no doubt?'

I nodded.

'You wouldn't have waited even an hour, say?'

'You have to draw a line somewhere, don't you? We couldn't even have been certain he was coming. I'd given him a deadline, and that was it.'

'So you weren't sure that he was positively *intending*—'

'From what he said – as I understood it – he did at that time

24

intend to come.' I glanced at the electric clock – on the bulkhead above the conning position . . . 'Is this going to take much longer?'

'Did he sound – well, in good spirits?'

'Christ, I don't know! This was the middle of the bloody night, I was fast asleep when the thing rang, I wasn't analysing—'

'Would you say – from as much as you *can* recall – that he was sober?'

'I've no idea. He made perfectly good sense.'

'Emotional, maybe?'

'How d'you mean?'

'Well. Such a sudden decision, in the small hours of the night, might have been precipitated by some kind of emotional crisis or' – the ballpoint waved – 'a row of some kind. Domestic upset, for instance. In which case you might have had some inkling—'

'No, I didn't.'

'No – inkling . . .' Scribbling again . . . 'Now, Mr – Johnson . . . Being such old friends, one might guess you'd have few secrets from each other. So I wonder whether you can tell me anything about Captain Fountain's relationship with his wife.'

'I'm afraid I can't.'

'Did he never say anything about his marriage?'

'If he had, he'd have said it in confidence.'

'But surely—'

'And I wouldn't have – have made any mental note of it . . . Look, if you've asked all the relevant questions now, Inspector, ones that have anything to do with me or with this boat—'

'Ah, well, as it happens, the question of Captain Fountain's marriage is *very* relevant . . . You – er – know his wife, I take it?'

I nodded. No need to tell him I'd never liked her.

'Did you see her during your recent stay in England?'

'No.' I held his stare. 'And I still can't see the point of—'

'The point, Mr Johnson, is that Mrs Fountain is dead.' His pale eyes held mine, intently: he told me, 'She died violently, last night.'

That flight of imagination I'd allowed myself earlier on came back in a rush. Although it still didn't add up, knowing

25

Tommy as I did . . . I heard my own voice repeating those last words – 'Died – *violently*—'

'Of a broken neck.'

That fell flatly into the silence – which lay strictly between him and me, Will Wyllie mightn't have been there at all . . . Harrison added – timing these pronouncements carefully, doubtless for effect and for my reactions – 'According to our initial estimate, not long before Captain Fountain telephoned you.' And then – well, I suppose this impression was actually retrospective and part of the sense of confusion that a shock can bring, but at the time it was as if I'd pre-heard this next bit, known it was coming before he'd begun to ask it: 'You'd maybe correct me on this, Mr Johnson . . . In your SBS – you'd know how to break a person's neck?'

2

That evening, while *Lady Be Good* was making her rather frustratingly slow progress up the Seine, playbacks of that long question-and-answer session with the police inspector kept flickering through my mind. In conversation with Will Wyllie too – with some variations in our respective memories, exactly what had or had not been said, as well as the implications.

I kept telling myself that I was certain Tommy Fountain couldn't have murdered his wife. I told Will too – probably for about the fourth time, wanting him to accept it, *believe* it.

He grimaced . . . 'Yeah, I know. Your old chum. Fellow Marine. Never let it be said, etcetera . . .' A shrug: 'You may be right, too . . . They have any kids, by the way?'

They hadn't. I've no idea why, the subject hadn't ever come up. If I'd had to guess at a reason I'd have thought maybe Penny hadn't wanted her style cramped.

Will muttered, 'Just as well, you might say.'

I knew Will was thinking we should have told Harrison the truth. After the policeman had left us – so late that we didn't get anywhere near Rouen before we had to stop for the night – although he didn't actually say it, it was obviously in his mind, so I mentioned it, saying that *I* wished we could have come clean with Harrison – except it would only have amounted to admitting we'd lied in the first place.

'Then we'd have been saddled with trying to explain the inexplicable – what *did* happen to him. And *why* didn't we admit he'd been on board? He'd have found all this very difficult to believe, and he'd have learnt nothing from it that could have helped him much, anyway.'

'Except the guy was *there*, in Southampton, at that time.'

'But he knew it. All that stuff about the car.'

Harrison had told me, latish in the interview, 'It's *very* surprising to me, Mr Johnson, that he never did join you. It's more of a puzzle than I think you realize.'

'I was surprised too. I thought he'd make it easily. With about three hours, and empty roads.'

'Oh, but I'm sure he *did*. That is, timewise.'

I glanced at Will, saw he was lost too. Harrison said – smooth as silk: 'You see, his car was in the marina's car-park. Peugeot, silver-grey, this year's registration.' He added, his pale eyes on mine like probes, 'Still there mid-morning.'

'Well.' I looked at Will again. 'What d'you know . . . Must have just missed us.'

'What time did you start, Mr Johnson?'

'Five-thirtyish. It's in the log.' I pointed. 'There.'

He went to the inside conning position, opened the soft-covered log and copied the exact time of departure into his notebook. Returning, he murmured – as if communing with his own thoughts, although of course it was for me to hear – 'If the night watchman had that vehicle's arrival time logged – I didn't talk to him myself, but I think he would have, maybe, a car arriving at dawn or earlier, wouldn't you say?' I shrugged; he went on, 'I mean, if we could prove the car was parked there *before* you left – well, how would you react – Mr Wyllie?'

Will started – like a kid in class, inattentive and suddenly jumped on . . . He was already having his doubts, I guessed. Thinking that this guy Fountain surely *had* done his wife in, and that he, Will Wyllie, had now become an accessory after the fact of murder . . . He shook his head, and passed me the question: 'Huh?'

I said, 'I'd wonder what the hell Tommy had been playing at. It wouldn't have made any sense.'

'More likely' – Will muttered – 'he arrived after we went. Maybe got lost or something, couldn't find the place.'

'Then what? Just left his car, went walkabout in Southampton?' Harrison asked me, 'When you saw him earlier in the week, he said he'd like to join you – that's what you told me, right?'

'Not quite. I told you he said *in general terms* how he'd have liked to be in my shoes, free to swan off to the Med with us.'

'To escape from a marriage that was – somewhat less than happy, might one guess?'

'I thought we'd finished with that line of questioning.'

'Well, we left it, didn't we . . . But are you quite sure he didn't mean it more – more positively? More like would you take him along, please?'

'Damn sure he didn't. If he had, I'd have said yes, and he wouldn't have had any reason to make that call, would he?'

'Oh, last-minute check, maybe, making sure you hadn't left without him . . .' Harrison turned back to Will: 'I take it *you* had no idea there'd be a passenger, until he rang?'

'No idea at all.'

'It's so coincidental, you see. I mean, the way it strikes an outsider's eye.' Quiet, thoughtful, taking us into his confidence . . . 'You meet him in London, tell him when you're expecting to leave, he says how he'd love to go along with you . . .' A new thought struck him: 'He'd have known *where* you were going, would he?'

'Yeah. The Med. Cassis, to dump this, then from Marseilles back to Menorca, then a charter party to be picked up in Malta . . . But tell *me* something, would you?' Harrison raised his eyebrows, waiting for it; I asked him, 'How did you know Tommy Fountain had any idea of coming down to Southampton?'

'Well, his call to you—'

'How did you know about it?'

'From that friend of yours – the agent, Mr Loder. Captain Fountain telephoned him, shortly after two a.m., to ask where he might find you. Loder gave him your telephone number in the marina, and went back to sleep. Then he was thinking about it while he was shaving, and certain aspects worried him to the extent that when he got to his office he rang your number – getting no answer, of course, that extension having been disconnected, I suppose, since you'd started out several

29

hours before that . . . So, he looked up the Fountains' number and tried that.'

'What for?'

'Your friend – Captain Fountain – had sounded like he was in a panic. In some kind of fix, not just *wanting* to get hold of you, but – well, sort of desperate. Mr Loder says he felt responsible, having given him your number; my guess is more likely he was – well, say *curious*? And you see, *we* picked up his call to the Fountain house. We were there, Mrs Fountain's maid had arrived just after eight thirty and found her body, dialled nine-nine-nine, and – that's it, that's where we come into the picture.'

'So you had it from Loder.'

'Right. And *your* questions get full and frank answers, Mr Johnson, did you notice?'

By this stage he'd got all he could hope to get out of me; at least, it was obvious that scratching away at the same spots wasn't getting him anywhere. He'd already said, as a preliminary to departure, 'We know where to find you if we need to, anyway.'

'Loder. He'll know where.'

'Exactly . . .'

But I took him up on that remark about getting complete answers to questions, and he backed off, more or less apologized, but then we were back at it again, beating around the same old bushes . . . 'Dead-ends are frustrating, aren't they? I'm facing several – one being Captain Fountain's recent movements, and since we know he was coming to join you – and that he did get there—'

'Presumably, after we'd gone.'

That pale stare: he repeated, his tone mildly sardonic – '*Presumably* . . .'

There was something I wanted to check on, a detail I hadn't consciously noticed earlier but must have done because it was in my mind's eye now like a snapshot. Unless I'd imagined it, just *thought* I'd seen it . . . It would only take seconds to check, but not with this guy around. He'd just murmured, 'Well. That's about it, I suppose. For the time being . . .'

Actually on the move, he'd shut his notebook. Then opened it again. 'Look.' Scribbling numbers on a blank page: he tore it out, slid it towards me. 'That's my place of work, and that's home. In case *you* ever wanted to telephone at two in the morning . . . But if you heard from him, or of him. Or for that matter – ' a pause for effect ' – if you happened to remember anything you haven't told me.'

A small, quick smile: and the unspoken words being something like *the truth, for instance* . . . I'd had the feeling, surprisingly, that although we were on opposite sides of the fence in this, we quite liked each other. I put in a final word for Tommy – an appeal, really – as we filed out into the cockpit: 'One thing I *can* tell you – because I'm certain of it – is Fountain didn't do it. *Couldn't* have. I really do know that guy, and I swear to you—'

'Not an uncommon reaction, Mr Johnson.' He murmured – preoccupied, looking up at the iron dockside ladder, plainly not relishing the fact he was going to have to climb it – 'People do often find it difficult to see their close friends as murderers.'

He made it, all right. Then stayed on the quayside, keeping the French waiting, until one of them had cast off our lines. He waved goodbye then: an odd thing to do, I thought, considering it was fairly obvious he thought I'd helped a killer to get away.

He'd only been doing his job, of course. For Tommy's sake, I hoped he was good at it. This started a different train of thought – which I shelved for the moment because I had that other item to see to. I waited until Will came up to join me on the flying bridge, having coiled the mooring lines, and asked him to take over for a minute.

'Have one for me, while you're at it.'

I went down, and forward, hearing the diesels' note thicken as Will opened the throttles. And why not, we'd be in the river soon and down to that limit of eight knots.

Then I was in the forward cabin, the one we'd put Tommy in, and at a glance I saw that the image in my mind had been accurate. The transparent overhead hatch was shut but not clipped. The two short clips hung loose; reaching up one-handed I could easily push the hatch open.

It wasn't intended as a way of entry or exit – no more than a car's sunroof is. It was primarily a skylight, but hinged at its leading edge, and rubber-seated, you could open it upwards,

31

engaging that raised edge on a metal strut, so in harbour you'd have ventilation, and under way – in a reasonably calm sea – you'd get a wind-suck effect. When it was shut, though, you'd fasten it with the clips; and before Tommy had come aboard it *had* been shut and clipped. When a seaman shuts any hull or deck aperture he shuts it properly; otherwise the unsecured hatch or scuttle, whatever, can easily be overlooked – until a strong blow, let alone a heavy sea crashing over the bow, flips it open.

I happen to know that it had been shut. We'd been preparing the boat for sea, and having turned out, vacated the cabins, checking that sort of item was instinctive, second nature.

Pushed right up, it left an aperture big enough – at a pinch – even for Tommy Fountain's width of shoulder. Standing there in the cabin I could see it happening – see him pushing that hold-all out then grabbing the edges and pulling himself up, wriggling out. In the marina at Southampton, this would have been, in the half-hour before we sailed: it had to have been then, because once we'd shoved off one of us had been permanently on the bridge, ninety-five per cent of the time looking out over the bow.

So he'd jumped ship, surreptitiously, decided to sneak ashore, stay in England. God only knew why – what could have been in his mind, and how come he hadn't passed out within seconds of thumping his weight down on that bunk.

Or why he couldn't have just come along and told me he'd changed his mind.

I fastened the clips, and went up to join Will.

'Feeling better?'

'I'll take her, if you like.'

I didn't tell him what I'd found. I knew he thought Tommy probably *had* killed his wife, and he'd already backed me up with a lie – at least, in not telling Harrison the whole truth; it seemed wiser not to burden him with yet more information which I didn't intend offering to the police. And he confirmed his own view of the situation, that scepticism about Tommy, at dusk that evening, when we'd secured to some riverside pilings for the night and were busy dismantling those aerials and other removable bits and pieces, to reduce *Lady Be Good*'s height in the water. He broke a silence with: 'What that Harrison guy said about how people see their friends – I reckon it makes sense, Matt. I'm not saying your pal did it, but – well, he's scarpered, hasn't he ... And the timing of those phone calls—'

'I know how it looks. If I was in your place I'd have the same idea. I just happen to know him – and he'd need to have been bombed out of his mind.'

'Maybe was ... People don't usually kill each other when they're calm and collected, do they? Well, some might ... Finished with that wrench?' I passed it over. He muttered, grunting as he put some weight on it, 'Anyway, if you're right, he probably won't have to worry. Blokes like that Harrison know what they're about, I'd say.'

I hoped he was right. And wished to God there was something I could do. The feeling I had was of leaving a friend in the lurch.

It was dark before we'd finished dismantling the gear. We went down and cleaned ourselves, and had a little fortifying Scotch while Will made supper – scrambled eggs and sausages – and while he was slaving over his hot stove I tuned the radio to catch a late BBC news bulletin – thinking there might be some mention of the Fountain murder.

There was. The first part of it was about the Gulf, the peculiar antics of the Iranians. Then – startling in its immediacy – *Police in London, investigating the death of Mrs Penelope Fountain in her Chelsea house last night, are anxious to trace the whereabouts of the dead woman's husband, former Royal Marine captain Thomas Fountain. Captain Fountain, an insurance underwriter at Lloyd's of London since leaving the Marines seven years ago, has disappeared after driving his car from London to Southampton in the early hours of this morning. Aged 38, he is described as six feet four inches tall, of powerful physique, with brown hair and blue eyes ...*

We were into a weather forecast, then. Rain-showers from the south-west, bright intervals ...

'Jesus, Will—'

'Yeah.' Stirring his egg mixture, he reached left-handed for his whisky. 'Couldn't doubt it, could you, just hearing that?'

Even the 'powerful physique' bit added its own quota,

33

impression of a dangerous killer on the loose.

I switched off the radio. Admitting to myself that in fact it wasn't easy to think how else it could have been worded. A woman had been murdered, her husband had vanished, the police wanted to talk to him: nothing but the truth . . . Will said, 'Beats me how that bloke Harrison doesn't bloody *know* the guy sailed with us. Why else would he have left his motor in the park there? When they knew he was planning on joining us – so bloody obvious, isn't it?'

'I suppose . . .'

'So Harrison knows we weren't being straight with him. He *must* do . . . Here you go.'

Food, in lavish amounts.

'Marvellous, Will!'

'Well. Must say I'm ready for it.' He sat down with his own. 'Tell you what I think, shall I?' I nodded, with my mouth full, and he pointed aft with his knife. 'Went over, finished it. Sorry, Matt – your old chum, all that – but I can't see how else.'

'OK.'

'You agree?'

'No, fuck it, I do not! I say he didn't kill anyone, so why should he kill himself? Another thing – when you saw him, when he came on board, OK, he was like some kind of spook, but by the time he went to turn in he was definitely on the mend. He even talked about coming to Turkey with me on this charter, for instance, he was all for it. *That's* not suicidal, is it?'

Will only grunted; then we were silent for a while – if two hungry men eating scrambled egg and sausages can be called silent – and with my mind on Tommy as I'd last seen him, disappearing into the forward cabin – where I'd assumed he'd have passed out immediately – I wondered if that half-tumbler of brandy might have kept him awake. As drink can, even when it's called a nightcap, when you're very tired. I imagined him lying there wide awake, his mind suddenly clear and active: deciding to sneak ashore, stay in England . . .

And leave this false trail, have the fuzz believe he'd left the country?

Or Will's theory – that he'd drowned himself.

Or – maybe much more likely – wanted it to look as if he had . . .

34

Leaving his car in the marina park would fit well into either scenario. Mightn't be a bad dodge at all, for someone who needed to disappear. And if this was as logical a solution as I thought it was, wouldn't Harrison see it the same way?

Over mugs of instant coffee, I muttered something about this feeling of running out on a friend when he was in trouble; and the still rather vague idea of getting in touch with Harrison – he'd given me his phone number, after all – and trying to convince him Tommy wasn't the type to go around killing people, that SBS training wasn't all that likely to turn a perfectly decent bloke into Jack the Ripper.

Will put his mug down, stared at me. 'Can't see much mileage in it, Matt.'

'Well, maybe not, but – look, you heard the broadcast, didn't you? At least there'd be someone on Tommy's side, arguing his case for him . . . OK, I'd have to come clean on one or two points, but – might be a lot better than unanimous, total acceptance of "Former Marine captain Fountain murdered his wife" – when anyone who *knows* him could tell them he wouldn't hurt a bloody fly?'

Will shrugged. '*I* don't hurt flies, much, but I could've bust Liz's neck for her, a few times.'

He and his wife Liz are separated – not in the legal sense, but by mutual preference. She has her own business, somewhere in Surrey, mail-order women's fashion, which I think originally he set up jointly with her.

'Look, Matt.' He began to speak slowly and carefully, as if he might have been addressing a halfwit. 'It's in the cops' hands, they know their business, they aren't going to shoot him on sight, you know . . .'

Etcetera, etcetera . . .

I didn't argue with him. He meant well, but there were a couple of things he couldn't have understood – especially as he is, frankly, a rather selfish man – and I wasn't going to waste time trying to explain. The first was that like all Royal Marines of comparatively recent vintage I'd been brought up to respect what's called the buddy-buddy system – which may sound unhealthily cosy but amounts, broadly speaking, to sticking by your friends. And in my own case there was a much more personal motivation, too. It's to do with that horror on the motorway; only three people, apart from me, knew about it. One of them is the girl who was the reason why Alison – my wife – was in such a rush to get home that night, and what it adds up to is *I* killed my wife and daughter.

Then opted out, and ended up with the *Bird of Dawning* and living – in Tommy Fountain's view, for instance – what might be called the life of Reilly.

What I'm saying is that for a long time I'd felt I owed somebody something.

We didn't sit around for long. It had been a long day, and the idea was to make another early start, squeeze as big a mileage as we could out of each stretch of daylight hours.

I thought I *would* telephone Harrison. But right now the sensible thing to do was sleep on it. I said goodnight to Will, and that was that.

Or should have been. In fact I'd been turned-in for about thirty seconds when I heard him blundering aft, yelling at me. Then the cabin door crashed open, the light came on, and there was Will with a look of excitement on his face and some object in his hand. Holding it out towards me: 'Found this in my bag!'

A money-belt, as advertised for use by people travelling and wanting to keep funds safe from pickpockets. About two inches wide, soft leather with a fabric lining and a long zip-fastener in the fabric. Will displayed it to me: pulling the zip open over a long bulge of contents, folding back the edges with his thumbs so as to tip those contents out onto my bunk. A wad of sterling notes – it was in tens and twenties, and when I counted it it came to exactly £250 – and a sheaf of American Express dollar traveller's cheques in denominations of $50, each of them already signed once by T. Fountain: total, $1500.

If my guess was right, he'd only have been in that cabin for maybe ten or fifteen minutes; and in that time, for some reason of his own which at this moment I couldn't guess at, apparently he'd stuffed this bundle of currency into Will Wyllie's hold-all.

'Take a look at *this*.'

A sheet of off-white paper with computer printing on it and the letterhead of a bank in Zurich, Switzerland. It listed not cash, but securities, international bonds. Total value – the figure in the bottom right corner – I shifted it so the light would fall on it better—

'Well, well . . .'

At two-and-a-half Swiss francs to the pound, which I thought would be near enough the going rate, it came to about seventeen thousand pounds.

No name on it, just a number.

Will said, 'Now we *know* he drowned.'

I didn't sleep. At any rate not for a long time. Then it wasn't real sleep but that kind of half-waking, half-conscious mental battle between rational thought and way-out reaches of the imagination, flickering in and out of dreams like an aeroplane alternately in and out of cloud.

Some of it made sense.

I saw Tommy in that bow cabin – needing the full length of the bunk, as he would – with the brandy driving his pulses fast, heart thumping and brain hyperactive with images of what had been and thoughts of what might lie ahead.

And maybe the feeling that being here on board the *Lady Be Good* was a mistake. The police weren't stupid, they'd trace him here. The car, for instance – they'd have its description, registration number, and the marina people might be on the ball – a motor they hadn't seen here before, apparently abandoned in the car-park. Then the police would want to know which boat or boats had left early this morning: name of skipper, destination . . .

Even if it took them two or three days, they'd have this boat targeted long before she was out of the French waterways.

I saw him shift on the bunk then, reacting to the discomfort of the money-belt's thickness under him. Hands moving to the buckle, unfastening it, raising himself on the bunk to get it off, then groping through the dark for his zip-bag: jerking it open, pushing the bundle in.

Unaware he's put it in Will Wyllie's bag, not his own.

Flopping back: staring up at the slow beginnings of dawn in the glass panel overhead. Working out what to do, whether to stay or go: and if to go – where, how . . .

How – the first part of *how* – is easy. He's looking at it, at that hatch. Lying still, mustering energy and resolve. Hearing

37

me and Will working somewhere aft, our voices low in the early quiet. Pearly dawn-glow putting a shine into that rectangle of glass.

Must not be tempted to take the car. Leave it, hitch a lift or lifts. And start *now* . . .

Bag out first. Shove it out, then follow it. Maybe noticing the zip's closed, thinking he'd done it subconsciously while his mind was busy . . . But he's pushing his own bag out, having stowed the money-belt in the other. Then reaching up, getting a grip on the frame of the hatch, heaving himself up and out.

3

Sleep had intervened and there'd been some weird additions to that sequence, footage connected with deaths by drowning and snapped necks. Neck, singular – slim, white where it wasn't purple-bruised – blonde head lolling, eyes wide and glassy and a whisper from the slack, dead mouth accusing me of having always hated her. This wasn't true, 'hate' was far too strong a word, and when I woke it was in my mind, it seemed important to impress upon her that I hadn't. Just hadn't liked her: no question of *hating* ... Waking, then, to the river sounds, and *Lady Be Good*'s creaky motion against the fenders – Will had rigged our gangplank as a fender-board, between them and the pilings – and from up top the drumming of heavy rain.

It certainly was raining. So our loss of the open-air steering position – we'd taken down the windscreen and the surrounding rail as well as the antennae – was no deprivation; we'd have been driving her from inside in any case.

But – back to Tommy Fountain ... Will had his own theory – unchanged since last night – and in his view it would be only a matter of time before Tommy's corpse was washed up on some English beach.

'Tides would've been westbound?'

He was asking me this because I'd done the small amount of

navigation that had been necessary the day before; and the answer was that we'd motored out through the Solent two hours before low water at Dover. I had a mental note of this not only because it had been a basic factor in setting courses to Le Havre, but also because of that original hope of making the trip from Le Havre to somewhere above Rouen on one tide. I confirmed, 'Westerly for the first two hours, then slackish, then eastward.' I shrugged. 'Much as that may tell you.'

'Well, they can tell how long a body's been in the drink – pathologists can – then working back from where he fetches up – Weymouth Bay, say – according to the tides, you'd get a fair idea where he went in.'

'I don't believe Tommy's dead, Will.'

'So why'd he leave his bankroll with us?'

'Must have put it in your grip by mistake. Intending to stick it in his own, picked the wrong one.'

'Yeah, *likely*! Would you be so careless with that much cash?'

'In his state of mind, I might. Anyway, it's no less unlikely than a guy who's about to drown himself taking his luggage with him.'

I saw that one strike home: it was obvious, but until now he'd missed it.

'I think he must have got ashore before we sailed. When we were looking the other way, or something, I don't know, but I don't think you can make sense of it any other way ... OK, Harrison said – you know, SBS, strong swimmer, etcetera – but firstly, why bother? and second – toting a soft bag that'd be waterlogged in the first minute and weigh a bloody ton – huh?'

'Suppose he's going to swim for it. *Why*, I don't know. Well – he guesses the fuzz are waiting for us in Le Havre, doesn't he? So, he wants us all – and them – to think he's done himself in. He takes the grip – you're right, it'll sink, and—'

Gazing at me: realizing he'd got it wrong. If Tommy had wanted anyone to think he'd drowned, he'd have left his gear behind. And if he'd been contemplating a long-distance swim he'd have left it behind, too.

But he'd have taken his money-belt along. Even saturated bank-notes dry out eventually.

'I think he stayed in England, Will. And the money was just a

40

cock-up. When he looks in his own bag and can't find it, he'll throw a fit.'

As if he didn't have enough problems already, I thought.

I found a telephone, in a village on the Paris side of Mantes. We'd made good time throughout this foul, wet day; needing to, because we had time to make up and because our progress would be a lot slower after we left the Seine and took to the canals. The speed limit in the canals is a miserable three and a quarter knots, and there's the tedious, time-consuming business of getting through the locks.

We'd have had to stop before dark anyway, as Seine navigation isn't allowed at night without a pilot on board. It wouldn't be all that safe either – there's a lot of traffic, especially barges and lighters, whole strings of heavy lighters moved around by very large pusher-tugs. Up as far as Rouen, of course, there'd been full-size ocean-going freighters; but the river was wider, too, down there.

Anyway – we'd been in a good place to tie up, the daylight had been on its last legs and there'd obviously be a public telephone in the village – also no doubt an *estaminet* where, by forcing myself to buy a drink, I'd get some small change to make the call with.

Then in the glass booth at last, I hesitated – with the coins ready to hand, and the choice of two London numbers – wondering whether this was crazy, whether I'd be taking a risk I didn't have any right to take.

Supposing he'd done it. Lost his head, lost control. Suppose Tommy *was* a murderer . . .

But this was just the point. What I'd be doing – if I went ahead and called Harrison – amounted to backing my own judgement, faith in Tommy's innocence, in the logical conclusion that since he was no killer, someone else *was*.

And if she'd had a boyfriend . . .

It was after nine, now, so chances were Harrison might be at home. Unless he worked at night . . . It was a toss-up: I picked the home number, dialled a lot of digits and felt like a public-bar punter with four cherries in a row when a woman's voice told me yes, hold on a minute, and then – gruffly, as if maybe interrupted in a meal – 'Charles Harrison.'

41

'This is Matt Johnson, in a French callbox.'

He reacted quickly, even eagerly. 'Give me the number. When we're cut off I'll ring you back.' I gave it to him, and he repeated it as he wrote it down. Then: 'Well, Mr Johnson?'

'Something I thought of about Tommy Fountain. But tell me – any news of him?'

'Not yet. Early days . . . What is it you thought of?'

'Well, when he and I met in London – look, I stalled your questions about his marriage. Sorry, but it seemed to me it was his own business, no one else's. Even now I'm not sure I should be talking about it. But the fact is you were right. His marriage was falling apart – which is why he was going on about how he wished he could get away, come to the Med with us, and so forth.'

'Right. Thank you. Anything else?'

'In confidence?'

'As far as it may be possible, in the context of a murder investigation.'

'Not for leaking to the Press, for instance?'

'Oh, I can go *that* far.'

'He told me his wife was playing around. Whether with one particular individual or more than one, I don't know, but—'

We were cut off at this point. It took him several minutes to get back to me, and I spent the time wondering whether I was doing the right thing, or dropping Tommy right in it.

Making myself feel better, maybe at his expense?

Tommy had already done himself the worst damage, of course – by scarpering. Would he have, if he hadn't killed her? Well. The *old* T. Fountain wouldn't have. But—

The phone rang, I picked it up and said 'Johnson here', and Harrison's voice said, 'Here we go again . . .'

'That was it, really, I've said it.'

'You've given me a motive. Would have, if I'd needed one. I'm wondering why.'

'Because you'd have got wind of it anyway, sooner or later. But also I'm damn sure he couldn't have done it. But someone did, and if she was involved with another man – or other men – well, the sooner you do know it the better.'

'Why, if he's innocent, has he run away?'

'I don't know. But I want to help him, and the guy you met –

42

Will Wyllie – made the point that you wouldn't be just looking for someone to arrest, you'll want to get to the truth. I happen to believe the truth would clear him, so if I can help—'

'Like telling me where I'd find him?'

'I haven't the least bloody idea—'

'—or admitting he did embark at Southampton?'

'He did *not*!'

'Well . . .' I heard him sigh: a tired man, no doubt with a long day's work behind him, displaying controlled impatience, letting me know I wasn't pulling any wool over *his* eyes . . . 'Thank you for as much collaboration as you *have* seen fit to provide . . . I take it from what you said that we may hear from you from time to time?'

'I'll call from Menorca. Or Marseilles.'

I felt better for having made the call. Although we weren't seeing exactly eye to eye, I thought the air between us had been cleared to some extent, and there was a chance it might pay off. And at least I'd done *something* . . .

We pushed on south as fast as we could move the boat along, passing through Paris on the day after that call. I didn't want to stop there, partly because we didn't have any time to spare but also because I'd been warned that the berths provided by the French Touring Club are very uncomfortable to lie at.

There's not much worth recording about the journey. It would be an enjoyable trip to make as a holiday, maybe with family or friends, taking plenty of time and making the most of the scenery, towns and countryside – including the Rhône wine country, of course. But our concern was only to get to the south and not hang about: which makes for hard work, with the passage of countless locks absorbing a lot of time and effort. There are various other hazards, requiring a certain amount of care and concentration: like the tidal swirls around the massive stone supports of bridges, and some of the traffic – such as the *peniches*, the barges which in narrow canals create an enormous amount of wash as well as driving a tidal wave in front of them. You have to cut in across their sterns, take the wash bow-on.

Then we were into the Rhône, which is a mighty river and

needs to be navigated with caution if you're a stranger to it, and our last night was spent on the very doorstep of the Mediterranean, at Port St Louis du Rhône, where we refitted the flying bridge. In a yacht, this would be the place to re-step your mast, which you'd have taken out either at Le Havre or at Rouen and carried lashed to the deck or coachroof. You need a crane, of course, and there's one available here.

Personally I'd rather not bring a yacht through by this route. The outer sea passage is faster and far more enjoyable. Maybe between autumn and early spring you might want to avoid Biscay – some yachtsmen do, I know – but I wouldn't insult my *Bird of Dawning* by pulling her mast out of her, all that messing around.

It was a relief to get out into salt water. A short coast-hop east to Cassis, where *Lady Be Good* was inspected, accepted and signed for, then a high-speed taxi charter to Marseilles and thence in Will's ketch to Menorca, where we secured stern-to in the fine old port of Mahon nineteen days after departure from Southampton.

I'd left the *Bird* in the care of Haemish McAllister, who with his wife Lorna owns and runs the café-bar called Lorenzo's. Café-bar is what they call it, but they're being modest; it's a bar-restaurant and a good one, and good value too. It's right on the quay, and I had the *Bird* moored less than fifty metres from it, and Haemish is not only an experienced sailor but also a very conscientious, painstaking sort of guy. How he has the time to spare for doing a friend this kind of favour I'll never know, because that place of theirs is a very full-time occupation. Yachtsmen patronize it, of course, British yachtsmen especially.

From Will's boat I walked along the quay to the *Bird*, stood looking at her for a minute or two, from this angle and that, before I boarded her. I was telling her, in my thoughts, *What you and I need now, old Bird, are some charterers . . .*

It was getting to be a bit of a worry, frankly, and coming to a head now because I was counting heavily on good news from Harry Loder.

The *Bird of Dawning* is a Swan, and she's no chicken. That's not intended to be funny: the fact is she's a Swan 48, which

44

means they don't build this kind any more. *Bird of Dawning* was hatched in 1971, her builders were – or I should say *are* – Nautor of Finland, who build all the Swans – and she was designed by Sparkman and Stephens of New York. Nautor build about a dozen different kinds of Swan today, to designs from such world leaders as Ron Holland and German Frers, but they no longer produce the 48. Which gives the 48 a certain distinction, of course, and this one was distinguishing herself in top-class international races long before I'd ever dreamt of owning anything so beautiful. About the time I was sweating my guts out to earn a green beret, in fact, in the Commando Training School – which is quite a while ago . . . Then in more recent years she went through a bad patch – a bad time, in bad hands: and this by chance was just about when I left the Corps to become a farmer and – that motorway crash. So you might say – fancifully, maybe – we had something in common. Fanciful or not, I've felt this from the moment I first set eyes on her.

And she really was in a mess, at that time. I'd had a letter from a friend who's in the yacht business in Gib, telling me this Swan was coming up for auction – Customs auction, she was an impounded boat and they'd just about gutted her, stripped her to find the narcotics she'd been carrying when arrested. And cutting a long story short, I got out there fast, made the auction with minutes to spare and bought her at what was really a knockdown price.

For a Swan, anyway. And she was basically sound, the damage was all really cosmetic. I did put in a new engine, replaced the mast and all the rigging, and installed electric anchor-winches forward and aft – in her former life as an ocean racer she'd managed without any; they'd have led the anchor warp to one of the winches abaft the mast, but I was fitting her out for single-handed cruising and I felt this expense was justified – but most of the work was on internal joinery. I did a lot of it myself, though, then moved her to Malta where the bigger jobs were completed in the yard on Manoel Island.

I paid £55,000 for her at that auction, and fixing her up cost about another £12,500. This included the new 48-horsepower diesel, and the secondhand mast which a helpful Swan agent found for me and cost £2,000. I could easily double my money now, if I wanted to. Swans are the Rolls-Royces of production yachts; they're built to last and they don't come cheap.

I went on board. In the next few days I'd be checking over every inch of her, overhauling every fitting and all the loose equipment too, but just from a quick once-over now I could see she'd come to no harm during my absence.

To describe the *Bird* and her layout, briefly, she's 47′ 1″ long, 39′ at the waterline, with a beam amidships of 13′ 7″, draft 7′ 9″, and she displaces about 30,000 lbs. Her hull is fibreglass, decks and interior all teak except that I've used some mahogany which I found lying around in Malta. For the cockpit doors, for instance. She's sloop-rigged, and her hull is white with the Swan traditional blue stripe, and on the transom is her name in blue lettering above her port of registry, which is Plymouth.

Right aft, where you step off the gangplank on to her stern, is the hatch over a lazarette that holds cordage, the stern anchor and various other gear. Then you're in the steering well, the after cockpit, with a smart wooden wheel, concealed now in its blue nylon cover. The wheel came off an older yacht and I was lucky to find it in Gibraltar. The original one, and some other metal fittings such as lifeline stanchions, had been pulled apart or perforated by searchers who'd overlooked nothing that might have been stuffed with narcotics.

There's a second cockpit a few feet forward, and at the front end of it my mahogany doors give access to a ladder leading down into the *Bird*'s interior. Down we go, now . . .

Galley to your left, navstation (radio and radar gear, Loran, depth-sounder, chart table, etcetera) on your right. Turn right around, move aft past the down-sloping ladder (the diesel engine's here, inside a teak-and-mahogany enclosure) and here a door leads into the stern cabin, which most of the time is mine. There's a small compartment off it, on your right, containing head, shower and washbasin – you're facing aft, so that's the port side – with stowage and hanging-space for clothes opposite, starboard. Originally there were two quarter berths in here, but I changed that when I refitted her, substituting one good-sized double berth on the port side and a narrow settee with lockers under it to starboard.

All the woodwork, by the way, all the panelling and

46

furniture right through the boat, is honey-coloured with a
satin finish. It's really very pretty; and there's good headroom
everywhere.

Now we're heading forward. Passing the ladder, galley and
navigational space, we come into the midships accommodation area, the big cabin in which there are berths for four
people but otherwise is just living space, the saloon. This is the
widest section of the boat, of course. There's a settee with two
short right-angle ends enclosing a dining-table on the port
side, and a straight settee to starboard, with ample room to
walk straight through between them; both the settees convert
to bunks, and up behind them at a higher level are fixed but
extendable (pull-out) bunks set against the boat's sides port
and starboard. On all four of these berths bunk-cloths are
provided, material that's stowed under the mattresses and can
be pulled out and hooked up so you can't fall out of bed.

At the forward end of the starboard-side settee there's a
chest of drawers with a cupboard above it. Then a door
leading forward into a short passage from which on your right
you have hanging and locker space, on your left the head with
shower and basin. Another door faces you: it leads into the
bow cabin, which has two bunks set at rather sharp angles
to each other into the narrowing forepart. It's not all that
narrow; there's room for an upholstered seat between them at
that end, with more lockers and drawers there and under the
bunks. And on the after bulkhead, immediately on your left as
you come in through the door, is a vertical ladder leading up to
– or for that matter down from – an overhead sliding hatch.
This forward (forepeak) cabin can be used for charterers, if
they need the extra space – for children, for instance –
although it's really crew accommodation. If one carried crew –
which I don't normally but might have done for instance if
Tommy Fountain had come along – he or they would use the
forward hatch for entry and exit, thus not disturbing the
paying customers amidships. Alternatively, two couples or
even three can be berthed in the stern and midships cabins, and
then I'd vacate my own and use this forward one.

But that's the *Bird of Dawning*, what you might call a
visitor's first impression of her.

Thinking about Tommy – on my way back to Will's boat – I

47

was going to try to get through to Harrison this evening. I'd tried from Marseilles, the one evening we'd had there, but no one answered the telephone at his home – flat, whatever – and at the police station they'd told me he was off-duty and I should ring again in the morning. Which of course I couldn't do because by morning Will and I had been at sea, the start of a 200-mile southward reach with a moderate north-west blow that held steady all the way. It was the wind you'd expect, at this time of year, but expectations aren't always fulfilled quite so happily; I was hoping to be as lucky – touch wood, the same wind ought to be near enough dead astern – from here to Malta in about a week.

(I told myself, not wanting to count chickens, that as likely as not I'd have a gale, right on the nose.)

On the way back to Will's ketch I passed Lorenzo's, which was still shut up tight. Haemish and Lorna had a routine of clearing up at night when they'd seen the last customer out, and they rarely stirred before noon. They lived a few miles out of town, not over the shop as they could have done if they'd wanted.

Will had been ashore and bought bread that was still warm from the baker's oven. He also had some eggs on the boil, and coffee heating, and he'd got a copy of yesterday's *Daily Mail*.

'Nothing about your chum in it . . . Seeing Susan tonight, are you?'

'Susan?' I was leafing through the paper, glancing through in case there was some mention of the Fountain case and he'd missed it. 'Maybe. Hadn't thought, really. I want to call Harrison, I know *that* . . . I expect I'll make the call from Lorenzo's, probably eat there.'

The McAllisters are extremely kind people. Naturally one pays one's way, and a couple of times when they've felt like it and I've had no charters they've shut up shop and I've taken them on short cruises to the other islands; but both those trips have been as much for my own pleasure as theirs, very relaxed holidays, and I'm sure that by and large I get the best of the deal. For instance, they give me storage space when I need it, for sails and other gear. The McAllisters in fact are basically the reason I spend as much time on Menorca as I do; I winter the *Bird* on Manoel Island where she gets taken out of the water to have her bottom scraped, and anything else that needs doing, and in both the previous two winters I've done skippering jobs for a yacht-charter company in the Caribbean. This last winter I stayed in Malta; by early spring I was ready for a change and this was the obvious place to come to.

Susan, by the way, is a girl Will's seen me with a couple of times. That's all.

He asked me as we were finishing breakfast, 'Be taking your gear now, will you?'

'Might as well.'

'Don't leave that cash behind.'

'No. I won't. But if he doesn't show up to claim it, eventually—'

'Uh-huh.' He shook his head. 'I'm not interested, Matt. Not now, not later, don't even *tell* me.'

'I doubt we'll be stuck with it anyway.' I'd know more tonight when I called Harrison, maybe, but meanwhile I was still counting on Tommy being alive; and only dead men have no use for money. I asked Will, 'When are you pushing off?'

'Couple of days. Contract starts next Monday, there's no rush.'

I envied him – in a way. Not really, only at this moment because he had work lined up and I didn't. I was *very* anxious for news from Loder, and I couldn't get any – if any did indeed exist – until the McAllisters showed up at their place of business so that I could get my hands on any post that might have come.

I had to keep reminding myself that I did have the Lawries' charter, to keep me going for a few weeks; even if he hadn't set anything up yet, a lot could happen in that space of time. And I wouldn't have wanted to operate as Will Wyllie does, anyway. He lives on day-chartering, attaching himself to hotels or tourist companies; he prefers this, he told me once, because with different people on board each day he doesn't have to get to know them or pretend to like them; the company couriers take all that strain. Actually I think he likes it because it's steadier work, one contract lasting all season, and he doesn't have to think about passenger comfort the way I do. Just as well, since his boat wouldn't be up to standard, anyway, for longer charters.

I collected my gear, first checking that the money was in it, and strolled back to the *Bird*. There were quite a lot of people around by this time – locals, yachtsmen, tourists – and with the sun high now, glittering bright in shop and restaurant windows, the place was beginning to warm up and also to smell a bit, the way old seaports do. I was wondering, as I passed Lorenzo's again – still shut – what Tommy would be doing for money, if he was still at liberty. Which I thought he was, probably; I'd missed several days' newspapers, but there'd been nothing in any news broadcast, and if he'd been arrested or given himself up there surely would have been. I guessed he'd have had other money – ready-use cash; for instance he'd surely have had a wallet in a pocket in the anorak he'd been wearing – and he might have access to other funds as well. With the police broadcasting their interest in him he could hardly walk into a bank and cash a cheque, I imagined, but with a numbered Swiss account – there'd have to be a cash account attached, to receive interest payments on those bonds – maybe he could arrange by telephone for money – cash, bank-notes – to be sent to a poste restante address.

He'd get along somehow, but meanwhile he'd be expecting me to keep this bundle safe for him. Which, since I'd done most of the *Bird*'s internal joinery myself, and exercised a certain amount of forethought when doing it, presented no kind of problem.

My problem was whether Loder had come up with the goods. I could have telephoned the McAllisters at their villa, but they're hard-working people who have to stay up half the night and I didn't like to break into their well-earned rest with my private anxieties. So by midday I was getting to the nail-biting stage.

They rolled up at three minutes past. I'd managed not to be waiting actually on the doorstep, but I was in sight of it, saw them coming round the corner from the alley where they always parked their vehicles, and was with them by the time Haemish had the door unlocked. I knew them well enough to cut the greetings short: I asked, with my arms still round Lorna – for which let me say you need long arms, there's plenty of her – 'Any mail for me?'

'Only junk.' Haemish lurched off towards the rear of the

premises. 'Love letters and that. I've had a good read of 'em, of course.'

I spotted the long yellow envelope that had come from Loder's office, ignored the rest, ripped this one open.

'Beer?'

'Thanks . . .'

He had two more charters signed up. The first to start a week after the Lawries' three-week cruise. From Athens: which meant a bit of a long haul – disembarking the Lawries in Malta, then to be ready in Athens inside the week. But – the hell, I'd cope with it when the time came.

Relief was – well, it felt good. I looked up, saw Haemish about to rip open some glistening cans of beer, and grabbed his wrist: 'Hang on. Got any champagne on ice?'

At the Chelsea police station that evening they took my name and checked with Harrison before they put me through to him. I'd called his home number, and his wife had said he was working late.

Not all that late. Getting on for 9 here, but it would be only about 8 p.m. in England.

'Charles Harrison . . .'

'Matt Johnson here. I tried to call you a few days ago from Marseilles, but no joy. I'm in Menorca now. D'you have any news of Tommy Fountain?'

I heard him clear his throat, or it could have been a mutter – like inviting a colleague to listen in or to start a tape running. That was OK – I was asking the questions, not answering any.

'Mr Johnson—'

'Why not shorten it to Matt, save money?'

'All right – Matt. Since it's *your* money . . . Straight answer to a straight question – no, I don't have any news. What have you got for me?'

'Not a hell of a lot, actually . . . But – OK, Charles, that's all I rang to ask you. If you want to keep this going now, you'd better call me back. The number's—'

A grunt – derisive in tone – was followed by second thoughts: 'All right, give it me – case of future need. Right now I've no reason—'

51

'Are you saying you've made no progress at all – in three weeks?'

'No. I said I had no news of Captain Fountain.'

'Ah – so the investigation—'

'I really can't discuss it, Mr – er – Matt . . . But if you want to give me that number—'

Want was too strong a word – mostly because I didn't expect he'd bother to use it. *I* was the one with the axe to grind. But I gave it to him; then hung up, conscious of money down the drain. Except I felt that having started this, if there was to be any mileage in it at all I should keep it up, try to keep Tommy's interests – meaning his innocence, or at least my own presumption of it – in their minds.

We'd had quite a session, at lunchtime, celebrating my good news from Loder. I could admit to myself now that I'd been quite seriously worried; only Tommy's predicament had kept it in the background. The detail of the new charters was that they were both from Athens and for cruises in Turkish waters, and the first was to start seven days after I dropped the Lawries back in Malta. It *would* be cutting things a bit fine, particularly as I'd have to allow adequate time for that return to Malta against the prevailing wind – no doubt mostly under power, therefore – but it was a hell of a lot better than being out of work. And Loder was promising more to come.

I bought a brandy and soda, and when Haemish came back from serving a *spaghetti Bolognaise* to a yachtsman whom I knew but couldn't have put a name to, he asked me, 'Be seeing Susan, will you?'

It was beginning to feel like some kind of conspiracy. I asked him, 'D'you think I should?'

'You'd be the one to answer *that*.' He added, 'I think Lorna saw her the other day, and she was – och, asking when you'd be back, or—'

'Who's Lorna talking to now?'

Haemish turned to see. His wife had brought a plate of something to a girl who was sitting by herself and far too attractive to do so very often, I thought. She'd be waiting for someone, probably. Haemish said, 'American. She was in here yesterday.'

'Alone?'

52

'Uh – yeah, believe she was. Excuse me, Matt.'

One of the other diners was wanting something. One of a row with their backs to the wall, four in line, four tables each with one guy sitting at it, all minding their own business. They're all single-handers, and they're four of the same breed, the kind who take to this life because they expect it to be glamorous, exciting, romantic – that 'freedom' bit, as promoted by old Tommy, but which doesn't always turn out so well.

With me, it's worked, it's fine – because I've no objection to being alone, and as for romance – well, I get by, and steer clear of anything that begins to look like a threat of permanence. Also, I make a go of the chartering business, by virtue of having a splendid boat and looking after her well, and ensuring that the customers get at least as much as they pay for.

(I could say this, now. Ignoring the fact that earlier in the day I'd been sending up prayers. The business *does* have its tricky moments: the point is that so far – touch wood – I've survived.)

But those guys: they start off with this daydream. They're mostly divorced, or widowed, or they've just run out on their wives – backgrounds vary, but that's the generality. The dream is they're going to pick up dolly-birds for crew, rollick around the world in seas of sun and sex, have the time of their middle-aged lives, live the way they'd always longed to live and never could – only better now than it would have been in days of yore because they're mature now, they can handle it . . . It's South Sea Island stuff, hula-hula . . . And the way it actually turns out – more or less, and with variations of course – is that – well, that guy at the middle table, for instance – late forties, going bald, he looks fit enough but if he goes on drinking at that rate he may not be for long – he'll have embarked some enthusiastic little darling in – say – Lisbon, romped with her in Gib and Tangier (at no small expense – she'd expect it, from an older man, and he wouldn't want to be thought stingy) but soon after he docks at Formentera he meets some guy her own age, and – the lone sailor wakes up alone again.

Money's another snag. It takes some, to run a yacht. Sails and rigging can need replacing, hulls require maintenance and

53

engines quite frequently need expensive spare parts. Fuel costs money too. If the cash-flow doesn't measure up to demands made on it, the boat gets shabby, which isn't good for business; and a man still has to eat, which is why some of these characters can't help looking gloomy even at the prices on the McAllisters' menu.

Will Wyllie tends to look miserable too, but not for any of those reasons, it's just his temperament and the way his face is arranged. He nodded morosely at one or two acquaintances as he came in, looking around before he spotted me and shuffled over to join me at my table. I say 'my' table, but there were some young Germans at the other end of it.

'Hi, Matt. I'll have a Carlos Primero and soda, if you're buying.'

'Terceiro. He's out of Primero.'

'Wouldn't you know it?'

If he'd given it a moment's thought, he'd have known that Haemish never runs out of anything he has a ready market for. But Carlos Primero is the best he stocks, too good to dilute with soda. Carlos Terceiro runs it a good second, anyway. I caught Haemish's eye, pointed at my own glass and held up two fingers. He grimaced – under pressure, looking round for help from Lorna, who'd paused for another chat with the American girl. Haemish yelled at his wife, and she glanced round, said something like, 'All right, all right . . .' – from her expression it must have been something of that sort – then she was moving on, and while I was still watching the girl turned her head and we were looking at each other.

Not for long; but for long enough to make it more than just an exchange of glances. It wasn't just flirtatious, either, that 'across a crowded room' routine, but – well, it's not easy to describe: but to put this plainly, it left me excited.

Interested may be a better word.

Will had been telling me something, and I hadn't heard a word of it. I looked back across the now *very* crowded room, saw the girl topping up her glass; she had a half-bottle of white wine and she was fizzing it with mineral water, paying close attention to what she was doing and seeming to take longer than she need have. Sick of being stared at, maybe. I told myself, *by people like you . . .*

54

To describe her as I saw her then, the first impression – well, she has glossy-looking brown hair which at that time she was wearing pulled back into some kind of knot at the back, she has a high forehead and her face widens at the cheekbones. It's still quite a small face – she has big eyes, too, rather wide apart – I couldn't see what colour, but as it happens they're brown, sort of golden brown. And she has a sweet mouth, a truly lovely mouth. And this doesn't even start to do her justice; I don't suppose an inventory of features ever can. What counts is the way it fits together: and she does have it all together, she also has this marvellous kind of *directness* which I suppose is what had intrigued me in that long moment when we'd been looking at each other, effectively seeing each other for the first time.

I made myself tune in to Will's sporadic utterances. Then Lorna came with the drinks I'd ordered. She asked me, 'You did say you're here for about a week, Matt, didn't you?'

'More like four or five days, I'd say now.'

'And you did say Marmaris as your base in Turkey?'

She was a bit on edge, aware of the demands for service and that Haemish was getting frantic; she always does like to stop and chat, and when they're busy it annoys him. I told her yes, Marmaris as port of entry and departure, cruising south from there . . . 'Why, want to come with me, Lorna?'

'Believe me, Matt, I'd love to!'

She waddled off, giggling, in time to save Haemish blowing a gasket. Will immediately began to talk about his holding tank – the one in his ketch, that is – and this is not the most gripping of subjects. I'd mention, in case it's not general knowledge, that a holding tank is a container, installed in a boat's bilge spaces and usually in the form of a very large plastic bag, into which the heads are flushed so that sewage isn't expelled into harbours or enclosed anchorages. You pump the tank out when you're offshore, in deep water. Will had a leak on his: it served him right, because when he'd had trouble with a previous tank he'd replaced it with a secondhand one. I'd thought at the time it was a false economy.

'Better put in a new one, double quick.'

'Well, the tank itself may be OK, could be just the connec-

55

tions. I'm not about to rush out and spend a lot of money—'

'Right. If a stink of sewage below decks is what you—'

'Matt.' Lorna. And beside her, looking down at me, that same unsmiling, thoughtful look on her face, the American girl. Tallish, very eye-catching figure. She had on a yellow T-shirt under a bright multi-coloured sleeveless jacket – sort of waistcoat, hanging open – and expensive jeans. *Brown* eyes . . . I got up, slightly fazed and probably showing it, hearing Lorna gabble, 'This is Matt Johnson, Gill. And that's Will Wyllie. Gill Paget, Matt. The thing is—'

'I'll tell him.' She touched Lorna's arm. 'Thanks.' Then to me, 'OK if I sit?'

'Very much OK.'

'Thank you.' She sat down, glanced at the Germans and then at Will and finally back at me. 'You're wondering what the hell—'

'Well, not exactly, but—'

'You're going to Turkey – right?'

I nodded. And caught on – sadly. There'd had to be some angle . . .

'Mrs McAllister told me. She also said you're picking up charterers from Malta and you always sail single-handed. So this is kind of a long shot, I realize, but – it so happens I need to get to Turkey, actually to Fethiye, which I believe may be on your route.'

'Yeah, it is, but—'

'I've sailed quite a lot, in the Caribbean mostly. And I cook, I mean I've cooked in boats, I could well look after your passengers . . .'

Her voice tailed off, into a silence that was like a hole in all the noise around us. I was suffering from conflicting inclinations – in other words dithering – and I could see disappointment in her honey-brown eyes. Well, I agreed with her, I *hate* indecision – in anyone, but especially in myself. Then I realized that half the reason I wasn't already begging her to sign on was the way it would be seen by other people, the talk amongst other yachtsmen – Matt Johnson, joining *that* club, acting like those slobs – I mean the scene I was just describing, lecherous lone sailors making bloody fools of themselves. Recognizing this – the idiocy of allowing oneself to be influenced by the possibility of silly gossip – put an end to the dithering.

Gill was saying, 'Look, OK, I'm sorry. It was – like I said, just a long shot, sort of a wild idea I—'

'But – it mightn't be such a *bad* wild idea, at that . . .'

4

Gill knew – she explained, when this story was being stitched together – that Matt Johnson would have assumed she was an impecunious globe-trotter looking for a free trip to Turkey. For whatever reason she wanted to get there – which he'd be expecting her to reveal pretty soon, and OK, she'd tell him. As far as she could make sense of it . . . She also guessed that if she'd been ugly he'd have stuck to his principles – which Lorna McAllister had touched on – of rarely taking any crew with him in his *Bird of Dawning*, and never taking on young female crew. This indicated another illusion which she'd have to clear up before arrangements were finalized – if they did get to finalize anything – otherwise he might be expecting what he wasn't about to get.

Not as a matter of course, anyway.

Although now he might be having his own second thoughts. She'd let him see her taking an interest in him, reciprocating his interest in her, and she guessed his male vanity would have had him jumping to conclusions. But since then she'd declared her *real* interest – getting a ride to Turkey. This might be a big disappointment, and if the penny hadn't dropped *before* he'd said 'Mightn't be a bad idea', negotiations might not proceed much farther.

She noticed him noticing her wedding band. Wedding ring,

as he'd call it. That was something she did *not* have to explain, not in the short term anyway, although she'd told Lorna McAllister about it yesterday. Just ordinary woman-talk, instant establishment of the basics.

The droopy guy – Will something – had excused himself and slunk away, muttering something about a problem with his boat. And now Lorna was back.

'You two all right?'

She'd brought Gill's wine bottle, which had a few inches left in it.

'If you're staying – as it seems you are, that old misogynist just pissed off, I noticed – and someone seems to have snitched your table, Gill, so you might as well . . .'

'She's staying.' Matt Johnson said it flatly. 'What's more, I'm hoping she's going to crew for me on this charter.'

'Well, I'll be!'

He nodded. 'Guess you *have* been Lorna. Several times.'

'Cheeky sod.'

She'd ploughed on, dispensing sustenance elsewhere. She and this Matt Johnson obviously knew each other very well, Gill noted. A short while ago – and this was something else, another illusion he'd have, she guessed, because logically by this time he *would* be under the impression that her interest in him had only started when she'd heard he was going to Turkey – just minutes ago she'd asked Lorna McAllister, 'Say, who's *that* guy?'

'Which?'

'Where the beanpole's just sitting down. Dark, middle thirties maybe, looks like if he was hungry he'd eat broken glass.'

'You mean Matt Johnson. Broken glass *nothing*, my dear, Matt's the gentlest of creatures!'

'Well, mercy.' She'd laughed. 'I mean, like it's a mercy Irish wolfhounds are gentle. Else you'd have problems, right?'

'Hey, *that's* something I might have thought of!'

Lorna had snapped her fingers: remembering suddenly that Matt was getting ready for a charter to Turkey – and not just Turkey, but the coast which Gill was now so keen to visit . . . Then after she'd told her, and Gill had naturally been interested, her expression had changed . . . 'Oh, Lord . . . Look, come to think of it – I'm sorry, I should've thought before I spoke – it's really *very* unlikely he'd take you . . . If it had been any of *that* lot – ' she'd moved her greying head, indicating the group of lonely-looking diners ' – any of them'd jump at the chance. And you'd know what they had in mind. But Matt's a very professional sailor, and – well—'

'Married?'

'Was. There was some frightful accident, though – road smash, his wife and baby daughter were both killed.'

'Oh, my God.'

'Long time ago now. But I think it's with him *all* the time. And professionally he's – well, he doesn't mix business with pleasure, or – look, you'd be safe with him if you wanted to be, if you see what I mean.'

'But he wouldn't take me.'

'He wouldn't take most people.' Lorna looked at her thoughtfully. 'On the other hand – I don't know, the leopard *might* change his spots, I suppose . . . Want to try your luck? He'll almost surely say no, but – shall I ask him for you?'

'Uh-huh.' She'd put her glass down. 'Thanks, but that's surely something I should do. If you wouldn't mind introducing us?'

She said to Matt now, about Lorna, 'She's very kind, isn't she? She was going to make my application to you on my behalf, if I'd wanted.'

'You make your own applications.'

'Guess I do.' Facing his blue eyes, mustering in her mind the items she needed to get straight. Starting with – 'Listen – I wouldn't want to be paid, for crewing for you. I don't need it, is one reason, and I want to get to Turkey is another, I mean *I'm* the applicant. I don't know if you'd have been expecting to or not, I'm just putting this on the record, OK?'

He nodded. 'Suits me.'

A wide, tough face with humour in it, she recorded. Remembering, by way of contrast, what her sister Anne had written to her not long ago from this island about a man called Raoul – no surname mentioned, just 'Raoul' and a reference to his charm and his delightful French accent, and then: *He's just beautiful. As well as crazy about me, so much that sometimes*

61

*he seems desperate with worry that I might not stay with him.
Crazy – all he'd need do is try to shake me loose, he'd find out
fast who's desperate! OK, I know you'll be thinking 'beautiful''s a strange word to use about a man, but it's the only word
that fits . . .*

It was not a word anyone would use about Matt Johnson.
Gill thought maybe she could detect signs of the alleged
'gentleness' behind the rugged assembly of features, but
'beautiful' he most certainly was not.

She said, 'There are some other things I better tell you, Matt.
Like why I want to get to that part of Turkey.'

'All right. But first, are you happy with that watery-looking
wine?'

'For the moment. Thanks . . . Don't let me inhibit you,
though.'

'You won't, don't worry. So who's in Turkey – your
husband?'

'No. Not – my husband.' She lifted that ring finger, let it
down again. Deciding not to explain here and now that her
husband had run out on her – in New York, several months
ago – run off to live with his girlfriend. She didn't want to have
to tell Matt about this now, because it might have seemed like
a come-on, a statement of availability which she certainly
didn't want to make, wouldn't have intended. And he'd
wonder why she still wore the ring. The answer to this – she
thought, trying to put her mind back to how she'd felt at that
stage, that evening in Lorenzo's, and wanting to be honest
about it – might have been that she wasn't accepting that her
marriage was irrevocably finished; although this wasn't the
case, it *was* finished, and she didn't *think* she'd been under any
illusions about it by that time. If she'd been hanging on to
anything it was maybe to the concept of being a married
woman, a state to which she'd become accustomed; that was
one angle, and another was that a wedding band was supposed
to afford some kind of protection – travelling alone, and
especially in the last couple of days when she'd been in and out
of bars, hotels, police precincts and other male-dominated
centres, looking for Anne, describing her, asking had anyone
seen her or did they know this Frenchman called Raoul who'd
be with her.

Not that the protection factor had been all that evident.

Although Lorna had made a wise observation: that if she took the ring off now, when her hands were sunburnt, the mark would label her as a married woman on the loose.

Lorna had said, 'Which I would *not* recommend. Not that it's any of my business.'

Gill told Matt, making the statement as complete as possible so as to get it over quickly, 'I'm looking for my kid sister, Anne. I was coming out here to be with her for a while, but she's vanished. She wrote that she'd gotten herself involved with a Frenchman called Raoul who had a yacht and was going to Turkey – well, Turkey's where I *think* they've gone, although she didn't actually say Turkey in her letter – and Raoul had said if I could get myself here fast he'd take the both of us. Then I didn't hear another thing – it took me a little while, I had some legal stuff to tie me down—'

'Are you a lawyer?'

'Hell, no . . . Listen, I got here – oh, three days, I've been here – and she's simply gone, left no message, just damn well *gone* – and Anne wouldn't have done this, we're very close, we always were more like twins than just sisters. I've had – well, problems, I wanted to be with her, and – well, it's just *incredible*—'

'Can't say I've heard of any Raoul in sailing circles. But we can put the word around. And on that Turkish coast – well, there are a lot of boats, but they know who comes and goes . . . How old is Anne?'

'Twenty-three.'

'Your kid sister, twenty-three? I'd have thought *you*—'

'I'm twenty-eight.' She knew she did look more like Anne's age, and that his surprise was genuine. She nodded: 'So now you know why I want to get to Turkey, Matt.'

She'd already had something to eat, but he hadn't; he ordered a bottle of wine, which she shared with him, and a Wiener Schnitzel, and they went on swapping information. He explained various things to her – like the Turkish regulations on crew lists and on foreign yachts engaged in charter work in Greek and/or Turkish waters, and passports and so on. And about the *Bird of Dawning*: she was impressed that he owned a vintage Swan.

'Come and see her in the morning. Just along the quay there, fifty yards from here.'

'Right. I'll look forward to it. Thanks. But not too early, because first I have to meet Lorna in town, about ten thirty. She's coming to the place I'm at, where Anne stayed. The couple who own it are trying to be helpful, but we have a language problem and Lorna talks good Spanish – right?'

'She's fluent.' He had fingers crossed, she'd noticed – obviously to remind him of something he'd had in mind to say; she waited for it, and he put the question now. 'D'you have family – well, your husband, maybe, but I was thinking more of parents . . . Anne might have been in touch with them?'

'Sure. Our father which art in California. I called him, first night I was here, but he hadn't heard from her. And Anne's his favourite daughter – you know, baby of the family.'

'But you've talked to him, so if he did hear—'

'Yeah, we said we'd keep in touch. But he's not worrying. He just said stay cool, she'll show, you know how scatty that kid is, keep me posted, will you? I guess he doesn't *want* to have to worry. He – you know, he loves us, sure, but – oh, he's a *very* busy man, last thing he'd want is me crying on his shoulder. In fact—'

She'd checked, abruptly. Stopping herself because it had occurred to her she might be talking too much, too much about herself, personal stuff that not everyone would want to know: and she didn't want him deciding she was a bore and then not wanting her on this trip.

Matt's eyebrows queried the sudden silence; she shook her head. He asked, after a moment, 'No mother?'

'Sure. Someplace. They split up, years ago, both re-married.'

'You don't keep in touch.'

'Right. I don't, she does not.' Gill had been toying with her glass: she glanced up, murmured, 'Life's *shit* – you know? I mean *really*—'

'Can be.' Her eyes were searching his: he added, maybe as a polite way of disagreeing, 'Can *seem* to be . . . What does your father do – I mean for a living?'

'Oh, there's a question.' She drank some wine – it was warm now as well as watery – before she answered it. 'The short answer is – computers. Very advanced, state-of-the-art stuff. He and two other guys started the business together – hardware, a mainframe that's had a huge success, the DBX they call it and it's still a big thing – updated, I think it's the DBX4 now. But early on he – well, he got to be on his own, and cutting a long story very short, he's now into billions, he breathes really thin air up there, you know?'

'No wonder you don't want to be paid for crewing. I'd have thought he'd have sent a private jet to fly you there.'

'Well' – this was one of the things she'd meant to explain, and she could do it now – 'it isn't like that, actually, but as I said, if Anne's gone east in a yacht I'd have a better chance of catching up with her if I went the same way. Same ports, same cruising area? OK, I *could* just fly, go straight to Fethiye, but then I'd just be put down there, like I am here – see what I mean?'

'I think you're right. But why Fethiye, if your sister didn't even get as far as saying Turkey?'

'The one letter I did have – weeks ago – she wrote, *Raoul is heading for parts exotically eastern, he says we can go along if we want.* But now also, the guy who runs the *pension* where she stayed – as I said, I'm using it too, thought I might as well – this Spaniard told me she was studying a big map of the Mediterranean they have stuck up in their foyer, one morning, and she asked him where the heck is Fethiye, and he helped her find it. He's not too easy to understand, but no mistake about Fethiye, he pointed it out to me just as he had to her.'

'And you think—'

'That's how I know where it is. I never heard of it before.'

'You think he may have more to tell you, if you get past the language problem?'

'Well – I *hope*. At least we'll get whatever he *does* know.'

'Any theories? If you had to guess what she's doing?'

'What's *being done*, is how I'd phrase it. Done *to her*. Because on her own, voluntarily, she would *not* have let me down as she has. Not in a millennium. The thing is, though – well, she's naive, she thinks people can be *trusted*, for God's sake . . .'

'You *don't* think so?'

The way he was looking at her, she said, made the question seem important. So instead of an offhand 'Bet your life, I don't' she hedged – rather as he'd seemed to, a minute or two ago . . . 'Meaning you do?'

'Meaning I wouldn't generalize. Depends on people, person. Well, obviously. But also, Gill, you've had a run of bad luck with people lately, haven't you?'

'You psychic?'

'Not that I know of. But that wasn't the first downbeat observation you've made ... Taking a chance – would I be wildly wrong if I guessed at marital upset?'

'I don't *believe* this!'

'Nothing psychic about it. You said you had some personal problem – apart from worry about your sister, this was some reason for coming out to spend time with her – then I asked if your husband was waiting for you in Turkey, and you said, "No, not my husband" – in a certain tone of voice.'

'But I'm wearing this damn ring, Matt, so—'

'So you're still married. OK, I take the point. But—'

'That was *not* the point.'

'Oh – right ... Anyway, the way you've looked at that ring—' He half smiled. He was really not bad looking, when he smiled, she thought. He was saying: 'that ring – or quote, that *damn* ring – gave me the impression – well, I don't know, but as if you weren't so sure of it, might have been in two minds about wearing it.' He smiled again. 'Go ahead, tell me I'm wrong.'

'You've surprised me. I'd no idea I was so transparent.'

'Perhaps you're not. Could be it's me that's brilliant.' He checked the time. 'And here's a brilliant suggestion now, Gill. I'll walk you back to your hotel, and on the way I'll give you a quick sight of the *Bird of Dawning*.'

Gill only saw the *Bird* from the quayside, that night. She'd expected to be invited on board, and it was a relief as well as a surprise that Matt didn't suggest it. She wouldn't have wanted to seem wimpish in declining such an invitation – as if she might be scared of him, or couldn't trust herself, whatever – but even less did she want to be rushed into anything – even like having to fight him off, for instance. She'd had the feeling even then, she said, that close involvement with Matt Johnson wouldn't exactly help with the tangle her life was in already.

5

I'd done a good morning's work before Gill turned up. I was living on board, of course, and I'd woken and started early, breakfasting in the cockpit and on yesterday's bread because the baker's wife wouldn't have opened her doors at that hour. It was a good time of day, though, the only other visibly moving humans resembling figures in some old marine oil painting – fishermen, they and their boats blending into the sea-mist that lay over Mahon's four-mile-long deepwater anchorage.

Psychic, she'd called me. A more appropriate term might be 'idiot'. She wanted a lift to Turkey, that was all.

She'd be asleep now, that glossy brown hair a dark mass on the pillow in the balconied room just a few hundred yards from this quay. She'd pointed the window out to me before I'd said goodnight, holding both her hands in mine for maybe twenty seconds – and that was all, the only physical contact there'd been between us, and the thought in my mind that when I did kiss her it wouldn't be trivial, and she'd know it wasn't.

Great stuff, imagination.

Except it would be up to me, wouldn't it? You can let a dream lie, or you can work at it, bring it to life.

Or run away from it. In the last few years I'd done some of that.

I worked on deck for the first few hours of the day, enjoying the morning's cool and performing such chores as taking shackles apart and greasing their pins, and servicing the hydraulic gear on the backstay and then the vang on the mainsail boom. I also ran the engine for an hour – having delayed this long enough to allow my neighbours a reasonable amount of lie-in time – to top up the batteries, from which pretty well everything in the boat is operated – lights, deepfreeze, electric winches, autopilot and all the navigational equipment, for instance. Not the stove – that's gas – or hot water, which comes from the engine.

Anyway, progress was being made, and this was only my second day on the island. I thought another two full days would be plenty, to get everything done and some stores embarked. Then I'd sail for Malta on Day 5, and if anything still needed doing it could be done either on passage or in the Manoel Island marina, where I thought I'd have several days to wait.

Where *we*'d have several days. The thought was exciting. And by way of reaction to it – to the feeling in my gut – I thought *Susan* . . .

She's blonde, vivacious, quite intelligent, and shaped like Marilyn Monroe. Her father runs the Menorcan end of one of the mass-market travel companies; he and his wife live on the island permanently, and their offspring come and go at various times of the year. Susan would be on the island now, and she'd have heard that I was back; I'd realized yesterday when first Will and then Haemish had asked about her that I'd have to get in touch, ask her out for a meal or to go swimming or something; I'd done nothing about it because people seemed to be assuming there was some long-term relationship developing, and in my experience this usually meant that the lady concerned was promulgating that idea.

Anyway, I went ashore, used a restaurant's telephone, found her at home and full of joy, and arranged to pick her up at nine that evening.

Insurance, this was: and probably self-flattery to imagine I needed any.

When I got back to the *Bird* there was a guy on the quayside staring at her, and I nodded to him and said 'Good morning' as

68

I went up the plank. He called, 'Excuse me . . . Am I right in thinking this is a Swan?'

'Yup. Swan 48.'

'Well. If she's yours, you're a lucky man.'

'Right. I am. You a sailor?'

'No, not really.' He didn't look like one either. Too pale, for one thing, too neatly dressed for another. Neat little moustache, and all. He looked like a thousand other tourists – except he was a bit tidy even for that, and should have had a wife and children with him. That age, that type; but maybe he'd given them the slip . . . He told me, 'I *have* sailed . . . Now I'm an armchair yachtsman, you might say. How big a crew do you have, on this boat?'

'None.' Then I thought of Gill, and added, 'Usually.'

'Single-handed, eh . . . And Blue Ensign. Does that mean you're on the naval reserve, or—'

'Means RNSA. Royal Naval Sailing Association. I have a warrant to fly it, and' – I pointed up at the spreader – 'that's the RNSA burgee.' It's a white burgee with a red St George's Cross and a blue naval crown superimposed. 'Now you know all.' I said it with a touch of sarcasm, and went below before he could ask any more questions or invite himself on board for a look round. He'd had that look, and I'd sensed that he was working round to it . . . I went down, and forgot him, worked below decks mostly on electrics until Gill arrived. It was only ten minutes short of noon when I heard her call from the quayside: I shot up on deck, and there she was.

I hadn't dreamt it. She was a one-off, absolutely. The world's full of Susans.

'Hi. Come aboard. Don't wait to be asked, the invitation's now permanent . . . You must have struck oil – right?'

With the *pension* people, I meant, because she'd been much longer than expected – about an hour and a half, since Lorna had been due to rendezvous with her at 10.30. She told me as she came aboard, 'Struck *something*, Matt . . .'

I saw then that she looked scared. At close quarters – somehow I'd come to be holding her, this was the smooth warmth of her upper arms under my hands – there was no doubt of it, her eyes were wide and – *definitely*, scared.

'Not good?'

'Not in the least good.' A lot of movement inside the T-shirt – a green one this morning, apple green, and shorts instead of the designer jeans – as if she'd been running. Beautiful, as well as frightened . . . She shook her head: 'I've been an age, I'm sorry, but – we went to the police, you see, and—'

'Better come down, sit, and—'

'Anne *did* leave a letter. This Raoul guy took it . . .'

Gill shut her eyes, enjoying a first swallow of ice-cold lager. Then she took a long, deep breath, swelling the green shirt; I dragged my eyes up just as hers opened . . . She said, 'Can't have been anyone but him. Incidentally, the Spaniards think he's probably Algerian – light-skinned, they said, but definitely not plain French . . . And the letter – they both swear there was one. When I arrived she'd forgotten but they'd had it there for me. Anne told them I was to get it the minute I walked in. This is the awful thing – she'd written some for posting, bought stamps for them at the desk in the hotel, and Raoul took them, said he'd get them into the post right away, so' – she was gabbling, still out of breath, wanting to tell it all at once – 'so she separated those from the one – mine – that didn't have a stamp on it, and he went off with them, but he must've come back before they finally left, and gone behind the desk, taken that one too – it's just this husband and wife run the place, they can't be on the desk all the time, I don't blame *them*—'

'But there's no certainty, you're *guessing* it was the Algerian who took it, right?'

'It's the hotel owner's guess, actually. But *somebody* did, for God's sake, and he'd seen it pushed into the slot under "P" for Paget – there wasn't anyone else around, no one else knew any letter existed – or that *I* did, even!'

'So she'd written to you – through the post, as she thought – and left a letter here in case you were already on your way.'

'Exactly. And she gave up her room at very short notice, they said, so he must've just sprung it on her that they were leaving right away. What else *could* she have done?'

'Well, since you ask – she might have telephoned . . .'

'To the old man, she could, if she'd wanted to, but she might not have relished the idea of telling him about Raoul. I doubt

70

she could've called *me*, I've been on the move a lot, might even have been on my way by then – uh?'

'OK . . . Now you've been and told all this to the police . . . Oh, wait, did Lorna think of checking poste restante, known locally as the *Lista de Correos*?'

'General delivery, sure, she did.' A shake of the glossy head. 'No dice . . . Matt, this is really nice, I *love* your boat, she's—'

'I'll show you round, in a minute. But tell me, which police lot did you go to? *Guardia Civil*?'

'God knows, Lorna simply—'

'What colour uniforms?'

'Oh, brown.'

'Brown. *Policia Nacional*. That's the national anti-crime force. So what's their reaction?'

'Well, they're putting the word out that Anne's disappeared, checking with the Immigration Department and so on. They've no record of anyone called Raoul, yachtsman or otherwise, but we don't have a surname for him anyway. The police captain pointed out they have hundreds and thousands of yachts coming and going, not only here at Mahon but shoals of them in the other yacht harbour, whatever it's—'

'Ciudadela. He's right, boats pack in there like sardines.'

'They're going to check on the boats, anyway, also with the Customs records and Port Health, all that. But just one guy with only his given name – I mean, they'd need to be damn lucky, wouldn't they? Especially as he'd have – well, wouldn't have been advertising himself, would he?' She drew a shaky breath. 'He asked me – did my family have money?'

'Kidnap. I suppose that's the obvious first guess.'

'Right. Especially since my father *does*.' She shook her head. 'But how anyone out here would have known—'

'If they'd had her targeted, and known she was coming?' Another thought struck me: 'You haven't told me what she was here for in the first place, why she'd have been here on her own. Is it possible she knew Raoul before?'

'She met him here, just recently. She told me she'd just met him, when she wrote, the letter I *did* get. But there's something else, Matt, before I answer that.' The honey-coloured eyes were fixed on mine. 'Something this cop said – he's a captain, Captain Cesar, d'you know him?'

71

'Can't say I do.'

'He knows *you*.'

'*Does* he . . .?'

'He'd asked me all about – well, things like why I came, where I'm staying and how long, etcetera, and I mentioned I'm hoping to leave here on your boat – because of Anne being in Turkey, maybe—'

'And?'

'He said, more or less talking to himself, but in English – "*Everybody* disappear, around this Señor Johnson." '

I stared at her. Drinking beer slowly but thinking quite fast. Harrison – or say Scotland Yard – must have asked the Spanish police to keep an eye out for Tommy. Keep an eye on *me*, therefore, in case Tommy surfaced in my vicinity. Because I was about the only lead they'd have to him. And they might strike lucky, at that – if he came to get his cash from me. Not that they could know about it: at least, I didn't believe they could.

'What did he mean, Matt?'

'Rather a long story. You're welcome to it, but there's no possible connection, so let's stick to your sister for the moment – why she was here, on her own.'

'She didn't *come* alone, she came with two other girls, touring. They were due to visit Rome after they left here, but then she met this bastard and the others went ahead without her.'

'Not very smart of them.'

'Well, she'd written to me, and I wired back to say I'd come as soon as I was free – I wanted to come for my own reasons, I told you about that – but anyway Anne is a very strong-headed person, Matt, they wouldn't've had much choice but to leave her here.'

'You're almost like twins, you said?'

'Not in that way, I'm not strong-willed like she is. She gets an idea in her head, that's it, nobody's going to change it.'

'Raoul changed it, though, didn't he? Persuading her to leave without you?'

'But she'd have thought she'd covered that commitment with the letters she wrote. She must have made up her mind she wasn't going to lose the guy – *that* would've been the strong

72

will at work . . . Who else disappeared, Matt?'

I was going to have to tell her, although in fact it wasn't anything she needed to know about, and that Spaniard should have learnt to control his tongue . . . I explained, 'An old friend of mine telephoned, a few hours before I left England in a motor-cruiser I had to deliver in the South of France. About three weeks ago. This guy's my own age, we were in the Royal Marines together. He rang to ask if he could come along – middle of the night, very short notice. I said OK, but I'm not waiting – because of a tide on the French side, mostly – and in fact he didn't make it, I sailed without him. Then at Le Havre, where we were entering the French inland waterways, we were stopped by police. For some reason they thought he might have been on board, and – well, turned out they wanted to question him in connection with the fact his wife got murdered.'

'Oh, *Jesus* . . .'

'That same night. But—'

'Are you saying this person—'

'I'm positive he couldn't have done it. He's – it's just so improbable, he simply could *not* have.'

'Because he's your old buddy?'

'No. Because I know him well enough to be bloody sure he didn't do it.'

She shrugged. 'Fair enough.' Then: 'But – despite being innocent, he was on the run?'

'Still is, apparently. I'm in touch with the fuzz who interrogated us at Le Havre.'

'Us?'

'Will Wyllie – you met him last night – was along to lend me a hand on that trip. It's hard work, going through the canal locks. I called this detective inspector last evening – from Lorenzo's actually, not long before we met – and if they'd caught Tommy he'd have told me. And, I got the impression he has an open mind – wants to question him, obviously, but – well, I'm only guessing, wishful thinking, but he did sound – open-minded.'

'So why – if your friend's innocent—'

'Why should he be on the run? I don't know. Obvious guess is the circumstances look bad for him, or *looked* bad,

73

and he panicked. But I don't know.'

'And you *can't* be sure he didn't do it, Matt, can you? You can say you are, and you'd *like* to be, but—'

'Well.' I finished my beer. She was right, of course. I didn't *know*, I *hoped*. But that crucial question – why did he run? – the truth was this wouldn't have been in character either. Admittedly he hadn't been his normal self, so maybe *that* didn't count for so much ... I said, 'Can't be completely certain, no. I suppose just about anyone can be driven – you know, over the edge ...'

I wondered why I was admitting to her what up to now I hadn't admitted to myself. There was an answer to this question, I felt sure, but I'd have needed time to get to it. I nodded. 'It's what I *want* to be the truth, but it also happens to be what I *believe* to be the truth.'

'OK. I didn't mean to—'

'That's all right. But you see, the British police must think there's some chance he'll turn up somewhere near me, so they'd have asked these people to look out for him, which may be how your Captain Cesar reacted to my name.'

'Maybe ... Only thing is, he made it sound like you had a police record or something.'

'Well – from his angle, I suppose I'm someone who may be tied up in a murder case. That's all he'd know. The British police certainly thought I'd helped Tommy to get out of the country, most likely still think I did, and once they start suspecting, that's the way they look at you ... Anyway, listen, now – what you have to do is call your father again.'

'To tell him about the letter?'

'And because – well, kidnapping for ransom's the most likely thing – isn't it?'

'Why not – well, white slaving?'

'Oh, come *on!*'

'What d'you mean, *come on*? We don't *know*, do we, we don't know a fucking *thing*, Matt! This Raoul could be *anything*! OK, ransom, that's the first thing anyone'd think of, my father's stinking rich and she's his favourite daughter, must be quite a few people know it too ... But in that scenario you need an organization with links back to the States and a team out here, it'd take time and a lot of money and logistical considerations, *all* of those things. But some shit of a white-slaver – or OK, just a kook, maybe it's for himself he'd want her, this "Raoul" creep . . . there *are* such animals, you read about them in newspapers just about every day, you know?'

'Yes. It could be . . . But – kidnap for ransom, in the circumstances—'

'*That* way it's simple, a one-man effort—'

'Gill,' – I put a hand on one of hers – 'I do think you should call your father.'

'He has the number at my *pension*. If he'd heard from her, or if he'd had any ransom demand, he'd—' She shrugged. 'He *could*'ve called me, if—'

'But from what you said about him he might not have, even if he *had* heard from her. And however much he may not want to know, even if he *is* that hard-nosed, he still ought to be told.'

She wasn't reacting. I shrugged. 'Well. He's your father and she's your sister, it's entirely your decision. Although I'd like to help you find her . . . Look, I don't know about you, but I'm ready for another beer.'

This started us on a tour of the *Bird of Dawning*'s interior – starting-point the fridge, where the beer was, and which is kept cool simply by having an only mildly effective insulation barrier between itself and the adjoining deep-freeze locker. This is in the galley space, of course, where the gas stove and the sink are, and another item in this department that pleased her was the Swan self-draining crockery cupboard. Washed-up crockery goes into this cupboard on racks through which it drip-dries itself into the bilge, so we don't need dishcloths.

She wanted to see everything, including the navigational electronics – Loran, radar, etcetera. She knew what she was looking at, too, although not having sailed in the Mediterranean she hadn't known that Decca doesn't work down here, which is why I've fitted Loran. Anyway, we covered just about every cubic inch and every piece of equipment therein, each switch and plug. I'd thought it might be good therapy for her when we'd started, and if therapy means getting a person's mind off whatever's tormenting it, then I'd guessed right.

'Your *Bird*'s fantastic, Matt. I really love her.'

She was close to me when she said this, really very close, and the proximity and sight of her triggered thoughts that were a long way ahead of their time. Or maybe not – as thoughts – but if they'd been translated into action they would have been.

I led the way back aft.

'I'll show you the gear on deck now, just to round off the tour, but I want to take her out this afternoon anyway – for an hour or two, couple of things to see about – if you are free, like to come along?'

'Why, yeah, I *would*.'

'Fine. We'll have a snack on board before we start. But another thing I was going to say is I don't see why we shouldn't leave for Malta a bit sooner than I'd thought. Two more days, then take off – if that'd suit you?'

'Sooner the better, for me.'

'Well, that's another point. I know how worried you are, but the fact is it'll be some while before we get to Turkey. There'll be several days waiting around in Malta, as well as the two sea transits. You're going to need patience.'

'I'll make out, don't worry.'

'Sure you will. And I'm delighted I'll have you with me.'

I hadn't meant to say that. Hadn't meant to say anything like it . . . I was face to face with her – *again*: we were in the saloon, the midships cabin, and I wondered how I was going to stand this when I had her to myself on board day after day and night after night . . . Then she'd turned away, fiddling with a chart I'd left out on the table, and talking rather quickly: 'I mean I'll *try* to be patient. I was thinking anyway that when we get to Turkey you'll have your charterers, you won't be free to – I mean, you say you want to help find Anne, and obviously I'd love that, it's sweet of you, but you'll have those guys to look after—'

'Not every minute of every day.'

'When we get to Fethiye – well, we could see how it goes, maybe you'll have to leave me there a while and—'

'See how it goes, as you say.'

There was something I had to do on my own account, anyway. That's to say Tommy's. His Turkish friends lived in Istanbul, had a business in Izmir and a hotel at or near a small place called Göcek, which isn't far from Fethiye. Tommy had talked about them that evening in London, so he'd know I knew about them, and they'd be an obvious link between us if he had any intention of making contact. If he was alive, and free, and half a dozen other 'if's'; and contact might be made by post, or telephone – word of mouth, messages via these Turks – or even, just in the outer fringes of possibility – in person.

Whatever his plans or movements might be, he'd be wanting his money back.

One way and another, I hoped these Lawrie people weren't going to be too demanding. But as the Lawries of this world provide my livelihood, they and their requirements would have to come first.

We had bread and cheese and fruit for lunch, and I nagged her again about calling her father. A check in the Nautical Almanac showed that if she called at eight in the evening – which she could do from Lorenzo's, or from her *pension* – she'd get him in his office at 11 a.m. Californian time. She said she'd do this – reluctantly, and maybe just so we could drop the subject – and I remembered that at about that time I'd be getting set to go and pick up Susan.

I wished I hadn't made that date, now. It had been a reflex action: like diving for cover.

The things I needed to do this afternoon were (a) check the compass, which I could do out in the bay, using various marks on the surrounding land, (b) go on out to sea and pump out the holding tanks, and (c) on return, top up with diesel. I thought I'd better take on some fresh water too, before Gill came to live on board and the frequency of showers, hair-washing, etc. increased.

I'd pulled in the gangplank and the stern warp, and Gill was up forward looking after the anchor winch, when I spotted that British tourist, armchair yachtsman as he'd called himself, on the quayside. Just standing there, watching – but well back this time, as if he didn't want to be seen. I had the engine ticking over in neutral and I'd looked astern to check that we were all clear, only happened to glance across the paving, and there was this familiar figure. He saw me recognize him, and his hand was lifting to wave – I had an impression of embarrassment, but that might have been in my imagination – as I turned away to go forward and give Gill a hand.

It occurred to me that he might be a colleague of Harrison's, sent to check on whether I had Tommy Fountain with me. It wasn't unlikely: he'd asked about crew, maybe with Tommy in mind, and if he'd just arrived, and contacted the local *policia* – which I supposed he would have done – it would explain my name having rung an instant bell with the Spaniard who'd interviewed Gill.

Anyway, if he was a copper, he was wasting his time. Turkey, not Menorca, would be the place – the only place Tommy had expressed interest in, and where he had these friends, also with a certain remoteness that would appeal to him. How he'd get there – well, in his situation getting anywhere at all would pose problems, but like me he'd had years of training in the arts of evasion and concealment; as long as he could sober up and got over the shakes, psychological and otherwise, I thought he'd hack it all right.

There was a point for *me* to bear in mind, though: if they'd sent a CID man here, the odds were they'd send one to Turkey as well, so if there was any prospect of contact with Tommy I'd need to watch my back or I might lead them to him.

Our sea trip went off satisfactorily – just on the engine, I didn't have the mainsail on her yet – and when we'd secured again Gill went off to her hotel with the intention – surprise, surprise – of washing her hair. This reminded me about topping up with fresh water, and I had the hose running while I got on with the next series of jobs.

I got into Lorenzo's just before eight. Gill was there, hobnobbing with the McAllisters, and she told me she'd booked a call to her father for eight fifteen.

'So you take young women out sailing now, Matt.'

Haemish, with a hand on my shoulder; several pairs of ears were tuned-in from neighbouring tables and from the bar, and there were smirks on one or two faces besides his. I said – because imitating his Scots accent always infuriates him – 'Och aye . . . Romantic as the bonny, bonny banks themselves, is pumping out holding tanks. Right, Gill?'

'Great experience. And your *Bird of Dawning*'s beautiful.'

'Glad you think so . . .' I asked Haemish, 'Listen, do you still have that old Renault, and if so can I borrow it this evening?'

'Sure. It's in the alley, help yourself.'

'You'll want it back here by about midnight, I suppose.'

'God, no . . . Lorna'd never get in that old thing now!'

She confirmed this. 'It stinks – of fish, among other things. We only use it for the market and suchlike. We've a much smarter job now for our own transport.'

'I always said this place was a goldmine.'

Haemish asked me, looking at Gill, 'Where'll ye be taking the puir wee lass?'

Gill looked away, and I frowned at him. '*Which* pure wee lass?'

Lorna made a snorting sound, and he slid away, before he could put the other foot in it as well. Gill was looking unconcerned and Lorna was gazing at me speculatively. I began, 'It's only a duty date I—' and Lorna interrupted with 'Sit down, Matt, something to tell you.'

'Why don't I get us a drink first?'

'Because we've already got drinks, and you can listen to this, first. There was a fellow in here asking questions about you and your boat. He asked a lot of other stuff as well but he kept coming back to you and the *Bird of Dawning*, that was all he was really after. Things like did I think you'd take a crew with you to Malta, and were crew usually paid or just friends along for the ride. That kind of thing.'

'Who told him I was going to Malta?'

'God knows. I didn't. But most people around here know it, anyone could have.'

'I think he's a copper. If it's the same guy, I was wondering about him earlier on. Would he be about thirty-five or forty, silly little moustache, pale or maybe by now pink complexion, and sporting a blue-striped shirt, khaki Marks and Spencers slacks, khaki sun-hat?'

'Spot on, I'd say.'

Gill murmured, looking at me as if I was some creature from outer space, 'Incredible . . .'

'Not really, I've had two good looks at him. He engaged me in conversation this morning, and when we shoved off this afternoon he was on the quay to wave goodbye.'

'So what did you do, Matt?' Lorna asked me. 'Rob a bank?'

'Yeah. How else could I afford to patronize this clip joint? Come on, now, let's have some drinks.'

Gill's call didn't come through until nearly half-eight. Waiting for it, we talked about various things including the Turkey cruise and the various complications such as having charterers to satisfy, and so on, and she also slipped in the information that she'd arranged to have supper at her hotel tonight; she wanted to get an early night, and she'd be down to help me on the *Bird* right after breakfast.

I was pretty sure that if she *had* made any such arrangements, she'd have mentioned it before.

When she was called to the telephone, Lorna came over and asked me, 'So what are you up to tonight?'

'Date with Susan. Why?'

'*Why* is a good question.' Disapproval followed her like a smoke-trail as she strutted off: and at that moment I saw the Armchair Yachtsman – at the bar, getting a drink from Haemish; he must have come in when Gill had been on her way to the telephone and I'd been giving her departure my full attention.

I strolled over to the bar. Thinking about Lorna's testiness. Only about 24 hours ago her husband had implied I *should* have been doing something about Susan. Evidently I wasn't supposed to make my own decisions in these matters.

And at that, it might have been better if I hadn't.

'Haemish.' Out of the sides of my eyes I saw the Armchair Yachtsman turn and identify me. Haemish muttering, 'Hang on, Matt, only got two hands, God's sake . . .'

'Don't want a drink, I've got one. Just the keys of your Renault, please.'

'Ah, shit . . .'

He'd given the AY a brandy – Terceiro, I saw the bottle as he put it back – and ginger ale to mix into it. Pointing at the ice-bucket with one hand while collecting *pesetas* with the other. I said, 'Carlos Terceiro's too good to put that muck in. He's got cheaper brands.'

'Ah, well.' The AY was wearing a blazer with silvered buttons and a badge which for all I knew might have been that of the Metropolitan Police. 'Only live once, don't we?'

'You mean the taxpayers get the bill, so what the fuck?'

Haemish had fetched the keys; he tossed them to me across the bar. 'Must be a few litres in the tank. Get you to her house and back. Sorry about that, Matt.'

'We can't all be clever.'

'Thought you were keen on—' He jerked his head, rearward . . . 'Eh?'

'Keen as mustard.' I put my empty glass down, and asked the policeman, 'Planning on trailing me to Malta, next?'

'What say?' He *had* got a bit pink from the sun today. 'Beg pardon, didn't catch—'

'Give my regards to Charles Harrison, will you? Excuse me now.'

Gill was on her way back from the telephone, and I steered an interception course. 'All right?'

'Well, I told him.' She shrugged. 'He – what's that phrase diplomats use? – "took cognizance" of it.'

I didn't want to leave her. And a table had just been vacated, one of the small ones near the door. I gestured towards it. 'Let me get us a drink. If you have a minute?'

'What about your date?'

'There's no rush.'

'Well – OK . . . That brandy you drink, with ginger and a lot of ice?'

The Armchair Yachtsman had gone. Haemish growled, 'Bugger asked did I lend my car or rent it out, and where might you be going in it. I asked him how was it any of his business, and he said he'd thought you might have been going to Ciudadela and he could've cadged a lift . . . Which brandy d'you want?'

'Primero, please. Some detective, that.'

'Detective?' Then he did a double-take: 'Primero, with ginger ale?'

'It's for a delicate palate.'

He glanced over. Like some kind of terrier – chin out-thrust, eyebrows bristling . . . And reaching for the bottle, getting the right one without having to look. 'Ought to make up your fucking mind, Matt.'

I took the drinks over, and sat down. Wyllie had just come in, and was sort of teetering, looking at us, but getting no encouragement he continued glumly towards the bar.

'Your father wasn't all that concerned, then.'

'I told you, Matt, he's a busy man. In his office too, working hours, minions creeping in to lick his boots and crawl out again . . .'

81

She shook her head. You could see that talking to her father made her miserable. Made her – I saw this suddenly – *lonely*.

'But he got the point, did he – that she's at least been conned into disappearing with the Algerian?'

'What he said was "Anne's free, white and over twenty-one. If I hear from kidnappers I'll know she's been kidnapped. Until then I'm continuing to assume she doesn't know where she's at, where she's come from or where she's going." I did tell you, Matt.'

'Funny sort of father.'

'Funny's *one* word for it.' I was looking at her in close-up as she spoke, and her face at that moment seemed to shudder, a tightening of the facial muscles, I suppose, but so fast you'd have needed a very high-speed film to have caught it. Then she was sipping her Carlos Primero and ginger ale, murmuring, 'Nice drink, this, Matt' – and I wished to God I hadn't made that bloody date.

6

After weeks of abstinence, to have the *Bird of Dawning*'s wheel in my hands – her lively, lunging response to every touch on it, the feel of her in my hands and under my feet, and the music she made, the beauty of her plunging hull and the straining swell of jib and mainsail – it was wildly exhilarating, deeply satisfying.

You can add one other feature to the picture: Gill, near me in the cockpit, in profile against bright blue sea and the sky a lighter shade with streamers of white in it. Brown hair loose, windswept; she was wearing shorts and a shirt that left her midriff bare. I guessed she'd have acquired her tan in California but I hadn't asked, didn't want to probe into the background of her marital break-up, who'd walked out on whom, where from or where to.

It wasn't my business. I thought it would be a mistake to try to make it my business.

We'd sailed from Mahon eighteen hours ahead of even my revised estimate. Gill had been helping me – as she'd promised, from about breakfast-time on the morning after my date with Susan – and in fact most of the essentials had been done by then, we'd only had final touches to apply, like arranging the stowage of this and that, getting things generally straight for the trip and acclimatizing her to where things were kept and how everything worked. There were still a few jobs I had to do myself, but if I'd had to I could have finished it all that day. And she was terrific, I don't believe I'd had to tell her anything twice, she absorbed information instantly and in any case she'd sailed recently in modern yachts, in the Caribbean. The Hercules computer, for instance, which was under the chart-table and gives me print-outs of speed and distance logged, and wind speed and angle relative to the boat's course, held no mysteries for her – in fact I got the impression she might have thought it was rather old-hat and was just too polite to say so.

Anyway, she'd turned up that morning ready for work, and she was kind enough – or wise enough – not to ask me what sort of an evening I'd had. In fact I'd only returned the Renault to the McAllisters' alley at about 4 a.m., and I dare say I was showing the signs of it.

'So, what's to do, Matt?'

One of the snags of not having been in the habit of employing female crew is that I wasn't used to putting daz-zlingly attractive girls to work. Her working clothes, I might explain, were short denim shorts displaying her long brown legs, and a T-shirt with an anchor on it, the anchor's flukes pointing with unnerving precision at her nipples. After the night I'd just spent I shouldn't have been as susceptible to this general effect as I found I was.

I told her, 'Personally, I'm going to get busy on the sheet winches. The oil bakes hard in them, you know. They have to be stripped down and cleaned. I soak the ball-races in boiling water then put 'em together again with fresh grease in them.'

'Couldn't two of us do that?'

'Could, but—' Genius stirred, at last. 'Look, how about a clean-out inside here? The forward cabin specially – if I get all that junk out of it, which I'll do now. Then if you're going to be cook, you might like to sort out the knives and forks and things, so you'll know where it's all at. Then, there's some brain-work required – work out a list of what provisions we want.'

'For how long?'

'Ah – well, let's see . . .' I had a chart out already, on the saloon table – Admiralty chart 165, Menorca to Malta – which I'd been looking at while soaking up strong, sweet tea in lieu of breakfast. 'Here, look. To make Valletta in one hop's about 600 miles. That's no problem – 150 miles a day average, four days, say. With the wind from west or north-west – touch wood, it *may* hold – plus some help from the engine when or if it doesn't – if it all went absolutely right it *could* be done in about 70 hours. But 100 hours is more realistic, so let's say four days.'

'Leaving – day after tomorrow?'

'Or tomorrow after lunch, even. If you could make that?'

'Sure. The hotel's no problem, I'm on a daily rate.'

'So you could move in tomorrow forenoon.'

'I get to inhabit the forepeak, do I?'

'Or use one of these bunks here. Suit yourself.'

'But your charterers, won't they—'

'Not for a week, they won't. I think I'll give them my cabin, anyway, they'll be more self-contained in there. Doesn't worry me, I'll sleep on deck mostly, it's mainly where to stow one's gear.'

The question of who slept where was a tricky one, in the circumstances – meaning, in the delicate state of our relationship. At least, *I* felt it was delicate, and until now I'd avoided the subject. She hadn't raised it either, I'd noticed, not even when I'd been showing her round the boat, when it would surely have been natural to have asked 'Where do I sleep?' And while the Lawries would be more comfortable in the stern cabin, with their own head and shower *en suite*, this would put me and Gill in the midships and forward cabins with the other head and shower to share between us. With very little between us, in fact, and I didn't know how she'd react to this if I proposed it.

I let it ride, for the moment. We were still nervous of each other. Silly, but that's how it was. On that particular morning, as I've said, I wasn't too clear-headed either.

'Anyway – this transit to Malta – we can do it in one hop, alternatively make a pit-stop in Sardinia. Here – Porto Ponte Romano, or the more obvious place is Cagliari. Like to see Sardinia?'

'Matt, I'm your *crew*, remember?'

'You can still have a preference, surely?'

'Well, Lorna was right, you're a kind man, but—'

'Lorna said that?'

'*Gentle* was the word she used. But look – Malta's where we need to be, why don't we just get there?'

'Right. Why don't we . . . I'll have a word to Lorna . . . Let's clear out the fore cabin now.'

The biggest item in there was the mainsail in its bag, and I wanted this out anyway, to rig it, and she could help with that. The genoa was already where it belonged, furled on the forestay; I'd done that yesterday afternoon. But there was also a lot of loose stuff like life-jackets and foul-weather gear, and my Scuba equipment, and spare bedding, and so on. I was scratching my head over where to put most of it, when Gill solved the problem – *two* problems, actually . . . 'Matt, if I take this cabin for mine, I don't have much stuff with me and I only use one bunk – believe it or not – so a lot of it could stay. I'll stack what we won't be using, maybe lash it, and set up the lee-cloth that side.'

'You're a genius.'

'Not all that noticeably. Maybe you aren't *quite* yourself, this morning.'

It was the only reference she made, then or later, to my 'duty' date.

I hadn't taken Susan anywhere. It had been a Sunday night, and she'd prepared the materials for a barbecue – they have a stone fireplace which her father built close to his swimming pool – and we spent the evening in and around the poolhouse. Listening to music, swimming, and so forth. Her parents were out, and when they got back they didn't come near us.

She'd said at some point, 'Rumour has it you're taking a girl crew to Turkey.'

'Oh?'

'*Oh.*'

'Well. There you are, then.'

'Bastard.'

'She needs to get to Turkey. Her sister's vanished, she thinks she's gone to Turkey in some boat, so going there in mine may be the best chance of catching up with her . . . Ever hear of a French-speaking, light-skinned Algerian answering to the name of Raoul, by the way?'

'Can't say I have. Have we changed the subject?'

'He may have kidnapped this girl, that's all.'

'Wow. Thrill after thrill.'

'Well, now, you listen—'

'No.' She put her fingers over my mouth. 'No, I'm sorry. Really – I was only teasing. It's entirely your own business, Matt.'

'I *had* thought it might have been.'

'On this little island?' She laughed. 'Well, don't worry. *I'm* not worried. Nobody ever pretended we were going steady, did they?'

'Not that I know of.'

'And you'll be back, won't you?'

'Sure to be.'

'As someone just said – there you are, then . . . Let's dance to this?'

But Gill had been in my head all the time. Literally, all night. I don't know whether it would have pleased her to have known this, but I do know it would have made Susan spitting mad.

I was re-assembling the last of the winches, one of the two big ones – the 65s, which handle the foresheets and would have been used for the spinnaker in the days when the *Bird* had worn one – when Haemish McAllister stopped his new, smart car in the roadway and walked over to the quayside. It was just after noon, the time he usually gets to his restaurant and starts work. He came over the plank and told me, 'Telephone call for you last night, from London.'

Harry Loder, I guessed. To tell me the Lawries have cancelled. I tend to anticipate the worst: it's safer.

'Guy called Frewin, Chief Inspector. Wants you to call him back. I said I doubted you'd have the money, and he said you can reverse the charge. Here's the number.'

'Thanks, Haemish . . .'

'Soon as possible, he said. Detective Chief Inspector – *really* after you now, eh?'

'I'll be along in a minute and use your phone, then.'

He was in his out-of-hours work clothes – check shirt, baggy old trousers, sandals. Bristling crewcut, eyebrows like wire-wool gleaming in the sunshine. 'How d'ye make out last night?'

Gill spoke from the hatchway as she came up the ladder. 'Good morning, Haemish.'

87

'Why, *hello* there!'

Startled, flushing deep red across the cheekbones; elsewhere, since he hadn't shaved yet, you couldn't see it. I told him, 'The car seems fine. Bit rough, but – it goes, doesn't it . . . I put some petrol in.'

'Good man . . . So he's put ye to work, Gill?'

'He's a slave-driver.'

'Ask me, I'd say he has the luck of the devil.'

'What a *nice* man you are.'

I said, 'If you two carry on like that, I'll tell Lorna. Gill, I have to return a telephone call, from his place. Like to come along? We'll persuade him to make us a Spanish omelette; there's a dry rosé he has that goes just right with it.'

She nodded gravely. 'I think I'm going to like it here.'

Detective Chief Inspector Frewin thanked me for calling him back. He was in charge of the investigation into the death of Mrs Fountain, he added. I asked what had happened to Charles Harrison, and his answer was a stuffy 'We aren't quite a one-man band, you know.'

'Ah. Right . . . So how can I help you?'

'You last saw Mr Fountain when you met him for an evening meal in London four nights before your departure from Southampton . . .'

I waited. There was a bit of a silence. Then: 'Mr Johnson?'

'Was that a question?'

'No, I'm leading to a question.'

'Good. I wouldn't want to have to answer that one again. I've told Harrison a dozen times that's when I last saw Fountain.'

I didn't like the fact I *had* just been asked it again, even though he'd backed off. It reinforced an earlier feeling that they knew for sure I'd seen Tommy in Southampton, only lacked proof of it.

Frewin was saying, 'What I'm after, Mr Johnson, is your view on one particular aspect of Fountain's attitude to his marriage. You've told us – you volunteered the information, and we appreciate your desire to help us as well as to exonerate your friend – you've told us the marriage was failing, at least part of the cause being that Mrs Fountain was involved with another man, or men.'

'She was screwing around. Yeah.'

'What I want to ask is this . . . Would you say that Mr Fountain would have been disposed to try to save his marriage if that had been possible? If there'd been any chance of reconciliation, do you think he'd have wanted it?'

What I thought was that this guy was testing *me*. Whether or not I'd give him an honest opinion. Because the opinion itself was surely valueless: surely not worth two long-distance calls.

'Well. Difficult question – for anyone but *him* to—'

'Of course. But as he's – absented himself, and I gather you were close to him . . . Give it some thought, tell me what you think.'

Or, I guessed, he wants to be convinced that there was – is – another man, potentially the killer: that I didn't invent this scenario as a red herring for Charles Harrison.

So – the truth – as far as one knew it . . .

When he'd been in love with her, he'd have bust his guts trying to hang on. But he'd talked about 'the great turn-off': I'd forgotten that bit, but it came back now. Also, though, that he'd been worried about the fall-out, business angles . . . Which – well, as he *had* been, the real Tommy Fountain, this wouldn't have come into it for a moment: and one had to assume such spinelessness couldn't be permanent . . .

Frewin's voice: 'Like to think about it, call me back?'

'No. Not necessary. You recording this, by the way?'

Pause . . . Then: 'Yes, as a matter of fact—'

'I'd say the answer is no, he would *not* have tried to hang on. The whole thing was unstable, he didn't fit into her world, her father's world, and I'd think he'd have had to if they were going to stay together. Then the fact she'd been cheating on him – which I think he said he'd found out quite recently – that was the last straw, I think he'd finally had it, wanted out.'

'Well. I'm impressed with that forthright answer. You must realize it would give an edge to what any judge and jury might see as motive.'

'But that's a risk I've already taken. When I phoned Harrison.'

'Oh, indeed . . . And my reason for putting that question to you is not unrelated to – to just that area of inquiry, you might say.'

'So you *are* looking into other—'

'I'd like to put this to you now, Mr Johnson. When a man – a possible suspect – runs away, disappears – a grown, mature individual with special training and experience behind him, not the sort of person you'd expect to panic – well, I'm sure it's as obvious to you as it is to me, it would be *very* much in his interests to come forward. If you should have any means of establishing contact with him—'

'How the hell could I—'

'—or if he were to contact you, for instance – *please* do whatever you can to persuade him of this.'

'I would, sure, but I don't see how it could happen. You've got this idiot hanging around out here, calling himself an armchair yachtsman, and *that's* a waste of time and money, I can tell you.'

'I'm by no means sure who this is you're—'

'Little moustache, pink face, goes around asking silly questions and wasting good brandy. For your sake I hope you don't have many like that.'

'You've lost me. But – anyway, thank you, and if we need to contact you again, Mr Johnson—'

'Leaving for Malta day after tomorrow. Then Turkey, but I'll be on the move there, port to port. Addresses from Harry Loder – in the City, he's my charter agent, Harrison knows him.'

That evening we were in Lorenzo's when Loder called. The Lawries hadn't cancelled – I'd had that same foreboding, *en route* to the phone – but part of what Harry had to tell me did concern them. They were going to be in Malta – at the Hilton, where else? – a few days earlier than they'd planned, so if I could do the same they'd be happy to adjust the schedule accordingly. This was a stroke of luck; not only would we not have to hang around for so long in Malta, but Gill could get to Turkey earlier than she'd expected and I'd have about ten days instead of seven between landing them back at Valletta and picking up the next charter at Athens. The Malta–Athens trip

90

involved a transit of about 500 miles via the Corinth Canal, and I was relieved to know that I wasn't going to have to sweat over it. And that would be the last long haul; from then to the end of the season I'd be in the Aegean.

Gill was pleased with the news from Loder. Then she asked, 'But you mean you've got to ship them all the way back west to Malta, then turn round and flog back to Athens?'

'It's the trip west that'll be the hard work. Into the weather instead of with it. Unless I'm bloody lucky. But you see I wasn't getting any charters, a few weeks ago, so when the Lawries offered themselves my agent grabbed them for me. Quite right too. Since then, these others have come up – and he's got some more now, he was telling me it looks as if I'm booked right through into September.'

'You do *earn* your living.'

It didn't seem such a rugged life, though, when we were running eastward, that first morning – second day – out of Mahon, making close on eight knots in the ideal conditions of an almost cloudless sky and just the wind I'd been hoping for.

On the second morning, she appeared on deck in a bikini. From the start I'd worn only bathing shorts, during the heat of the day, and I'd wondered when or whether she'd come down to my level. Now she had, and it had been worth waiting for: it was an orange bikini and there wasn't much of it, and she looked – well, I won't try to describe how she looked, I'll only record that I wondered seriously how long I was going to be able to continue behaving in my present saintly manner.

Even why I *had* been.

I began to think it out. Gill meanwhile exposing her lovely body to the sun, reclining on the teak deck, port side. *Bird of Dawning* was on the port tack but again we had the wind well back on the quarter so the mainsail was well clear and there was no shade to spoil her sunbathe; it was a suitable time to remind oneself of established principles and good resolutions, such as why I'd very nearly not agreed to bringing her along, and what I'd seen of other single-handed sailors and their futile sexual adventures, and the extent to which it got in the way of their performance as charter skippers; also that I hadn't the slightest intention of giving up my present way of life, therefore had nothing to offer in the way of security, which is what most women want – need – so that my sexual partners had to be girls like Susan who weren't yet ready to think about settled lives and families.

Relating this to Gill now, a basic factor as I saw it was her loneliness. Parentally – well, we've covered that, but now on top of it she had (a) a failed or failing marriage, (b) good reason to be scared stiff for whatever was happening to her sister, the one person she'd ever been really close to.

I remembered her saying, 'We're very close, we always were more like twins than sisters . . . I'd had problems, wanted to be with her . . .' And – that same evening – looking at me searchingly, as if it was important to her to know whether I understood or agreed with her: 'Life's *shit* – you know?'

It would be difficult to imagine anyone more vulnerable, I thought. All I'd be doing – if I followed my natural inclinations – would be taking advantage of that vulnerability and loneliness, and in the long run doing her no good at all.

She wasn't wearing her wedding ring, I noticed. There was a band of white, untanned skin where it had been.

Bikini on, ring off?

'Hey, crew!'

Her head tilted, a hand up to shield her eyes. 'Hi, skipper.'

'Want to practise man overboard?'

'OK . . .'

She gathered herself up and came to join me. She'd sailed the boat yesterday for several hours, and taken her share of watchkeeping last night, but I wanted to know she'd be competent to handle emergencies on her own. This exercise now, for instance – if I went overboard, I'd like her to be able to come back and pick me up; one of the more aggravating situations for a boat owner is to be in the drink and watch his boat waltzing off into the sunset. But more likely, if a passenger went over the side and I happened to be taking forty winks when she was at the wheel – it's immediate, virtually reflex reactions that save or lose lives.

She took the wheel. Slipping in behind it – beside me, near naked. I could name people who wouldn't believe I'd have the self-control to keep my hands off her. In fact my hands were employed in separating the waterlight from the man-overboard pole, which is an eight-foot grp marker pole with a weight on one end, a float a couple of feet above it and a flag on top, also this strobe light with a mercury switch, and there wasn't any point wasting its battery now. The pole is attached upside-down to the backstay, and turning it right way up as it goes into the sea activates the switch.

'In real emergency you'd chuck *that* over, right?' I was freeing one of the horseshoe-shaped life floats: then I slung it overboard to leeward. 'But that's me in the water now. All yours.'

She whipped the pole off the backstay and tossed it over. If this had been for real she'd have ditched a few other articles too – cockpit seat cushions, for instance, bright yellow, show up well in the drink – so as to have a whole line of markers for guidance. I saw her check the compass course – so she'd have the reciprocal in mind – and reach to start the engine: which was an option, she could have done this under sail or power, or both . . . She let the *Bird* run a few lengths farther, furling the genoa while gaining that much stand-off distance: then we were coming round fast to port, hardening into the wind – increasingly violent movement on the boat as she swung beam-on to the sea – still swinging, turning her bow up into it, Gill sheeting the mainsail in as the boom swung over, and steadying her close-hauled, starboard tack, ploughing in to it with the red flag in sight over wavetops up ahead. Finally she brought my *Bird* up into the wind, pitching like crazy with the genoa furled, diesel running, mainsail flat: we were virtually stopped, close to windward of that float.

She'd done it just right. Wind-direction had been helpful, of course, allowing it to be concluded in just the one tack, but it had still been a neat job. I watched her dart forward, snatch the boathook out of its stowage and scoop up the float. Then, back at the wheel, she let the *Bird* fall off a little and gather way until we had the flagged pole scraping along the side: I had only to reach out, to lift it on board.

'Congratulations. You saved my life.'

'Oh, any time.' She smiled: she was bringing the *Bird* round, and resetting the genoa. 'She's a dream to handle.'

The phrase struck a spark in my mind and lingered. I couldn't help it: watching her with her slim hands on the wheel, legs straddled, balancing herself against the motion as the boat turned back across steep, fast-running sea. I'm in vigorous health, and she was damn near naked as well as – well, the way she looked . . . It flashed into my mind that she'd be easy to go mad about. Hearing myself telling her, 'Only thing I'd mention is when it's for real you'd do best to bring the body to the stern and use the swimming ladder. That's the easiest way out of the water, and you could even use that anchor winch if you had to – if you had someone heavy, unconscious . . .'

She'd said, a day or two earlier, 'I didn't know I was so transparent.'

But she is. She'd be no good at telling lies, and she'd find it difficult to say anything she didn't mean. It must make life difficult for her at times, but on that count alone she's a one-off. And it *rubs* off; it was that quality of directness, for instance – it really hits you when she's talking to you – that had made me admit to her that Tommy Fountain could have killed his wife. (Obvious enough, but until then I'd barely admitted it even to myself.)

Maybe this was what had come between her and her father. It mightn't be too comfortable to face her frankness, that clear-eyed way she looks at you when she wants to know something, if you're a wheeler-dealer of the kind who squeezes his partners out of a business when it's beginning to look like taking off – which, reading between the lines of what she'd said and the way she'd said it, was what I gathered Brennan had done.

I asked her that evening – in the stern cockpit, the sun dropping towards the horizon and the sky tinting gold behind us, the *Bird* on autopilot and fairly romping along – 'Tell me about your marriage.'

'Not much to tell.' She raised her glass: Carlos Terceiro and ginger ale, a drink on which she seemed to have become hooked, since that first one in Menorca. 'Here's to divorce, and other happy endings.'

'Getting one, are you?'

She raised the hand that had had a ring on it, waggled that finger at me.

'I guess so. It took a bit of getting used to the idea, but' – she

94

shrugged – 'no point trying to hang on to something that isn't there any longer, is there?'

'I'm sorry.'

'No need to be. Guy just walked out. Forty, and he's shacked up with this kid of nineteen. I'm sorry for *her*.'

'He must be awfully stupid.'

'I'm only a little concerned nineteen may still be a little old for him, might've suited himself better with something more like *fifteen*.'

I laughed. But you could bet there'd be some truth in it as well. Glancing at the time: 'Hey, log time . . .'

I write up the log each hour, taking the Loran position in latitude and longitude from the dials and noting it down with course and speed and updating the position on the chart. This isn't just some old maritime routine, it's so that if the Loran should happen to go on the blink I'd have a comparatively recent fix from which I could run-on a dead-reckoning position – thereafter *working* for my living, using D/F bearings if stations were handy and meanwhile blowing the cobwebs off my trusty sextant.

I put on a shirt, switched on the navigation lights and went back up to check that they were burning before I rejoined her. She asked as she moved back to where she'd been before, 'Making progress?'

'You bet. But I'll be surprised if this wind doesn't die on us before morning.'

'Does the forecast say so?'

'Forecast is hedging its bets, but it feels like it, don't you think?'

She shook her head. The sun was splashing down and the sails were pink now. 'Your brandy must've dulled my weather instinct.'

It was more guess than instinct. At this time of year in this part of the Mediterranean you'd expect to average about one day in three with little or no wind. I asked her – she was wearing a sweater over the bikini, legs still bare but in shelter in the cockpit – 'What's your husband's business or profession?'

'Stocks and shares. Money.'

'Is he good at it?'

She shrugged. 'When the market's going up, he thinks he's brilliant.'

'Does he get on with your father?'

She frowned, thinking about it. 'Well, Dad approved of him, to start with – I suppose for taking me off his hands, one less daughter cluttering the place up.' She reached down, put her empty glass between her feet, on the cockpit sole, turned one of those forthright looks of hers on me as she straightened. The sunset was staining her face, and her eyes were more pale gold than brown, almost glowing, reflecting that last light. 'What about *your* marriage? Car-smash, I know and I'm sorry, Matt. Lorna told me – I mean, I appreciate it must have been quite dreadful, but – years ago now, right?'

It was typical of Gill, I thought, that she'd raised this subject. I said, 'Lorna does talk, doesn't she?'

'All she told me was there was this smash-up and your wife and child were killed in it. I'm not asking about that, I'm asking about now – *you* – and what's this defensive cage you live in?'

'Defensive – cage?' I looked round – at the smoothly lunging *Bird*, the vast surrounding spaces of darkening sea and sky: 'I'm in a cage?'

'You're – oh, outgoing, you're exceptionally kind, you're great with people – I wouldn't for a moment call you an introvert, and yet—'

'Heaven's sake, girl—'

'You *hide*. And you never say anything about yourself. OK, I've heard a few things – like you have some girl on Menorca, maybe one in every port, ha-ha, but—'

'I'm so exceptionally kind I'll rip Lorna's tongue out.'

'*She* didn't say anything like this. It's my own feeling that this life you lead's like – well, sort of a refuge, isn't it?'

'Can't say I'd thought of it quite that way. It's how things turned out, that's all, I just sort of cut adrift, and—'

'Why?'

I drew a long breath . . . 'Gill, you're beautiful – *extremely* beautiful, and—'

I'd been on the very brink of saying 'And I'm falling in love with you' – but I caught that in my front teeth, swallowed it and substituted – 'and very quick on the uptake, percipient, surely you can understand that a thing like that, a man's wife and baby daughter—'

'I can see it would have been ghastly, for a while even unbearable, but I can also see you're no weakling, you'd have ridden the punch as well as anyone, as most guys would – because, as we all know, life has to go on, right? But obviously you have *not*, so – well, I don't want to pry, Matt, but tell me, what were the special circumstances of the accident?'

'Lorna told you.'

'No, I swear—'

'She hinted, then.'

'Matt. If I perceive something, I must have been tipped off to it, but if you do you're Sherlock Holmes *cum* Sigmund Freud?'

I allowed a pause, then told her, 'Lorna and Haemish are the only people out here who know, and only one person in England does. It's old, Gill, over and done with, it led to my adopting this life and now I – well, I like it, it *suits* me, damn it!'

'I just get the feeling you're on the run from your own past, Matt.'

'I'm not on the run from anything. I told you, the life suits me, I happen to enjoy it.'

But she was like a terrier – straining forward, peering at me through fading light, determined to get it out of me . . . 'Makes you seem – don't get me wrong, but sort of older than you are. All that *cautious* shit, the way you figure it all out before you—' She paused: it was about dark now, she was a black cut-out against the phosphorescence around the *Bird*'s creaming hull. 'Why *not* tell me, Matt? Might even be good for you, to—'

'It might. Except—'

I caught myself on the verge of telling her I didn't need any kind of therapy: something like that, and all the more pompous – *old*-sounding – for knowing it might not be true, that maybe she was right and I was, in a sense, 'on the run' . . . I substituted, 'I do appreciate your – your concern, Gill. As a matter of fact I think you're very, *very* special.'

'Why, thank you.' She was motionless, facing me through the dark. 'I guess you mean it, too – or you wouldn't say it, right?'

'Right . . . But also, believe it or not, that's exactly what I've been thinking about you, Gill – that you'd never say anything you didn't mean. I was thinking it might complicate your social life more than somewhat.'

'My.' She moved: my personal radar told me she was wriggling the sweater down over her hips. 'We *are* being mutually complimentary. But it's a red herring, isn't it? I have to admit I'm not *that* unsmart.'

'It wasn't, actually.'

'But since we've now confessed we like each other – Matt, I truly would like to help, if you'd let me. Tell me about it?'

'Better idea, I'll get you a fresh Caballo's Neck.'

Horse's Neck: mixed with Spanish brandy, therefore a Spanish horse. She queried, 'Should we? Boozing at sea?'

'We've only had one, and taken a long time over it. One more, then it'll be time to heat up Lorna's Irish Stew.'

'You're the skipper.'

'Never forget it. Move up here again?'

There wasn't much to bother with. Apart from the prime, basic necessity of keeping a sharp lookout for other ships. Apart from that, all that was called for was a glance at the compass occasionally, to check the autopilot wasn't going mad, and at the now softly illuminated close-haul indicator, which was in the console of dials in the forward bulkhead of this cockpit and saved one from having to strain one's sight to know what the sails were doing.

She took my place at the back end and I went down to get our drinks – mine in fact being no more than brandy-flavoured soda, and hers mostly ginger ale.

She'd said, 'We've now confessed we like each other.'

Understatement, as far as my own feelings were concerned. And where did we go from here?

She'd also observed, 'Makes you seem older than you are.' I'd been told this before – by Lorna, for one – and it bothered me, when I thought about it. Besides, forty-one to twenty-eight was enough of a gap without making it any worse . . . I went back up with the drinks, and she moved over to make room for me beside her.

'D'you always sail on the autopilot, not your wind-vane?'

We had a technical discussion, then. I do have a wind-vane,

98

home-made, but I'd only use it if I was taking the *Bird* to England, or across the Atlantic, that kind of transit. Strong winds and rough seas, then the vane self-steering came into its own; but it couldn't steer a compass course, it's no use in light winds or when motoring, and that's why I was keeping it dismantled in the lazarette.

When I'd finished answering her question, she didn't say anything for about half a minute. Then when she spoke, I had the impression she mightn't have been listening to a word of it.

'You don't want to tell me. OK. I understand. I think with me you wouldn't be that *self*-protective. So it's not about you, is it, it's to do with your wife, some kind of situation *she*—'

'You're absolutely wrong, Gill! Believe me, you couldn't be *more* wrong!'

I can't say there was a silence then. In a strong wind, a boat like the *Bird of Dawning* with that blow behind her wasn't anything like silent, no more silent than the sea was, or the wind, and the three of them together provide a whole orchestra of sound, over which I'd more or less shouted that denial. Because what she'd said had touched a nerve, stung me to defence of Alison; Gill responding physically, then – with both her hands clutching my arm, and her face pressed against my shoulder, and I was wondering not *whether* to explain it to her but how, and where to start.

7

'I was thirty-four when I switched from Marine to farmer. Nineteen eighty-one – bought a place in Devon, near Torrington – OK, you never heard of it, but it's lovely country around there and our house wasn't going to be at all bad when we'd finished doing it up. Strictly nightwork, DIY, I had a mortgage, no reserves, one wife and one child – daughter Sally, then eighteen months.

'Incidentally, the family angle was why I'd opted to leave the Royal Marines. I'd decided I had to make a choice – either leave the family side to Alison and concentrate on the job, or get out, into some occupation where I could be husband and father as well. I was SBS, you see, Special Boat Squadron; it's a small, specialist outfit and you often have to take off at no notice at all to – well, pretty well anywhere. I could never have said to Alison, "OK, we'll do this or that next week" – not without her knowing as well as I did that she couldn't count on it.

'So, that was the choice I'd made. It wasn't easy: there's a high degree of job satisfaction in what I'd been doing, and I can't say I was happy to leave. It just seemed wise in the long run, the best thing for Alison and Sally.

'I had sixty acres – good land, but that's not much, except in terms of man-hours of work. I couldn't have afforded help . . .

Incidentally, I'd been brought up on a farm, and directly after my release from the RM I did a six-month course at an agricultural college – also in Devon. Six months was maximum, either in cost or time – had to start earning a living, then. Trying to, anyway. It was a mixed farm, but the main thing was sheep – which you really do need to know about – more than I knew – because they tend to get things wrong with them all the time. I took advice wherever I could get it, but I found I also needed a lot of veterinary help – and when you're starting out that can be a big overhead . . .'

'Hey. Wind's backing.' I got up, to lean forward over the wheel for a look at the close-haul indicator, which confirmed it . . . 'Hang on, I'll ease the sheets a little.'

I cleated them again, and came back to her, this time slid an arm round her. 'Cold?'

'Not yet. Get on with your story. Farm economics, we were on.'

'Did I mention that I'm in love with you?'

'Oh, mercy . . .'

I'd paused. Went on now, 'This vet – local guy, I'd asked one of my farming neighbours and he'd recommended him—'

'Matt – you did say, *in love*?'

'Want proof? Or shall I tell you this first?'

'I guess . . .' It was her turn to be short of words for a moment: she moved around, her head ending against my neck, 'Best finish the story.'

'Right. The vet – name of – well, his name doesn't matter. But after I'd been his customer, not at all prompt with payment of bills, for about a year, despite this he was doing well enough to take on an assistant, newly qualified girl vet called Joanna. Early twenties, dark, pretty, very pale blue eyes.'

'Oh, *you* . . .'

'If you still insist on hearing this—'

'Sorry . . .'

'All right. Next thing is Alison goes to see her mother, who lives up in Essex. Devon's way down in the south-west, and Essex is north-east of London, so it's quite a distance. Not worth the effort and expense – cost of petrol, gas, being by no means insignificant when you're living close to the breadline –

for just a day's visit, so she'd gone up, taking Sally, for a couple of nights. She wouldn't have gone at all except the old bag was grinding on about her ill-health, always on the verge of expiry, complaining that nobody bothered with a sick old woman, etcetera. She's still going strong, of course. Alison was emotionally blackmailed into going, is what it comes to, although the sheep were lambing and that means being up half the night on top of working all day . . . Hang on a minute.'

I wanted to check the sails again. But it was all right, the wind seemed to be holding steady where it was – blowing from about due west now.

'Gill, you're shivering.'

'Only because you let go of me.'

I put my arms back round her, and my mind back to that early spring with its atrocious weather – high winds, sheets of rain. I'd had the ewes in a big old barn that must have been there about a hundred years and wouldn't stand for many more; it was long, low-roofed, and although I'd patched it up a bit it still let rain in here and there. I described it to Gill; and how sheep need help, or can do, when lambing, the complication of triplets – because a ewe only has two teats – and the oddities of their behaviour such as the facts that no ewe will foster a lamb that isn't hers, that some reject even their own and try to kill them rather than let them feed – and so on.

'I always thought sheep were just dumb.'

'Psychiatric cases, some of them . . . Anyway, Joanna – the vet girl – was a great help, turned up sometimes even without being yelled for. And there was – you know, sort of a thing between us.'

'You astonish me.'

'Right from the start . . . But it was only *potential*, I mean I did nothing about it, in fact I was bloody careful not to get – involved . . . But she used to come round a lot, and – well, it was always exciting to see her, although I never did anything about it and – well, I certainly didn't realize that Alison was aware of the – er – mutual attraction.'

'How *wouldn't* she be!'

'Yeah. I know. I've had time to think, since then. But – look, a little more background . . . Life in the SBS was – had often been exciting. Very active, and even in training it was

103

sometimes quite dangerous. It kept you on your toes: and despite the disadvantages I've mentioned, that was good for Alison too, I mean one was – you know, *alive* . . . I missed it, a lot. And farming on such a small scale and on a shoestring, I was more labourer than farmer, and I felt like one. No excitement, no stimulus, damn-all in sight except years of slogging on. And Alison, you see – well, she'd been a sexy young wife, and now she was very much a farmer's wife – small-time farmer, at that – wrapped up in domesticity, an occasional excitement like making cheese.'

'Poor Alison.'

'Yes, absolutely. And entirely my doing. I'd made the decision, decided what was best for us . . . But in sharp contrast to all this, you see, Joanna was pretty, very sexy, lively, young, she was ready for some excitement too, a change from working long hours with her arm up a cow's arse or – well, you can imagine.'

'Vividly.'

'So – Alison away in Essex. Joanna's day off, night off. She arrives – early evening – saying she didn't have anything else to do, maybe I could use some help. She knew Alison wasn't at home.'

'Right.'

'I didn't send her away, as I should have done. And she did help, with the lambs I was having to bottle-feed. But she wasn't dressed for that stinking old barn, sheep-shit and mud, and milk splashing around and rain dripping in – mud floor, of course – so I'd sent her back into the house while I finished up. Alison chose that time to telephone, Joanna answered the phone and – I suppose wasn't entirely convincing about how she happened to be there. Anyway if she'd been making a professional call she'd have been with the animals, not in our house while *I* coped outside.'

'Why did she answer the phone, heaven's sake?'

'I suppose she just didn't think. But worse, she didn't tell me Alison had called. She said afterwards she'd forgotten about it, but I think she didn't want to – you know, spoil things. She'd have told me in the morning, she said; but the *first* thing she said was that it didn't seem important and then she forgot, but in fact she didn't volunteer the information at all, ever. I got it out of her a few days later. And Alison's mother told me how her daughter had made this call, then seemed very upset, rushed off to pack and get Sally up – crying, and not telling the old woman anything . . . God, I can *see* her – me coming back into the house, rain driving horizontally, same weather all over England and that was what she was going out into. I can see her behind that wheel, Sal strapped in her seat in the back, ninety miles an hour with *that* scenario in her mind.'

'Matt – you don't have to go on with this.'

'I was woken – *we* were woken – at about five a.m. Doorbell. I thought it was the alarm clock – I'd set that for five thirty. And just for that few seconds, coming awake, I thought it was Alison in the bed with me. I've had it happen – repeats of it, the same bewilderment – I don't know, maybe half a second, but that's more than enough – time and time again. Two realities break through in the original – first, it's not Alison, it's Joanna; second, it's not the alarm, it's the doorbell. That's how it *was*, but in the replays, instead of "it's not the alarm, it's the door", always the other way about – a flood of relief and "only the alarm, not to worry, that was all a dream", then the realization it was *not* a dream—'

'*Still?*'

'No – no, I don't wake with the shakes. I *do* wake remembering that to all intents and purposes I killed them.'

'Oh, nonsense—'

'It's a fact, Gill!'

'I'd say it's nothing of the sort . . . But go on – obviously it wasn't your wife at the door, so—'

'I thought it had to be. So did Joanna. Seemed unspeakably awful, the absolute pits, but – how I've wished since it *could* have been . . . No, it was the police, a car from Torrington. They'd had a call from Basingstoke – which is a town up on the M3, the motorway, near where it had happened – the police there had made the identification through the car's registration plate, only way they could have done it. She'd been doing about ninety – heavy rain, gusting west wind, she'd passed a truck too close and clipped it, bounced off and—'

I'd stopped. Gill sighed; then murmured, 'I shouldn't have made you tell me.'

'That's it, anyway.'

105

Neither of us said anything for a while. Then Gill stirred against me.

'She crashed, Matt. *She* did.'

'If I hadn't had Joanna in the house, Alison wouldn't have been on the road that night – and in an emotional state that made her unfit to be driving on a motorway, at that. Just *think* of that state of mind.'

'That's something else, though, isn't it? Sure, one thing stems from another, but you're guilty of adultery, not murder.'

'Manslaughter? Culpable homicide?'

'Look. Suppose we hit a rock and I drown – is that homicide?'

'No. You asked to come along, you take your chances.'

'Here's another one. You have this girl on Menorca, right? Now she gets to hear I'm with you on this trip, it throws her so she gets plastered at some party, and on her way home she drives over a cliff. Did *you* kill her?'

'Of course not. No way or reason she'd give a damn.'

Sea noise, boat noise . . . Then her voice in my ear again: why Alison should have been so thrown . . . 'OK, so if it was that tight a marriage . . .' Then: 'Look, all right, so it was shattering – but that was *then*, Christ's sake, doesn't have to lock you into premature middle age . . . Matt?'

I was wishing I hadn't let her cajole me into telling her. If I hadn't, there was a chance that by now we'd have been making love, but as it was I was seeing Alison – and oncoming lights blinding, exploding one after another like gun-flashes in that white, hurt face: then the truck looming, and seconds later – jar of impact, screaming tyres . . .

Now a break from the personal narrative – two extraneous scenes that are best placed here because they'd have been happening at about this time, when the *Bird of Dawning* was at sea between Mahon and Valletta.

First London: Charles Harrison in conference with Chief Inspector Ronald Frewin.

'Awkward bugger, is he?'

Charles Harrison showed surprise. Facing his chief across a heavily loaded desk. 'Awkward?'

'Doesn't seem to exert himself much to make friends and influence people, does he?'

'He does have a – bit of a forthright manner, yeah. Sort of bloke if you tried pushing him around you'd get nowhere fast. He was a Marine – well, you'd know that.'

'SBS, same as Fountain.'

'Right. And consequently inclined to be over-defensive of his chum – all that "couldn't have done it" stuff, and swearing black and blue he never saw him at Southampton. Got on his wick when I pressed that, touchy at anyone calling him a liar.'

'Do you believe *now* he didn't get Fountain away, somehow?'

'Affirmative, sir. I mean I believe he didn't.'

'You've changed your mind, then.'

'I just can't see any way he could have.'

'Although we now have to conclude that Fountain did *not* drown himself?'

'That's why, really. I'd been reckoning on – well, call it assisted suicide, but as you say, since no body's come up—'

'How do you account for the car being in that marina's car-park – after Fountain had *said* that was where he was going – as Johnson himself admitted?'

'Only guessing, sir – I'd suggest he got down there, Johnson refused to take him – for some reason, maybe Fountain confessed what he'd done and that was too much even for the old pals' act – so he'd have left his motor there – as a blind, and if so it wasn't a bad idea; it worked, didn't it, I mean we were sure that was the way he'd gone, we didn't look anywhere else, did we – and – well, must've took off some other way.'

'You checked the addresses of known friends and former Royal Marine contemporaries, didn't you?'

'As far as we could, we did.'

'Malta – or Turkey. Turkey mightn't be a bad bet, since he did a spell out there, military duty . . .'

Frewin had a way of switching off, clicking on again with some different angle. He said now, 'If we were to accept your theory that Johnson refused to take him, shouldn't we discount Johnson's movements from there on?'

'Well, yeah, if—'

'And *in re* this Matt Johnson – I'm inclined to believe his

107

statement – this last one, *and* his voluntary telephone call to you. I think – *think* – we might assume he's going to tell the truth whenever he can afford to.' Frewin shrugged. 'Definition of twentieth-century morality, maybe ... Another thing he said – opinion, I'd asked him for it – was he thought even if *she*'d wanted a reconciliation Fountain wouldn't have – have accommodated her ... Well, she'd have known it – even if she did have any such inclination – which doesn't seem exactly probable ... See where I'm getting?'

'The champers and caviar—'

'Right. Wouldn't've been provided by her for him, or by him for her. Despite having to consider the possibility, we can be positive it wasn't – right?'

Harrison nodded. 'So—'

'So we do have a lover on our hands. At least, that's how he looks to me. Lover of Fountain's wife, lover of fine wines and exotic food. I'd say it's odds-on he laid on the provisions ... Well, more *likely* he did – not certain, I grant you, but more likely.'

'But she could've gone along to Fortnums and bought it for the occasion, or they might've had it in the house already. I mean, to them it mightn't – well, weren't short of a bob or two, sir, were they?'

'What did you say it cost, that little pot?'

'Sixty-four quid. One hundred grammes.'

'And Fortnums couldn't say who'd bought it or when.'

'No, unfortunately.' Harrison nodded towards the pile of paperwork on Frewin's desk. 'This is all in my report, sir. As I recall, though, it's not deep-frozen, although it's fresh, it's just kept refrigerated. Cash purchase, no serial numbers on the tins or labels, there'd be no record unless it was booked to a customer, and this wasn't, not that they could tell.'

'So on its own, that's a dead end ... How about the champagne?'

'There's lots of it in the house.'

'Lots of that same brand?'

'Well ...' Harrison, uncertain, reached for notes. Frewin added, wanting the answer but not waiting for it, 'Under lock and key, I hope.' Leafing through the file ... Harrison assuring him that the Fountains' cellar was securely locked – as it had been before they'd inspected it, along with the rest of the house, right after the murder. They'd had a job finding the key; the daily woman (who'd found Mrs Fountain's body and called the police) had had no idea where it might have been, and it had been Mrs Fountain's father, Hugh Benedict, who'd told them to look in one of the drawers in Fountain's desk.

'She was in her négligé, they'd polished off one bottle downstairs – with the caviar and toast . . . Where had the toast come from, by the way?'

Harrison said, glancing up from his continuing search through one of several notebooks, 'Toaster in the kitchen. Last use it had had, crumbs all around.'

'Right . . . But just thinking, off the top of my head – having had one bottle, if she or – whoever – nipped off to fetch the second – in those circumstances would she or he have bothered to lock up again behind them?'

'Earlier, sir, they'd have got out both bottles and stuck 'em in the fridge to cool.'

'I was thinking of an ice-bucket. In which case . . .' Frewin flicking through his file, busy looking for some passage or other and talking, as he'd admitted, off the top of his head . . . 'But there wasn't one, was there? You'd have thought in a house like that, and taking a bottle up to the bedroom, they *would* have had . . . Incidentally, all that data on the fingerprints, that's something else doesn't add up, to my mind. Come to that in a minute . . . Ah, here it is. Krug – Krug Collection 1961. Never heard of it, have you?'

'Krug, yeah, but—'

'Is this the kind you said there's a lot of in the house?'

'In that cellar. I couldn't say, sir, exactly.' He'd thought he had a note of it, but he'd failed to pin it down, as yet . . . 'I mean not the exact type or—'

'The same *marque*, I should have said.' Frewin read a paragraph or two, then shut the file. 'Better check. People who keep cellars tend to buy by the case, or so many dozen, they'd very likely have more than one *marque* and maybe different vintages, but they'd have 'em in quantity, not just the odd bottle like you or I might have under the stairs. Check it out, it's important. Question of did lover-boy bring it with him, or was it in the house to start with. If it was brought in, that'd be

109

another pointer to the existence of the lover – right? Then, where'd he get it? Fortnums, maybe, same time as the caviar?'

'Right . . .'

'See if there's more of this one, Charles. My guess is there may not be . . . Let me know the answer, will you?'

From London, now, to Suffolk. Ford Fiesta, woman driver, male passenger hunched beside her. Hunched because it's a small car and he's a big man. Gaunt, bearded, not enough flesh on him for his six feet four inches of height and big-boned frame, but she'd said to him this morning, 'You look so much better than you did when you blew in here. Not *quite* your old self, but at least I'd know it was you, now.'

'Let's hope not too many people will.'

'The beard'll help, I'm sure.'

Growing a beard had been part of the reason for having stayed this long. That and to recover health and spirit and let things quieten down – the police to have a few more recent cases on their hands, and the public to forget the face that had stared at them out of their newspapers and from TV screens.

Her husband had asked him last night, 'Have you got some kind of cover story, if anyone asks who or what you are?'

'Oh, sure. No problem there, James.'

The main worry was any passport inspection on this side. His intention – because he'd had no option – had been to show his own and chance it. A month had passed, and it was a fair bet that the police here in England would have concluded he was either dead or out of the country: they'd have his name on some list, but it wouldn't be anywhere near the top of it. Touch wood . . . But now, they wouldn't see that name, they'd see James's: he'd come up trumps, in this as in several other ways.

Eileen, James's wife, didn't know – because James had begged him not to tell her. 'She'd worry herself sick. Criminal offence, all that. Just post it back to me as soon as you're ashore – or first chance you get. Deal?'

Post *his* – James's – passport back to him. The differences between them weren't all that striking, and the photograph didn't look all that much like James anyway. If the guy in the photo had grown a full beard, as Tommy had now, nobody could have sworn that it was or wasn't him – or Tommy . . .

110

Might take a second, closer look before they shrugged and gave it back.

As long as the official wasn't sharp enough to compare the given height with Tommy's, five-ten against six-four . . .

He glanced sideways at the dark-haired driver. Eileen was about thirty now, and a long time ago he'd asked her to marry him. She'd stalled: they'd gone on having fun together, and he'd been very genuinely and urgently in love with her, but she hadn't wanted to marry a serving officer – with all the separations, and the moves, and – in Tommy Fountain's case, since he was SBS – anxiety. She'd still been hesitating when she'd met James, who was in the City but had plans connected with financial journalism, was very intelligent and reasonably good-looking, and who 'swept her off her feet'. Tommy had agreed with her that James was a hell of a nice guy, he'd been sincere in wishing them luck and happiness, and attended the wedding – behaved, in fact, exactly as anyone who knew him would have expected Tommy Fountain to have behaved. But he'd said later, 'Taught me a lesson. Service life's great when you're young, or if you're a real hotshot and you're going to the top, but I'm not getting boxed-in again like that!'

(This was at the time he'd met Penny and decided that to marry her, if she'd have him, he'd resign his commission. Then he too, having learnt the lesson, would become a high-flyer in the City. I'd forgotten that piece of background, which explains his readiness to cut loose. I'd already sent in my own resignation – for quite different reasons, which I've gone into – and it was difficult for me to give him contrary advice, therefore, without it being obvious that my main reason for telling him he was being a bloody fool was my opinion of Penny Benedict, as she was then. There's never any dividend from such frankness: the sucker goes ahead and marries her, and all you've achieved is the loss of a friend. Tommy pursued her for a year or so before she said yes, she'd have him if he left the Corps and took the job which she'd persuaded her father to offer him. And that was his full ration of bad luck.)

Eileen was trundling her Fiesta down the A134 towards Colchester. Ultimate destination Harwich, the ferry port.

'Can't begin to say how grateful I am, Eileen.'

'Silly . . .'

'James has been bloody marvellous, too.'

She smiled, her eyes on the road and the traffic. 'James is all right.'

Tommy had virtually fallen into the hall of their house when James had opened the door to him, at night and more than three weeks ago. James had called out for Eileen to come quickly: Tommy was told later that he'd mumbled, 'Don't worry, you want to call police, call 'em, sensible thing to do. But something to eat, hot drink or – oh, *Eileen . . .*'

At sight of her, he'd passed out. Not much of a compliment, she'd teased him, a day or two later when he was beginning to sit up and make sense and partially explain things.

The reason he'd come to this house was that he'd realized the police would probably be calling on all his known friends, from former Royal Marines to business acquaintances and others from earlier days. But he'd thought they wouldn't know of Eileen Briscoe's existence, and the few people who did – mostly ex-Bootnecks like me – weren't going to be racking their memories too hard anyway. And, nobody'd expect a former girlfriend, now a married woman, to be likely to give him shelter.

Luckily their son, aged eight, was away, in his first term at prep school.

Eileen had asked Tommy, on the morning after he'd arrived, 'Did you do it?'

James had been standing behind her, and Tommy's eyes shifted to hold his for a moment before returning to hers. He'd said, 'Don't be damn silly, of course I didn't.' Eileen had said – according to James – 'Well, that's something, anyway', and then turned to her husband. 'He can stay, James, can't he?'

'Of course he can. No choice really, is there?'

She'd kissed him. It wasn't a small thing he was doing. Later she asked Tommy how he'd got here, when the police bulletin had said his car had been found in Southampton, and he'd told her, 'Hitched, mostly. I was heading for Harwich, but then I thought of you: not being in great shape at that stage, and – had this brainwave . . .'

Drifting off. It had taken the best part of a week before he was really back to normal, able to keep his mind on one subject for more than about a minute. 'In shock', he'd heard Eileen

whisper, and James had murmured, 'Give or take some degree
of alcoholic poisoning.' Because to start with he'd wanted only
sweet things – chocolate, orange juice, cocoa. James had
mentioned that he'd had the same experience, answering
Eileen then: 'Yes, *long* before I knew you, stupid.'

On about the third day Eileen had asked Tommy – bringing
him soup – 'Are you going to be able to *prove* you didn't do it?'

He'd looked vague: then hopeless: literally, without hope.
He'd said quietly, 'Not a chance. Unfortunately.' Looking at
them both, facing them with that lack of hope and his own
acceptance of it . . . Then a week later he told them, 'When I
leave here I'll be going abroad. Better you shouldn't know
where. Guy I want to see – I can trust him, he's got something
that belongs to me, and he's sort of – out of orbit, he could –
well, act for me, I hope . . . Besides, he's right on the way to
where I'm going.'

'To do what, Tommy?'

'Disappear. Out there, I know how to.'

'Permanently?'

'God knows. Depends what happens here, I suppose. But a
lot better than going to prison.'

James offered help, in one important area, which Eileen
didn't have to know about, for the time being – to save her
from worrying more than she had to be worrying already.

Not that she showed it much. Tommy told James he was a
luckier man even than he'd known he was, way back.

'There is one thing, though. Trouble is, you've been so good
already, I hardly like to ask.'

'You'll want funds, won't you?'

He'd only had three pound coins when he'd fallen in the
front door. So on top of everything else, including the big,
really dangerous favour he'd agreed to, James lent him two
hundred pounds. It was more than enough, Tommy said, and
it would be repaid in cash through the post within a couple of
weeks of his leaving England. James demurred at this: cash
through the post might lead to questions being asked –
Revenue, Customs, whatever. There'd be no urgency for
repayment anyway; Tommy could wait until he was home and
dry and in a position to write a cheque. But also, they'd bought
him a new anorak and a soft suitcase, both entirely different

113

from the gear he'd brought with him, and a moleskin fisher-man's hat. The object was to change his appearance from the publicized description, and in the case of the suitcase because Tommy recalled there'd been some other guy on that motor cruiser, who'd actually handled the zip bag he'd had with him then and whom he didn't know, might for all he knew have talked to the police.

The Ford Fiesta had bypassed Colchester some time ago and had since covered a dozen miles of the A120. Somewhere between Wix and Ramsey, with only three or four miles to go to the ferry port. Eileen had been driving very slowly and circumspectly, in order to run no risk of confrontation with the Law.

'Eileen, listen. If by some unforeseen chance the fuzz should bother you, say yes, I was there and you looked after me, you never saw anything about me in the media, I just arrived looking done-in and you took pity on me. You said you'd call Penny to tell her where I was, and I asked you not to so you didn't. OK? I shouldn't think they could prove you knew anything – would you?'

'All right. But take care now, Tommy . . .'

She'd equipped him with a parcel of sandwiches, a thermos of coffee and a flask of malt whisky, and James had booked him a cabin on the Hamburg ferry, in James's name, so that once he was on board he could hole-up in it throughout the 21-hour passage, minimizing the risk of running into someone who might recognize him. It was a very long 21 hours, he found. Like being in a comfortable prison cell. Thinking, trying to remember detail of this and that, dropping asleep then waking and struggling to put the recollections back in order, motion . . . It was a major effort because at the time one had been dazed, punch-drunk: one had hardly known what was going on *then*, when it *was* happening: and drink had come into it too, confused it even more. Maybe *mostly* drink. But like – well, after that evening with Matt – and the other fellow, Loder – getting home, having problems with the door, stumbling through it finally and groping for the switches: Penny'd gone to bed and hadn't bothered to leave a light on for him. Usually, he came into the house through the garage: it was a mews house, the garage integral to it. He'd given himself a couple of drinks – nightcaps – wanting to think, get his intentions straight in his mind so as to be clear in what he'd say to her. In the morning – let her sleep now . . . It was a matter of knowing for sure what one wanted: and it wasn't easy. On the one hand you had something that would take a lot of facing up to, and on the other – but he wasn't so sure he could face the other.

Come on, Christ's sake . . .

Deciding he'd try the old dodge of putting it on paper. Sheet of paper, line down the middle, alternatives each side of it, balancing lists of pros and cons. The bottom line had to be either try a new start, or – Matt's advice – wrap up, get out.

Want to get out. That was the basic, the gut-feeling. Top of left-hand column . . . Trying to get it down: but writing wasn't any easier than thinking. Wouldn't be legible in the morning either. A mutter: 'Can't fucking read it *now* . . .' His arm swung out sideways, for some reason, knocked over his glass of whisky. Staring at the mess: 'Oh, shit . . .'

'You *said* it.'

Penny, in the doorway. Lacy dressing-gown over silk night-dress, blonde hair flowing, face oddly naked without make-up.

'What on earth are you doing, Tommy? Except getting drunker? D'you need to be drunk to come to bed with me? There are some who don't . . .'

'So you tol' me, ni' before las' . . .'

'You can barely *speak*!'

'I know. I know. But look—' Pointing at her – 'Loved you, y'know, been abs'lutely faithful to you, never's much as *thought* of—'

'Tommy, I don't give a damn, you can go and be faithful to someone else – all right?'

'Wha's done this? Eh? Wha's—'

'Talk about it when you're next sober, shall we? Use the spare room, please, I can't bear the smell. But be careful of the stairs, you could easily fall and – *break your neck*, the state you're in.'

She'd slammed the bedroom door.

Break your neck. Her idea, her taunting voice, implying – heavy accentuation on those three words – *why don't you?*

He'd remembered it when he'd been standing on those same

stairs with her body in his arms, limp and lolling. Head lolling on – coincidentally enough – a broken neck. Long, slim neck, very white . . . Wondering how, when . . . Recent memory all shot – well, confused, erratic – but recalling a time when he'd found this neck irresistible – so delicate, ultra-feminine in its smallness, frailty, he'd longed to kiss it, smother it with kisses, and then he'd found himself doing exactly that and she'd loved it, it was one of the preliminaries she'd most enjoyed. Even now he could put his mind back and recall the thrill – thrilling to *this* body – white, limp as a rag doll, négligé fallen open exposing pink-tipped breasts, blonde pubic hair light as cotton-thread, slim white legs dangling to scarlet toes, blonde head falling back across his forearm so suddenly and heavily it was almost a surprise the damaged neck checked its fall.

He'd told her father – as good as told him – that if he hung around, something like this *could* happen . . .

Carrying her slowly up the stairs, looking down into a face like a sleeping child's, he'd trodden on something – a bottle, champagne bottle it turned out to be – swayed backwards in an effort not to drop her, and fallen – backwards – gone crashing and thumping down with her soft weight clutched to him – as if there was some reason to cushion her from contact with the hard edges of the stairs.

After that, things were *really* vague for a while. He'd talked to her father on the telephone. Then soon after to Matt's friend Loder, and finally to Matt.

That night, though, she'd gone up on her own slippered feet into the bedroom, and locked the door, he'd slept on a spare-room bed fully dressed, woken to find a half-tumbler of whisky on the bedside table. No recollection of having put it there, but remembering the plain hatred in her face, matching it to things she'd said in the course of a previous row – about some other man – he'd realized in that cold morning light that she probably did hate him.

And known then for sure that he didn't have any decision left to make, except on points of detail, because she'd made the decisions for them both.

Tell old Matt? Give him a bell, tell him he was right in what he'd said last night, absolutely spot on, and that his advice was about to be acted on?

No idea where he'd be, though. At the club, or with some dancer he'd been screwing – wherever the hell *she* lived – or back on the boat that he was taking to France soon.

Better – much more practical in the circumstances – get on to Don Phelan – of whom Matt had reminded him last night – or maybe he hadn't, maybe he'd just happened to remember him, on his way home maybe . . . Anyway, Phelan was running a Defence-orientated business in Swansea and had once suggested that Tommy might consider joining him. Some time ago, that had been, but as Matt had said, worth a try, be right up one's street . . . And the next thing would be to have a talk with Penny's father. But before any of that – he was still a bit tight at this stage, hangover hadn't set in yet – he had to pound on the bedroom door to make her open it: his dressing-room was off the main bedroom, and he needed a shave, a shower, some clothes. Penny had unlocked the door, after a few minutes, gone quickly back to bed without even an exchange of glances, let alone of words. He'd stood staring at the bed, at her shape in it, the mound of her hip and the back of her blonde head, in deep and growing anger and with an urge to yank her out of it and slap her: then he'd controlled himself, turned away.

From his office, he put a call through to Phelan, who sounded welcoming and said he'd be delighted to have him come and see what they were doing.

'If I come today – get to you early evening, say, spend the weekend there, can you put me up?'

'Oh, Lord, that's *not* easy, old son. House full of kids – you'd go mad, even if there was room for you, which frankly there ain't. But I could book you at one of our local pubs and you'd eat with us, obviously . . . What d'you prefer, four-star or a smaller place with reasonable comfort?'

He chose the second, made a note of its name, said he'd be there late afternoon or early evening. This was a Friday; Phelan suggested staying over until the Monday, if he could.

The Monday – May 24th – was a public holiday: and this would be as good a way as any of *not* being in the house in Chelsea . . . Hanging up from the talk with Don Phelan, he called through to his father-in-law's PA and made an appointment to see him at eleven.

The chairman's suite was on the top floor. When Tommy walked into the sumptuous, walnut-panelled private office, Hugh Benedict was at the wide, plate-glass window, gazing across acres of rooftops towards the gleaming dome of St Paul's. A tall man, grey-haired, elegantly tailored: turning from the window . . .

'Tommy.' A pleasant but wary smile. He'd know, of course, he'd probably have had a good idea of how things were going, and the odds were that he'd have talked to his daughter this morning, knowing Tommy had asked for this meeting. 'Do sit. Coffee, or—'

'No, thanks . . . It's me and Penny I have to talk about. Primarily – unfortunately it has to involve the firm too.'

'I see.' He sat down behind the desk. 'You and – Penny . . .'

'It's no go, sir. One has – as you know – *tried* – and in the early days I'm sure she did too, but – that doesn't apply now.' He could hear an annoying shake in his own voice, and knew he was gabbling. Recalling how Matt Johnson – and even more so, that other guy – had looked at him last night. He was aware of being off-balance, of nerves fraying thin . . . 'Plain fact is, the situation's intolerable. No point going into whys and wherefores, we're – well, I'm sorry, but there's nothing for it except – pack it in.'

The grey head moved, sadly. 'After such a fine start, and all our hopes . . . Couldn't you perhaps – I mean *both* of you, of course—'

'No.' Seeing the danger of being trapped, trapped in the inaction that had led to this – in a way – to Penny's current – *attitudes* . . . 'No, sir, absolutely pointless. Truly . . .'

Waffle, waffle. Fresh start, sustained efforts, back to the golden promise . . . Tommy unwilling to tell him, *Look, she's a bitch, always was, now she's also a tart* . . . Because this was her father, and because on some fanciful level he himself felt the real Penny was still in there somewhere, a prisoner looking out through the barred windows of the present Penny Fountain's contemptuous eyes . . . And Hugh Benedict wasn't a bad old stick, there'd have been no justification for hurting him in lieu of taking a swipe at Penny herself.

'To avoid any misreading of the situation – you're talking of separation? Divorce?'

'I suppose – ' he nodded ' – divorce.'

'Should I take it there are cogent reasons' – expression of distaste – '*grounds*—'

'I – just have to get out – right out, *now*. Before something pretty awful—' He checked, shook his head: 'I'm sorry to say this, but she's – well, *highly* provocative . . .'

Stopping short of spelling it out, he saw alarm in the older man's expression, and a slow nod then, acknowledgement of message received. Tommy hadn't purposely exaggerated the dramatic potential of his marital situation: but what he'd indicated was true to a fairly minor extent and he said nothing to mitigate the impression he'd just given. He wanted to get this over, anyway, convince Penny's father that a break was inevitable and that there'd be no point in any attempts at peace-making or delaying tactics. Having made his decision – been pushed into it, by Penny, but in his own view he'd made his mind up – the sooner it was over and done with, the better. In fact he wasn't inclined to violence, never had been, but he was well aware that it was inadvisable for a man who was capable of killing with one bare hand – as he was – to allow himself to be provoked. It was axiomatic that such a man should never remain in a bar where some drunk was throwing his weight about, for instance. And he'd felt the potential in his brain and muscles: not last night, but this morning, in the face of her silence, that display of mute abhorrence. And to Hugh Benedict just that hint of violence would be enough to set alarm bells ringing: he'd always been intrigued by Tommy's SBS background, maybe because of the stark difference between that way of life and his own ultra-comfortable, sedentary existence. He'd more than once raised the subject, asking questions about the skills and techniques of that specialist brand of commando work – and of course getting very sparse, evasive answers.

He was looking – maybe speculatively – at Tommy's hands. Tommy moved them, clasped them together in his lap. Benedict said, 'I did suspect that – things weren't going as well as they should have, between you two, but not – not to that extent, such *extreme* . . .' He spread his own hands. 'If your relationship with Penny is as – as bad as you've indicated, I agree the best course would be physically to separate –

119

pending whatever kind of legal arrangements—'

'Yes.' Tommy swallowed. 'But also – hardly keep my job here, in those circumstances. Any case, haven't exactly set the world on fire, have I?'

'Well. I do know you've done your best. You've worked hard – a lot harder than most, in fact – I've admired your persistence, Tommy, but as you say – with typical frankness, I might add—'

Tommy interrupted: 'Friend of mine – same background – is helping to run a business in Wales that's in line with my – my previous experience. It's to do with – well, underwater defence systems. Some time ago he asked me if I'd like to come in with him – didn't seem to be on the cards then, but I telephoned him this morning and he suggested I might spend a long weekend, see what's happening and whether I'd fit in. Thought maybe I'd take off now, get back Monday night.'

'*Splendid* idea. You'd certainly be more in your own element. And what could be better for you than a complete change, after all this? I've noticed you haven't been looking all that well, Tommy – you've been under strain, of course. I'm sorry – very sorry . . .'

And relieved, of course, that he wasn't going to have to say *I'm letting you go . . .* Tommy saw this, but was still glad to spare him that embarrassment; none of it was *his* fault. He said, 'I could clear up outstanding work during the rest of the week. And give you my resignation, of course.'

'Heavens, no urgency about that. Arrange it to suit your own convenience. Except I do agree that you and Penny – that's to say – physical separation, I'd suggest sooner rather than later?'

Waking in the early hours of the morning in his cabin in the Harwich–Hamburg ferry, he'd felt an urgent need to get out on deck, breathe fresh air.

It was an inside cabin, and it felt like a prison cell. Maybe because one had thought quite a lot about prison: about a life sentence. Having told James as much as one remembered about the events of that night – night of Penny's death – James, with a hard head on his shoulders and an objective, pragmatic

120

outlook, had agreed it couldn't be ruled out. The Law wasn't infallible, juries were made up of ordinary people well capable of confusing circumstance and coincidence with proof, and some eminent judges had in recent memory made pronouncements and awarded sentences which had been – to say the least – idiosyncratic.

Besides, when you'd run away: were *still* running . . .

Prison could certainly *not* be ruled out.

It would be dark on deck, and below decks everyone would be asleep. He dressed, locked the cabin behind him, made his way up – past the reception area and entrance to the duty-free and cafeteria, stepping over blanket-wrapped bodies here and there – up again, then out of a side door into the clear, cold night.

There wasn't a soul out here. Only windswept deck, metal fittings wet and icy with sea-dew, and – a very long way down – the boil of white sea along the ship's side. Leaning over the rail, peering down: thinking what a hell of a long drop it would be.

Habit of thought, recently acquired. Better to get out of that now, get back to normal . . . He turned away from the side and began walking – to keep warm, get the blood circulating, get at least *some* exercise after so long with very little. He'd been doing a lot of PE – press-ups and so on – and he'd had two night walks, on his last two nights at Eileen's and James's house in Suffolk. James had gone with him, but they'd only made brief excursions because on the whole people didn't go for walks at night and they might easily have run into some busybody who'd report suspicious-looking prowlers – one of them well over six foot . . .

But no one was going to think twice about some outsize insomniac passenger pacing round and round a ferry's deck.

He remembered the sense of shock with which he'd realized that Hugh Benedict would almost certainly have had that conversation on tape. It was well known that he recorded just about everything. And the recording would include his son-in-law's gratuitous statement to the effect that he couldn't trust himself not to do some physical harm to the man's daughter.

The realization had hit him when he'd been flat on his back in the cabin in that motor-cruiser in Southampton: he'd gone out like a light, woken abruptly after only a few minutes and with his mind clearer than it had been for hours: he'd seen that rather frightening probability, and woken up to several other things as well, the sum of them being that he'd be crazy to stay aboard the *Lady Be Good*.

He'd left the money-belt where he'd thought it was, because it was going to be a tight squeeze through the hatch even without it. The loss of the money – which he'd only discovered hours later – had been another, pulverizing shock . . . Now, he hoped to God Matt did have the money, that the other guy hadn't hung on to it. It had been *his* bag, in the cabin . . . He couldn't remember whether it was £200 or £250 in sterling: £250, probably. He'd cashed a cheque for two hundred on his way back from the office after that face-to-face with Penny's father, and he'd found he had over a hundred in the house, and the Swansea trip hadn't taken much cash at all. But also, there were the dollar cheques, obtained several months ago before a planned Christmas trip to Antigua that hadn't come off because Penny had decided she wanted to spend Christmas in her father's house – with other guests, none of them Tommy's friends. He'd hung on to the cheques, thinking they'd come in useful before long, and they'd been bought when the exchange rate had been favourable; stuffing them into the money-belt he'd thought, *Thank God for small mercies* . . .

Looking back on it now, on that excruciatingly frightful night, it might have happened ten years ago and to someone else. The brain's way of protecting itself, he guessed: the effort of recollection was like looking through the wrong end of a telescope with dirty lenses.

The trip to Swansea had been a waste of time. The work Phelan's team were doing was interesting and had already produced results – one system actually in operation, deployed, and another undergoing MoD trials. Being so well in hand, but with no immediate prospects of expansion, it became obvious quite early in the visit that Don had only reacted so positively to the telephone call because he'd wanted to show an old chum what a success he'd made here. Tommy could understand this, but actually he'd been conned into making a very long drive to absolutely no purpose.

There would certainly have been no point in hanging around. He booked out of his hotel on the Sunday morning, lunched with the Phelans and their brood of incredibly noisy children, and set off back to London that afternoon instead of staying over to the Monday.

8

I'd guessed right about the wind. We were in a flat calm by dawn, and the *Bird* was making six knots on her diesel, instead of yesterday's eight under sail. It didn't matter, we'd done better than anticipated, a six-knot transit was just about par for the course anyway, and barring accidents we'd be in Valletta tomorrow forenoon. The engine's range is 300 miles, we hadn't used much fuel so far and there were only 160 miles to go.

So the Loran told me. At Loran's last way-point I'd had the light on the offshore-Sicilian island of Isole Egadi 25 miles abeam to port; I'd seen the loom of its double flashes four hours ago – confirming the Loran's accuracy, which is always pleasantly reassuring. Now in another four hours we'd have Pantelleria about the same distance abeam to starboard, although of course its light wouldn't be visible in daylight and there wasn't much prospect of seeing the island either, at that range and in what I guessed would be hazy sunshine, the kind of swelter that goes with a windless day out here.

The sun was up out of the sea in a red flush on the *Bird of Dawning*'s port bow when Gill came up, looking stunning in shortie pyjamas, cream silk with a golden Chinese dragon straining his head up in a frantic effort to look inside. He did actually look frantic, wild-eyed and I didn't blame him. Gill

was gazing around, getting her bearings on the new day . . .
'Motoring – wind did leave us . . . Hey, it's already getting
warm. Matt – you didn't wake me!'

'Didn't need to. I dozed a bit, on and off. I like the dragon.'

'Isn't he cute?'

'Like a swim before breakfast?'

'San Francisco, he came from . . .' Then the suggestion
registered, and she repeated, '*Swim?* D'you mean it?'

'Why not?'

'You going to?'

'One at a time's best. Other one minds the store. When
you're ready I'll stop the donkey and fix the ladder.'

'It'll be cold, won't it?'

'Good for us, wake us up.'

In June, and out here in deep water – the depth-sounder told
me there were eighty metres under us at this moment – it might
even be colder than she expected. She went below, came back
up in her orange bikini, and I switched off the engine, let the
Bird drift, gradually losing way.

'Want to go in by the ladder?'

'God, no.' She shivered. 'I'm not brave enough for that.' I
agreed with her: I always like to get into it quickly. 'Matt, if I
pass out from the shock, will you pull me out and force brandy
between my stiff blue lips?'

'I might. Go on, now.'

She stepped over the life-line on the port side, balanced for a
moment with the plastic-coated wire pressing into the backs of
her calves, and dived. Very neat, hardly any splash. Surfacing,
she screamed: then began swimming – a fast crawl, not all that
stylish because she was swimming as hard as she could, to beat
the cold. I watched for a few moments, then got the ladder
ready. It has to be folded down, the top part opening and
extending downwards into the sea below the transom.

She was there after only one circuit of the boat. I reached
down, whisked her up on to the stern. She gasped, 'It's torture.
Really, it's freezing!'

'Can't be *that* bad.'

'You'll see.' She passed me, found her towel. 'Now *I'll*
laugh.'

I was reaching down over the stern to unclip the ladder –

above the waterline – where the joint snaps rigid and catches have to be released before you can fold the thing back up. Hearing Gill shout, panting as she dried herself, 'What are you waiting for?' I'd fixed the ladder: I pressed the starter, and she whipped round as she heard the electronic bleep before the diesel purred into life.

'Had second thoughts. We shouldn't waste *too* much time.'

'Matt, you yellow *bastard*!'

She came flying at me and I had to hold her off with one arm while I started the autopilot with the other hand. Same course as before, it was already set, a true course of 130. She screamed, 'Matt, honestly, that is the fucking *limit*!'

'I know.' She was in my arms. The impetus of her attack had faltered, petered out, and we were kissing. Salt on her cold lips, cool body in my arms, cold arms round my neck, her voice – a lot less strident – telling me I was a shit, I really and truly was an absolute fucking shit. She was still wet, and my shirt was soaked, of course; I kept my left arm round her, used her towel in my right to get her a bit drier. The bikini bra came off, somehow: I heard her ask me what about last night, why *now*, and I muttered something about certain kinds of recollection acting like – I stopped myself just in time from saying 'like cold water', apologized instead, admitted I'd spent half the night regretting it. She said into my ear, 'So you're a *damn-fool* shit, at that' – and it was true, I had been, although not by choice: and anyway, I wasn't now, now I was just an *ordinary* shit, more than ready to make up for past deficiency. The sea around us was empty, horizon clear; we had the central Mediterranean to ourselves, the *Bird* was working up to her standard six knots and the autopilot was on the job: I took Gill down to the stern cabin, to that 'queen-sized' berth.

The only thing that could have improved that day would have been some wind. The *Bird*'s diesel is very quiet running, even when you're below decks and near the mahogany box which encloses it; but it goes against the grain to burn oil all day, polluting the sea air, after having the clean wind for free.

There was nothing else to grouse about.

I'd told her, 'I daren't believe this. In case I wake up and it isn't true. You – there's no way of saying it, Gill, you're—'

'Married woman is what I am. *Rejected* married woman.'

'Could a rejected married woman spend the rest of her life on a boat?'

'Doubt it. Especially if she got to be treated very often like you did this morning.'

'I *am* in love with you, Gill.'

'Not referring to *that* treatment. That was OK. In fact—'

'I'm going to swim now.'

'You're *not?*'

'Then make breakfast.'

'No, I'll do that . . . Matt – since you raised this subject – if you had to choose between me and the *Bird of Dawning*—'

'Choice wouldn't arise. the *Bird* is a boat, you're a girl.'

'If you did have to, Matt?'

'Wouldn't make sense. I couldn't take the *Bird* to bed, and I couldn't sail you to Marmaris.'

'You wouldn't give the boat up, would you?'

'No, I wouldn't. I'm not giving you up either.'

'Better go swim. Clear your head.'

'It's as clear as it ever will be . . . Look, I'm going to shower, not swim. I'll take a look up top first.'

'Take a look up there, then come back here.'

I took a look at her, first. A long one. Loving every square centimetre. Also the way she didn't put on a smile when she was saying something she meant or wanted, didn't pussyfoot around, half pretend she didn't mean it or care about it.

And that was how the day went. No wind, no sight of land, only a passing ship from time to time. I slept for a few hours, and did some maintenance jobs on deck, and – well, the *Bird* plus Gill added up to my idea of heaven: except a lot of it wouldn't be allowed, in heaven.

That evening at sundown, close together in the cockpit and Gill with ice tinkling in one of her Caballo's Necks, she brought the conversation round to a grimmer theme. Doubtless she'd have had her sister's disappearance in her thoughts during the day, just as I had, and I'd done some thinking about old Tommy Fountain too, but neither of us had chosen to interrupt the idyll until now. Sunset would have triggered this: after sunset comes sunrise, and not long after that we'd be in Malta, back in touch with our various problems.

'Something I'd better tell you about my father, Matt.'

I'd thought she meant in the context of our relationship, how difficult I'd find him, or whatever. I said, 'I know. He's a direct descendant of Geronimo. I don't care, I'm no racist.'

'Seriously. I'll call him again, tomorrow, incidentally. But this is something that makes the kidnap scenario more probable – or it might do. They could've done it for something else besides money. I told you he's a big noise, important, rich, etcetera? Well, three-quarters of the reason is Defence contracts. In particular the computer I told you about, the DBX. The 'DB' bit stands for Digby Brennan, by the way – his name.'

'You mean you're Irish?'

'Way back. *His* people. But the DBX is on the embargoed technology list – know what I mean?'

I did. Certain high-tech equipment with military applications is not allowed to be exported from the US except under special licence to NATO allies, who are then barred from re-exporting it. The reason for this is that for many years the Soviets have been hyperactive in their efforts to get hold of such equipment, by any nefarious means they've been able to dream up but mostly by employing intermediaries, crooked middlemen in the US or Europe, and chains of bogus company addresses. They've been successful too: a KGB section known as 'Directorate T', set up by none other than Yuri Andropov, organizes and orchestrates it all, and the net result is that a large proportion of the more effective Soviet weapon systems is based on Western technology.

I hadn't heard of kidnapping as a tool of this activity, but I could see what had to be in Gill's mind. Send us your DBX mainframe computer, or you don't see your daughter again.

'You didn't mention this angle before.'

'Because it's secret, I shouldn't know about it. In fact I dare say it's public knowledge, but I was *told* it's secret that he does Defence stuff. And another thing I shouldn't know is that a DBX did go East, about two years ago, eighteen months maybe.'

'So they've got it already?'

'Got *that*. Sure. Dad told me, in one of his expansive moods. Seems his company sold it to some other firm – legit, someplace in the States – and they sent to collect it, one of those big articulated trucks, that reputable company's name

129

all over it and so forth, then later – I don't know, same day or same week, whatever – the OK company sent their *real* truck for it. The FBI nearly went mad, Dad said. So much stuff gets shipped out every day of the year – a thousand containers, maybe. You can't see what's in every one of them: and next stop East Germany, USSR, you name it.'

'And you're suggesting he'd have other embargoed products they'd want.'

'Most likely. Software, for instance. Besides, he's a multi-millionaire, wouldn't do that on just one mainframe, huh?'

I had no idea. 'But if he's so rich, it could be just money, anyway . . . And whichever—'

'Right – makes no difference to us here, does it?'

'I was going to say, to your sister.'

'Oh, you're *so* right.' Her hand, well iced from holding the Caballo, pushed into mine. 'And I'm so glad I found you.' Then she spoilt it: 'Even if you *are* a bit of an old fogey.'

A breeze came up from the north-west after dark. We kept going on the engine until after midnight, but by the early hours the wind had freshened to around 12 knots, and as it was dead astern I had the genoa poled out to port, mainsail starboard, we were goosewinging along with the Loran telling us we had only 70 miles to go: say 10 hours, 12 if the wind dropped again. I brought her round 20 degrees to port, then – trimming the sails to match, to a true course of 110 to pass north of Gozo, knowing that in not much over four hours we should see the Gozo light. It has a range of 25 miles, for a 15-foot height of eye, so I reckoned on picking up its loom before we were within, say, 20 miles of it. And at sunrise we'd have Gozo itself in plain sight on the bow.

Gill came up at about 0300, in her dragon suit.

'Like me to take over, Matt?'

'Thanks, but I'm not sleepy.' I'd slept through some of the forenoon, between periods of love-making, and a couple of hours after lunch as well. 'But you can certainly come and keep me company, if you like.'

'Changed course, haven't we?' She was still in the process of waking up. A slim, pale shape swaying to the boat's motion, pale against the background of black sea. 'Hey, wind's up.

And no motor. No wonder it felt different.'

'You have a sailor's instincts. Gill, tell you what you *could* do—'

'I know. Coffee.'

'Spot on. Brilliant.'

She asked me while we were drinking it, bundled close together at the after end of the cockpit, 'Will the Lawries be joining us today?'

'Tomorrow, or more likely the day after.'

'Good. We don't have to move out of your cabin right away.'

'Not today, we don't.'

'When they're with us, are we going to – well, be open about us, or do we pretend we're just good friends?'

I'd been thinking about this myself. They wouldn't be expecting me to have a crew-girl, I was supposed to be a loner, but I thought they wouldn't object to getting a somewhat better service – on the cooking side, for instance. On the other hand, Loder had said they were middle-aged, and they might not approve of our relationship. People varied so much these days, you never could tell; and having adhered to those principles of mine until now, it wasn't a situation I'd experienced before. I thought the best answer might be to explain that Gill was with me because she was concerned for her sister who was supposed to be on some other yacht in Turkish waters, etcetera; there'd be no need to mention anything frightening like kidnapping. And as for our personal relationship – well, as long as we didn't make love in public, and the service didn't suffer, I didn't see why it should concern them.

I put these ideas to Gill. Adding, 'They do have to get their money's worth. That means I'm at their beck and call pretty well from the moment they board until the time they leave. Unfortunately, that's the nature of the job.'

'Sure, I understand. And really it's only the getting there, isn't it? I mean, once we're in Turkey I'll be hunting for Anne and you'll – as you say, you'll have your hands full.'

'I'll help you, though. I'm not leaving you to do it on your own.'

'I know you'd *want* to, Matt, but I don't see how you'll have the time.'

'Well, I have friends – Turkish – who generally know what's going on. Very decent, helpful people. If they can help at all they will. And if the Lawries run true to type they'll want to go shopping, eat in different restaurants, go on excursions to ancient ruins, and so on. You don't often get charterers who're round your neck *all* the time.'

'Right . . .'

'Although they do have to come first. If I let them go away feeling they'd had a bad deal – which I'd hate to do anyway, this is my job after all – when they got back to the UK they'd beef at my agent, the guy who booked them, so he'd lose confidence in me and maybe book the next prospects with Joe Soap instead of Matt Johnson. What it comes down to is, this is a competitive racket, to make a go of it I have to do better than the others.'

She squeezed my arm. '*I*'ll charter you. When are you free?'

'How about all winter?'

'Really?'

'There's no business here in the Med in winter, obviously. Two winters – not this last, but the two before – I went to the Caribbean and skippered a company boat there. There's plenty of work like that because there's a shortage of yacht captains with tickets. You get lots of young guys who're great at sailing but aren't anything like seamen. And when you have a boat worth a quarter of a million or more, you'd want to know she was in safe hands, wouldn't you?'

'I take it you do have this ticket – meaning a yachtmaster's certificate, right?'

'Coastal Skipper's and Yachtmaster Offshore certificates. And I'm qualified in radio.'

'I'm in safe hands, then.'

'I'd hope so.'

'It's a nice feeling . . . But – you're all booked up, aren't you, after this Lawrie charter – I mean, right through the summer?'

'Right into September.'

'And you couldn't get out of the next one, obviously.'

'Hardly.'

'No . . . Otherwise, you see, if I didn't find her or get news of her in this fortnight, I *could* have chartered you.'

132

'Keep our fingers crossed, that's all. But also, remember she may not be at this end of the Med at all, they could've changed their plans since she wrote that letter, she could be in Algeria getting married, or something. Anything . . . It's very slim info you're working on.'

Whether it was this night or the night before or the one after that Tommy Fountain was on the Harwich–Hamburg ferry I don't know, and the calendar date doesn't matter, but since we left him there we might go back to him at this point, see him again on that empty, darkened passenger deck in the small hours of a cold North Sea morning. Stooped over the guardrail, staring down at the shifting pattern of white as the ferry's bulk thrust through the dark water with ponderous, apparent slowness. Like gazing into a fire: and remembering his drive back from Swansea, the M4 teeming with high-speed traffic which would be a lot worse when the evening rush back into London got into its swing. He'd been well ahead of that, should be in the West End by about eight, he'd reckoned; and this thought would have led to another – that the last thing he wanted to do was go home to an evening with Penny.

If she was there, not in Daddy's house or some boyfriend's country cottage . . .

Drive to Chelsea, check whether she was in the house or not?

Two objections. One, it might be difficult to get away – without yet another screaming row. Recriminations, tears, temper, threats, taunts: or, maybe worse, pleas for a new start, pretence of continuing affection, etcetera. She wasn't predictable in her moods: and he knew he might have fallen for something of that sort a few days ago. He wouldn't now, one dividend from the weekend on his own was that he knew for sure that it was over. And the hell with old Benedict and his business: Tommy knew he'd been a fish out of water in that *milieu*, they'd had him feeling useless, believing he shouldn't ever have left the Corps because as a civvie he was no damn good. That was all balls. He had more than adequate financial resources, he'd take his time and find something – or start something – that would really suit him.

Penny wouldn't be expecting him home this evening. He'd

intended staying away until Monday night. He'd told her father this – and father, you could bet, would have been on the blower to his precious little daughter within minutes of that interview – and he'd also left her a note when he'd gone back to the house to pack a bag.

He wondered if she did have a boyfriend, or whether that had been only a taunt. He thought she probably did have. If so, she might well have taken off for the long weekend, with – well, not Tom, but Dick or Harry, or – he'd muttered aloud, getting in to London's outskirts now – '*some* City prick . . .'

He could think of several likely candidates. But it didn't matter now, oddly enough. Having decided they were through, the thought of her in transports of delight with some other man or men didn't bother him. Which surely proved there was nothing left worth keeping.

The question was, where to spend the next few hours. He'd have gone to the Special Forces Club if it hadn't been a Sunday; but on Sundays the bar and dining-room were shut. And any club that did have Sunday bar service would be morgue-like. So, some pub or other . . . Or – sudden thought – there was a club in Knightsbridge he *had* belonged to for a while, a place people joined mostly because of its Sunday opening, bar and restaurant. He'd joined about three years ago, at the end of a rather boozy evening when he and Penny had been taken there by one of her father's junior partners, a man called Jeremy Martin-Smith – and others including Martin-Smith's frumpy wife, and a merchant-banker called Graham Calderwood and a few others, all of the same stamp and mostly people who'd known Penny when she'd been a schoolgirl.

All or any of them could be her lovers now, Tommy thought. He'd had nothing in common with any of them, but he'd had to mix with them because of his work and because they were Penny's friends and her father's. And he'd allowed Martin-Smith, or Calderwood, or both, to make him a member of this club, but he hadn't used it after that or bothered to renew his subscription and he was clearly not a member now. But it would be less gloomy than a Sunday night pub with its handful of morose beer-swillers, and if he told them he'd lost his membership card – which was the truth – they just might let him in, he thought. Lost his card and forgotten to renew his

134

membership: if they suggested it, he could renew it on the spot.

Traffic thickened in the last few miles. It was getting on for nine when he parked his Peugeot in one of the small streets behind Harrods, near the Special Forces Club, as it happened – walked up into Knightsbridge – it was drizzling now – and found this place near enough to where he'd remembered. The manager, or whatever he was, on duty in a dark suit in the vestibule, greeted him as if he was a regular and valued customer, didn't ask for identification or a card, simply ushered him through. And that was it, no problem.

Unfortunately. He was there until midnight, and nobody knew his name or would know him again. There was no member whose name he knew or who could have been traced to confirm that he'd been in the place that evening, and that guy at the reception desk surely wouldn't have owned up to having admitted a non-member. Whose name in any case he didn't know: and when Tommy had left the club – it shut at midnight – it wasn't the same man on duty.

He'd drunk a lot more than he'd eaten. He'd also done a good bit of thinking – about where he'd live, and the move itself, the grim but unavoidable mechanics of physical separation. As so strongly urged by old Hugh Benedict, scared for his daughter's neck . . .

Just as well, Tommy thought, that it wasn't a very long drive, down into Chelsea. He was conscious of being a long way over the drink-drive limit. But if he'd left his car where it was and taken a taxi they'd have had it wheel-clamped by the time he got to it in the morning.

Anyway, no hurry. The later he got in, the better chance of Penny being in bed and asleep.

He drove into the mews, its cobbles glistening from recent rain, stopped the car outside his house, left its engine running while he unlocked and opened the garage, switched the inside light on. There was a light burning upstairs behind the curtained window of his and Penny's bedroom; he'd seen this from the mews and thought she'd be reading in bed or watching television. In which case he'd come home too early, after all. Thinking about this as he drove the Peugeot as quietly as possible into its stable, switched off and then went round behind it to shut and lock the doors, he found that he was

135

actually dreading the prospect of seeing her, having to talk to her, listen to her.

Music, from inside – upstairs. More likely radio than TV. So she'd be reading. He got back into the car, sat with the driving door open, wondering how long he might have to wait. Then, whether he'd not wait at all – sleep right here, in the car?

Could be the best answer: acceptance of slight discomfort so as to avoid what might otherwise be hours of wrangling.

It seemed a bit daft, when there was a comfortable bed up there just waiting to be flopped into. And he was extremely tired – as well as fuddled – but this applied both ways; he didn't think he could have faced her and her bitching.

Well. Make your mind up, one way or the other. No point just *sitting* here.

Maybe another five minutes passed before he got out, opened the rear door and climbed in, tried to dispose his length as comfortably as he could. In earlier days this would have seemed like luxury: when one recalled what real discomfort could be, how one had passed *some* nights – and thought nothing of it, at the time ... There was a rug on the rear window ledge, which he pulled down and spread over himself: it would have been a lot easier if one had been six inches shorter. But in any case, he was tired enough to fall asleep immediately.

He thought – recalling it afterwards as he'd done several hundred times by now – he *thought* he'd only just dropped off, slept maybe for a minute but maybe only seconds, when a loud crash inside the house jerked him awake.

He reached to wind down the window. Listening for further sounds but also re-hearing that one in his memory and concluding that it could have been the front door slamming. But a few minutes later – maybe as much as ten – he heard what surely *was* the front door shutting – not quite slamming but shutting with a thump – and it wasn't the same sound at all.

She'd had a – visitor. Who'd now left, hurriedly. She'd been in the bedroom and one might guess the visitor had been with her.

Heard the car, got dressed, taken off?

If so, he'd taken his bloody time about it ...

136

Should've gone up, kicked his balls off . . .

He thought he must have waited about twenty minutes before he did go in. So this would have been about 1 a.m. or a little after. Still not wanting to see Penny. Even if the construction he'd put on it was correct – a lover, now departed – he didn't want to see her, speak with her, discuss this or their imminent separation. He said – much later – 'I think I didn't want her to exist any more. I wanted to be done with the whole bloody shooting-match, never have to even think about her again. Something like that . . .'

But of course he'd had to go into the house eventually. And he'd found his wife three-quarters naked and entirely dead – although in the first moments of shock he hadn't accepted that she was dead, didn't for some reason believe she *could* be. But – she'd fallen on the stairs – that crash he'd heard – and then . . . Reality was dawning, to some limited extent, and he was checking the one vital, essential starting-point for any further action or decision: whether she was only unconscious, knocked out, or—

No breath. No heartbeat.

After that crash, he remembered, he'd heard the door shut violently.

His head was thick, thought-processes slow and confused by drink, tiredness and maybe shock. Shock may actually have set in during the next hour or so, but in any case he wasn't thinking straight. Someone had left the house in a hurry, banging the door as he ran out. *Or,* someone had rushed *in* . . . Crouching beside the body, looking around – down into the hall and up to the landing – feeling the stillness, then, the house empty except for himself and – and his wife's body. He began – gingerly – to examine her head: found no obvious sign of a blow . . . Trying to remember how long it had been between hearing the fall and his coming into the house: it was puzzling, he really didn't know, but the thought in his mind had been that if he'd come in quickly he might have saved her.

He picked her up, and started up the stairs. Having first assumed that she'd been hit, the most likely thing being a blow on the head, he'd then thought maybe she'd fallen – either in a struggle or just plain fallen – and struck her head: on the banisters, or – whatever . . . Then, lifting her, he saw the

137

damage to the neck. It would show bruising before long, but right now it was the unnatural angle of neck and shoulder, and faint beginnings of contusion – a discolouring that was almost imperceptible: and this was the result not of a blow but of a wrench.

Not necessarily the work of any other person. You could kill someone with a forearm round the neck and an expert jerk that would leave this kind of damage, but it could happen in other ways too. Hangover of esoteric knowledge, once essential but now potentially dangerous – as Hugh Benedict knew – and therefore burdensome.

She looked so – withdrawn. A child at rest in its own childish dreams: with a look of childish innocence and peace. Only the observer's eye and insight could find pathos in it, *she* wasn't feeling sorry for herself . . . She'd have died, he decided, from her head's violent impact against the banisters – or the wall where the stair curved in an elbow – so that it had been wrenched sideways, snapping vertebrae.

Echoes in his mind: her voice, on Thursday night: 'Be careful, you could fall – *break your neck* . . .' And his own telling her father next morning, *She's highly provocative* . . .

Implying, *Can't promise not to break her neck*?

Climbing . . . The body a deadweight in his arms. Still warm: but once fiery, passionate . . .

With whom? *Recently*, with whom?

Near the top, he'd trodden on what turned out to be a champagne bottle, struggled to keep his balance, fallen backwards.

Clutching her still, protecting the dead body with his own, jarring down the stairs. Even drunker than he'd thought he was. It wasn't a long flight but it was steep, and with that bend in it . . .

Then – some moments later, in the abrupt cessation of noise he heard a shout of '*Every* bugger's falling down fucking stairs!'

His own voice: *he*'d said that . . .

Start again . . .

Pausing to put the champagne bottle on the small corner table in the hall. It had come bouncing down with him and his wife's body and he'd picked it up, squinted at the label. A very

138

special wine from Krug, probably expensive too; for the second time that night he thought of Jeremy Martin-Smith – because amongst other things Smith was a wine-snob, often held forth on the subject, quoting – Tommy had once annoyed Penny by alleging this – bits of articles on wine he'd read that morning in the *Financial Times*.

That ponce?

He carried Penny upstairs, put her on her own bed, covered her near-nakedness. Straightened the bedclothes too: it was something that had to be done, while trying unsuccessfully to ignore his own perception of why it was necessary, what his wife had been doing in this bed with bloody Jeremy – or someone like him – while he himself had been getting quietly soused in Knightsbridge . . . Seeing then another, identical champagne bottle on the bedside table: and admitting to himself that if she hadn't been dead he might have been shaking the truth out of her, here and now – who, and who else, how many . . .

Whoever had shot out of the house, *that* was who. One, anyway. Got pissed with her – got her pissed, at least – and then—

Then what? And for that matter *now* what? He felt – dazed, inert: looking round, thinking about – about *nothing*. Seeing one glass beside the bottle, wondering where the other was . . . But knowing one had to do something: doctor, maybe, or—

The telephone began to ring. Before he'd had time to decide whether to call the police first, or the doctor. Ivory push-button telephone bleeping quietly but *still* bleeping, plaintively insistent although it was getting on for 2 a.m.

He picked it up. It wasn't only his hand that was shaking, his whole body – like a bad case of malaria . . . 'Yes?'

'Who's that?' A pause. Hugh Benedict's voice was sharp, high with alarm, suspicion . . . 'Eh, who's that? Penny there?'

'It's Tommy.' He swallowed. 'Bit late, isn't it, for—'

'Tommy? I thought you weren't coming back until *tomorrow* night – isn't that what—'

'Wasn't much cop, at Swansea. No point staying, so—'

'Is Penny there?'

'Yes. Yes, of course—'

'May I speak to her, please?'

139

'You want me to – wake her up, and – look, d'you know what time it is?'

'Of course. One forty-two.' Cold-voiced, as if insulted. At twenty to two, for God's sake. Then: 'D'you mean she's slept through this ringing and you talking now?'

Tommy felt himself sway: feeling as if he was about to pass out, he sat down on the bed beside his wife's body and told her father with his eyes shut, 'Separate rooms.'

'Oh. Oh, well, I'm sorry . . . Yes, of course, you *would* have. Sorry, Tommy. I was – worrying. Penny being on her own, you know. Concerned for her because – well with you away, and the strain she's – well, it's a strain for you as well, of course, but' – a sigh – 'you'd understand, I'm sure . . .'

'Yes. All right.' Flat tone: but nerves about ready to snap, and a desperate urge to slam the phone down . . . 'Right, then.'

'Sorry I woke you, Tommy. Give her my love, would you? I mean, in the morning, of course. Well—'

He put the phone down carefully, whispered 'Oh, Jesus Christ . . .'

Aware of what he'd done. Roughly like writing a confession and signing it. Telling his wife's blonde, pillowed head, 'But I didn't – you *know* I didn't!'

Difficult to see how anyone else would know it, though. In the first place he'd told her father he might be tempted to do something of the sort. Then it had happened: and he'd been on the spot and pretended she was alive, asleep. *Why?*

Because he could hardly have picked the phone up and said 'Oh, hello there, so glad you called, someone just broke your daughter's neck . . . No, I'm wrong, actually she broke it herself, I was sitting in the garage at the time . . .'

No proof he hadn't been here in the house all evening. Nobody in that Knightsbridge club knew him: he shouldn't have been admitted, they'd broken the law, with a club licence, allowing a non-member to buy drinks. Don Phelan and his wife could only say he'd left Swansea after lunch: he could have been here in the house by eight, and there wasn't a soul who could prove he had not been.

Except whoever it was who'd been screwing Penny.

Small tin on the dressing-table, one spoon and two pearl-handled butter-knives, a platter with some scraps of toast on

140

it. The tin was empty, scraped clean, but its plastic top with a round blue label lay beside it. He picked it up, held it to the dressing-table lamp: *Fortnum & Mason, fresh Beluga Caviar, MALASSOL. Keep cold, do not freeze. 100 g 3.52 oz. Product of the USSR.*

They'd been pampering themselves, all right. And now he'd put the icing on their cake. It was staggering, bewildering, how effectively he'd set himself up. Framed himself . . . Glancing round at Penny, he almost expected to find her smiling. Then – groping for straws to clutch at, it came to him out of the blue – *Matt Johnson* . . .

It wasn't a straw, it was a godsend of a thought, a lifeline snaking to him out of shock and bewilderment. Snatching at it, forcing his dulled brain to work for him . . . Matt would be leaving about now: but from where?

Loder. *Harry* Loder . . . Loder, H. – in the phone book . . .

9

By dawn we'd lost the wind again and were motoring. I'd had a sleep while Gill had presided over the *Bird*'s progress during the last hour and a half of darkness, but we were both on deck to see the sun rise, a blaze of gold on the slow-heaving, unwrinkled surface, blinding if you looked straight at it – as Gill did, while I looked at *her*, at her eyes narrowed into slits of pale amber like a cat's looking into a fire.

My last morning alone with her. I wondered if I'd ever see a dawn as heart-filling as this one.

Gozo was a dark hump on the beam, an undulating profile with its highest point at the western end where the lighthouse was – still circling, group-flashing twice each circuit. Between it and Malta itself are about three miles of sea, with the little island of Comino stuck in the middle; then the wedge-shape of the main island, a wedge about ten miles long with the slope from south-west to east. It was a familiar landfall to me, by this time, almost a homecoming. In recent years the Maltese authorities haven't been all that welcoming or helpful to visiting British yachtsmen, but things are a lot better under the new regime and the warm feelings that existed before between Brit and Malt, dormant as they may have been for a while, have re-surfaced, leaving everyone happier.

This was new territory to Gill, and I risked boring her with a potted history of the island as we drove along its northern coast. The great siege in the sixteenth century, for instance, when the Knights of St John held Valletta against the hordes of Suleiman the Magnificent and human heads were fired as cannon-balls; and the siege of 1941 to 1944, in which an uncle of mine was drowned, nearly ten years before I was born.

'Glad it wasn't your Daddy.'

'Why, *thank* you, Ma'am!'

'I mean it, though.'

Extraordinary. Really, bewildering.

We breakfasted while the light was growing, then tidied the boat up a bit and made some lists of stores that we'd embark here, and we'd cleared the Marsamxett customs and were secured alongside in the marina by ten-thirty. Door to door, the trip had taken four hours less than four days.

I had to go to the office first, to pay the marina fees – £M20, which would have allowed the *Bird* to rest her wings here for four weeks, with no reduction for the fact that she'd be spreading them again in a couple of days. I did my best to pave the way for not having to pay it again when I brought the Lawries back here – in less than a month – but it didn't seem I could count on it. And the next thing was to call the Hilton, which is at St Julian's, to find out when the Lawries were due to arrive; also, I had to order fuel – diesel oil – which would be brought to our berth in a tanker, and get the stores we'd listed – including a gas cylinder to be changed for a full one – and arrange for a mechanic from the Manoel Island Yacht Yard to come down and give the engine a once-over. In most Med harbours I'd have done this myself, but while we were this close to expert assistance it seemed sensible to take advantage of it. And – and – and only about a dozen other things: as well as some long-distance telephoning, to the Metropolitan Police (me, to check on any developments in Tommy's business) and California (Gill, to get an up-date from her father). Those calls could be made this evening, I thought maybe from the Yacht Club, where I was thinking I might take Gill for supper.

I'd been reckoning on having the rest of today and all tomorrow in which to complete all chores and have the *Bird* in immaculate shape to receive her guests; and it was on the cards we might have another day or so to kill after that, in which case I'd show Gill around the island, take her swimming, generally relax on *terra firma* before the long trip east. But I called the Hilton first, from the marina office . . .

'You have reservations for a Mr and Mrs Lawrie, I believe. Could you tell me—'

'One moment, sir, if you please.'

I waited. Then she said, 'I'm putting you through, sir.'

Through to reception, no doubt . . . A new female voice chirped a bright 'Hello?'

'Ah – I think you have reservations for a Mr and Mrs Lawrie. Would you mind telling me when you expect them?'

There was a murmur that wasn't addressed to me. Then: 'Look, this *is* – Mrs Lawrie . . . Who's—'

'You're Mrs Lawrie?'

A giggle . . . 'D'you have some reason to doubt it?' Then a man said something in the background, and she asked, 'Oh, this couldn't be Mr Johnson, could it?'

'Matt Johnson, yes.' With a spinning brain, at that, a rushed screening of numerous jobs all having to be done at once and completed by this time yesterday, God help us . . . 'Of the *Bird of Dawning*. We docked half an hour ago, didn't think you'd be here yet. Sorry, I thought I was talking to the hotel reception.'

'We didn't expect *you* this soon. But this is wonderful . . . Mr Johnson, would you hold on, here's my – my husband.'

I don't pretend to be Einstein – or Sherlock Holmes, as Gill had once suggested – but my antennae had picked up two very brief hesitations which I thought might be significant: one had come between 'this is' and 'Mrs Lawrie', and the second, just a moment ago before 'my husband'.

'Matt Johnson?'

'Mr Lawrie.'

'Ted Lawrie. You made good time.'

'Well, I got the word that you were a bit ahead of schedule, and there was no reason to hang around. Only thing is – as I mentioned to your wife, we've just this minute arrived, I'd like a day for such things as refuelling and so on.'

'No problem. D'you want to leave tomorrow – or day after?'

I would have preferred the day after, but I thought of Gill

145

and her anxiety for Anne: and she was right, if Anne was there, the sooner we were there too, the better. I suggested, 'How about tomorrow after lunch?'

'Fine. Suit us down to the ground. Like to come up here for a meal tonight?'

'Well, *very* kind, but there's rather a lot to do, and—'

'Don't worry, I understand, you have your hands full.' Mr Lawrie was from Lancashire, I guessed. He added, 'So we'll come to you, ready to go, at – say two p.m. tomorrow?'

'I'll be looking out for you. Incidentally, I have a crew with me, this trip, a girl – good sailor, and she can cook. Usually I'm single-handed, but—'

'Right. Right. Tomorrow, then – Manoel Island marina, two o'clock.'

'Just one question, Mr Lawrie – choice of accommodation: do you prefer a double bunk, or two singles?'

'Oh, *double*, please.'

And no doubt about *that* . . . I told him, 'You get the cabin in the stern, then. It'll be all ready for you.' I went back to the boat, deciding to ask Gill which she'd like to hear first, the good news or the bad.

It was a busy day. Fuel arrived, and I took all she'd hold, knowing we might need every litre if the wind continued as capriciously as it had just lately. Malta to Marmaris is about 750 miles, five days' normal transit; I thought I'd make a stop in Crete, probably at Iraklion, but even that was a run of 550. Easy if we had the winds we should have at this time of year, but winds didn't always go by the book and our range on the diesel was only 300. Touch wood, we'd get at least *some* good sailing days.

I checked the level of fresh water in the tank, and was glad to find we'd be able to last out until either Crete or Marmaris. We'd been careful with it, because the water available in Malta tends to be brackish; I've even known it to be undrinkable. If I'd had to I could have taken some, and relied on the clean water in the barricoes for drinking – barricoes, pronounced 'breakers', were originally small barrels, but in the *Bird* they're plastic jerrycans, lashed to the rail in the stern – but this wasn't going to be necessary, thanks to Gill not having washed

146

her hair too often . . . And the stores arrived, by van, from a shop that's in walking distance from where we were berthed. Come to that, everything's in walking distance, there are only fifty acres of Manoel Island. But it was still good service. Also the mechanic turned up, did his stuff and assured me we had no problems, and while I had him there I got him to service the Yamaha outboard as well. It's stowed aft, in a smart blue plastic jacket and clamped on a transom-board that's bolted to the rails; the Avon inflatable which it drives at satisfyingly high speed is stowed, deflated, in the stern lazarette, and this had to be brought up and inflated so that the motor could be run on it. I hadn't used the inflatable at all in Menorca, so it had had a long stand-off and it was as well to be sure it was in good order. This too I could have done myself, but there were plenty of other jobs, and neither of us was standing around and watching.

The stores, for instance, had to be stowed away. When there's a chance you might hit rough seas you can't just throw stuff in a cupboard as you might at home; but you still need access to it when you want it. Then the *Bird* needed a good clean-out internally, and her teak decks scrubbed. Four days at sea leaves decks salt-stained, and where the sheets are led across the coachroof you get unsightly marks which become permanent if they aren't periodically removed.

All this we did by sunset that evening: at which hour I lowered the Blue Ensign and put it away. The *Bird of Dawning* would be under charter to the Lawries from tomorrow onward, and a boat plying for hire isn't allowed to fly the Blue Ensign, only the ubiquitous Red.

I asked a neighbouring yacht's skipper to keep an eye on the *Bird* for me – but locked the mahogany doors too, just to make sure of it – and took Gill up to the yacht club to do our telephoning and have one good shoreside meal while we had the chance.

It used to be called the Royal Malta Yacht Club. Then the word 'royal' became unfashionable, for some reason, and the name was changed to Valletta Yacht Club. It's on the eastern promontory of Manoel Island and less than half a mile from where the *Bird* was lying; it's an old fort, Fort Manoel or *Il-Fortizza Manoel*, and it's a fine old building. I have reciprocal membership through the Royal Naval Sailing Association, but as I spend so much time on the island and use the club quite a lot I'd recently become a full member.

Just to the south of it, incidentally, below sheer limestone cliffs and facing right on to Lazzaretto Creek, is another fairly ancient pile, the quarantine hospital which during the Second World War was the base of the 10th Submarine Flotilla, from which my uncle was operating when he was drowned – lost, anyway – in the Strait of Messina in 1942. It's a hospital again now: as it was in May of the year 1811 when the poet Byron carved his name into one of those soft stone walls, and wrote shortly after his incarceration, *Adieu thou damnedest quarantine/That gave me fever and the spleen.*

(Through that uncle, I have a special interest here, obviously, but I like to tell my customers these things. They can get the standard bullshit from the guide-books, of which there's a shelf-ful in the midships cabin, but I regale them from time to time with a more personalized variety.)

The Maltese barman didn't know what a Caballo was, so Gill had to settle for a brandy and ginger ale. Then she went to telephone her father, while I had a couple more Scotches and chatted to a guy who was in transit westward, taking his boat from Athens to Gibraltar *en route* to the UK. He'd come via the Corinth Canal, and told me it had taken him three days and cost about £300 – just that little stone's throw – so this changed my plans, there and then. After I brought the Lawries back here I'd go to Athens the longer way round, save both time and money. In fact it would be only about a hundred miles farther, through the Kithera Strait, so with that sort of delay in the Canal I'd win hands down.

Comparing notes like this with other yachtsmen can be a valuable exercise; it also provides the best of excuses for hanging around in bars.

Gill came back. She was wearing a dress tonight, the first time I'd seen her in one. There wasn't a terrific amount of it, and it was very simply cut, but I guessed it had cost her quite a lot of money and she looked absolutely fantastic in it. She told me, 'He's heard nothing from anyone, including Anne.'

We couldn't talk then, as we had this other guy with us. I got some more drinks, and went to make my call to Charles

Harrison: having debated whether to call him or his boss, Frewin, and picking Harrison not only because I had his home number but also because I felt there might be some degree of *rapport* between us by this time.

He was at home. I said, having told him where I was calling from, 'Business must be slack, Charles.'

'Eh? Oh – well, they let me out sometimes. Only at night, of course . . . What can I do for you – besides saying no, no news of Fountain?'

'No developments at all?'

'Can't even be sure he's alive, can we?'

I didn't comment. Maybe it was what Tommy had wanted them to be unsure of. Harrison tried, 'Didn't give *you* any idea where he might be going, did he, when you saw him at Southampton?'

'Come off it, Charles . . .'

'Well, you might have had another of those attacks of memory, mightn't you . . . Oh, here's a little puzzle you might solve, too – initials GC, mean anything to you?'

'George Cross.'

'Who's he?'

'It's a medal. This island I'm at was awarded it after the war . . . No, nothing else I can think of. Someone's initials?'

'You wouldn't know many of the Fountains' London friends, I suppose.'

'None. Except for any former Royal Marines we'd both know. GC: I'll put my mind to it, but—'

'Here's another, while we're at it. Would you say Captain Fountain was a wine expert, wine lover, whatever you'd call it?'

'May have become one, but not to my knowledge. Why?'

'You'd need to be a bit of a connoisseur, to pay £121 a bottle for champagne – eh?'

'Or an idiot.'

'That's what was in his house, though.'

'That much a *bottle*?'

'Right. Had his prints on it too.'

'How come you'd have a record of his prints?'

'Matched some on the wheel of his Peugeot, and on the telephone from when he made his calls to you and your agent.

149

At which time, incidentally, it's beyond doubt his wife was lying dead beside him.'

'Oh, Jesus . . .'

'Yeah. Best way I can put it, Mr Johnson—'

'Matt, please . . .'

'Matt – best way I can put it is our inquiries would be greatly facilitated if we had your friend where we could talk to him.'

Meaning – I supposed – that they still thought Tommy was a murderer. That bit about telephoning with the body right beside him: couldn't have meant much else. When *I'd* been talking to him – Penny lying there dead . . .

It was a shivery thought. More comfortable to latch on to another one – that there did seem to be some kind of investigation still in progress. I asked Harrison, 'What's this GC initials business, then?'

But he wasn't going to tell me anything else about it, and the conversation wasn't getting anywhere except expensive. I told him I'd be in touch, and that was how we left it – nothing learnt or achieved, and several quid down the hole.

I went back to Gill. She was surrounded now, all that guy's friends had closed in like hungry sharks. I extracted her – rather like plucking a rugger ball out of a scrum – and took her through to the dining-room.

'No change at your father's end, you said.'

'He hasn't heard from Anne or anyone else either. I told him I'd call again when we got to Turkey, but he's still – you know, unconcerned.' She had that vulnerable look she gets when she's talking or thinking about her father. She asked me, 'How about your guy?'

'Nothing new there either . . . But if your father's unconcerned, Gill, I'm sorry to say he must be stupid – as well as whatever else.'

'What d'you mean?'

There was a break while the head waiter bowed us to the table I'd reserved. When we were alone again with menus under our noses, I explained, 'Because having missed you in Menorca she surely *would* by this time have got in touch with him. The one point of contact she'd have with you . . . OK, no ransom demand, so presumably no kidnap, but it's ten to one on that she's not – not free.'

'Raoul.'

'Right.'

'I've been thinking the same way.' She was fumbling for a handkerchief; I thought tears might be coming, blamed myself for having expressed that thought so bluntly. Even if she *had* been thinking on the same lines. She spoke tensely, almost whispering: 'He might have taken her to Algeria, Turkey could have been a blind – could have told her Turkey to put me off the scent, he could be – what I said when we first talked about it, remember, white slaving? Or just some pervert—'

'Gill.' I reached over and took her hand. 'This is all supposition, imagination – and it's a vicious circle, the nastiest scenario's the one that sticks in your mind . . . Honestly, it's better not to keep making guesses, they're bad for you and they're probably nowhere near the truth . . . Listen, I had an idea just now, I think quite a good one. Means another little job tomorrow morning, but—'

The waiter coughed. He had his pad and pencil ready.

'Right. Let's decide what we're going to eat.'

It was a splendid meal, and we had a Chianti Classico that went down well with it. Then we went back to the *Bird* and turned down the bedding on the double berth for what looked like being the last time.

But – I thought, when I was peeling that slinky little dress off her – this couldn't end. There'd be an interruption to it, inevitably, but if I had anything to do with it there'd be some longer-term arrangements made. Some kind, somehow.

We slept in each other's arms until the alarm buzzer woke us at six-thirty – ridiculously early to get up, on our one and only morning in harbour and our last in a comfortable bed, but we did have a lot to do before our passengers arrived: and the waking itself, the overwhelming thrill of finding her right there – *here* – where she'd dropped off to sleep – well, it's a waking that I'll remember all my life.

But – from the sublime to the boring essentials now – the cabin, *our* cabin, had to be emptied of gear, cleaned, polished, the bunk remade with clean sheets, etcetera.

'Bloody people . . .'

She smiled at me. 'We'll be all right up in the sharp end, Matt.'

'You're absolutely right.'

We'd be all right anywhere. As long as it was 'we'. I told her this and added, 'I suppose you do realize I'm not letting you go.'

'Do you think I'd *want* to leave you?'

It sounded all right at the time, the way she said it, but afterwards I thought maybe she'd been implying that she might *have* to. And the problems were still there, the same ones – like the fact I live on a boat and wouldn't know how to live any other way, and Gill obviously with different ideas, anyway having to go back (I supposed) to get her divorce – and only God knew what other complications might come out of whatever was happening to Anne . . .

'Breakfast now?'

She made it, while I stowed my gear in the midships cabin. Then when we'd finished our eggs and bacon, toast, honey and coffee, we got dressed and I asked the same guy to watch the *Bird* for me, and we took a cab into Valletta and visited a photographer. This was what I'd thought of last night. At some earlier stage Gill had said something about herself and Anne being more like twins than just sisters, and I'd taken this to mean they looked alike. I'd asked her, after we'd ordered the meal, and she'd confirmed it – up to a point.

'You wouldn't doubt we were sisters, sure. Not *entirely* alike, her face is a little narrower than mine, and her mouth isn't as – well, her lips are sort of thinner.'

'Could you make yourself more like her – compress your lips, for instance?'

'Well . . .'

She tried it . . . 'Like that?'

'If her face is narrower, maybe a shot that's not quite full face would hide that difference.'

'Photograph, are we talking about?'

I nodded. 'Here's what we do. First thing in the morning we go into town and get you photographed. In the kind of clothes you think she'd be wearing on a boat – shorts, T-shirt, your kind of gear?'

'Near enough the same, I guess.'

'Is her colouring like yours?'

'Oh, sure. And both of us tanned now—'

'Colour prints, then, and we'll get a couple of dozen. Postcard size would be best. They're for Turkey, by the way – harbour authorities, for instance. And the police ... As in Spain, there are several different kinds, and the crowd we'd do best to nobble are the coastguards. They have boats – motor-launches, and small ships – guns on them – and they're in all the ports and pretty smart, sharp-eyed ...'

The photographer was so shocked at the idea of producing two dozen prints in one hour flat that you'd have thought we'd asked him to shoot his mother. Eventually he calmed down enough to quote what I thought was a ridiculously high price, but to which Gill said 'OK' – she'd insisted on paying for it, which I suppose was fair enough, and she did have quite a wad of dollar travellers' cheques.

Then she re-arranged her hair, and posed in semi-profile, slouching slightly and pressing her lips together as I'd suggested, and the Malt took his picture, and that was that. I made a point of synchronizing watches with him, and repeating 'One hour!' and then we went and saw the sights of Valletta. As much as was possible in an hour, anyway. Then back to the shop, and of course the prints weren't ready, so we went to look down on Grand Harbour from a different viewpoint ... Finally we got back to the *Bird* just before noon, with a bulky package of photographs of a girl who might have looked something like Anne Brennan, but wasn't a bit like Gill Paget.

Ted Lawrie – late forties, maybe pushing fifty – had greying dark hair and the sort of tanned, muscled face you see on a lot of professional golfers and suchlike. Including – I suppose – yachtsmen ... And his wife Emma was petite, dark, pretty. I guessed at the high thirties, but she looked good enough to stave off having to admit to the next round number for quite a while yet.

They'd both started well – said the right sort of things about the boat, and enthused over their cabin and its fitments. Well – Emma Lawrie enthused, her husband expressed satisfaction. Mainly with nods and grunts, in answer to her promptings. This isn't a snide comment, it's only to say he's not a voluble sort of character. And so far, therefore, so good. I'd had a bottle of Spanish sparkling wine in the cooler, to welcome them aboard – it's a custom the clients always appreciate – and we were drinking it now, the four of us, in the midships cabin.

Lawrie saw the package of photographs, which we'd been looking at just before they'd arrived: he slid the top one out and frowned at it for a moment before asking Gill, 'This wouldn't be you, would it?'

'I'm afraid it would.'

'Feller who took it must be a highly skilled passport photographer, I'd say.' He passed it to his wife, and asked Gill, 'Why'd you want so many?'

She said, 'Well, it's a long story.'

Emma put the photo down. 'I agree, it's rotten.' She smiled at Gill. 'But I like long stories.'

Lawrie tapped the package of photographs. 'I'd shoot the guy who took these, if it was anything to do with me.'

I decided I rather liked him.

'Fact is' – Gill had decided to satisfy their curiosity – 'I've signed on as Matt's crew because I want to get to Turkey – a mutual friend on Menorca knew he was going there and introduced us, and I do know something about boats, you see – because my kid sister's disappeared and I think that's where she may be. On a yacht with some Algerian . . . Well, in these photographs I was trying to look like her – so it wouldn't be fair to shoot the poor guy, he only did what he was told. Anne and I are quite alike – this could easily be her, it's come off better than I thought it would – and the idea – Matt's, he's the genius – is we hand these out to police and harbour officials, so if they see her—'

She looked at me. 'What would they do, Matt?'

'The coastguard would arrest the boat and hold it until we got there so you could identify her.'

'Would they *do* that?'

'I'm sure they would. Turk police and these coastguards are no pushovers, but if you're on the right side of the law and they know it – and if we've told them she's almost certainly being held in that boat against her will—'

'My poor darling.' Emma Lawrie went over to Gill and put her arms round her. 'How *dreadful* for you . . . Look, we'll help, any way we can. *Won't* we, Ted?'

154

We'd struck lucky, I thought. On present indications. I crossed my fingers, hoping it would last. And Gill was noticeably touched.

I asked them if they'd done any sailing before this, and Lawrie said he'd always wanted to, never found time for it, but might take it up if they both found they liked it. And his wife told me she'd done some dinghy sailing, years ago, but never in a boat this size. She asked a few questions about the *Bird*, and about Swans generally, and then commented, 'It's a lovely name, the *Bird of Dawning*.'

'She was called that when I bought her. Far from original – I belong to the RN Sailing Association, and there are two others listed under members' boats. It was a John Masefield title, of course.'

'Right.' She nodded. 'He wrote it sometime in the thirties, didn't he?'

'Before you and I were reading books, Mrs Lawrie.'

'Well, that's true.' She laughed. 'Just.'

Ted Lawrie muttered – 'Masefield – Poet Laureate, was he?'

He was asking his wife. She nodded – approvingly, as if it pleased her that he'd got it right. The Sherlock Holmes in me had now decided that (a) they hadn't been married long, (b) Ted had made his own way, made a success of some kind out of obscure beginnings, while Emma had been more fortunate, had had a better education and was concerned to conceal or bridge that difference between them. Also, they were in love with each other: it was unmistakable, and I thought – liking them both, and seeing that Gill did too – *Join the club* . . .

I spread out a chart, showed them our route and explained that if we didn't get good winds and had to do much motoring we'd need to put into one of the Cretan ports to refuel. Otherwise, if conditions were right and if they didn't think they'd get bored or cramped from a stretch of about five days and nights at sea, we could make Marmaris in one hop. They both said they'd prefer this. Turkey was the chosen cruising ground, and with only three weeks for the whole round trip they didn't want to waste time elsewhere.

'Unless you do need to.' Lawrie shrugged. 'You're the skipper.'

Gill looked pleased, said, 'Great, let's say prayers for a

following wind,' and Emma immediately caught on: 'Of course, you must be dying to get there, Gill.'

'Sooner the better. But I won't interfere with your cruise, don't worry about that. I expect I'll move ashore when we reach Fethiye.'

Ted Lawrie asked, 'We don't have a fixed itinerary, do we?'

I confirmed no, we didn't; but explained that there's a stretch of coast that's well worth seeing, and I hoped to show them the best of it, with plenty of time for days or part-days at anchor in quiet coves for swimming and sunning; how much of that, and how much sight-seeing, was something they could decide for themselves. Lawrie broke in, 'That's a point. You're taking us to Marmaris, I know, and that's fine with us, but a feller I was gassing with in England said most yachts put in to Bodrum, for starters. Marmaris better for you, is it?'

'Yes. They're both legitimate "ports of entry", but for one thing I think the best cruising area's south from Marmaris, and for another Bodrum can be a pain in the neck, from the point of view of officialdom, red tape. There's one guy there who just loves paperwork, and it can take for ever.'

'Right.' He nodded. 'You know the ropes.'

'Speaking of paperwork, I have to make out a passenger list, for clearance here and then for when we get to Turkey, so I need to see your passports. If you don't mind?'

I saw the quick glance she gave him. He said evenly, 'Right, I'll get 'em, in a minute. I'll warn you, though, we only got married a week ago, wasn't time to hang around, so Emma's travelling in the name of Masterson, you'll notice.'

'Right. And congratulations.'

Gill enthused to Emma, 'How lovely! You're on honeymoon!'

She said to me later, when we were clear of Malta and heading due east – engine at rest, main and genoa set and straining to a north-westerly blow of about force 4, pushing us along at a fraction over seven knots – 'Just as well you didn't give them single berths, Matt.'

'So what about us?'

She glanced at the hatch, checking we were still alone; then patted me in an extremely intimate manner and murmured into my ear, 'We can do it *anywhere*.'

156

That morning, Charles Harrison reported to his boss, Chief Inspector Frewin, that Matt Johnson had called the night before, and had not been able to help with the initials GC.

'Only thing I did wonder, sir, was that brolly might've been left in some restaurant by owner "GC", and left in the Fountain house by someone who'd purloined it or taken it instead of his own, whatever.'

'Not so many with gold bands on 'em, these days. That'd come more like theft than a swap by mistake.'

'Might go with champers at £121 quid a bottle, though?'

'And it was still wet, wasn't it?'

'Well – damp.'

'But Fountain entered the house through the garage, straight out of his motor.' Frewin opened a file. 'Now, I had your memo about the champagne – Krug Collection 1961 – and Fortnums sell a fair amount of it, you said. Bloody amazing, isn't it . . . But – yeah, here we are – would have been a cash sale, just two bottles, sales by the case they'd have a record of charge and/or delivery . . . Doesn't take us far, does it?' He changed the subject as he glanced up from the paperwork. 'Would a man who was going to murder his wife make a point of telling her father he might be tempted to do so?'

'Short answer, sir – no. But—'

'There's some more here doesn't exactly add up.' Frewin began turning pages in the file. 'Like – as you said, his prints were on the banister, and on the telephone – and on the wheel of his motor – and on the champagne bottle that was in the hall. But no prints at all on the other bottle, the one upstairs, nor on either of the two glasses or the handles of the knives or the spoon . . . There's only one answer to all that, someone wiped all those articles, *must* have. Right?'

Harrison nodded. 'No question.'

'Wiped every fucking thing, but your prime suspect didn't wipe the items *he* touched?'

Frewin gazed at the younger man. Blinking slowly, hands spread flat on the open file. Waiting for comment: or maybe thoughts still running on . . . Then: 'I'll tell you something for free. If we had Fountain here and we charged him, and he went up for trial, any defence lawyer worth his salt'd have the case

157

thrown out on that count alone . . . I'd go so far as to say you couldn't *bring* a case.'

'Mightn't he have just lost his head, sir? Killed her – cleaned up – then the father calls, and that's when he decides to bolt for it – right? Panic stations, and he forgets the rest?'

Frewin lost in thought: with the blank, inward gaze of one who's switched off, is dreaming dreams . . .

'No.' Patting the file. 'No, Charles . . . This "GC". Let's not take it as a maybe, stolen brollies, all that cock. Dig a bit deeper, get us a run-down on every business contact – clubs too, maybe – but specially business. You've been looking too hard at Fountain: because he scarpered, I know . . . Leave him to Interpol now, plenty of time for second thoughts, let's have this "GC" where we can get a good look at him – right?'

'But *whose* business contacts?'

'Christ, you're not with me, are you . . .'

'Benedict's – but he was – *emphatic*—'

'And you take that as gospel . . . Daughter killed, Daddy'll want her killer caught. Right? No question he'd mislead you, any *other* motivation?'

Fountain was in Zurich.

Big guy, bearded, just off a train – he's casually dressed, and a head taller than most of the crowd pouring in and out of the Hauptbahnhof.

He crosses Bahnhofplatz, stops to look around as he realizes he's misread the street sign – Bahnhofplatz, not Bahnhofstrasse. Searching around, he finds the road leading off at right-angles: but it's surprisingly narrow, a slit of a road, not at all the kind of thoroughfare on which he'd expected to find his bank's headquarters.

Long-strided, loping walk . . . He's checked his bag in at the station, hoping he won't have to spend a night in this town.

Four blocks east, puzzlement fades. A triangular junction, small *platz*: from here on Bahnhofstrasse has become the broad, busy street he'd expected. Big, solid-looking, Germanic-Swiss buildings, constructions fit for gnomes to lurk in.

He finds the bank a couple of hundred metres farther east, on this north side of the street. A uniformed doorman approaches him, eyebrows raised in polite enquiry: Tommy murmurs, 'Herr Klennermann, bitte.'

Trying to look calm, self-assured, but aware that this is where the best-laid plans may be shot full of holes. It's unavoidable, he's tried to think of alternative ways of getting at his money but nothing seemed better than taking it head-on. British police *might* have put out a call to Interpol, who *might* have circulated all banking establishments – if that's possible, and maybe in the computer age it is – and this one *could* have asked its computerized records of numbered-account holders to look for the name Fountain, T.

If so, there'd be a noticeable delay now: and then, if one was silly enough to be still hanging around, some kind of confrontation with Swiss lawmen.

He crosses some fingers. Clock-watching, and encouraging himself with the thought that nobody can know he has funds here. He picked the bank from a whole list of them in the office files, and transferred the money from a Channel Islands unit trust company, early in the New Year, as a hedge against the forthcoming general election being won by Labour with subsequent imposition of exchange controls.

A girl approaches. A somewhat steely blonde: eyes sharply appraising through ornamental spectacles ... If it's 'Herr Klennermann will be a little while: if you would be so good as to wait?', he decides, that will be the signal to take off, face up to some very long-distance hitching.

'Mr Fountain? Herr Klennermann is free now. He will be pleased to see you ...'

Forty minutes later he emerges: well-equipped now financially, and also having arranged for a cheque for £500 to be sent to James in repayment of the loan and the other expenses he and Eileen incurred. He turns right, back towards the station, because on his way to the bank he's passed a travel agency and he's now in a position to make use of it. Inside the expanse of plate glass a dark girl with soft, inviting eyes asks him in German what can she do for him; he tells her in French that he'd like her to book him on the first available flight to Istanbul. An open return in the name of Fontaine, initial T.

'Un petit moment, Monsieur ...'

She plays with her computer for a few minutes, then tells

159

him in her slightly Italianate French, 'This afternoon, four-twenty?'

He pays with Swiss banknotes, inquires where the airport bus starts from and at what time he should be on it. Checks the paperwork – he's bought a return because he knows that Turkish immigration officials, like most others, frown on foreigners who arrive on one-way tickets – and thanks the girl for her assistance. He'll be showing his passport at the airport, and again of course at Istanbul, but from Hamburg to this point at least the only tracks he's left are French.

10

The wind was up to about 20 knots within a couple of hours of our departure from Valletta, and from the general indications I was beginning to wonder whether the forecast we'd had just before sailing had been all that accurate. And sure enough, the corrected version that came over Malta radio on 2625 kHz at 2103 GMT promised us a wind veering to north and increasing to seven or eight – meaning 30 to 40 knots.

I had a presentiment that by morning our guests might be having second thoughts about taking up sailing as their recreational pursuit. Emma Lawrie, in fact, had already retired, and Gill was keeping an eye on her, offering advice and dry biscuits and so on. I'd offered Stugeron, which I personally find is about the best of the anti-seasick pills, but the Lawries had some other favourite brand and apparently they'd been taking it since before we'd left Malta.

Ted seemed to have taken root in the forward cockpit – I'd rigged the hood that shelters it and the hatch, the companion-way – and before the light faded he'd turned paler than he'd been to start with, hadn't wanted any supper and wasn't encouraging conversation.

They both had my deep sympathy. It's a horrible way to feel and I know all about it; it just so happened that the *Bird*'s gyrations this evening weren't affecting me. It does help to be busy, have something else to think about and to be in the open air – as well as dodges like wearing your belt a notch or two tighter than usual.

Gill had taken some Stugeron, but she was grim-faced when she didn't know she was being looked at. For all I know she might have been sick a few times: what I *do* know is that she wasn't giving way to it. She was helping me when help was called for, nursing Emma, keeping an eye on Ted, and – now – asking me what I'd like for supper.

As it happens, I don't have to be in love with a girl not to make her cook when she's feeling seasick. But anyway I'd just taken in that weather forecast – I'd left her on deck while I went below to catch it – and there were more immediate things than food to think about. I told her that when we had time for making supper I'd do it myself, but meanwhile she could help me shorten sail.

I'd brought three safety harnesses up with me; I gave one to her and another to Ted, suggesting that if he was staying up here he ought to put it on – please . . .

'Routine precaution, Ted, nothing unusual. Goes on this way – can you see? Then clip it to any solid fitting near you.' He was fumbling a bit, not entirely on the ball, so I helped him with it, mentioning at the same time that it was going to get worse before it got better, that therefore I was about to reduce the amount of sail the *Bird* was carrying – so we'd get a reasonably comfortable night – and that this would involve temporarily altering course, turning her a bit closer to the wind while we did it.

'The motion'll be – more noticeable. And it'll be noisy for a while, gear banging around a bit. Might be an idea to warn your wife – tell her it won't last long, and it's nothing to be scared of.'

Ted decided – as I'd hoped he might – to turn in himself, keep her company.

Furling the genoa – or as now, reefing by partly furling it – is dead simple. It's roller-reefed on the forestay, and all you have to do is winch in a line which operates the roller gear and wraps the sail around the stay, and cleat it. Then to re-set the sail the line has only to be released. As long as the sheets are clear so they don't snag on anything during the reefing process

162

it can be done without anyone leaving the cockpit. Gill started the diesel while I was seeing to this; we'd be using the engine presently, on autopilot, to hold her steady while we reefed the mainsail. With Gill helping, we'd do it a lot faster than I usually do single-handed.

I brought her round. Far enough to take some of the pressure off the sail, just so it was luffing a bit, but still with wind in it. And with the change of course the *Bird* was like a mad thing, crashing and jolting across the sea, rolling hard enough on the way round to make me hope Emma had her bunk-cloth rigged. Well, she would have, Gill would have seen to it. Except Ted might have released it, to get in there with her ... I thought of them both down there under our feet, probably clinging together and petrified as well as ill; I guessed they'd be asking themselves what on earth had possessed them to part with good money in order to be subjected to such a frightful ordeal.

Meanwhile it was a great luxury for me, to have an extra pair of hands – competent ones, at that – when one was used to doing it all solo. I'd decided to take three slabs out of the sail: two might have been enough, but better to make a real job of it; we'd still have enough sail on her to make good progress, in this blow. So the task was – well, first the vang has to be disconnected, and the halyard eased away – Gill took this job – until I could hook the ring at the reef-point to the boom, clicking it in. Gill's value was proved at this stage particularly: single-handed, one's had the experience of clicking-in the reef-point and then while you're moving back to the halyard the ring unhooks itself. Here and now, Gill took up the slack immediately: and I was busy then winching the reefing-line, to haul the clew down good and tight to the boom. The *new* clew: the sail having been shortened by three slabs, it has a new foot now.

Then the halyard needed to be winched tighter, and cleated again, and it was done. More or less – except for re-connecting the vang, and securing the loose bight of sail.

It *was* done, then. We were back in the cockpit, and Gill was at the wheel – autopilot disconnected, diesel stopped – bringing the *Bird* back to her course. Gill's hair streaming in the wind and wet, her face glistening, tensely alert and joyous-looking in the faint radiance from the cockpit dials and the glow of phosphorescence from surrounding foam, and the *Bird* responding to her helm, bucking and dancing as she came round but quickly settling down again: she was back on her easterly course maybe four or five minutes after we'd started the manoeuvre. Down below, Ted and Emma would have been telling each other *Thank God* that's *over*: and I had time to look some more at Gill, enjoy the sight of Gill in storm conditions, soaking wet and wind-blown, quite astonishingly beautiful.

During the dark hours the wind veered, as had been promised in the forecast, and blew hard from the north, the *Bird* making seven knots – heeling hard to starboard, dipping her bow in periodically and flinging back streamers of salt spray. I left her on autopilot and kept watch mostly down below, only occasionally going up into the forward cockpit, to take a look round from the spray-hood's shelter. The hood has see-through panels in it, for purposes of keeping a lookout, which when the boat's sailing herself is all one has to do – and at that, only every ten or fifteen minutes.

Gill took over for a three-hour stint just after midnight, and I turned in wondering what I'd ever done without her.

Or *would* do without her, when she left me.

At 0300 I was up again – everything was fine, she'd had no problems – and I was on deck to witness a bright and stormy dawn. Even reefed as we were we were still making better than six knots: the electronic log and our position by Loran told me this, but from the *Bird*'s way of throwing herself through the brightening sea, and the sound and feel of it, you'd have thought we were doing a lot more.

Gill came up, and we kissed good morning for about twenty minutes, then she went down and made breakfast. The Lawries didn't stir, but during the forenoon she persuaded them to take in some beef tea and dry toast, and around noon Ted appeared on deck in red-striped pyjamas.

'My God, it's beautiful . . .'

'If you can appreciate that, Ted, you're on the mend.'

'Reckon I am. So's Emma. Sleeping it off now.'

It *was* a marvellous sight. Brilliant sun, and dark-blue sea

with the white flying in pennants from the crests, the *Bird*
listing less now because the wind had backed by about a point,
and she was dancing through it, revelling in it. Exhilarating, as
well as beautiful; Ted was drinking it in like medicine.

He looked round at me. 'Had a dreadful time last night, did
poor Emma.'

'I'm sorry. Bumpy when we were reefing, I dare say.'

'If that's what you'd call it. I went arse over tit twice. I'm so
bruised I look like a bloody Dalmatian.'

Gill made ham-and-egg sandwiches for lunch. Emma stayed
below, but the wind was dropping and still backing, and by
four in the afternoon she was with us on deck, pale and a bit
unsteady but ready to absorb tea and biscuits. I'd shaken out
the reef hours before that, and re-set the genoa, and we were
fairly belting along. Emma said, 'Thought I was going to die.
Several times . . . Didn't seem such a bad prospect either,' and
Ted told her, 'You try dying on me, my girl, I'll bloody shoot
you!'

I thought that in retrospect there might be something to be
said for having had to endure some discomfort, first night out.
Gill and I hadn't seen much of the Lawries, but that didn't
matter, what counted was the fact that they'd been through the
ordeal and weathered it – and had confidence in us, one might
hope. But the benefit was that we'd been through it and now
we were all relaxed, at home with each other.

By sunset the wind was astern and had dropped somewhat,
the *Bird*'s motion was rhythmic, regular – barely noticeable,
after the earlier banging around – she was making seven and a
half knots and the forecast was for present conditions to last
for a day or two. Loran told me we were nearly 200 miles east
of Malta, so I'd given up thinking about any need to stop in
Crete.

Our charterers had brandies and ginger ale, at Gill's suggestion, by way of pick-me-ups, and Gill then weakened and had
one herself. I made a point of telling them that she'd been sick
too, and she broke in quickly with 'How d'you know that?'

I said something like, 'Never mind, I think you're bloody
marvellous. Best crew I ever had.'

'You never had one.'

'Well – right . . .'

'Some compliment, huh?'

The Lawries were amused. And agreed wholeheartedly that there should be a medal struck for anyone who could be seasick and still look after others who were in that extremity. While I was remembering how she'd looked in that gale. I know I kept looking at her, wanting her: probably looked too often and too obviously, because at one point I met Emma's thoughtful, knowing gaze, saw her reading the situation as if it was right in front of her in large print.

Embarrassing. Meeting Gill's eyes a few times, and guessing – from the fact she seemed to be on edge, rather, and each time glanced away quickly but still looked back a minute later – that our thoughts, inclinations, weren't so far apart.

We went below, when they'd finished their drinks, to dine on a chicken pie which Lorna McAllister had made, and followed it with fruit and coffee. Emma said, over the coffee, 'I'll tell you one thing, this is a great improvement on *last* night.'

Ted suggested, 'Have a natter about where we'll go after Marmaris, shall we, Matt?'

'Yeah, why not . . .? But I'll just take a look up top first.'

I'd been up three times during the meal, to check that all was well. It still was. The lights of two other ships were visible but they weren't coming anywhere near us, and the close-haul indicator showed that the *Bird*'s sails were set about right. I was on the point of going down to rejoin the party, when a new thought hit me.

Thought isn't quite the word for it. Wasn't exactly new, either, it had been building up for some time.

I called into the hatch, 'Gill, lend a hand?'

She came up quickly, as a good crew should. I led her forward, where the dark and the mainsail's intervention between us and the hatch afforded privacy, and took her in my arms not all that gently.

'Matt, you're *crazy* . . .'

An infectious brand of lunacy. I'd never known anything like this. The force of the need, for one thing, the mind-blowing release of passion – as if all day we'd been caged, with bars between us – and the surroundings for another: black

166

night, swell of black sea streaked and leaping, flying white, racket of sea and wind and the *Bird*'s own racing, thrusting violence . . .

Then we were back: still, clinging to each other while all the surrounding noise and movement continued – as if we'd been part of it for a while and now – washed up, high and – no, not so damn dry – wet deck juddering under us and the *Bird* rushing on, wind suddenly cold, spray-laden: Gill in my arms, and enfolding, tasting of salt. I said, 'Better go – go down, and—'

'We're crazy, Matt!' Her breath short in my ear, words in the puffs of breath. 'They'll *know* – soon as they *see* me – Emma will for damn sure! And besides – oh, *damn* you—'

'Down here.' The sliding hatch over the fore cabin: we'd been *on* it, although I hadn't thought about it until this moment . . . 'In quick, I'll shut it over your head. You got wet – foresheet had snagged, you were up here to clear it, got soaked, had to change into dry clothes – OK?'

'I – suppose . . .'

'Here you go.' She slipped in as I slid it open: only about a pint of sea slopped in with her.

I made essential adjustments – belt, as well as zip – and went aft, back down into the saloon. Thinking *without safety harness, too* . . . What a way to go over the side: the *Bird* sailing on through the night untended, and these two sitting, waiting . . . Intriguing to guess how they might have coped . . . They watched me as I came from the ladder into the saloon: and looking past me, for Gill. I told them, 'Problem solved.' And that was no lie. I added, nodding towards the fore cabin, 'Gill's getting dry. Bit damp, up on the bow.'

'Oh, poor Gill!'

'She's a sailor, she's OK . . .'

I found the chart I wanted, the Turkish coast eastward and south from Marmaris, and brought it to the table, spread it out. 'Here now. Here's Marmaris . . . I think – if you agree – one day there would be enough. We'll need to take on fuel and water, of course, and some provisions – and you'll want to see the shops I dare say, but—'

'Get to a bank, change some money,' Ted said. 'That's about all.'

There was a Turk I had to see, too. On charter business, but also I thought he might help in the search for Anne.

'They have marvellous carpets, don't they?' Emma was talking winningly to her husband. 'I'd love to take home a really good Turkish carpet.'

I said, 'You'll see thousands, every place we go. Including Fethiye. They hang 'em over walls and on street corners, let alone in shops. Best place might be Fethiye – from Gill's point of view, since that's where she wants to be, mostly, and you see you'd need time, you don't want to buy the first carpet they show you. Actually, you need either to know a lot about it, or have expert advice.'

Carpets are mass-produced now. Only a few villages produce them in the traditional, painstaking way, and using their own locally-produced vegetable dyes, not chemicals. Crushed grasses, for instance, for the greens . . . I've been told that if you want a really good, expensive carpet, the best place to shop for it is in London; in the tourist areas of Turkey what you get is a vast choice of very attractive but by no means special products, admittedly at quite reasonable prices.

Gill came through from forward. Looking determinedly self-assured, and wearing jeans and a sweater. Emma asked her, smiling, 'All warm and dry now?'

'You bet. But that water's *cold*.'

They were looking at each other like two cats. Emma's blue eyes, Gill's honey-coloured ones. Ted and I might not have been there. Emma still wearing that smile of hers: Gill had been dead right, I thought, she *did* know.

I wondered whether she also knew that I was feeling like the luckiest, happiest man alive. Looking at Gill, accepting the towel she'd brought through for me: and re-living . . .

Emma asked me, 'So what happens after this one day we spend in Marmaris?'

I pointed it out on the chart. 'Place here called Ekincik. About twenty miles east of Marmaris, by the time one's got round the corners. We could anchor in the bay – pretty surroundings, safe anchorage, good swimming and a restaurant that's not too bad.'

And there, as in Marmaris, I planned to enlist the help of a friendly Turk, in the search for Anne. I told them this, also that

168

the same guy, a great character by name of Abidin Kurt, ran a fleet of boats that took tourists up the Dalyan river – close by, just round the headland – which is a fascinating trip. Turtles in the river, ancient tombs cut into the cliffs, and a Roman amphitheatre above the ruins of an ancient port and settlement.

'It's an outing you'd probably enjoy.'

Ted shrugged. 'Maybe.' Nodding to Emma. 'If *you* want to. A little Roman rubble goes a long way, with me.'

Emma shook her head. 'Isn't he awful?'

'Man after my own heart.' I touched the chart again. Aware of Gill's restlessness – because it was Fethiye she wanted to get to, not some Roman amphitheatre ... 'Place here called Göcek.' It was where Tommy Fountain had told me his friends from Istanbul had built an hotel. There was no question of not stopping there, I *had* to see them.

'You're thinking of Fethiye, Gill, I know, but the point is, yachts cruise all up and down this coast, visit all these places, and if we can leave Anne's picture with a few key people who have business with the boats, yachts and *gulets*, we'll have the whole coast covered. They're all in touch with each other, you see – sort of a bush telegraph.'

'What about the coastguard?'

'Sure. I'll see them in Marmaris and in Fethiye, and anywhere else we see one of their boats.'

She nodded. 'OK.'

'What's a goolit, when it's at home?'

'*Gulet*, Ted. You'll see droves of them. Large, timber craft, some with one mast and some two, mostly 18 or 20 metres long. It's a traditional Turkish design, and plenty of them are available for charter, usually with a three-man crew.'

'So after this place – Fethiye *then*?'

'Yeah. And we can hang around there without actually staying in the port, if we don't want to. There are quite a number of good anchorages, coves and so on, where we could spend nights and have good swimming. Then from there on – well, I usually bash on south, stopping here and there and visiting these other ports – Kalkan, Kaş – on down to Kekova. If we're pushed for time we could miss out Kalkan and Kaş,

169

but at Kekova the Roman rubble's terrific, Ted. Really, it's fascinating.'

'Get to Fethiye and then decide, shall we?'

'I'll tell you what *I've* decided.' Emma tapped her husband's arm. 'You and I are going to bed.' And – Gill told me this later – when I'd gone up on deck and Ted had come up too for a nightcap of fresh air, Emma had murmured, 'Don't see why you two should have *all* the fun.'

We made Marmaris in four days and four hours, which means we'd averaged 7.5 knots over the whole 750 nautical miles. We'd had good winds right up to the last day, and *The Bird* had taken full advantage of them; then the wind died when we were between Rhodes and Cape Alupo, so we had to motor the last 30 miles, but I had her secured stern-to on the Marmaris yacht quay at 5.30 p.m. (Malta time), 6.30 p.m. (Turkey time) on that fourth day out.

We'd had no more rough weather, and our passengers were fit and loving it. Gill was fine too, although as the trip neared its end she was becoming a little tense – almost getting into her running shoes, when we entered Marmaris Bay through its narrow entrance, ready to sprint to the post office and put a call through to her father.

She and Emma had become very close, in these few days, having long, low-voiced conversations all by themselves, either sunning themselves up on the *Bird*'s bow or with their heads together in the saloon when Ted was on deck with me. Gill had obviously taken a great liking to Emma, and I thought Emma's attitude to her verged on the maternal, although there would only be about ten years between them.

One might have thought more than that, seeing them together. I'd have guessed at a fifteen-year gap, at least. Because Gill, even when she was all uptight with worrying, looked so damn young. Maybe Emma thought of her as being younger than she actually was.

With me, Gill talked quite a lot about Anne – naturally enough, when she was so worried for her – and I guessed this would be the subject of her conversations with Emma. It would account for Emma's mothering her, too. Maybe Gill's failed marriage and her father and the long-absent mother would come into it too, with the same effect on Emma: and for

170

Gill, in her basic loneliness, the shoulder willing to be cried on would fill a need.

But about Anne – on that second night out of Valletta, for instance, huddled close to me in the cockpit in the very small hours of the morning, Gill said suddenly – straight out of her own thinking, there'd been no reference to this in whatever we'd been chatting about – 'White slaving isn't the name they give it now. Now, they call them *sex*-slaves. There was a piece about it in some magazine I read – this guy was saying it's rife, especially in the Middle East and the Gulf. Women in cages. He'd seen them ... But Jesus, I never dreamt *I'd* have any reason to – I mean, my *God*, the very idea of that *kid*—'

'Gill, stop it. You're torturing yourself quite unnecessarily, there's no reason – God's sake, just because you read some lurid magazine article—'

'You through lecturing?'

'No, I'm not ... I happen to care about you – so please, for your own damn-fool sake—'

'Has it occurred to you she might be *dead*?'

'Of course it has. But again, there's no reason—'

'I keep wondering if my father's heard yet. From *her*, even. That's still a possibility, I guess.'

'You're right. It *is*. But Gill, why not forget it, until we get to Marmaris?'

'Because I *can't* fucking well forget it, that's why! How about your buddy who's supposed to have murdered his wife, you forgotten *him*?'

'No. But here and now there's damn-all I can do about it. Any more than you can about Anne. First chance I'll have – very longshot chance, at that – will be when we get to Göcek.'

'Göcek?'

'Last call before Fethiye.'

'And it has something to do with that guy?'

'He has – connections there. May have been in touch with them. It's a possibility because he knows I was coming to this coast, he'd have guessed I'd check with them.'

Her expression said, *So that's why we have to stop there ...*

It was an irrelevance to her, of course, at this stage. Some guy who'd knocked off his wife – or hadn't, if I was to be believed ... Her mind was full of Anne: and racked up tight, and the closer we came to Turkey the worse it was getting for her.

The Lawries, anyway, were determined to help as much as they could. Emma had said – a day or two after this – 'Priority number one is tracing Gill's sister. Doesn't matter if we don't see all the places you would have shown us, Matt – we'll still get lots of sun and swimming, and if we miss out on some of Ted's Roman rubble we can charter you again *next* year.'

'Care to make a firm booking now?'

'Not *quite* yet. And it'll be conditional that you have the same crew with you.' She raised her voice: 'Get that, Gill?'

Gill called from the galley where she was cooking something, 'Got it. You bet!' and I said – wondering if she meant it, and deciding that if she was true to form she wouldn't have said it if she hadn't – 'Gets better and better.'

Emma murmured quietly, 'She's adorable, Matt. And *so* pretty.'

'A lot more than pretty.'

'So what are you going to do about it?'

'It's – complicated. For one thing, she has a husband. Obviously she'll have to go back to the States after this trip – to set up a divorce, she says . . . And I live on a boat . . .'

'You don't have to. I mean, not for *ever*. Do you?'

'As I say' – I drew a breath – 'it's complicated.'

Ted growled, 'Leave the man alone.'

Gill, as it turned out, had heard every word. She said later, when we were on our own, 'Re what you and Emma were whispering about – me going back to the US, getting a divorce, all that—'

'Big-ears.'

'I have *sharp* ones, sure . . . Seriously, Matt – I don't know how *you're* thinking, but right now I can't see anything beyond finding Anne.'

'I know. I understand. And there's no rush. Not while I have you here with me, anyway. When there's distance between us, I wouldn't be surprised if I start frothing at the mouth.'

'How far ahead are *you* thinking, then?'

'How long's a piece of string?'

'What does that mean?'

'Means no limit. And no future that doesn't have you in it.'

172

On our last full day at sea, contemplating the call she'd make to her father next evening, she was once again speculating about Anne – Anne in the kidnap scenario, which was comparatively speaking light relief, after the visions of her in chains in some Arab brothel.

'Suppose it's aimed at his Defence contracts. I mean, forcing secrets out of him – you know, what we talked about?'

'Embargoed high-tech equipment.'

'Right. You see, he might not *tell* me. Could have had the kidnappers at him, and – look, two ways he mightn't let on about it. If he's not allowed to – the FBI, CIA or whoever, all *that* scene, Pentagon spooks breathing down his neck. But also – this is what I started out to say, Matt – it could be his own decision. It really could, he could've told them to go to hell, he's not paying, or whatever it is they want – I mean, irrespective of what might happen to Anne … He's well capable of it – and the very last thing he'd do would be to tell *me*.'

'You do tend to look on the black side.'

'Being realistic. I *know* my father.'

That night I was assembling the various items of paperwork I'd need for Turkish harbour authorities. As this was my first visit of the year to Turkish waters I'd have to get a new Transit Log, for instance, so I'd have to show the *Bird*'s Small Ships' Register papers, as well as crew and passenger lists (in triplicate), and the four passports, and so on. I'd typed a passenger list for clearance from Malta, but I did a new one now, having had a second thought about it, and applied my own rubber stamp to each copy. All port officials are reassured by rubber stamps: mine, which I designed myself and had made in England, has a handsome swan in profile and the name the *Bird of Dawning* in a scroll around it, and it's always much admired.

I warned Ted, 'As Emma's passport's in her previous name, I have to put her down as Mrs Masterson, I'm afraid.'

'Oh, aye?'

He hadn't even looked up from the paperback he was reading. Emma widened her eyes: 'We're living in sin, then. Naughty old us.'

'Better than getting stuck here for a couple of weeks while

173

they ask for guidance from Ankara, anyway.' I looked at Gill. 'And I'm putting you down as a passenger, not crew. Regulations are that a boat has to leave with the same crew it brings in: so if you didn't want to leave with us – I hope you *will*, but—'

'That's good thinking, Matt.'

The idea wasn't at all attractive. I said, signing the lists, 'Keep the options open, that's all.'

Ted changed the subject . . . 'In by five or six in the evening, did you say?'

'Could be later, if the forecast's right and we lose our wind. Touch wood, we'll be berthed in good time for you and Emma to take a look round and have your first Turkish meal.'

'You two'll join us, I hope.' He looked at Gill. 'You've cooked enough grub for us, our turn to feed *you* – OK?'

She glanced at me, passing me the ball. I'd planned on having her to myself, and I began, 'Kind of you, Ted, but—'

'You'll dine with us, no bloody option!'

'No bloody argument, then.'

Pleasing the customers is part of the job, and there'd be other nights.

Gill said to me, on deck that night when I'd remarked that I'd have thought *they*'d have wanted to get away on their own, after four days cooped up with us, 'And they aren't even married yet. How does *that* grab you?'

'They – what?'

'They're going to be. But she's in the middle of a divorce. Ted's a widower.'

'Be damned.'

'She's nuts about him, anyway.'

'I've wondered what you two gas about all the time. Does Ted know she's told you?'

'God, no. I haven't told *you*, either.'

Marmaris from seaward is a pleasant sight, right from the first glimpse of white walls and minarets, the rise of buildings to the small castle that tops the old town – walls and streets climbing a little hill that's surrounded by less antique streets and shops, restaurants and so on – from any distance like a bouquet of white against the background of wooded hillsides. You come

174

in from sea through a bottleneck entrance, into this landlocked bay which is roughly circular, diameter say two to three miles, and the town's on the north shore with yacht quays on both sides of a south-pointing, rectangular promontory. Boats are also moored offshore, and bigger ships lie at anchor out in deeper water.

I spotted a narrow parking space in the line of boats just to the west of the promontory, dropped anchor well out and where my warp wouldn't – or shouldn't – foul anyone else's, and swung the *Bird* around to slide her stern-first into the slot. An obliging Turk from the *gulet* lying next to us caught my stern line and secured it to a convenient ring, and there we were – except for minor adjustment, having Gill pay out a few feet of cable forward, then taking in all the slack aft.

I like to perform this evolution neatly, because the Turks, handling their rather clumsy, broad-beamed *gulets*, are so damn good at it. They slide those great fat ships into slots barely wide enough – you'd think – for dinghies.

Ted and Emma went ashore as soon as I'd got the plank out. He was anxious about getting some money changed into Turkish lira before the *bureaux de change* all shut their doors. I thought they'd be open for some time yet, although the banks would have shut; anyway I pointed him in the right direction, and Emma danced off down the plank behind him, obviously delighting in the prospect of spending the lira as soon as he got hold of some. Gill went with them. I'd told her where the post office was – a walk of five or six hundred metres – and that if she wasn't back on board before I was I'd come and find her. I had to drop in at the post office some time anyway, to check whether there was anything for me from Loder or Tommy Fountain. The Lawries were also to come back to the *Bird*, and we'd all rendezvous over a drink before we went to dine.

I locked the boat up, and went about my business. Locking up is no slur on the locals, but in any crowded tourist centre you have people of all kinds, including thieves, and it would be silly to make things easy for them. Anyway I got a Transit Log, and customs and health clearance, got the Transit Log stamped in the harbour master's office, and we were now legitimately in Turkey. The next thing was to walk about a quarter of a mile down the crowded quay to the yacht agency office where I hoped to catch Sefik Yeşilay at his desk. Which is where he very rarely is; that bulky, beer-bellied frame is hardly ever in one place for more than about five minutes.

And he was *not* there. But his assistant, a pretty Turkish girl whose name fortunately I remembered, greeted me warmly, told me Sefik had been looking forward to my arrival – I'd written to him from England as soon as I'd known I was coming here with this charter – and was due back tonight from Izmir.

'I'll see him tomorrow, then, Feriha. It's important, we've a lot to talk about.' I told her where the *Bird* was lying. 'I have to leave here tomorrow afternoon, unfortunately, so – first thing in the morning, as early as he can make it?'

'*Tamam.*' Bright smile, shiny black eyes. *Tamam* means OK. 'If he do not come, I speak Ayla, maybe, *she* tell him you bet!'

Ayla is Sefik's wife. I rather think she's the brain and he's the leg-man, but the combination works, anyway, they're nice people and they run an efficient agency with a lot of charter work involved. My aim, which we'd agreed in principle, was for the *Bird* to become – technically – a unit in his agency's fleet next summer; then I'd be legally entitled to base myself here. And – I hoped – I'd avoid a rather nasty tax they'd recently imposed on visiting charter yachts. This year the tax was having to be added to charter rates – which maybe was why I hadn't been exactly inundated with bookings earlier on.

And if the tax kept Greek-based boats *out* – well . . .

I went back to the *Bird*. Noticing as I reached her that a coastguard launch had berthed during the past half-hour, about fifty metres the other side. Those ships are easy to spot: painted grey, with a broad orange stripe diagonally on the bow and the Turkish for 'coastguard' – SAHIL GIJVENLIK – in large capital letters on both sides of the hull. As always there was a sentry, immaculate in white uniform, orange band on his white helmet, at the foot of the gangway with a submachine-gun in the crook of his left arm.

Tomorrow morning Gill and I might call on that boat's skipper, I thought. Maybe at the coastguard office ashore first.

She wasn't back. Nor were the Lawries. I'd said I'd go looking for her: she'd either be in a queue in the post office still,

I thought, or pecking round the shops with Emma. I rather wished I'd said I'd wait on board, as it would be only too easy to miss her in the crowded streets, but having promised – and she might have been having problems with the telephone – I set off, northward.

I'd passed the coastguard launch again, getting a stony glare from the sentry – they're adept at stony glares, I think they practise in front of mirrors – when I saw Gill. She was – the best way to describe it is *scurrying*. Half walking, half trotting. I called and waved, and she saw me, yelled '*Matt!*', skidding across the bows of evening strollers as she swerved in my direction.

She grabbed my arm. 'He's *heard*, Matt! Anne *has* been kidnapped! But the call was from Spain – *Madrid* . . .'

11

When she'd asked the girl on the company exchange to put her through to Mr Brennan, personal call, she'd been connected instead to some male functionary who'd asked her to identify herself and then told her she'd have to be transferred to another line: then, after a long wait, there were sounds of connections being made, and finally – 'Mrs Paget's on now, sit . . .'

'Gill?'

'What *is* this?'

'Security. You're on a line nobody could tap, now.'

'Well, hooray, but—'

'Good reason for it. That call you thought I might get, about Anne? It came this morning.'

She gasped. Then, as it really sank in – 'My God, what did they – *what* about her?'

She'd yelled it . . . Her father's voice growled, 'Take it easy, will you? Guy – Spaniard, I guess – said she's OK – usual routine, the way you read it – long as I cooperate, etcetera, give 'em what they want. The call was from Madrid.'

'My God, what'll you do?' She did a double-take, then: '*Madrid* – but—'

'It's being taken care of. I'm not about to give you any detail – fact is, I *can't*.'

179

'What do they want – money, or—'

'I can't talk about it, Gill, I just *told* you this. But everything's being done that can be done. Our friends – you know who I mean – are right on it. And listen – I'm glad you called, it's good timing – you're in Turkey, right?'

'Right. What I'm asking is – look, are you *going* to pay, or give—'

'Gill, listen to me. There was a time I didn't have to repeat everything over and over. *Get* this now: you don't have to concern yourself any more, it's being taken care of. Thanks to you, we had some warning – I'm grateful for that – but all I want you to do now is jump on the first plane home, get back here soon as you can. Will you do that?'

'You believe what this guy tells you? Do you have *reason* to believe him? That she's in Spain?'

'The call came from Madrid – not so far from where you lost her.'

'*Damn* it, I did *not*—'

'—other end of the Mediterranean from where you're at now – right?'

'Anne told me in that letter, and the hotel people in Menorca confirmed it, she'd—'

'They fed her a line of disinformation and it sent you two thousand miles in the wrong direction . . . What are you doing now, are you *with* anyone?'

'British couple, called Lawrie. On a yacht they chartered. Because *she's* on a yacht – I thought she was, so this was the best way – and I have photos to give the police and – oh, the coastguard—'

'Now, drop all that. Your sister is in Spain, not Turkey. Steps are being taken to secure her release, and meanwhile the last thing I want or Washington would tolerate is publicity like talking to police forces who don't have any business knowing anything about it. The material that's being demanded in return for her release does not *exist*, as far as anyone can be permitted to know – d'you understand me?'

'But the kidnappers must know, so—'

'The kidnappers, Gill – listen to this, now – the guy who called me spelt out very, very emphatically that if they were to see or suspect police anywhere near them they'd kill her

180

immediately, cut their losses and get out. He explained this sort of logically so I'd understand it's not just a threat, it's *fact*, I have no doubt at all it's what they'd do. So, *no* police will be called in: there are other agencies – right? You understand me?'

'Yeah. Oh, God, yeah, I—'

'Gill, drop whatever you're doing. Tell your Turkish friends, and the English, that it was a mistake, she's not in that area, you just received this positive information . . . Then, you have business of your own, don't you? In New York, a delinquent husband. You need lawyers on that, right? Don't worry about what it costs, I'll look after it – give me a call soon as you get back.'

'How d'you know *yours* isn't disinformation?'

'Oh, God have mercy!' He'd bellowed it: now he paused, spoke in a normal tone again . . . 'I spoke to this guy, Gill. I *do* know. Also I take advice from the FBI, and that's a lot better than chasing fucking shadows like *you're* doing. The reason I say get on the first flight home is *you* could now be in danger, I have one daughter a hostage and I don't need *two* – get it? You're running around showing her photo, talking to goddam Turks—'

'I thought you were sure it was all happening in Spain?'

'I *am* sure. But they snatched her out of Menorca, didn't they? So they could snatch *you* out of Turkey – or Timbuctoo . . . Second string to their bow. Gill, I have a guy here in this room with me who's a professional, an expert in this area, he heard what I said then and he's nodding, he knows it's a goddam *fact* that if they were in a position to do it they damn sure would – and you're out in the back of fucking beyond, advertising who you are and where you are! I want you home – *now*, d'you hear?'

I took Gill back to the *Bird*, switched on the electric fans to get some air circulating, and gave her a stiff, well-iced drink – which she needed – and thought about putting the awning up, but decided to leave that until the morning. The awning's not only for shade; it has sides that enclose the cockpit area to give some privacy when you're alongside a crowded quay like this one, but it was getting late now and we were planning to eat ashore in any case.

On the subject of her father's certainty that Anne was being held in Spain, she was in two minds. He'd almost convinced her: she said twice, 'If the FBI believe it too . . .' But she was also still strongly influenced by Anne's letter, and by what the Menorcan hoteliers had told her – told Lorna McAllister – about Anne's interest in the geography of this coast. Lorna had had to work hard to get the detail out of them, Gill said, *that* couldn't have been disinformation.

I pointed out that what Anne had believed at that time might have been what Raoul had wanted her to believe: this was where the disinformation would have come in, surely – when it had been fed to Anne.

She took a long drink of Caballo's Neck, and said 'OK. It *could* be like that, I know, but it's not proven and it doesn't *dis*prove what I've felt sure of up to now.'

Nothing was proved or disproved. There was no *proof* Anne wasn't in Algeria, either. Or Libya, or Marseilles.

'What do you think, Matt?'

'I think this is where we are and have to be for some while, and your sister *may* be here. Or she may be in Spain – although the call coming from Spain proves bugger-all – but if she's there, your father or the FBI will be taking care of it, so – well, I say we should carry on as intended.'

She nodded. Her eyes on me over the glass as she sipped at it. Then: 'It's some kind of technology they're demanding. He said so – he used the word "material".'

It wouldn't make anything any easier. It would impose severe restriction on Brennan's and/or the FBI's room for manoeuvre or delay. When the demand's for a finite object there's no latitude, no bargaining: you deliver, or you face the consequences. Consequences like Anne Brennan never being seen again.

Gill didn't mention to me, incidentally, what she revealed later, that the FBI thought she herself might now be in danger. I did have a slight sensitivity in that direction myself, but I was attributing it to my personal interest in her, concern for her. I wasn't thinking of it as any real threat. She *should* have told me: the fact is, she didn't.

'One thing, Matt. It's terribly important. In that call, he

182

explained very clearly – Anne's life would be very much at risk if they thought any police were on to them. They gave him good reason to believe it. OK, maybe she's not here: then we're losing nothing by *not* going to them – right? If she *is* here – well, that's *it*, Matt, no way do we bring in the Turk police.'

'Surely the coastguard – who are not police—'

'No uniforms at all. *None*. Matt, promise me, now?'

The Lawries joined us about then, and eventually we all went ashore again to dine. Emma had picked out one of the sea-front restaurants she liked the look of – one of many, all side by side, open to view under awnings and with their offerings mostly on display in glass counters so that you see the actual food, not just a menu, before you sit down to order. It was a reasonably good meal, with rather a lot of wine – which Ted asked me to choose, as I'm familiar with the local plonks, and we had *Villa Doluca* which is about the safest red to go for. (Its white counterpart is also good; I'd be embarking a case of each in the morning, as well as a few other things, Scotch for instance. There's a rather better dry white wine called *Kutman*, but the red by that name is sweetish, not a patch on the *Doluca*.)

Ted raised his glass: 'Here's to Anne and taking her home with us', and Gill looked for a moment as if she was going to cry: I put my hand on hers and squeezed it, squeezing a small smile out of her. She'd told the Lawries about that telephone call, her father's news, and explained to them about not going near the police, that we should keep our enquiries private.

'So when we're asking your Turkish friends to help look for her, Matt, we don't have to say anything about kidnap, only that we think this shit Raoul may be holding her against her will.'

That got it about right, I thought. It stressed the private nature of our concern, justified not asking for official help.

Gill said later on, 'Look, I wouldn't ask you to hang around in Fethiye any longer than you want. It's such a long shot now, isn't it?' I gave her hand another squeeze and murmured, 'Keep changing our minds, don't we', and Ted said, predictably, 'Woman's privilege', then Emma chipped in with *her* change of mind: 'Oh, one thing *we* decided, Matt – we don't particularly want to go up that river – the boat trip you were telling us about.'

183

'Ah. Well, now . . .'

This would save most of a day. I did some figuring on distances, speeds and times, then suggested, 'Suppose we buzz down to Ekincik tomorrow, late afternoon – nice swimming there, and the restaurant I mentioned – then next morning it's a short trip to Göcek. I only want a couple of hours, and we could push on into Fethiye that evening. With stops for swimming here and there?'

I thought, while we ate, drank and chatted, about the call at Göcek – day after tomorrow, maybe word from Tommy, or word of him. I'd decided not to call Harrison before then; might do it from Fethiye . . .

Might. But all this telephoning was a bit much for my carefully controlled budget. Gill had some American telephone credit card that she used; it meant her calls were billed at US rates – a lot more reasonable than most – and charged to her account in the States. But I had to fork out hard cash each time.

I'd have to call Harrison again before long, but I'd see what came out of Göcek first.

The fore cabin wasn't too bad, with the hatch open and the fan running, in fact it turned cool during the night and we didn't need the fan from then on. Despite this, Gill didn't sleep well: I woke twice to find her awake, and at about 3 a.m. I reminded her that it was surely better that Anne had been kidnapped than lured away by some sex-maniac. Kidnappers, after all, tend to look after their captives, maintain their value as properties. At some other time Gill asked me, 'Why would they have waited so long before they contacted him?' I suggested, maybe in the hope of softening him up. Give him time to get really worried, and receptive? She'd snorted, muttered that nothing short of a bulldozer stood any chance of softening *him* up . . . 'I don't think he'll lift a finger, Matt!' I tightened my arms around her – we were only using one of the two quite small, single bunks, both by choice and because the other was still stacked with sundry gear – and whispered, 'Leave it to the morning, *sleep* now . . .'

I slept. I don't think she did much. So when I was ready to turn out, not long after dawn, by which time she finally was asleep, I disentangled myself from her very gingerly, crept up out of the hatch and started work – moving around bare-footed so as not to wake the lovebirds aft, either. Trusting mostly to their being heavy sleepers: there was a lot to do and it couldn't all be done soundlessly. There was the awning to be rigged, and the inflatable to be brought out and inflated by footpump and then eased down into the quiet water, the Yamaha fitted to its transom and the full tank connected to it. There was some work to be done on the winches, too – lubrication, and – well, plenty, as there always is after a few days at sea.

I was thinking, while I worked, about Gill's father and the ransom demand. Thoughts I couldn't easily have expressed to Gill. Because although I was deeply in sympathy with her and her feelings, the plain truth was I couldn't have damned him, as she was doing, if he didn't play ball with the kidnappers.

Even if the demand had been only for money – of which he had plenty. Because surrender to kidnap demands leads to more kidnappings, just as surrender to terrorist threats encourages terrorism.

I wanted Anne free, and this terrible anxiety off Gill's mind. But in their father's shoes I wouldn't have given way. There'd be various ploys to try, in collaboration with police or other security agencies, but surrender wouldn't be part of them. And in the circumstances – demand for technology, not cash – even if Brennan had been so inclined, the FBI would surely have blocked any such move.

At eight o'clock I went below, switched on BBC World Service and started making breakfast. Sounds of movement told me the hint was being taken: Gill first, limp and sleep-warm in my arms while bacon sizzled: then we went to get dressed and the aroma brought Ted out, and finally Emma looking pretty in a kimono. Then, when we were all tucking in, there was a hail from the quayside and I went up and found Sefik Yeşilay, fat and beaming as he came waddling over the gangplank.

Introductions, everyone shifting around to make room for him. Like making room for a medium-sized elephant, while Gill put more eggs and bacon in the pan. Sefik purred, 'The English breakfast, this I very much adore.' The women loved

185

him, Ted looked as if he thought he must be some kind of practical joke, and I explained, 'Sefik's a yacht agent and he operates a fleet of charter boats. He and I have a business arrangement to make for next season – right, Sefik?' He nodded with his mouth full: I said, 'And I'm going to ask him to help trace Gill's sister.'

He swallowed, then asked me, 'Please, what is Gillsister?'

I explained, and he listened attentively, finally frowning and tut-tutting. I showed him the mocked-up photo, he studied it, told Gill her sister was not as beautiful as she was herself, and asked, 'You have more, please?' Gill looked startled, thinking she was going to have to start cooking again, but he'd meant more copies of the photograph. He promised to call various yachts and *gulets* on VHF, alert them and ask them to pass the message on: French yacht, American girl . . . He wanted six of the prints, and I counted them out absent-mindedly, thinking that this was now a fairly hopeless cause; now they'd been on to Digby Brennan she surely wouldn't be anywhere afloat or visible; they'd have her locked up somewhere.

Somewhere like Barcelona.

Ted said, 'You're going to need more prints than you've got there, Matt.'

'Doubt it, since we don't need any now for the coastguards. But Gill has the negative. If necessary we could get some made in Fethiye.'

'From here you go to Fethiye?'

Discussion of itinerary followed. Likely date of return to Marmaris, later charter arrangements, etc. Sefik made notes.

'Very adorable breakfast, Matt, I thank you very much, most kindly.'

'Great to see you again, Sefik. And please give my best regards to Ayla. Some other time, we could talk about next year?'

'Yes, *lunching* time. You lunch with us, please? Also is coming Ayla, I have arrange this with her, OK?'

He invited the others too, but they excused themselves: they'd let us talk business on our own. Which was fine. He manoeuvred his bulk back down the narrow plank, and Emma said, 'What a *lovely* man!'

Gill asked me, 'What's to be done now, Matt?'

186

A whole lot of things . . . I mentioned a few of them, then made tracks for the post office, poste restante, where I found a letter from Harry Loder about charter bookings – one cancellation, but another replacing it – and a few other items, but nothing concerning Tommy Fountain.

From Marmaris to Ekincik is a run of about 20 miles, and we had the north wind known as the Meltemi on our beam – fairly light, so I used the engine too, some of the time. Everything had been done that had needed doing, and before we left I'd telephoned to Abidin Kurt's office at Dalyan and left a message that we'd be at Ekincik by about eight that evening, hoped he'd join us for a drink on board the *Bird* and then dinner, and would he very kindly book us a table at the restaurant for nine o'clock, four of us plus himself and whoever he might have with him.

Abidin Kurt is the guy who – amongst other things – runs the boat trips up the Dalyan river. He knows everyone, and everything that goes on; he's an outgoing, charming character and a prime-mover in local tourism.

Ekincik has two good anchorages and it's an attractive place, a sheltered bay surrounded by pine woods. For convenience in getting to the restaurant I moored the *Bird* in the cove right below it – turning in to starboard, dropping the hook in about fifteen metres and then running a stern warp to a rock on the shore. I had the inflatable in tow, but over a short distance it saved time to dive over with the line and swim with it – with, also, a careful eye out for sea-urchins when landing.

There's only one thing that has to go on the record about our night's stay in Ekincik. It was the start of everything that happened later, and it stemmed from something Abidin Kurt told us – or to be more precise, put us on to, having half-remembered . . . He arrived on board, coming from around the headland to the east – Dalyan direction – in one of his own tourist boats, only about 20 minutes after we'd anchored: he came over the side like Tarzan – except for loincloth substitute minuscule bathing trunks – and looked at Gill as if he had some idea she might make an ideal Jane. We'd all been swimming – in water like silk, warm and so clear that swimming over the anchor you could see it shimmering fifty

187

feet below you – and Gill and Emma were in bikinis, both of them looking marvellous but Gill – well, Gill's something else, there aren't words.

'Abidin. Great that you could come.' I made introductions. We'd already opened the bar, and he accepted a beer, regretting that he wouldn't be able to join us for supper as he had to get back up-river, some previous engagement; but he'd booked us a table at the restaurant and he hoped my charterers – and if I'd spare her, this beautiful young lady also – would accept *his* hospitality next day, a river trip which would be conducted by his brother Mehmet.

Well, the Lawries had already decided against making that trip, of course. We compromised by suggesting what Gill called a raincheck – on our way back to Marmaris in a week or so, maybe, if the offer was still standing.

I told Abidin about my plans for the next year, how I expected to be working out of Marmaris right through the season, so I'd be bringing him a lot of custom. (The lunch with Sefik and Ayla had clinched the deal, in principle. I'd technically be a unit in his fleet, which would legalize my remaining in Turkish waters, although I'd continue to operate independently, as always, and in return the bookings I couldn't handle – in fact any surplus business emanating from Harry Loder – would be passed on to Sefik's agency. These arrangements were subject to confirmation from both sides before the end of the current year; obviously I'd have to tie it up with Loder.)

Then I told Abidin about Gill's sister. He listened, asked questions, promised to put the word around. As I've indicated, he's an influential guy; if there *was* anything to be seen or heard, his eyes and ears would stand a good chance of picking it up. I told him roughly what our itinerary would be, so he could contact us – as Sefik also had promised he would – by radio, if any information reached him.

(Radio via the nearest port, on channel 16. For instance, if we were in the Kalkan area he'd ask Radio Fethiye to request Radio Kalkan to call us up. All the boats are talking to each other all the time, in about all the languages there are but mostly Turkish and English; we'd been listening to some of it on the way down from Marmaris.)

So, I told him where we aimed to be, more or less. Couple of days in Fethiye, then south, and turning round at Kekova.

He was staring skyward. Looking puzzled, fingers stroking his big jaw, eyes narrowed in thought . . .

'Funny. Some bell ringing. Kekova. American young woman. Bell ringing in here.' He banged the heel of his hand against the side of his head. 'I don't know, maybe I dream it. American young woman, French yacht, Kekova, that's the combination. Some most peculiar anecdote. My God, my *memory* . . .'

12

We still hadn't got the story when we up-anchored in the morning, but we did know where to go for it. At least, we hoped we did: depending on a guy by the name of Ahmet Çevik being where he was supposed to be and knowing where someone else was. As both of them were ships' captains, it might take some time and mileage to nail the second guy. And with reservations, anyway – awareness that the effort might well be wasted, that the story was unlikely to relate to Anne Brennan anyway, if ever we did get it.

Abidin had tried hard but he hadn't been able to recall the detail. He heard so much talk from transient skippers, crews and passengers, a constant Babel of Turkish, English, German, French, Italian, Dutch, and his recollection was that this had been a conversation in which he hadn't been taking part himself, had only heard in snatches, and he thought second-hand; it might have been chat around a dinner table, or random conversation in some group like ours that evening, friends loafing around on some yacht's stern, voices and music drifting across still water in the dying light.

He'd said before he left us, 'I will think hard. Also I will ask some people who perhaps remember.' Turning to Gill: 'But I should not raise hopes, I don't suppose it would have been your sister. Although I *very* much hope you find her.'

Then some more joking. I'd been asking him where the hotel was at Göcek: the problem was I'd forgotten the names of Tommy's friends, I only knew that they lived in Istanbul, that one of them had a carpet emporium at Izmir, and that they'd very recently built the hotel. That was as much as Abidin had needed: their name was Çerçi, brothers Halim and Nazmi. But what did I want with a hotel – I was a sea-creature, wasn't I, couldn't live long out of water, could I? He had a laugh that might well have been audible in Fethiye, let alone Göcek.

Gill said as we watched the boat puttering off, Abidin waving energetically from the stern, 'He's right, nothing to get excited about, I guess.'

'Could be, though.' Emma wanted to see everyone happy. Glass in one hand, fingers crossed on the other: '*Could* be, Gill.'

'Any case, it doesn't amount to much.' She shook her head. 'I'm going to forget it . . . Better get clothes on, huh?'

We were breakfasting next morning when one of Abidin Kurt's boats appeared round the headland and approached the anchorage. There were half a dozen other yachts close by and I didn't take much notice, but when it turned in towards us and I recognized the brother, Mehmet, at its helm, I thought maybe Abidin's memory really *was* going, maybe he'd forgotten we'd declined his invitation.

Mehmet brought his boat alongside, passed a line up to me and climbed on board. He explained as we shook hands, 'My brother was asking about the American girl at Kekova. I can maybe help a little, not much, but I come to tell you what I can.'

I welcomed him, and made the round of introductions, but he wouldn't accept even a cup of coffee: 'I can only stay one minute, I have to take people from that *gulet*, up to Dalyan. And it is very little I can say. I remember only that it was a French yacht this person mentioned – I don't know any name, nothing – and the girl was American, and there was some arguing about a camera. *Something* concerning a camera, I do not know what.'

Gill sighed. 'Thanks, anyway.'

'Please.' A hand up, to tell her he hadn't finished. He had a pleasant smile, too. 'I am sorry, excuse me—'

192

'Excuse *me*, Mehmet, I thought—'

'Sure. OK. What I can say, when you are in Fethiye, you should go to see Ahmet Çevik. Do you know him, Matt?'

'Not sure . . . Name's familiar, but—'

'He is captain of the *gulet* called *Keyiflioğlu*. His father was the captain, until last year, now *he* is. *Keyiflioğlu* belong to the Çevik family, huh?'

'I do remember. Father's a small guy – Ahmet was with him. Young, smart, talks good English.'

Mehmet nodded. 'But you should understand, it was not Ahmet who was telling about it, it was a friend, another captain, this other man who was at Kekova and knew about it was telling him – right here, two day ago, no more. He is from Bodrum, I think. I don't know his name.'

'And the *Keyiflioğlu*'s in Fethiye now, you say?'

A nod. 'Ahmet was returning some Italians to Fethiye, and Germans are coming there to him in one week. So although *Keyiflioğlu* is based Marmaris, he wait for them there, where he is. You understand?'

'Perfectly. Your English is very good now.'

He smiled. 'Thank you.'

'We're very grateful. Going to all this trouble.'

'Sure are,' Gill told him. 'You and your brother too.'

'Oh.' He was embarrassed. 'It is nothing . . .'

It was a windless morning – you get a lot of them, on this coast, this time of year. The wind tends to be a late riser, so if one wants to take passengers from A to B outside the shelter of bays or islands one tries to get them there, back into sheltered water, by lunchtime. Anyway, we motored all the way and it took about four and a half hours. From Ekincik to the Peksimet lighthouse and the headland where I turned *The Bird* to port to enter the Gulf of Fethiye is about 20 miles, and from there it would have been another 10 to Göcek, which is at the northern extremity of the Gulf; but I'd decided to give my customers a break, and we anchored before that, in an inlet to the west of the Yassica Adalari islets, where they could enjoy the swimming and have lunch in peace, then push on to Göcek. Göcek's a small place and getting to be popular with yachtsmen, especially with the flotillas, therefore it gets crowded; besides, no one except maybe the village kids would want to swim right in there where the boats are, and inevitably a certain amount of village refuse.

So we all swam, and sunbathed – which the girls and Ted had done all the way down from Ekincik – and I moored *The Bird* with her stern to Göcek's little pier at about two-thirty.

'If you want to go ashore, snoop round the shops, remember to lock the front door, will you?'

'I'll stay on board, don't worry,' Gill said. 'Good luck, Matt.'

Abidin Kurt had explained to me where the Çerçi brothers' hotel was. To the west of the village: up the short main street where most of the shops are – I called in to say hello to a guy called Mohamed who runs a general store and with whom I'd done business on previous visits – then left, past a few more shops and a couple of *pansions* – and a newish hotel on the left behind the commercial jetty – and still a long plod on: past the timber yard, and patches of cultivation which extend into wide, lush plantations up the valley northward – fruit trees, tomatoes, corn, aubergines . . .

Half an hour's walk, maybe, and oven-hot all the way. But the hotel was in view on that flat landscape long before I got to it. Long and low, with sunshaded balconies around its single upper storey, modern and cool-looking in the blaze of sun. There were quite a few cars parked behind it, all with Turkish plates – holidaying Turks from points west and north and the sunbaked hinterland.

I walked round the building, to get an idea of the set-up before I went in to find one or more Çerçis. The long south front opened on to paving which in turn led to the beach and the shimmer of blue water. Bodies were strewn here and there, children played in the shallows, windsurfers were enjoying a surface-ruffling breeze they wouldn't have had earlier in the day. There was a bar on the terrace, stone-built and with a thatched roof, tables with bright sunshades surrounding it. With a thought of ice-cold beer, but manfully resisting temptation, I went on by, passing through glass doors into the surprise of air-conditioning – and thinking as I walked in that the brothers Çerçi clearly knew what they were about.

Display cases, boutique windows: and a desk at the end where a short, plump Turkish girl regretted that neither of the

brothers was in Göcek right now. American intonation ...
Would I care to speak with the manager? I said yes please, I
would; she asked me for my name, and wobbled away on her
high heels, leaving me to prowl around the foyer, looking at
such things as carpets – a whole lot of them, doubtless from the
Çerçi business in Izmir – and women's dresses, necklaces,
ornaments of beaten silver, leather skirts and jackets ...

'Mr Johnson?'

A short, square-built guy, middle-aged: he introduced himself as Kemal Firat, hotel manager. Was there something he
could do for me, in the absence of the proprietors?

'I'm looking for a friend of mine, name of Fountain, who's a
friend of theirs. He'll be expecting me to ask for him here –
because if he's in Turkey at all they'll have heard from him. I'm
Matt Johnson, by the way, I have a yacht here, the *Bird of
Dawning*.'

'A beautiful name for a boat, Mr Johnson.' We'd shaken
hands. He told me that so far as he knew both Çerçis were in
Istanbul: if I liked I could call them, use the telephone in his
office. I thanked him, and asked him to be even kinder – if he'd
do the talking, as I spoke no Turkish.

'If you wish.' He shrugged. 'Both the brothers speak fluently
in English, but – I am sure they would wish me to assist you.
Please – this way ...'

Within minutes he was talking to one of his bosses. A stream
of Turkish, then a pause, and one of the few words I knew:
'*Tamam* ...' He held the phone away from his ear: 'Do you
have some personal identification, Mr Johnson?'

I had my passport. I usually bring it ashore with me, if I'm
going more than a few yards from the boat. He took a look at
the photograph and my name, then murmured affirmatively
into the phone before passing me the receiver: 'Please.'

'Mr Johnson?'

'Mr Çerçi ... Forgive this intrusion, but I'm hoping to get in
touch with Tommy Fountain, thought there was a chance you
might be able to help me.'

'So I have just been informed. I must say it is puzzling – so
many people looking for him, and for some reason assuming
he might be with me or my brother!'

'You say there've been other—'

'Indeed so. Although why it should be imagined – after all, it's years since we – well, I am sure you must know this, you're a good friend of Tommy's, he has mentioned you—'

'He has, eh?'

'In the past, of course. The distant past.'

This was unlikely. He'd have mentioned me *now*, all right, in the present circumstances, but he'd have had no reason to a few years ago. Nor, if he had, would this guy have been likely to have remembered it.

I caught on. Better late than never. Çerçi had told me two things: one, he *had* seen or spoken with Tommy recently, and two, the Turkish police were looking for him: doubtless at the request of Scotland Yard. Or of Interpol, I supposed.

'Mr Çerçi – if he should by any chance get in touch with you – at some time in the future, just in case he does – would you give him a message from me?'

'Well, it is so unlikely, you know. I suppose that – *at a pinch*, as you say in English – he might at some time wish to contact my brother – Halim, he's in Izmir, maybe you'd like to leave your message with him, rather than with me?'

'If you think he'd be more likely—'

'Kemal Firat will introduce you to him. Put it like this – if Tommy is coming to Turkey and wanted to be in touch with either of us, it would be Halim. I do not have reason to expect it, but – well, I am glad to have spoken to you, Mr Johnson, and if at some time you do see Tommy, please give him my salutations.'

'I'm very grateful for your help.'

'It's nothing. But if ever I *could* be of service to a friend of Tommy's, I should be honoured. Goodbye.'

Obviously Tommy *was* here. Incredible. I'd hoped for this, but I hadn't, deep down, expected it. Such a hell of a long way to have come – especially in the demoralized state he'd been in when I'd last seen him.

I certainly hadn't foreseen the Metropolitan Police knowing enough to have been able to link him to the Çerçis. Correspondence, maybe, in his house: obviously they'd have searched it. And knowing Turkey was where I'd been coming – the notorious Matt Johnson who'd smuggled him out of England . . .

196

Dialling again, Firat was murmuring, 'In Izmir, Mr Halim Çerçi has a substantial interest in carpets of the highest quality. *Only* of such quality. If you should have any interest in . . . Ah, excuse . . .'

It was a female voice on the other end. Then a pause, and it must have been Halim then, Firat talking nineteen to the dozen, obviously explaining who'd said what to whom up to this point. I wasn't sure whether the stuff about carpets had been just patter, politeness, or the inveterate salesman never missing an opportunity . . . But now he was offering me the telphone again.

'Halim Çerçi? Matt Johnson.'

'Yes, Mr Johnson – you want to leave a message for Tommy Fountain. Do you have some reason to believe he will be coming to Izmir?'

Halim's voice was more nasal than his brother's.

'I thought he might be. And you were the only contact I could think of. I'm sorry if I'm wasting your time, but—'

'No, not at all. Only that I have no expectation – much as I should *like* to renew our old friendship – did you know that I was in our Turkish navy when he was stationed in Ankara?'

'No, I didn't. I know he has a great regard for you, that's all.'

'And I for him. My brother also . . . So, Mr Johnson, if you wish to leave a message, simply against the happy chance that he may – what d'you say, pop up?'

'Thank you. And yes, please. Incidentally, I gather there've been others trying to get to him through you. Your brother mentioned—'

'Mr Johnson, we both have his interests at heart. I hope very much that if he has any – any current problems, you may be able to assist him with them.'

'That's the object of the exercise. Why I want to get in touch, I mean. Shall I give you the message?'

'I will record it. Then there can be no misunderstanding. One moment, please.'

Cagey. Obviously – to coin a phrase – fuzz-conscious. But he'd as good as told me Tommy wasn't far away.

'Please, speak now.'

'Tommy. Matt . . . I'm at Göcek, moving over to Fethiye in an hour or two, and I'll be there about two days. I have

197

charterers on board whom I have to take south as far as Kekova, then back, but I can hang on at Fethiye for – well, say three nights maybe, and I'm leaving this message with Halim Çerçi just in case you should happen to be in Turkey, in which case I imagine you'd be in touch with him. I've some property of yours, also I've spoken to the boys in blue a couple of times, and I *think* your position may not be as bad as you must have thought it was. Anyway, we have to talk ... Listen – at Fethiye, now or later when we get back there, the *Bird of Dawning* will be either stern-to at the quay or if the customers prefer it I'll move out and spend nights at anchor somewhere close. Most likely Tersane island, the little cove in its north-west corner: but if I'm doing that, I'll leave word for you with a guy by the name of Ahmet Çevik, skipper of a *gulet* called the *Keyiflióglu*. As long as you can make it in the next few days – I think he'll be in Fethiye all this week.'

I spelt out the *gulet*'s name. Not being too sure of my pronunciation of the Turkish. Tommy did talk it, a little, or had done, at one time.

'But look, I won't have room for you in the *Bird* – sorry, but I have these charterers and a crew this trip too. You could ask Çevik, if he's in port, that *gulet* has four cabins in it, he might let you use one ... One other thing – the Met want to know who has initials GC. As in George Cross. Someone you or Penny might've known?'

Not so fuzz-conscious. But you can't have your cake and eat it. I had to trust in Halim, in his not letting anyone but Tommy hear that tape.

There was a little wind from the north-west, right up the *Bird*'s tail in fact, for the 12-mile trip to Fethiye – which is in the south-east corner of the gulf and, like Marmaris, has the protection of its own landlocked bay, *Fethiye Limani*. But it was a fitful wind, so I used the diesel as well and we made it in just under two hours – losing the wind altogether and therefore dispensing with sailpower as we passed *Fethiye Adasi* – *adasi* means island – which lies across the entrance to the bay and is also known as Snake Island because it's long, narrow and wiggly in profile. The harbour was crowded, as it always is in summer, but I found a vacant niche on the yacht quay, slotted *The Bird* in stern-first between a *gulet* and a Moody 33 with Majorcan registration.

Emma was all ready to go shopping. Ted rolled his eyes and muttered, 'Bloody carpets', and I came to his rescue, telling them we might have expert advice available to us in a day or two – thinking that I might take them to the Göcek hotel on our way back westward, later, and that Kemal Firat would be only too happy to give us the benefit of his expertise – and as a friend of a friend of the bosses I might hope *my* friends wouldn't be short-changed.

Anyway, the Lawries took off, and after we'd tidied up the boat I locked the doors and Gill and I went in search of the *Keyiflioğlu*.

It wasn't exactly difficult, as she was lying only about three boats down, to the east of us. There was no sign of life on board, so I went up the plank to where its end rested on the timber stern, shouted 'Captain? Captain Çevik?'

(That accent under the 'C', by the way, means you pronounce it 'Ch'. So it's 'Chevik'; and 'Cherchi' for Çerçi.)

A young Turk appeared, but it wasn't Ahmet. A narrow face, large eyes, the face of a poet or a musician. He smiled, told me something reassuring in Turkish and trotted away down the plank, returning a minute later with the man we wanted.

Ahmet Çevik was about twenty-five – by the time this yarn sees the light of day I suppose he'll be twenty-seven – with a sharply intelligent face on which there was a slight frown as he looked at me – looked then with greater interest at Gill, for which one could hardly blame him – then back at me again, I guessed wondering where we'd met before.

'I'm Matt Johnson: yacht *Bird of Dawning*. This is Mrs Paget.' We all shook hands. 'You and I met in Marmaris last year – you had your father with you then.'

'Of course.' The smile lit his face up. 'Yes, I do remember – *Bird of Dawning*, sure!'

'We just got here, Ahmet. Last night we were at Ekincik, though, and Abidin Kurt was telling us – well, he doesn't remember much of it, but his brother Mehmet thought you might – an American girl on some French yacht, some fuss about a camera?'

199

'Sure!' Ahmet laughed, put a thumb to his head, a screwing motion . . . 'Some crazy woman, that one!' He looked quickly at Gill, then: 'Oh. You are American?'

'Right. And the crazy one just *might* be my sister.'

'I am – *very* sorry.'

On the verge of more laughter, though: and a comical expression – self-mockery – glancing at the other lad, shrugging as if to say *There goes my big foot in it again* . . . The crewman – Ahmet had introduced him, name Mustapha – was giggling – at the pantomime, I doubt if he'd understood any of it: and Gill smiling, assuring Ahmet it was OK, her sister *was* slightly nuts. Not that the girl in the French boat had necessarily or even probably been her.

I don't think either of us thought it could have been, at that stage. As far as I was concerned – well, I was still receptive to Gill's belief in Anne being at this end of the Mediterranean, but I have to admit that looking for her here was largely a matter of 'going through the motions', now. For Gill's sake, of course. At heart, I thought it was far more likely her sister was in Spain.

Ahmet said, 'My friend who was telling about it will be in Bodrum now, I think. When we were at Ekincik I was coming to Fethiye with *Keyiflioğlu* and he going the other way. He is captain of a *tirhandil*, name *Unos*.' He asked Gill, 'You know what means *Unos*?'

Gill frowned at him. 'How could I?'

'Means' – Ahmet made weaving motions with his hands, imitative of a dolphin's motion through the sea – 'what you call him – dolphin?'

I told her, 'And a *tirhandil* is like a half-sized *gulet*. Cross between a *gulet* and a *caique*.'

'I stick around here, I'll be bilingual pretty soon.'

'Yes.' Ahmet extended the lesson: 'Tell me what is the meaning of the name of this ship, *Keyiflioğlu*?'

'Please, Ahmet, don't be silly.'

He pursed his lips: as if shocked by her ignorance. 'Means *Son of a Happy Man*. That's a good name, huh?'

'Sure. Unusual, anyway.' I could see she'd taken a liking to him. 'It's your papa who's happy, right?'

'I don't know. You better ask him.'

'Ahmet – the guy we want to ask about is this *tirhandil* skipper. Since he's not here and we certainly don't want to flog all the way up to Bodrum, how much of his story do *you* remember?'

'You want me to tell it to you?'

'It's what we're here for.'

'Ah. OK, then.' A sideways glance at Gill. 'I was hoping you came only to see me.'

'We'll come *back* only to see you, Ahmet.' Gill nodded. 'But right now, what was it about a camera?'

'You know Kekova?'

'No, she doesn't. We'll be going down there, though.'

'OK. But you know it, Matt. And Tersane Bay, you know?'

Not to be confused with Tersane Island, right here in the Fethiye gulf. Tersane Bay is an anchorage at the western tip of Kekova island. I nodded: 'Where that big ruined archway is.'

'And the small girls who come out in rowboats to sell their' – his hands delineated a square – 'you know, in the baskets, what d'you call them—'

'Scarves.' I explained to Gill, 'Kids from some nearby village, they row out to visiting yachts and *gulets* with baskets of these brightly coloured scarves. Dozens of different colours, and little cowrie shells sewn into the edges.'

'Right.' She looked at Ahmet. 'So?'

'The French yacht lying at anchor, and the girls around it in their boats, but the Frenchman is not letting them come on board. My friend is watching this, his *tirhandil* is lying close by, and he sees – he is also hearing, you know how sound is heard across the water – some arguing, the American girl is on deck and wants to see what it is the girls are selling, but the Frenchman makes her go down inside and he's shouting at the boats to go away . . . Then my friend is seeing her again, at a – how d'you say, a window, in the side of the yacht? She goes like this' – beckoning motions – 'to a boat the other side from where the Frenchman is trying to make the others go away. It is not so easy, you know? But the boat *this* side – the girls are holding out their baskets for the lady to see all the scarfs, but she doesn't take any, instead she is reaching out and she has a camera – looks like a good one, you know, 35 mm? – and she push it

201

in one basket . . .' He paused, asked Gill, 'You understanding this?'

'Sure.'

'Go on, Ahmet.'

'They don't know what to do, you see. And the Frenchman has seen there is this boat the other side, he's getting really mad, shouting "Go 'way, go 'way" – making like so . . .' Ahmet waved his fists. 'So they – back off, huh? Then one girl holding up the camera to him: she is calling, "We don't want this, what did she give us this for?" But he's not understanding Turkish, he think now they try to sell him a camera – you see?'

'Right . . .'

'That is nearly all. You see, they can't get the camera back to the girl, this man won't let them near. Then he pulls up his anchor and he goes. North, my friend said, maybe to Kalkan or here to Fethiye, he didn't know. But the camera – the girls row to the *tirhandil*, they want my friend to take it. They don't know *nothing* about cameras – except the tourists all the time wanting to take their pictures . . . But also, somebody – *jandarma* maybe – is going to say they stole it – because they don't have money for such a camera, huh?'

I explained to Gill, '*Jandarma* are soldiers, regular army, who're billeted in all Turkish villages, usually two to a village, to police it. Very tough and unsmiling, nobody argues with them.' I asked Ahmet, 'So what did they do with it, finally?'

'Maybe they still have it. Hide it, maybe – if they don't throw it away. Throw it in the sea maybe.'

'Wouldn't they sell it?'

'No, I don't think so. They are simple people – nice people but not – you know, sophisticated? If the *jandarma* say they must have stole it, they would not know how to – I mean, to prove it was *not* so.'

'So they *might* still have it.'

'It's – possible . . .'

I looked at Gill. 'Suppose that was Anne. She's being held against her will. Maybe just when there are other people around, the rest of the time it's OK and she's infatuated with this guy so it was all sweetness and light—'

'Right—'

'—and of course he's getting her here on the hoof, as it were, no need to lock her up, or keep her gagged – or drugged, whatever ... But she's catching on now, it's not the great romance she thought it was – and she's trying to get a message out – hoping you'd be on her tail?'

'She'd *know* I would be.'

'But *he* wouldn't. If he didn't know about the letter – the one you *did* get—'

'Or about her talking to the people at her *pension*.'

'Right ... Listen, you've said she's crazy – scatty, whatever – but is she clever – I mean smart?'

'Oh, when she chooses to use her brains, yeah.'

'So the ploy with the camera would make sense, wouldn't it? She'd expect it to attract attention – and what Ahmet said – possibility of theft, it might bring the police, or the coastguard?'

Ahmet was watching us, listening closely, and his rate of blinking had accelerated noticeably ... 'This guy – you think he is holding her prisoner?'

I nodded to him: and Gill let out a rush of breath: 'Matt – if you're right, any film in that camera might tell us something.'

After we left the *Keyiflioğlu* – I had to visit the poste restante, then back to *The Bird* and later we went ashore for supper – Gill and I agreed that although it was a longshot chance we should definitely try to get that camera. It would mean going down to Kekova, but this would suit the Lawries too. There was obviously no certainty we'd get it – it might have been sold, or thrown away, and even if it was still in those kids' possession they might have opened it up and exposed the film.

More likely still, it might have absolutely no connection with Anne Brennan.

But even without the camera, if we could find the kid who'd been that close to her, we might get an identification – or otherwise – from the photograph.

I'd showed Ahmet that mocked-up portrait, asking him if he could get a print to this *tirhandil* skipper in Bodrum, to see whether he could identify the girl who'd been on the French yacht as this one. Ahmet didn't know whether or not his friend had had a clear sight of her; he suggested that he might get him on the telephone, ask him about this. He had his doubts, as there'd been no description given, and he thought there would have been. The *tirhandil* man hadn't known the name of the French boat, either – Ahmet was sure of this, he'd asked him, thinking he might have kept an eye out for it and seen if the girl was still acting crazy.

He'd promised to make enquiries here in Fethiye, meanwhile. He was going to be here for the rest of the week, and he'd show the print to a lot of skippers he knew and maybe a few he didn't, and ask them to ask *their* friends – in other ports, and so on. The sort of intelligence network I'd thought of setting up in the first place, in fact, a web that would quickly cover the entire coast – and which would already be forming, incidentally, with Sefik Yeşilay and Abidin Kurt on the job. Ahmet seemed genuinely concerned for Gill's sister, indignant at the idea of some Frenchman holding her against her will: come to think of it, his reaction was the same as Sefik's and Abidin and Mehmet Kurt's had been.

He'd told us that as well as asking around among his seagoing friends, he'd make enquiries – and post copies of the photo, if they'd let him – in places like the harbour master's office and customs, and with the waterman and the guy in charge of the fuel pumps on the quay. Gill had started to protest, when he'd started talking about recruiting these officials, but I'd suggested he need only tell them this Yankee girl had lost a valuable camera and someone at Kekova had found it.

'My God, Matt.' Gill sighed. 'D'you think we *dare* hope for that much luck – that it could be hers?'

'*Let's* hope. Got to get lucky sometimes.'

But maybe I should have been satisfied with the luck I'd had already. With having Gill here with me: with being in love with her and having her in love with me. In this big, rather glossy restaurant – it's a restaurant although it's called the Yacht Club – there were quite a lot of good-looking girls, but there wasn't one to compare with her. She was in pale yellow tonight – simple, just perfect for her style, and she looked absolutely wonderful. I had to keep looking at her: it was positively difficult to look anywhere else: and one of the things that had me baffled was how some guy who'd had the luck to marry her could possibly have walked out on her.

I'd locked up the *Bird* – having given the Lawries a spare key in case they were back on board before we were – and I'd also asked the owner of the Moody alongside us if he'd keep an eye on her for me; he'd said he'd be glad to and maybe I'd do the same for him some time. That's how it works: and as I've said before it's not the locals one's bothered about, it's the horde of drifters from all over.

So here we were, having a very good meal for about a quarter of what it might cost in England, and waiting for the floor-show, a belly-dancer whom Gill had said she'd like to see – which was really why we'd come here, having seen the advertisement posted outside. It's right on the waterfront, this place.

I'd said – earlier, on board – 'Her belly won't be a patch on yours, I guarantee it.'

'I don't *have* a belly!'

'Yes, you do. Just a little one. It's beautiful.'

'So I'll learn how to do it, too. Then when you're all tired and jaded I'll know how to get you sparking.'

'Not to spark around you, Gill, a man'd be needing a whole new ignition system.'

This conversation had led to a delay in our getting dressed to go ashore. She'd tried out her belly-dancing there in the saloon, and it had been more than I could stand. Anyway – in the restaurant – her saying what huge luck it would be if that camera did turn out to be her sister's – she added, 'And wasn't it a stroke of luck your friend Abidin thinking of it, when he did?'

'We'd have heard about it sooner or later. After all, we were canvassing – American girl, French boat – and among the locals a story like that's a diversion, another crazy-foreigner anecdote. But it's why I wanted those photos – eyes and ears all up and down the littoral, all you have to know is where to put your ear to the ground.'

'I suppose . . . But Matt, your theory – luring Anne here, then she has to catch on to the truth because when they're getting close he can't have her talking to people or being seen too much – d'you realize it'd explain why they took so long to get through to my father? Waiting until they had her – had her locked up someplace?'

205

'I suppose it would . . .'

Kidnappers tend to use busy, crowded places, where comings and goings aren't noticeable. Towns. Fethiye, for example. After all, it's the only fair-sized town anywhere near Kekova, and they wouldn't have had time to get much farther; one might also guess they wouldn't have come all the way to this coast if it hadn't been their ultimate destination. Also, Raoul *hadn't* sold Anne any disinformation, he'd baited his trap with the promise of a trip to the exotic East . . .

He'd delivered on his promise, too.

I realized that I'd begun to count on that camera being Anne's. From private scepticism and a leaning towards the Spanish theory, this yarn stemming from Abidin Kurt had swung me the other way. Wishful thinking, mostly, wanting it all to turn out right for Gill's sake. Not that picking up Anne's tracks would necessarily bring us to some happy ending: in fact that was when things might get *really* difficult. Like having found the haystack, start looking for the needle.

I told Gill, 'The camera probably *isn't* hers, you know. Odds are heavily against. I agree we have to check it out, but let's not bank on it.'

'I know.' She reached for my hand. 'I know, Matt.'

What I *had* been right about was the belly-dancer. She was a pretty little thing, but she couldn't have taught Gill anything at all. While I was watching her – when she'd almost finished her act and was dancing between the tables so that diners could stuff money into her bejewelled bra – it was interesting to see the eagerness of some guys to part with their money – I was thinking about a separate problem, namely that while our obvious move now was to make tracks for Kekova, Tommy Fountain might already be on his way here. I certainly didn't want to let him down, and it put me rather on the spot.

But I could brief Ahmet Çevik about him, and if he did come while we were away, he'd just have to stick around.

'She really gets to you, doesn't she?'

I'd had my eyes on the dancer and her fund-raising activities while I'd been pondering this dilemma, and Gill had got a wrong impression. I smiled at her: 'Want to hear what I've been thinking about?'

'*That* might best be kept to yourself.'

She was smiling too, but she meant it. I had to talk for about ten minutes before she'd accept that I'd had a few thoughts, as distinct from sexual fantasies, running through my head. But in the course of the explanation yet another line of thinking developed, on that subject of kidnappers preferring urban environments in which to hole-up with their victims. One, these kidnappers had acted in a very off-beat way. (If that girl in the French yacht *had* been Anne.) The idea of getting her most of the way under her own steam, so to speak, was original, as far as I knew: so maybe Raoul and Co. were new to the business, not professional kidnappers, might therefore not conform to established procedures. And among the options that would be open to them would be to transport her into the interior: not into some easily accessible coastal town, but into that huge hinterland, camel country. If this was the truth of it, we didn't stand a chance, there'd be no possible way to trace her, follow her, without getting the police to do it: and we weren't allowed to go to the police . . .

But the police, in that case, *would* be the people for the job, it would even be easy for them. In a huge, sparsely populated area, and with a pair of *jandarma* in every village, a team of kidnappers with a girl prisoner would hardly go unnoticed.

Unless they – Raoul – had had it really organized, someone from the interior lined up to rendezvous with him on the coast, whisk her into the interior and oblivion . . .

'You off again on your wild scenarios?'

'Well . . .' I prevaricated: 'One obvious thing we should do is check on all the French-flag boats around here. Ahmet might help with that. They won't all be in the port, they'll be in the little anchorages too. And *we* ought to get off down to Kekova, so—'

'Let's go tomorrow!'

'We *could*.' I frowned. 'If the Lawries are agreeable, I suppose—'

'Sure they will be.' She frowned. 'What else is bothering you?'

'Only that Tommy Fountain may put in an appearance. I've just no idea; the guy I talked to – well, I told you, he gave me the feeling Tommy's around, but how near or far or what he's doing, I've no idea at all. He could show up at any time.'

'Would it matter so much – since we'd be back in – what, three or four days?'

'Well. Maybe. Although I don't want to rush the Lawries – a cruise should be a leisurely procedure, not a blind rush from A to B and back again.'

'I don't think they'd mind at all. They're – well, they're *involved*, Matt.'

'There's another angle too.' I'd just got to this. I'd been aware there was some snag, the wine must have slowed my brain. I explained, 'The main thing's to find your sister. And if we're lucky we may get some kind of clue at Kekova. But one thing for sure is she and Raoul won't be there now – and they could be *here*, in Fethiye. Or nearby. And Ahmet's putting that photograph around – incidentally, we'd better get some more prints made – but if we take off now and anything comes out of all that, and we aren't here—'

A waiter was giving us more coffee; and in the pause I saw the answer. I didn't like it much: and Gill was going to hate it. It was an easy solution to arrive at logically, though. We needed to be in two places at once: so, in military terms, we'd have to split our forces: and as to how to do it – well, I had to sail the *Bird of Dawning* down to Kekova, the Lawries would obviously come with me, and that only left Gill.

Leave her in the care of Ahmet Çevik, as a paying guest in the *Keyifliöglu*?

13

It made for a subdued end to our evening at the Yacht Club. What it came down to was that this was our own private business, in particular of course Gill's, and it wouldn't be either fair or reasonable to leave so much of the weight on Ahmet's shoulders. No matter how willing, well-disposed, competent, etc . . . In fact through his efforts in showing the photograph around there was a chance – no more than a chance, but it wasn't so remote as to be ignored – that if that had been Anne with the camera, and she'd been trying to get away – if she succeeded, and through her picture being around the town and waterfront she ended up somewhere around the *Keyiflioğlu*, she'd need someone to look after her – and the one and only candidate for that job would be her sister.

Gill agreed that this made sense, although the prospect of being left here didn't exactly fill her with enthusiasm. The same went for me; I didn't want to be away from her for ten minutes, let alone two or three days.

But she'd have Ahmet to look after her. Might also have Tommy, before long. And – objectively – it seemed silly to have any qualms about it; after all, she'd been knocking around on her own for quite some time before *I'd* come into the picture.

I was acknowledging to myself that for me it was utterly

impossible now to take any such objective view, when she broke in to ask me how far it was to Kekova.

'From Fethiye – about sixty, seventy miles. Take us between ten and twelve hours each way. I'd start at dawn if I could, but we need fuel – my fault, should've kept her topped up ... Anyway, let's see what Ahmet thinks about it.'

Lights were showing from the *Bird*; we went on past her, found Ahmet and his crewman in the *Keyiflioğlu's* saloon, and I asked him whether he'd look after Gill while I made this Kekova trip. He was obviously delighted to be asked, and hurried to show her a cabin; there were four, and two heads-cum-showers of which she'd have one for her own use.

'Hotel rates, Ahmet?'

'But of course. All world travellers hear of the five-star *Keyiflioğlu*. How many meals each day you like?'

'You're a cook, too?'

'I very much like to cook. You will see – then *you* say if I am a cook.'

'Right. I'll try you out. Thanks, Ahmet.' She nodded to me. 'Just fine.'

Fine, but also slightly wretched.

But it was the obvious thing to do. And the Lawries had no objections. Emma very sweetly offered to stay behind to keep Gill company, but of course Gill wouldn't hear of it, and I saw Ted trying not to show his relief. Over a nightcap we finalized our plans: we'd get to Kekova, and back with the camera if possible, in the shortest possible time – twelve hours there, another twelve back, with as short an interval between as could be managed. Meanwhile Gill would get some more copies made from that negative, Ahmet would get all the info available on French boats in the area – particularly any with an Algerian skipper, and/or any whispers of an American girl on board – and Gill would collate whatever he got hold of, and follow up any likely leads.

'But be careful ...'

'*You* take care, too.'

She slept in my arms all night, on our narrow bunk in the fore cabin. Not that this, *per se*, was exactly novel, but for both of us it was different from any time before: a quieter, deeper appreciation of each other, and that sad, verge-of-parting atmosphere – as if we were about to be separated for much longer than a day or two. The night passed too quickly; one's inclination was to cling tighter rather than let go when the morning came.

Sixty-five miles, this trip would be, if I cut the corners fairly fine. Not as fine as some of the local boats cut them, passing so close to some sheer, steep-to headlands that if they'd shoved an oar out they'd have lost it. I don't know the inshore waters as well as they do: anyway, if one happened to break down in the wrong place, and the wind decided to amuse itself by shifting, one would end up wishing one had been less of a bloody fool.

Put at its simplest, that's seamanship.

Anyway, we were clear of the Fethiye quay by 10 a.m., having filled up with diesel. Gill waving to me from the *Keyiflioğlu*'s bow . . .

Once out of the gulf, the *Bird* spread her wings to a light northerly breeze which after midday increased gradually to about force 4, backed to north-north-west and stayed with us all the way. There was quite a big swell running, rolling in from the north-west to put a lot of motion on the boat and slow us somewhat, but we had seven knots on the dial at times, averaged better than six and a half and made Kekova island at about eight-thirty that evening. The Lawries had sunbathed all the way – having to grab for handholds at times so as not to get rolled overboard by that swell – and they'd enjoyed intervals of food and drink, taken snapshots of each other and of scenery when we'd passed close to any, like for instance the Greek island of Kastellorizo; they'd behaved, in fact, as charterers are expected to behave – relaxing, getting what they'd come a long way and paid a lot of money for. I was very glad to see it, because I had them on my conscience, rather; I told them so, and they both assured me – Emma with bubbling enthusiasm, Ted with a few of his grunts and nods – that they'd loved every minute right from the moment they'd stepped on board.

'That first night out of Malta? That night and day?'

'Ah, *well* . . .'

In fact on this quite bouncy run down to Kekova they hadn't come anywhere near feeling even queasy. I'd seen them laughing, Emma howling and clutching at Ted for support, in one stretch when we'd had the swell at its most powerful, the *Bird*'s bow soaring and thumping down again, and the twisting roll that was her speciality when she had her nose in it and a new mountain of sea running in under her quarter. I thought I was darned lucky, with these two.

Lucky with the *Bird* as well. The feel and the look of her, her instant response to even the lightest touch on the wheel: it's something I'll never tire of, never fail – please God – to react to with a sense of joy in being alive and in exactly the right place . . . You'd have to experience it, I'm sure, to know what I'm talking about.

Anyway – Kekova, now: eight-thirty p.m., light fading as the sun died behind the small peninsula jutting from the mainland; we'd turned in to port around it, turning northward into the channel between it and the island and then to starboard, passing round Kekova's western tip. Kekova Adasi is about three miles long and a mile thick at its widest, and Tersane Bay is just inside this western end: it's a good anchorage, and there are some interesting ruins right on the beach at the head of the cove, but there was no sign of what we'd come to see – rowing boats containing small girls selling scarves.

I'd have anchored, if the Lawries had wanted to, and we could have spent the night here; I'd have produced some kind of supper and a bottle of this or that. But the kids would have rowed themselves back to the mainland by now and they'd hardly be coming out again this late, and for just a single yacht; so an alternative now – I put it to the Lawries as their choice – was to motor over to Kale, which is on the mainland and almost right opposite, less than four thousand yards away. Half an hour ago one could have seen it from here, at least have seen the crenellated walls of the Roman fort that crowns the hill above the little harbour: and from up there in daylight, looking down into the clear water, you can see the underwater outlines of the ancient Roman harbour, the straight lines and right-angles of drowned quays. I told Ted, 'It's one area of Roman rubble I think you'd agree is worth seeing. And there are several small restaurants. *And*, some of our scarf-sellers might be around. If they aren't, I could bring us back here at dawn without disturbing the first-class passengers, and we could have breakfast and a swim while we wait for them to descend on us.'

Emma put her hand up: 'Roman rubble is my choice', and Ted put on his long-suffering look: 'You heard, skipper. Let's go.'

We'll leave the *Bird* at Kekova now. To keep more or less in step with events elsewhere I want to go back to Gill, see her that morning on a sight-seeing trip which Ahmet Çevik had laid on for her.

He'd sprung it on her, like a surprise treat for a child, when she'd been eating the excellent lunch he'd prepared for her – little twists of pastry with spicy fillings, then meat balls with an aubergine salad and a side dish of yoghurt and olives. Purely out of the kindness of his heart, in case she might be bored or lonely, and also out of sympathy for her in her anxiety about Anne, he'd arranged with a friend of his who had a car to take her to see Fethiye's Likyan tombs – which are cut into the ironstone cliff-face above the town – and the remains of the Byzantine city walls, and the deserted village of Kaya Koy. The whole thing would take less than a couple of hours, he assured her, and while she was away he'd stick around the *Keyiflioğlu* to deal with any information that came in.

Gill didn't want to disappoint him, and just that short absence couldn't do much damage. She'd already ordered the extra photo-prints – despite this being Sunday they'd been promised for noon next day – and Ahmet had made his rounds of places where he'd left them on display, and talked to a few *gulet* skippers who'd come in since last night; there'd have been nothing else to do except sit around and wait. So she accepted, gratefully, and a few minutes later the driver arrived and honked his horn at them from the quay.

Kaya Koy was the bit she found fascinating. *Kaya* means stone, and *Koy* means village; what was once a community of 150,000 people is now a sprawl of 4,500 stone ruins covering an entire hillside. Tracks which in steeper sections still have wide stone steps in them lead uphill between the tumbledown dwellings, some of which still have timber remnants – doors and sills, shutters, split and crumbling . . . The place wasn't totally deserted, she realized: there were sheep-droppings everywhere, she could hear plaintive bleating from somewhere close by, and from one comparatively intact hovel near the road a television aerial projected incongruously from an embrasure at first-floor level. She guessed it must be there to hang washing on. The driver – name Ali – confirmed that a few people lived here: squatters, she gathered, gypsy-like, some of them beggars preying on the tourists. But areas of quite richly fertile-looking ground down in the valley were in cultivation; she guessed – sick of asking questions all the time – it would be the work of local farmers, not squatters, and then indeed saw a group of women in bright clothes, by no means ragged, sitting around in a tree's shade and working with some crop or other. The driver told her in his fragmented English, and using a cigarette as illustration, that they were stripping the leaves from tobacco plants.

Kaya Koy, he explained – sporadic bursts of explanation later amplified by Ahmet – had been evacuated in 1923. It was much older than that; village after village, down the centuries, had been built and rebuilt on the foundations of earlier ones. But in 1923 the inhabitants had been Greek, and by edict of Kemal Atatürk they'd been ordered off the mainland – allowed to re-settle on the islands close offshore – and Kaya Koy became, and has remained, a ghost town. It's about five or six miles out of Fethiye, in a setting that feels remote because the steep-sided hills enclose it, isolate it from the sea. This is typically Greek – you can see the same thing all over the Greek coastline and on their islands, how the ancient villages were sited on the blind side of hills or ridges so they wouldn't catch the eyes of prospecting seaborne raiders.

Kaya Koy's being left to rot had to do with Turks not wanting to live where infidels had throughout the centuries. The explanation Gill got was vague, but she construed it as something like this. It seemed such a waste: climbing the hill, up one of those steep tracks, she tried to visualize it as it might have been, when it had been a living, thriving, working community . . . Ahmet's friend climbed with her: she wanted to get a wider view of the desolation, from up there. There was a chapel – almost intact and easily identifiable by its shape – and much higher, right up on the skyline, more like a lookout

214

post in its lofty isolation – was a small cube which he told her was another.

From up there – a height of maybe two thousand feet, she guessed – you'd have a fantastic view southward, over blue sea right down the coastline: and if you'd been up there now with a pair of binoculars you'd maybe have seen white sails, the spread wings of the *Bird of Dawning* flitting to Kekova.

She climbed on, with the driver following, in burning heat, scent of wild herbs, and a sense of intruding: as if the people who'd lived here might be watching, wondering – passive in their helplessness – why she'd come, what she'd want of them.

'Ali. What in God's name . . .'

A human skull, right at her feet. One side of it had been crushed in; from the dirty-yellow colour, it was very old. Other skull-fragments lay around: this was level ground near the chapel, a flattish area of earth and weeds between her and the dark, doorless entrance. She stood still, looking around her feet, seeing other human debris – yellowish bones that might have been shins, thighs, arms . . .

She was standing still because she didn't want to tread on any of it, hear the *scrunch* of what had been parts of living people.

'What happened here?'

'Maybe all bury in one place, then' – he waved his hands around – 'some landslide . . . But also, until maybe one, two year ago is many – many *these* . . .' Skulls. He gestured, suggesting a mound of them. 'People take for souvenirs, huh?'

She shivered. 'Well. My God, some—'

She'd been going to say some people must have peculiar tastes in souvenirs, but as she'd turned, glancing away from the grisly scattering of relics – glancing *up* – she was confronted – it was sudden, almost like a blow – by an old woman on the path above her – a dozen feet away, glaring . . . She'd gasped: glancing round then at the driver as he moved up beside her, then back at the harsh, uncompromisingly personal, brutish stare.

Blocking the route upward. Heavy, wide-set figure, one arm crooked to balance a flail – a pole with a length of chain dangling from its end – across a massive shoulder.

215

To continue, Gill would have had to walk round her, through thistles and over rock.

'Ali—'

He said something in Turkish – some kind of greeting, by the sound of it – but the woman didn't answer or shift her furious stare from Gill's face.

Expressing – it was unmistakable although Gill was trying to rationalize, tell herself it wasn't the old woman's fault she looked as she did – crude malevolence.

'What does she want?'

Ali tried again, but she continued to ignore him so completely that Gill might have been alone. He muttered – close at her side – 'Maybe if you seen all you want—?'

'Have I *ever* . . . Come on, let's go . . .'

She'd moved the flail. Not by much: but she'd seen Gill's eyes return to it and she'd responded by sliding that thick hand up its shaft, as if to say yes, what *about* this . . . And – Gill wished afterwards she hadn't seen it, could convince herself she'd imagined it – the creature's mouth had opened, a slit in the dirt-coloured face, stumps of teeth the same shade as those bones: a smile, of sorts, prompted by Gill's interest in the flail . . . Gill with her back to her now, wanting to get away and to shut her out of her mind let alone her sight – picking her way down the slope carefully, resisting the urge to hurry, show her fright, maybe stumble . . .

'What's she carry that thing for?'

'Huh?'

Describing it with hand gestures: 'That pole and the chain?'

'Oh . . . For corn. For beat corn.'

'Threshing – this early in the summer?'

'I don't know.'

She'd carried it like a weapon. And when she'd seen Gill *seeing* it as such, it had made her day.

In the car, driving back into Fethiye, Ali said, 'I think she – scaring you, that woman.'

'Some, I guess.'

'She look like she hate you. Why, for—'

'I know. I mean I *don't* know . . .' Gill thought – still shaking – *Wish to God Matt was here . . .*

*   *   *

In London – Kensington, to be more precise – Detective Inspector Charles Harrison had called at the residence of Mr and Mrs Graham Calderwood. He'd come by appointment, and she'd let him in – Calderwood himself was away – but the welcome wasn't anything like warm.

'I've not the remotest idea how I could help you, Inspector.'

'Oh, just by answering a few questions, ma'am. Shan't keep you long, I promise.'

'Why it couldn't have waited a day, so you could've asked my husband – when it's purely a business connection?'

A nod . . . 'No doubt we *will* have a word with him. But this investigation's been in progress some while now, we don't want to hang about . . . if you don't object *too* much, Mrs – er – Calderwood?'

'You'd better sit down.' Vague gesture of one hand . . . A pale, thin-faced woman, tired-looking, in a house worth about a million, everything in it antique and wall-to-wall. He'd have guessed she might be forty but he'd done his homework and knew she was thirty-four.

'Like some coffee?'

'Very kind, but – no, thank you . . . Mrs Calderwood – you just said "wait a day", for your husband's return from the USA; I thought the day *after* tomorrow?'

'Tomorrow evening – quite late, so—'

'Ah, right. Sleep off the jet-lag.' Harrison peeled back pages in his notes. 'Now, here we go. You said the connection with Mr and Mrs Fountain was purely business. I'll just make a note of that . . .'

'I personally met them precisely once. At a function of some kind – well, one of those awful business things. I'd say my husband might have known who they were, but it would have been Hugh Benedict – that's Mr Fountain's chairman – who'd have introduced us. Actually – now I think about it – my husband *might* have met the man's wife before, because she's – she was Hugh Benedict's daughter, it's possible that they'd have met in earlier years, when she'd have been a schoolgirl.'

'But not *since* then?' Jotting neat shorthand. 'Neither you nor your husband saw the late Mrs Fountain since that function?'

'Not as far as I – remember.'

'So there's no question of any close friendship having developed between you and your husband and – and the Fountains?'

'Certainly not. I mean, why should it? One meets *hundreds*—'

'Quite.' He glanced up from his notes. She looked scared, he thought . . . 'And if your husband on his own *had* made a closer friendship with them – to the extent of calling at their house not infrequently – you *would* have known of it, I dare say?'

'Are you suggesting—'

'Not suggesting anything, ma'am. Matter of getting it all straight, knowing who's who and who knows whom, all that . . . Sorry if I've offended you, but—'

'It's really too nonsensical . . .'

'I dare say it might seem so . . . But now one final question, Mrs Calderwood. The night of Mrs Fountain's – er – demise: it was a Sunday, and the date was' – flipping through notes again – 'May twenty-fourth . . . Would you be *very* kind, check in your diary or engagement book and tell me what you and your husband were doing that night?'

She'd gasped – with more amusement than shock: 'You surely can't suspect *us*?' Throwing up her hands . . . 'What of, anyway? D'you think my husband helped that man to get away, or something? Why should he, what possible connection—'

'It's simply – well, *no* to all those questions, it's a matter of having all the little ends tied up. If you see what I—'

'Frankly, I do not.' She was tight-lipped, angry. 'I'll see if I can give you the information you want, but it's quite, quite monstrous.'

Harrison got up too. He said as she left the room, 'Then, I'll leave you in peace, Mrs – er—'

She'd gone. But she was only away about a minute. Returning, she found him with his notebook open, ballpoint poised: while she had a red leather engagement book open in her hands and a look of satisfaction on her face. Still breathing hard, agitated . . . 'Here we are. Sunday May twenty-fourth. My husband left for New York on Concorde flight BA 179 from Heathrow at 6.30 p.m. He was away five days, that trip . . . While I, that evening, had a bridge party here. Would you like the names of my guests – so you can check I'm not *lying* to you, Inspector?'

I used the searchlight, getting into the little harbour at Kale. The harbour-front was lit up, of course – the restaurants make sure of that – but the approach is somewhat cluttered, not only with rocks on both sides but also outcrops of masonry which the Romans left, watchtowers or somesuch pointing upward from the ancient harbour wall which is now submerged.

I don't take risks if I can help it, with the *Bird*.

But I was taking a risk with Gill. Nobody except me seemed aware of it, but I had this worry nagging at me pretty well all the time.

Anyway – having got past the navigational hazards, I let an anchor go on the swing, well out from the quay, and took her in gently stern-first to where I wanted her – the quay wasn't as crowded as it often is – while Ted obligingly led the inflatable forward, out of the way, and an aproned girl from the restaurant took the stern line which I tossed to her and deftly secured it to one of the iron rings set into the concrete for that purpose.

OK. Stop engine. Up to the bow to ease out another couple of fathoms of anchor warp and then cleat it, and aft again to make all fast and put the plank out – with help again from the waitress. Finally, unplug the searchlight and take it below: that's just the sort of gear that gets nicked, if anything's going to be. Nothing would be here, certainly not by any of the locals, and as we'd be having our supper within a few yards of the gangplank there'd be no risk of other kinds of predator either; but it's a principle, a habit worth cultivating so you don't forget when it *does* matter.

No scarf-girls in sight.

'Ted – want to climb the hill and inspect the castle?'

'Not effing likely.' He glanced at Emma. 'But this one might.'

'How long would it take?'

'Quarter of an hour to get up there, same to get down again.'

'You sound like the grand old Duke of York.'

'Yeah. And you wouldn't see much, this time of night.'

'Might give it a miss then.' Emma patted her tummy. 'I *am* peckish.'

'Next year?'

'Yes, Matt. *Definitely* next year. Agreed, Ted?'

'You'll have divorced me before that.' He nodded to me. 'Proper flibbertigibbet I've got here.'

'I'd say you've got her for life and you're damn lucky.'

'*Thank* you, Matt.'

'You're welcome. Another thing I'm not taking argument about, Ted, is this is my party, tonight.'

'Bloody hell it is!'

'You took Gill and me to supper in Marmaris, so it's my turn. Also, with our various preoccupations I'm not treating you in the style to which I'm accustomed, I have a guilt-complex which you ought to let me – what's the word, expiate? *And* – please let me, because I'll have to sooner or later and it happens to be cheap here.'

'Well.' He put an arm round Emma. 'We'd best let him. This once. Only I buy the wine – how's that?'

We had a deal, and we ate well. It was relaxing to have the *Bird* right under my eye, and the waitress who'd secured the stern line spoke good English; she was waiting, she told Emma, to hear whether she'd won a place at the Izmir university. Emma chatted to her, getting the lowdown on intelligent young Turks' attitudes to this, that and the other, and Ted took interest too; the spoiler as far as I was concerned was this continuing worry about Gill. It annoyed me that I couldn't get rid of it: it wasn't based on anything I could have explained, it was simply *there*, the way I felt. *Felt*, as distinct from *thought*.

And then I did forget it, for a while. About halfway through the meal, and into the second bottle, it went out of my head completely when out of nowhere a wide basket heaped with colour was nudged against Emma's arm.

'Oh, how *pretty*!' Then a double-take, realizing what this was: 'Matt, see what—'

'Yeah. We're in luck.'

I hoped. And while Emma fingered through the scarves – which would be much better seen in daylight, some of the colours differ only quite subtly – I enticed our waitress to come over, and asked her if she'd do some interpreting for me.

Because, because . . . I simplified the story, made it more

straightforward and comprehensible. A friend of mine, an American girl now in Fethiye, had asked me to try to recover a camera which she'd left here with the scarf-sellers. She was a bit over the top, this girl—

'Over the top?'

'Wild. Gets cross with her boyfriend sometimes.'

'Ah.' She understood that, all right. 'The boyfriend is also peculiar. He's French, and they fight a lot. I mean quarrel, argue . . . And when they were here – over there, at Tersane, anchored in the cove – they have a boat, you see, a yacht . . .'

My story was that they'd been having a row because he didn't want her to buy any scarves, said she'd spent too much already. She flew into a temper, snatched up his camera and shoved it into one of the girls' baskets. The Frenchman didn't know she'd done this, and when the kids tried to give it back he thought they were trying to sell him a camera, and he drove them away. Now he was raising hell, the American girl regretted what she'd done and she'd asked me to try to get it back; I'd pay a reward for its recovery.

'She was good and mad, huh?' The waitress laughed, clapped her hands: she'd heard about the camera incident, she said, everyone had been talking about it, discussing what the scarf-girls should do – sell it, give it to the *jandarma*, whatever.

'Do you know if they still have it?'

'Oh, *sure!*' No doubt at all . . . 'I tell her, she will be very glad, I think!' She began to murmur rapid Turkish in the scarf-girl's ear. This was one of the older ones: might have been sixteen. Emma, who'd picked out eight or nine scarves – presents for Christmas, maybe – and was haggling over the price, was still talking into the other ear. I interrupted: 'Might help if you'd pay what she's asking.'

Ted observed quietly, 'I'd never've credited you with being such a bloody liar.'

'Frightening, isn't it . . .'

But the scarf-girl seemed to like it. It would be a triumph for her, I supposed, to return to her sisters and cousins with the solution to the great camera mystery.

'She is saying they still have the camera, no problem, in the morning they bring it for you.'

I pointed out across the dark water where the Romans had

moored their galleys . . . 'Would they bring it over to the cove – Tersane?'

If so, I'd move the *Bird* over there when we had finished this meal. The Lawries would get their breakfast swim, and we'd be away bright and early – back to Gill.

Ted murmured, 'Looks like we struck lucky.'

'If it's Anne's camera, and if there's a film in it.'

But also, starting back for Fethiye soon after breakfast – depending of course on how early the kids came, but say ten o'clock latest, maybe nine – motoring all the way, the wind wouldn't be much use to us – well, we'd be there maybe seven-thirty or eight: and the film – if one existed – would still be undeveloped.

Not too good. And there *might* be an alternative. Although I wasn't sure I had the nerve to suggest it, having already traded on the Lawries' good nature rather heavily . . .

I had the *Bird* anchored at the mouth of the cove by midnight, and ran a stern warp out to a rock on the foreshore. There were several boats moored farther inside the cove, but it would have been a tight squeeze in there for us, and there was perfectly adequate shelter where we were.

We had a nightcap, on deck: agreeing without words passing on the subject that the night and the surroundings were too beautiful to leave too soon. The new moon had set hours ago, not long after dark, dropping behind the mountains to the north, but the sky was alight with stars and the sea agleam with their reflection. A velvet night, very warm considering we were still in the month of June, and absolutely quiet, only the rustle of the sea along the *Bird*'s sides as a background to our low voices and the clink of ice in Emma's glass. She'd caught the Caballo's Neck habit from Gill; Ted and I were soothing our fevered brows with whisky.

Emma said, 'You must be missing Gill, Matt.'

'Dead right I am. Should've brought her along, left Ahmet to mind the store.'

'If her sister turned up?'

'I know. That was it, really. Small chance, but – not one that we could have risked.'

Ted said, 'Let's hope there's a film and it's hers and tells us something.'

222

'I'll drink to that.'

I'd been thinking some more about it too. Getting to Fethiye the next evening, late, we wouldn't have the thing developed before noon next day, no matter how big a surcharge we paid or how successfully Ahmet might twist the pharmacist's arm for us. So even though we'd have it in our hands, we'd have nothing from it, we'd just be sitting around, while Anne—

Well. God only knew . . . And Gill's nails would be bitten down to the quicks while she let that imagination of hers run wild.

'Ted. A thought just struck me – about the film, if there is one.'

Second lie of the evening. It hadn't just struck me, I'd been pondering it for an hour. Emma asked, 'Going to let us in on it?'

'*If* there is one, we'll get to Fethiye with it late tomorrow – except now it's today, but anyway late – and it'll take them a few hours next morning to develop it. If there's anything in it that'll help us to locate her, having to wait that long is – well—'

'Fucking bore.'

'Neatly put, Ted.'

Emma said, 'Go on, Matt.'

'I wondered if you two might like a little variety in your lives. A few hours on *terra firma*. I could put in to Kaş two hours – two and a half – after leaving here, and there's a bus service that passes through, links Fethiye with Antalya. Alternatively – I don't have the timetable, unfortunately – you could hire a taxi. Road distance'd be about a hundred kilometres: you'd be in Fethiye for lunch and we could have the film developed that – *this* – afternoon.'

Ted asked Emma, 'What d'you reckon, girl?'

'Same as you do, obviously, it's what we *must* do. It's a *very* good idea, Matt.'

'Ted?'

'I'm not bothered. And we'd see a bit of the countryside, and all . . .'

'*And* we'll be there that much sooner to keep Gill company. Right, Matt?'

'You two' – I said this with absolute sincerity – 'are bloody fantastic.'

223

14

I was up before dawn, to get a few jobs done while I had the chance. Barefooted, and not even muttering to myself, for the sake of the Lawries' slumber, also confining activities to the fore part of the boat. A boat's like a drum, acoustically, even when it's as rugged as Nautor build their Swans.

If I *had* been doing any talking it wouldn't have been to myself, it would have been to Gill. I missed her dreadfully: in fact I'd decided that this was the only reason I'd been worrying about her, just that I'd got used to having her around. It was extraordinary – in about a fortnight I'd moved from total independence to *this* condition. Objectively, you might say it was catastrophic . . . But I'd first set eyes on her on the evening of the day Will Wyllie and I had got into Mahon, and the log told me that had been Saturday June 13th. Today was the 29th: sixteen days, in which time I'd become unaccustomed not only to sleeping alone but even to watching the sunrise on my own.

I knew I'd have to get used to it again soon, anyway. Longer-term, it didn't bear thinking about.

'Hi, Matt!'

Emma, coming forward along the port-side deck on *her* bare toes. Bare legs too, under a towelling robe. She leant with a hand on the boom, the bundle of the mainsail in its blue cover . . . 'Been to bed at all, have you?'

'Lord, yes. Hope my scratching around up here didn't wake you.'

'I've been awake ages. I think I'm a bit tensed-up for what's in that film. And our safari overland.'

'I'll make tea in a minute. Just polish off this chore.'

'What is that thing?'

'Called a vang. When you sailed a dinghy you may have had an item they called a kicking-strap. Does the same job, but on a craft like this you need something a lot more powerful. Holds the boom down when we're on a reach or running – and when she jibes . . . Have you and Ted decided yet if you're going to take up sailing?'

She'd moved to sit down, then sprung up again. The coachroof was awash with sea dew, which is always ice-cold. After a minute of anguish and bad language, she answered that question: 'No, not really . . . But more to the point, have *you* decided if you're going to take up Gill?'

'I *have* done. I never felt like this about anyone in my life.'

I didn't *think* I had.

'Well, then!'

I looked up at her. Still rubbing herself with the towelling, wriggling attractively. She demanded, 'What are you going to *do* about it?'

'There are a few – imponderables.'

Standing, wiping oil off my hands, I wondered whether Gill might have told her anything about my past – my marriage to Alison, and how it had ended. She might have done: they'd spent a lot of time with their heads together, and women do trade confidences; for instance, I didn't suppose Emma knew that Gill had told me she and Ted weren't married . . . But that miserable background of mine was part of the equation: it had to be, in any thinking about permanent relationships – past, present or future.

But 'permanent' means 'for ever'. You can't separate present and future, if you're using that word. It took a lot of getting used to, even as a concept, when it had been unthinkable for so long.

A vision in striped pyjamas was approaching.

'Morning, Ted.'

'What about some tea, then?'

Emma said, 'I'll get it.'

'No – my job. You're paying for all this, remember?'

'Oh, get stuffed.' She shimmied away to the hatch: most likely needing to change her pants. Ted stretched and yawned, resplendent in his stripes: 'My word, what a light that is . . .'

Sunrise. Sun*burst*: brilliant pale orange blazing up from behind the island's bulk to the east of us. Across a flickering dazzle of sea the mainland was already floodlit, all the way from the Roman battlements on the hilltop down to the village at the water's edge.

'Worth coming for, Ted?'

'Oh, I reckon.'

'Going to take up the sport of sailing?'

'Might, I suppose. Teach us, would you?'

'Next year?'

'Maybe. If *she*'s willing, we might, at that . . . Would you take us on, as pupils?'

'Be delighted to.'

'Have Gill along, and all?'

Back to *that* . . . And I didn't have any immediate answer for him any more than I'd had a minute ago for Emma: the best I could do was mumble something about hoping so . . . The sun, pushing up over the island's crest, was more like the nucleus of a furnace than a crystal ball. I'd looked too long, was temporarily blinded: and the answer wouldn't come from crystal balls anyway, it would have to come out of my head and Gill's. Heads, hearts, and extraneous influences too. Gill's husband, for instance, maybe other circumstances or connections I didn't know about. People don't come vacuum-packed.

The scarf-sellers came when we were about finishing breakfast. We'd all had a swim before that – the water was pleasantly warm, to Emma's surprise – and the sun was well up now, with hardly any breeze at all.

Only one boat came, with a young woman at the oars and two girls clutching baskets. The boat edged in alongside and all three swarmed up like monkeys.

'You ask for this?'

One Nikon 35-mm. I took it from her hands, and thanked

her. She was about thirty, and there was a strong family resemblance between her and the youngsters. She – mother or aunt, whatever – was dark, attractive, with black hair drawn back under one of her own scarves; she had on a man's shirt and a voluminous skirt, or skirts. The children were pretty, one of them outstandingly so; I'd heard Emma murmur to Ted, 'If this one keeps on as she's going, she'll be a knock-out . . .'

I said, 'There's a film in it, all right', and the Lawries both more or less cheered. Assuming it had to be Anne Brennan's film: of which there was no indication whatever . . . If the camera had been in a case there might have been a name-tag on it, but it wasn't. Just one Nikon containing a film of which 16 frames had been exposed.

Emma was into the scarves again, the two kids twittering competitively, elbowing each other aside, each displaying her own wares. I told the mother, 'My American friend will be very grateful to you. It's most kind of you to have kept it safe for her.'

A smile . . . 'She get angry with her man, huh?'

'Very angry . . .'

'He make trouble for her?'

'Too damn much . . . Look, she'd want me to give you something for all *your* trouble.'

I had three 5,000-lira notes in the back pocket of my shorts, and she would have been happy enough with just one. She looked pleased when she got the second, and tried to give me the third one back. But 15,000 lira worked out at only about £12, which in the circumstances and for a camera worth several hundred didn't seem excessive. Meanwhile Emma had acquired a few more scarves; she'd had to buy the same number from each of the two little girls so they wouldn't claw each other's eyes out.

One point: I just observed that there was no indication the camera did belong to Gill's sister. But in fact, the way in which it had been forced on these people was bizarre enough to call for some kind of explanation, and if it was Anne's we *had* one, whereas God knows how you'd even begin to explain it otherwise. On this line of reasoning it seemed almost *likely* it was hers.

Except she was supposed to be in Spain.

228

I docked in Kaş – pronounced Kash – at about half-ten and stayed for only minutes, just the time it took to put the Lawries ashore. They'd decided to hire a taxi, not hang around for the bus, and by the time the *Bird* and I had cleared the little harbour they'd have been hurtling westward. Having some experience of Turkish taxis, *hurtle* would be the right word for it: if they survived the shocks they'd be in Fethiye in a couple of hours.

Fethiye is where it was all happening, that morning. If I'd had any idea what was going on, while I was stuck out there at sea plugging along at six knots on the diesel with the wind right on the *Bird*'s nose and nine hours to go, I'd have been in agony.

To start with there was a crowd in the harbour master's office – which is on the landward side of the seafront road pretty well opposite the commercial pier, roughly two hundred metres from where the *Keyiflioğlu* was berthed – because there'd been a number of boats in and out, the guy who stamped transit logs had gone out for a beer or a *raki* or something else, and several skippers were hanging around looking fed-up, awaiting his return. There'd have been other business in progress as well, of course; Fethiye's a busy, crowded port, at this time of year.

Hans Schreiber looked like just another yachtsman, in the mêlée. Early thirties, rather beefy, tanned, crewcut fair hair, sunglasses hiding blue eyes: jeans, T-shirt hanging loose, sneakers, red-and-white striped baseball cap ... Pushing the cap back with a thumb as he stood gazing at the notice-board on which Ahmet Çevik had pinned a photo supposedly of Anne Brennan. The hand-printed notice didn't name her, only stated – in my English and in Ahmet's Turkish – *Missing person: information concerning this lady's whereabouts to Ahmet Çevik, gulet Keyiflioğlu, please.*

Schreiber's lips moved as he practised the name *Keyiflioğlu* in a whisper to himself, getting his own German-accented version of it into his memory.

Shouldering his way out, then. The sunglasses hid his frown. Turning left to where the road bent south-westward, crossing it there and continuing over to the quayside, threading his way through the sauntering, noisy crowd and reading the names of the boats as he passed them.

Turkish flags everywhere, an overlay of scarlet on all the others – British, German, French, American, Dutch, Swedish, Italian, Swiss . . . And languages of course to match, mostly at the tops of people's voices. Registrations Hamburg, Villefranche, Rye, Valletta, St Helier, Boston . . .

And Marmaris, under the ornamentally scripted name *Keyiflioğlu*.

He walked on past, just as a girl's back view vanished into the *gulet*'s interior. A young crewman – or it could have been Ahmet Çevik, for all Schreiber knew – was sitting in the open stern, filleting a large, pink-fleshed fish: returning his attention to this task now after turning to glance over his shoulder as the girl – tall, slim, with a lot of glossy brown hair, was as much as Schreiber had taken in – went inside. Schreiber stopped, leant his shoulder against a corner of the building containing public showers and WCs: there was a patch of shade here, and a clear view of that *gulet*; sooner or later the girl was bound to reappear, and the first thing he wanted was a good look at her.

That fish wouldn't take all day to fillet. The lad would remove himself, some time soon. Schreiber took off his sunglasses, polished them on the loose edge of his T-shirt, put them back on again and reached to his hip pocket for a cigarette.

Tommy Fountain saw him pull out a crumpled pack of Camels and light up. Leaning back against the wall in that patch of shade, which was as good a reason as any to have chosen that spot to wait in. It was only 11 a.m. but the temperature was well into the eighties, and climbing.

Didn't look much like a Turk, Tommy thought. Wouldn't have thought he was a Brit, either. But whoever, and *what*ever – whether or not he was police, was the question – he was undoubtedly watching the *Keyiflioğlu*. So it was just as well that old habits of caution, ingrained in years long past, in training and practice of the techniques of infiltration and evasion, had prompted this recce before boarding.

Tommy had come from Izmir in a vanload of carpets, the van had stopped at a wayside café a couple of miles short of the town – there'd been storks nesting on the café's roof – and from there he'd yomped. If the police had been watching the

Çerçis they might have been waiting in town to see the van unloaded. Might *not*, too: he wasn't convinced that they were expending very large resources in pursuing him. But there was no reason to take risks that were avoidable.

If this sweaty-looking guy was a policeman, it would mean that Matt's message passed through Halim Çerçi had been leaked – telephone bugged, or one of the office staff an informer. But – Tommy's powers of observation had been sharpening recently, out of necessity – that watcher in the funny hat wasn't acting like a man staking out an R/V in expectation of some known person's imminent arrival. On such a task you'd be looking at faces – those approaching, passing, in particular any that were just hanging around. Such as this face here – property of T. Fountain – this fine and noble countenance, complete with ginger beard trimmed to perfection by Halim's own barber: it hadn't drawn a single glance. All the guy was watching was the *gulet*.

Not for someone whom he expected to arrive, but for someone who must be on board already.

Like – Matt Johnson?

Well. One good turn deserved another. The cold shower to be followed by iced beer, to which one had been looking forward rather keenly for some time, would have to wait until this situation somehow resolved itself.

Ahmet, at the small table opposite his galley, was working out accounts, expenditure on stores consumed during his recent charter by the Italian family. And his crewman, who'd just come down into the galley with the dissected fish, knew better than to speak to him when he was doing his sums.

Gill didn't, though. She was talking as she came out of her cabin.

'Going to the bank to cash a cheque, Ahmet. Be about ten minutes.'

He closed his eyes, opened them again . . . 'Better I go with you.'

'Oh, there's no need, really . . .'

'Matt would say I should go with you.' He capped his ballpoint. 'To – *escort* you, is the word?'

'But I don't *want* to be escorted . . . Please, Ahmet, relax, I'll

231

be back in ten, fifteen minutes – OK?'

'What you want when you come back? Bloody Mary?'

'My God no, not in this heat. I mean thanks a lot, but –
lemonade, maybe?'

'OK. This evening, Bloody Mary.'

'When Matt gets here. Sure, you're on.'

Last night he'd made Brandy Sours, the best she'd ever
tasted, and powerful enough almost to have obliterated her
recollection of the woman with the flail. *Almost* . . .

She went out into the *gulet*'s stern, down the plank to the
quayside and turned left. The nearest bank was about 800
metres away – through the garden-café, then over the road
where it ended and along past the Turkish Bath.

Ahmet picked up his ballpoint and started again on the
column of figures. He'd reached about the point he'd been at
before, about halfway, muttering the figures to himself, when
he heard the thumping rattle of the plank again – much heavier
weight on it than Gill's – and then a shout of 'Matt? Matt
Johnson? Ahmet Çevik?'

He dropped the ballpoint, shot up the steps into the stern.
Remembering the name of the Englishman Matt had warned
him might appear at some stage . . .

A tall, bearded figure, in jeans and a loose cotton shirt and
trainers, back-pack . . . 'I am Ahmet Çevik. You Tommy
Fountain?'

'Right.' Shaking hands quickly: 'Hi, Ahmet . . . Matt not
here?'

'He went yesterday to Kekova, he will be back maybe this—'

'Who's the girl just went ashore?'

'Gill – Matt's girl—'

'Oh, Christ.' The big man swung away, telling Ahmet as he
dumped his pack and then started back down the plank,
'There was a guy watching this ship, then she came ashore and
he followed her. What's going on here, for Christ's sake?'
Bounding down the plank: on the quay he glanced back, saw
Ahmet following, turned left and began to trot. Ahmet stayed
with him, the two of them thrusting, dodging through the
crowd: Tommy shouted, 'Look out for a baseball cap, red
stripes . . .'

'I should have gone with her—'

232

'Any idea where—'

'Yes! The bank!' Pointing – towards the open-air café and the shopping area beyond it – 'That way!'

Gill turned in to the park-like café: the trees made it cooler than walking along the outside, the sunbaked paving. There were a few customers – more Turks than tourists – at the tables, consuming coffee, pastries, soft drinks, ices, and a waiter offered her a table, was rewarded with a smiling 'Not right now, thank you . . .'

At the eastern boundary of the gardens she waited while a truck loaded with melons rumbled by, heading for the market. Then a battered Ford with screaming tyres, and two high-snarling mopeds both with teenage girls on their pillions: behind that lot it was clear for long enough to get across.

Schreiber at her heels.

The Turkish Bath was the building on the corner, and the bank she was making for was just beyond it. But this side of it, and about forty or fifty metres up on the left, was the photographer's shop where the prints were being made from that negative. They'd promised to have a dozen ready for her by noon: it was only about eleven now, but it could be worth a try, maybe save another walk into town when it would be even hotter than it was now.

She crossed this road. The melon lorry was a block away, grinding up towards the market. She reached the pavement, turned to her right. Remembering that there was a bank along here too, near the next intersection. So no problem . . .

A slobby-looking guy, pushing up on her right, the outside of the pavement, was crowding her. She edged left, to let him pass. Baseball cap, jeans, T-shirt bulging, a shine of sweat on his face as he looked at her – level with her now, keeping pace . . .

'Hi . . .'

She turned away, and stopped to look in the window of a carpet shop. Thinking *Ugh* . . . and *Of all the nerve* . . .

He'd stopped too. But the carpet merchant was in his doorway, welcoming her. These guys didn't miss their chances, one spark of interest was all it took to get them going: she'd seen him hovering there before she'd stopped, guessing

233

the presence of a third party would be enough to shake this person loose.

'I have most beautiful carpets inside, my lady, most beautiful and best value in Fethiye. If my lady would care to see? Only to look, is no obligation . . .'

'Why, thank you.' She glanced, frowning, at the slob. 'Go away. Or I'll ask him to call a cop.'

'Oh – not to do *that*.' Damp hand on her arm. 'Look, baby—'

'Get *away* from me!'

A tourist couple stared in quick alarm, then averted their eyes and hurried on. She felt a prick on her arm – on the side away from the carpet salesman – recoiled as far as she could, but he held on to her, let her see the knife, its point against her ribs now . . . 'Make it easy for yourself, baby. We take a walk, a talk, is all. This way.' He nodded to the carpet man, said something in Turkish, something like – she guessed – 'Thank you. Another time . . .'

Walking – he was more or less propelling her, by one arm – towards the market. She was remembering Ahmet, hearing his voice insisting 'Best I go with you', and 'Matt would say I should go with you . . .'

Matt would have been damn right. *Ahmet* was damn right too . . .

Humour them – she'd heard that was the thing. She asked him – his left arm linked through hers, tightly clinched, and the knife in his right hand, that arm across his swollen belly and the blade out of sight under the bent left elbow – 'What do you want to talk about?'

'You have – put around a photo? Or your Turkish friend doing this? Photo of a young woman is looking like you? Also yesterday you are meeting with Selma?'

Selma . . .

That crazy woman: the flail . . .

Nothing accidental about this, then. It wasn't one of those encounters. Wasn't something you'd talk your way out of, either. Shock made her head swim.

Anne . . .

Christ, that flail . . .

'I don't have the least idea what – or *who*—'

234

'I have here a car. Not so far, here after the corner. We go to have some talk – with Selma fortunately I am speaking Turkish, so – hey, *damn*—'

She'd tugged away, a jerk to get distance between her body and the knife-point – then twisting aside, hacking out backwards at his shins, two guys close ahead of them, she'd begun it because of them, because it could be the last chance she'd get before he'd have her in some car. Schreiber grabbing at her, snarling '*Bitch*, goddam—'

'Gill!'

A bellow from behind: people running, there was a scuffle back there, more yelling and a woman's scream. The two Turks – middle-aged and dressed in dark business suits – were only a few yards away, shouting at the slob, who'd given up trying to regain control – couldn't use the knife now he had an audience – and decided to cut his losses. One of the two Turks made a futile attempt to tackle him as he charged between them, running towards the corner: he shouldered that one off, sheathing the knife on his belt as he ran – lumbering, no athlete – and then this big guy was sprinting right up the centre of the road, long-legged, *really* sprinting – large, bearded, limbs pumping like pistons as he came pounding by, caught Schreiber, a hand clamping down on one thick shoulder jerking him round and a kick tripping him, heavy body airborne then smashing down: and now *Ahmet* flashing past, for God's sake . . .

Ahmet was kneeling on him. The last seconds of the action had been a blur of movement partially obscured by bodies intervening, but she thought the big man had lifted the guy's shoulders and then slammed him down, bouncing his head on the pavement. Talking fast to Ahmet: then he – not Ahmet, the other one – wasn't there any more . . . People crowding round, she didn't have any view at all now until out of the swirl of people he was suddenly here beside her – hands grasping hers, bearded face peering down: 'You OK? Gill, is it?'

'Yeah. I guess . . . Who—'

'Friend of Matt's. Expect I'll see you later. Listen, I wasn't here – remember, please? Ahmet caught him, tripped him – OK?'

* * *

235

'Then' – she was telling Emma and Ted – 'the whole street was full of cops . . .'

And she'd been suppressing – just about – a nervous breakdown . . .

Now, they were in the *Keyifliöglu*'s stern, sitting with drinks around the table; Ahmet's crewman, the poetic-looking Mustapha, had already set it for lunch, the fish was baking in the oven and Tommy Fountain was down below, showering and hacking off his beard. Gill was still shaky, but a lot better than she had been. The whole thing had happened so fast, had been over so quickly.

Unlike Anne's ordeal. The harsh reality of it, of its continuance *now*, had been brought home to her in that spasm of violence and its aftermath; it was weighting her mind now, a constant, nagging discomfort.

The Lawries had been on board when she and Ahmet had got back from the police station, where they'd been interrogated for about an hour and finally signed statements. Ahmet had told them – these were the civil police, in blue uniforms – that he'd gone after Mrs Paget because she'd left her passport behind – in his care – forgetting she'd need to show it in the bank before they'd accept her cheque. She was his guest temporarily because although she was crewing in the *Bird of Dawning* she hadn't wanted to go on the Kekova cruise; Matt Johnson, skipper of the *Bird*, was an old friend and he'd promised him he'd take care of her.

'So. You went after her. And saw this person dragging her along the street. Much bigger man than you, eh?'

'Maybe. But this other fellow—'

'Yes, who was he?'

Ahmet had no idea. He'd appeared, then vanished. No, not British: maybe a Dane, Norwegian maybe . . .

Schreiber had told the police his name and that he was German, and he'd come to Turkey as crew in a cruising yacht. They'd asked him 'Name of yacht?' and he'd gazed around, looking baffled, muttered eventually that he didn't remember: then he'd forgotten his name too, and couldn't believe he'd been trying to abduct some young woman. They'd locked him up, and a police officer had intimated that he'd be staying until his memory improved. Meanwhile they'd be searching through crew-lists at all the ports of entry, looking for the name which he'd given them before amnesia had set in.

Emma said, 'It could be concussion. If he banged his head on the road – pavement – you said he fell—'

'Could be, I guess.' She nodded: getting a quick mental replay of the action, Matt's ex-Royal Marine friend lifting that guy like one end of a log and letting him clunk down again . . . 'No matter what, they're holding him. They had a lot of witnesses, not just us, who saw him trying to drag me to his car.'

It felt now as if she'd been in some kind of daze. Fright, anger, then desperation: but recollection was like seeing it from outside, an almost detached view of herself being hustled along that street. As if it might have been Anne, maybe, a form of sublimation. And every time she let herself go back over it she ended praying *Get here, Matt, hurry* . . .

In her own interrogation she'd told them that she'd stayed in Fethiye because she was looking for her sister, who'd taken off from Menorca with some Frenchman or Algerian, hadn't been heard of since and might, just *might*, be in Turkish waters. Just something she'd said in a letter, nothing definite: and being far from certain that her sister was even at this end of the Mediterranean she hadn't approached the authorities, with just a flimsy notion . . .

What connection did she think there might be – the police captain had asked – between the apparent disappearance of her sister and the attack on her this morning?

'I told him no connection at all that I knew of. That guy Schreiber tried to chat me up, then when I didn't want to know he turned violent, that's all. Only reason I mentioned Anne is because they may hear about the photos and the questions we've been asking, so better they should hear it from me than wonder why I *didn't* tell them.'

Emma asked, 'But you *do* think there's a connection?'

'I know there is. I know more than that, too – *now* . . . But we decided – *I* decided – no cops. Because they told my father – the kidnappers did when they telephoned him – from Madrid, for God's sake – that if any police came near they'd kill her. He was sure they meant it, and the FBI—'

Ted echoed, 'FBI?'

'My father called them in, Ted. Fact is – confidentially – he's in a position where the demand doesn't have to be for money, it could be for – well, material, technical stuff.'

'Oh, aye?' Ted's eyes were shrewd: as an industrialist himself he was quick to catch on. 'You didn't say, did you . . .? What kind of—'

'I don't know, Ted. Wouldn't be for public knowledge, you see . . . That's another reason my father didn't want Turkish police brought in on it – as well as being sold on the idea she's in Spain anyway . . . But you see why I didn't tell you two, I hope?'

'Not much the wiser now you *have* told us, are we . . . Does Matt know about it?'

'Sure.' Gill checked the time. Counting hours, minutes, wanting him back here *now* . . . 'Sure, Matt knows . . . well, not what I know now, what that shithead as good as told me . . .'

'Wouldn't mind if someone'd tip *me* off to what's going on,' Ted said. 'Like for starters – this bloke who's turned up – you say he's a friend of Matt's—' He'd jerked a thumb towards the cabins. 'Well, where'd he spring from?'

'Good question. But I don't know.' Gill called, 'How's that shark coming, Ahmet?'

'Shark coming one minute . . . Anyone want more to drink?'

Nobody did, immediately. This was the heat of the day, and hunger predominated. Ted had already had one of Ahmet's Bloody Marys, the girls had had lemonade and Tommy had taken a couple of fat bottles of the local beer down with him. Gill said, coming back to the subject, 'What you were saying, Ted – what's going on – I guess the first thing's to see what's in the film – which we should get between five and six, right?'

Emma nodded. 'That's what he said.' She'd taken it straight to the Kodak shop when she and Ted had arrived in their taxi: from there they'd come to the *Keyifliöglu*, finding only Mustapha, who since he spoke no English couldn't tell them where anyone was, or what was happening. Then this tall Englishman with the ginger beard had slunk on board and dived below, saying only that he was a friend of Matt's and that Gill and Ahmet were OK, don't worry.

Gill said, 'So we should have the film by six, and Matt by maybe eight.'

'Must say, I'm looking forward to seeing old Matthew . . .'

Tommy, in the doorway. Gill waved at him: 'Hi, Tommy. Here, plenty of room, food coming *very* shortly now' – she raised her voice, to reach Ahmet – 'We *hope*—'

'I'll have mine inside here, if you don't mind. Less public.'

'May be a daft question' – Ted craned round to look at him – 'but you saved Gill from that bloke, and now – now you're hiding? Reckon they'll be after you, do you?'

'Well.' Tommy stroked his newly-shaven jaw. 'Just sort of keeping a low profile, Ted.'

'Not too easy, the size you are.'

'Shaving-off won't have helped much either. Left me skew-bald. Stick out like a sore thumb, won't I?'

Tanned around the eyes, pale at lower levels . . .

'We told them we thought the guy had a *black* beard, Tommy. Couldn't say *no* beard, so many others saw you. But just to confuse it a little.'

'Good thinking . . . Where did Matt find you, Gill?'

'He didn't – I found *him*. On Menorca . . . Tommy, Ahmet wants to get past you.'

With the food: mouth-watering aroma . . .

Gill said, 'The thing is, Tommy, my sister Anne's been kidnapped, and – well, Matt'll tell you all about it, but here and now *I* can tell you – and for *sure* – which is a lot more than we've known until now, we've really been groping in the dark – *this* is where they've got her.'

Ahmet stopped. Holding the heavy, laden tray. Rock-still, staring at her.

'Here?' Rapid blinking . . . 'In Fethiye?'

'Close by.' She hesitated: began to say something, then stopped . . . 'Look – let's save it until Matt's here.'

Bringing the *Bird* into Fethiye as late as 9 p.m., I was lucky to find room for her on the yacht quay. The wind had got up, as it tended to, during the afternoon, and I'd been motoring right into a 20-knot headwind gusting 25, with a sea to match, until about sunset when it had eased off again – just as predictably. The result was I was an hour later than I'd hoped to be.

Ahmet's winger, Mustapha, was on the quay to take my

stern line; then he disappeared, and by the time I'd secured properly and got the plank out I had Emma, Gill and Ted filing over it, in that order. The Lawries said I was a sight for sore eyes (Emma) and better late than never (Ted), and yes, they'd had a terrifying taxi-ride up from Kaş; then they went down to their cabin, which was tactful of them, and a few minutes later Gill and I began to get our breath back. Until then I think all she'd said was my name, and all I'd said was hers: love's a very peculiar condition, if you consider it detachedly, at least its symptoms are. But now she said, in another gust of breath, 'I've a *hell* of a lot to tell you.'

'I've one thing to tell you. Never missed anyone so badly in my life.'

'Good. I've been hurting too . . . Listen – the boat Anne was on is called *L'Ecstase*.'

'Got that from the film? It *is* hers?'

'And how. Wait till you see my little sister . . . Matt, would you faint if I told you I was kidnapped this morning?'

'Oh, Christ, *no* . . . Gill, my darling—'

'It's OK, it's OK.' She began to cry – letting some of it out, at last – 'I'm *here*, Matt, no need to fuss, I—'

'Who – how—'

She told me: in short, jerky sentences while I cursed myself for having left her, for not having listened to my own instincts . . . 'Who is this arsehole, and how did you get away?'

'Guy called Schreiber. My guess is he'd be a friend of Raoul's – as of now he's in the slammer, downtown. Concussed, I guess. Tommy' – she giggled, like hysteria on the heels of tears – 'Tommy used the asshole's head to bang on the road with.'

'Tommy . . .'

'And Ahmet, they did it between them.'

'Where is he now – in *Keyifliöglu*?'

'Right. Quote keeping a low profile unquote, but he wants to see you to discuss *his* business – OK?'

'Anything else?'

'Only that I know where Anne is.'

'You mean – the boat, *L'Ecstase*?'

'No, I don't. Listen – yesterday – Matt, you know that spooky deserted village to the south here?'

240

'Kaya Koy?'

'Right. Well, yesterday . . .'

So I heard it all – about the woman with the flail who'd appeared to hate her – but had probably just recognized her, been stunned at the sight of her, *because she was by this time familiar with her looks – Anne's looks* . . . And what the German had said: which seemed to tie it all together. It was a lot to think about, left plans to be made: my first, virtually immediate conclusion being that one should on no account make any move without prior reconnaissance and planning, some hard pre-thinking to avert any risk of blowing it, getting Anne killed.

I went down to see the Lawries: to thank them again for the way they were helping, and to check they were generally OK, had had enough to eat and would help themselves from the *Bird*'s bar if they wanted, play the radio or tapes, whatever, but excuse me and Gill while we went over to Ahmet's *gulet* to talk things over with Tommy. Although first I wanted a quick look at those snapshots – which, had it not been for Ted and Emma, we wouldn't have had until tomorrow.

Gill spread them on the table, and added one which she'd kept separately. Close-up of kid sister – starkers. I made a quick recovery: concentrated on the others, particularly those featuring the French boat. Timber-built, I guessed about 36 feet; sloop-rigged, not very well maintained. One snap had been taken from right astern, probably from a dinghy, and showed the name on the transom: *L'Ecstase*, and port of registry Marseilles. Others – most of the pictures, in fact – were of Raoul – tall, slim, deeply tanned, curly hair on his head and chest and a smile that suggested he enjoyed posing, wasn't at all surprised at girls wanting to take his picture. Maybe it was why he'd been so silly as to allow these, which otherwise might have seemed careless. Except he wouldn't have expected them to have fallen into other hands: and it might have seemed odd to Anne if he had *not* allowed photography. Obviously he'd been conning her all the way along . . . Gill murmured, 'I wouldn't call him *beautiful*', and I said actually I wouldn't either; but apparently Anne had said in her letter that *she* thought he was.

There were several shots of Anne – the one I've mentioned,

which except for facial variations could have been Gill – and two others in which she was only topless. Areas normally covered were as deeply tanned as any other part of her, indicating that life on board *L'Ecstase* had – shall we say – verged on the informal.

'OK. We have the name of the boat, and we know we were right, all the way from Mahon to at least Kekova she must have thought she was only along for the' – I hesitated – 'for the beer. Then finally – moment of truth.'

Gill's expression was bleak. I guessed she'd be thinking of the old woman with her flail.

Some moment, that would have been. Some truth.

I said, 'Having the yacht's name, anyway, Ahmet can put the word round.'

'He's been doing exactly that. We decided on it as soon as we saw these. First he checked at the port offices, found no entry for any boat of that name, and since then he's been asking everyone he knows to keep their eyes open for it – including fishermen, who get around all these little coves, he said, and the day-trip *caique* skippers, and so on.'

'Why them? Any special reason *L'Ecstase* should be in any of those places?'

'Got to be *some* place – and she's not in Fethiye. He sent Mustapha to check on that, really scoured the place.'

'Right . . . And now what about the coastguards?'

'*No*, Matt. No way.'

I looked at her. Only questioningly, because I knew she could be right, the bastards could have meant exactly what they'd threatened. On the other hand the coastguard with their fast boats and their ready access to information on all boats either entering or leaving would undoubtedly have been the surest way to locate an individual, named yacht.

But what would be the point, if it ended with Anne dead?

'OK. I've taken one risk already that I shouldn't have. Let's find Tommy.'

Emma said, 'He's a sweety, isn't he?' She was referring to Tommy, not me: but Gill agreed, and Ted admitted that as far as he could see he was a decent enough bloke. I didn't tell them that the Metropolitan Police suspected old 'Sweety' of murder.

And thinking about it, I wasn't at all sure they did. For some time I'd had the feeling that while they'd still be only too pleased to lay hands on him, it was more a genuine desire to have him 'assist them with their enquiries' than to pin a murder charge on him. What was more, I hoped that in the early stages my prodding might have helped to encourage that kind of thinking. If not, I'd wasted a lot of cash on those long-distance calls.

'Gill.' We were walking towards the *Keyiflioğlu*. 'Don't get any idea I'm being callous about your sister, but now he's here I do have to try to help with Tommy's situation too.'

'OK. I won't . . . But – *about* Anne, what—'

'What'll we do . . .? Well, tonight, nothing.' I caught her hand as it swung. 'If we just blundered in there on spec we could really fuck it up. But tomorrow – tomorrow night, say—'

'Don't promise too much, Matt.'

'OK, I won't. Just keep your fingers crossed.'

15

Eleven p.m.'s a bit late for telephoning people, anyway it seemed so, especially at the end of what had been a very long day, but in England it would be only nine o'clock and if Harrison wasn't either working overtime or whooping it up in his local I thought that on a Monday evening he'd most likely be at home. Tommy and I were making the call from the hotel; it's a place I usually steer clear of, but it was a case of necessity – the post office, PTT, as they call it, would be shut, and I didn't expect to have time for telephoning next day – and as it happened we were in luck: the manager, with whom I have not always been on the most cordial of terms, was absent, and there was a friendly, efficient girl on desk duty who booked the call for us.

Another pleasing aspect of it was that Tommy was paying for this. So far, therefore, things were looking good – even better, when the call went through in just minutes. In the PTT a pre-booked call, for which you pay in cash at the end, can take an hour or more getting through, and the alternative is to have a sackful of tokens to feed the machine with after direct-dialling. Anyway, this went through like the proverbial dose of salts, and Mrs Harrison came on the line. Then, I thought the run of luck had ended: Charles was not at home: and no, she didn't expect him back tonight . . . 'Who is that, please?'

I told her, and she astonished me by sounding pleased about it.

'Mr Johnson – I was told to ask you – if you did call tonight, that is – would you give me the number you're at, please, and then wait there, and Chief Inspector Frewin will call you back at once. I mean as soon as I've rung him with your number.'

'Right.' It was on a card on the wall, and I read it out. 'But tell him this is a hotel telephone and I can't hang around here for long, would you? It's getting on for midnight, local time, I'll be thrown out if he isn't quick. Thanks, Mrs Harrison.'

I hung up, explained the situation to Tommy, and went out to the bar to get us a couple of beers. It was crowded and noisy out there – one of the sailing flotillas was in, about a dozen identical small cruising boats tied up at the hotel's jetty – and Tommy was staying out of sight, as far as possible. Not that either of us thought there was much danger of his being picked up by the police, particularly here and at this time of night, but there was no sense in taking unnecessary risks, and apart from this he was a bit self-conscious, with the upper part of his face tanned by Turkish sun and the rest City-of-London white.

He was on his way to Iraq, for God's sake . . .

We'd talked it all out, earlier, on board the *Keyiflioğlu* after I'd got there with Gill, and he'd explained that in coming to Fethiye all he'd had in mind was to collect his money-belt and its contents from me, then yomp east over the camel-trails and offer the Baghdad government his services as a mercenary, either operationally or as an instructor. This would be as effective a way as any of vanishing from Western sight, and he reckoned the Iraqis would welcome him: they had mercenary pilots working for them, very likely other categories too, so why not a former SBS officer?

I thought he was right; he'd have been worth a lot to them – especially in that kind of war, that watery terrain. But I'd suggested it might be a lot better to yomp back to the UK instead, take *those* chances.

'Like prison?'

'I think they want you back there – *now*, anyway – for what you may be able to tell them – to help with their investigation. On which subject, incidentally, any clues to someone with initials GC?'

246

'Graham Calderwood. Merchant banker, stinking rich, pal of old Benedict's. More to the point, he was sniffing around after Penny like a pig after truffles, the last few months.'

'May I tell them that?'

He shrugged. 'Don't let 'em fool you, Matt. *I'm* the candidate. They know you're batting for me, *obviously* they'd let you think I'm off the hook . . . Look – for instance – before it happened, two days before, I more or less told her father I couldn't trust myself not to do her in – then it happens, and I make a run for it . . . What would *you* think, after that?'

'Why on earth . . .?' I stared at him. 'What were you hoping to achieve, telling him such a thing?'

'Trying to make him see she and I really were washed up, that it was pointless saying "try again" . . . He's a widower, goes misty-eyed about the late Mrs B., true love and never a cross word, etcetera, and of course little Penny could do no wrong . . . What I was trying to achieve was make him understand – *without* having to tell him she'd been messing around, which might've given the old guy a heart attack – he had to be made to see I was – well, that I wasn't talking about some storm in a fucking teacup.'

'You *didn't* kill her, did you?'

'No, Matt.' He frowned, glancing at Gill then back at me. 'I did not.'

'Why did you run away, then?'

'Oh . . .' Another look at Gill, and a tired smile . . . 'Takes a lot of telling. It isn't even straight in *my* mind – not all of it, and *that* doesn't make it easy . . . But – well, I'd been away for the weekend – seeing about a non-existent job, actually – and got back on the Sunday night instead of Monday . . .'

He told me about sitting in his car in the garage, having had a lot to drink – which I could believe, having seen him a couple of nights before that – not wanting to have to cope with Penny, deciding to sleep there in the car . . . Then – he *thought* – hearing the front door slam. Or maybe not: he'd done a lot of dreaming since then, and he'd been half-cut at the time, nothing was exactly crystal-clear . . . But finally he'd gone in, and found her body on the stairs and realized she'd fallen down them and broken her neck.

He'd rambled on with a lot of detail – this was the first

247

chance he'd had, I realized, of getting it all off his chest. He'd fallen, for instance, when he'd been carrying her up to her room – their room – and he seemed to think this mattered, had some importance in the narrative: whereas in my view it only underlined the fact that he'd been drunk. I'd interrupted: 'You're getting side-tracked', and Gill had frowned at me: I asked her what was the matter, and she said, 'Let him tell it his own way, Matt.'

'You're right. Sorry, Tommy.'

He went on with it, and told us how, after he'd put Penny's body on or in the bed, the telephone had rung, it had been her father, and he'd told the old boy she was fine, fast asleep.

This, to him, was the real clincher. And I thought the same: as he himself put it, no innocent man would have told that lie.

Gill pointed out – making her own interruption, just after she'd told me to keep quiet – that there was another way of looking at it: that no one in the state Tommy must have been in, and in those circumstances, could easily have told the truth.

It was a good point, too.

Tommy said, having agreed with her, 'But I remember thinking at the time *God, I've framed myself* . . . And I had, hadn't I?'

'Then you called Harry Loder.'

'Yes. Thought of you, and – you know, like a rat in a trap, all one thought of was getting out – there it was, you and that boat. You've always stuck by your chums, and – Christ, if anyone ever needed – or say *felt* they needed—'

'But after you got on board, you ducked out.'

'Yeah.' He looked at Gill; muttered, 'I suppose *you* think I'm crazy.'

'I do not. I think you've been through a dreadful experience; I also think you're the guy who saved my life today.'

'Hardly *life*—'

'Sure of that?'

He shook his head. 'Quite a girl this, Matt.'

'I agree. *Why* did you—'

'I saw I was about to drop you in it. You'd have taken me across – you'd already said you would – and by not telling you what had happened – which I couldn't have explained even as semi-clearly as I just have – I'd have been conning you, wouldn't I? – and they'd soon be on to me, I'd be caught and you'd be an accessory to murder. Wouldn't have been easy for you to prove you hadn't known what I was running away from, would it? You know, I'd got sort of clear-headed suddenly – the brandy you gave me might've done it, I don't know, but I seemed to be thinking straight maybe for the first time in days – and I saw how I might make capital of it *without* getting you into trouble. If I left the car there, once they traced me that far they'd be sure it was the way I'd gone – so I could sneak out the back door – right? – and they wouldn't have anything on you, because you wouldn't have *done* anything.'

'OK in theory.' I was thinking of those coppers' certainty that I'd helped him get away. Despite having no evidence, they thought they *knew* I had, and as far as I could tell they still thought so . . . I asked him, 'Where did you go, then?'

'Made tracks for Harwich, for the Hamburg ferry. But I was really knackered – physically, mentally, the lot. Psychologically . . . I more or less collapsed, luckily in the care of old friends who were – I can't tell you how – but you know them, Matt.'

I could make a guess. Geography was one clue: and people of a kind who – to coin a phrase – don't grow on trees . . . I nodded. 'Go on.'

'Thanks to them, I got my act together, eventually went over on the ferry, then train to Zurich to get some money – which reminds me, Matt—'

'I've got it for you. Whenever you want it.'

'Tonight?'

'No problem.'

'Thanks. Once *again*, thanks . . . But that's about it. I went to these friends I have here in Turkey, then I got your message, and here I am.'

'Dropping by on your way to Iraq.'

'That's about it.'

I tried again to convince him that I didn't think he was wanted for murder, that various things Harrison had said had given me the impression of open minds – of at least partially open minds . . . 'Last time I called him was from Malta. Eight or nine days ago. That was when he asked about the initials GC. He had some question about champagne, too – were you a con-

249

noisseur of wines, would you have paid £120 a bottle for it?'

'Of course I wouldn't . . . But now you mention it, there were champagne bottles all over the place that night – I trod on one, on the stairs, that's why I fell – I think . . .'

'One bottle had your prints on it, Harrison said.'

He smiled: glancing at Gill, then back at me, an expression of friendly derision: 'That's the sort of thing makes you believe I'm in the clear, is it?'

'You're not denying you were in the house. Why wouldn't your prints be here and there? Like on a bottle you'd trodden on – did you pick it up, after you fell?'

I didn't mention the other thing Harrison had told me: that they'd also found his prints on the telephone beside the bed in which Penny must have been lying dead at the time he'd taken one call and made two others. I didn't say anything about it because I didn't want Gill to hear it. I wanted her to believe in Tommy's innocence as I did, and there was a grisly, seemingly cold-blooded quality in that episode that might shake confidence, especially I thought in a female mind. In fact, it was easy enough to comprehend: the body had been lying there, and the telephone had been beside it, and it had begun to ring, so he'd answered it. If you described it in a certain way – as a prosecuting counsel might in a courtroom, for instance – it could *seem* like the kind of ruthlessness one might associate with murder, but it didn't have to be, at all.

I said, 'I'm pretty sure I'm right, Thomas. Not a hundred per cent, I'll admit there's a bit of a gamble in it, but in your shoes I'd take the chance, and go back . . . There's no chapter and verse I can give you, it's how it's been shaping in my mind since I had that last talk with Harrison. I'm pretty damn sure they're still investigating, *not* simply chalking it up to you.'

'Wishful thinking, old Matt.' He told Gill, 'He's all right, though, under all that bullshit. If you've got any sense, you'll put your brand on him.'

'I might, at that.'

'I'll send you a wedding present from Iraq.'

At least he seemed to be back to normal. His brain was working, he wasn't weeping salt tears for himself as he had been – metaphorically speaking – in London, he wasn't even

250

drinking excessively. He was wrong, I thought, about the police investigation, Iraq, etc., and I hoped the call to Harrison might help to change his mind.

But a life sentence – which is what he thought he might be facing if he did go back – isn't something to be contemplated lightly. And he'd have had this in his mind since the night of May 24th – five weeks ago. I thought he was misjudging the situation, but I could see his point of view.

So, after that session on board the *Keyiflioğlu*, I took Gill back to the *Bird*, and retrieved the money-belt. Then yomped east to the hotel, where Tommy had already booked the call to Harrison. Now we were waiting for it to be returned by Harrison's boss, Frewin.

Didn't have to wait long, either. The desk-duty girl had taken several calls, but this time she held the receiver up, waving it above her head and calling down the length of the foyer, 'Mr Johnson? Call from London.'

There's a booth near the desk. Tommy and I crammed half into it with the door open, and I held the receiver so he could hear it about as well as I could.

'Chief Inspector . . . What's new?'

'I'll start by asking you, Mr Johnson, whether you're in communication of any sort with Captain Fountain.'

I'd been prepared for this question, and had a slightly ambiguous answer ready for him.

'I'd say I *might* be. If he turned up in Turkey, that is. He used to have friends here, he'd probably get in touch with them . . . Put it this way – if you had anything for him, I could *try* to – to establish communications.'

I knew he knew about Tommy's Turkish friends, because Interpol had told the Turkish police about them, and only the Met could have told Interpol. But Frewin didn't have to know I knew it: although he could guess his head off, and welcome . . .

He said in his rather dry, quiet voice, 'I'm going to pretend you *are* in touch with him. For the purposes of this conversation. Or at any rate that you have been, and could be again. And I'll ask you what Charles Harrison has already asked – can you put names to the initials GC?'

'Yes, I can. Graham Calderwood.'

'Ah-hah . . .'

251

'It cost you about a pound, saying that.'

'You're right. And let's not waste money beating about the bush: for instance, I won't ask you how come you're able to give me that answer right off the bat when you couldn't answer the same question to Charles Harrison a week ago ... Mr Johnson – would you accept my word that I don't believe Captain Fountain killed his wife?'

'Yes. *I* would. Not so sure he would, though. He might think you were trying to trick him into going back. I think that to have scarpered in the first place he must have been damn sure you'd have it in for him.'

'All we had was a great deal of circumstantial evidence. Which would neither convict him nor convince us. On the other hand I can tell you, in confidence, that we now have one strong suspect. You can believe me, and so can your friend. I *hope* he will, because I need his help.'

'I'll – see if I can pass that on.'

'This Graham Calderwood. He's just returned to this country and I expect to be interviewing him tomorrow morning. What would help me enormously – as well as being in Captain Fountain's interests – would be to know whether he had any kind of personal – well, say friendship – with the late Mrs Fountain.'

'Yes, he did. He was chasing her.'

Pause. Surprise. In the brief silence I could visualize the effect of what would have been an unexpectedly positive answer.

'D'you know this for sure, Mr Johnson?'

'I remember Tommy telling me. Must have been when I saw him in London. His description has stuck in my mind: he said Calderwood was sniffing after Penny like a pig after truffles.'

'Well, well ... It might surprise Captain Fountain, then, to hear that his former father-in-law, as well as an associate of his by name of Martin-Smith who is a personal friend of Calderwood's, *not* only a business acquaintance, deny emphatically that he – that's to say Calderwood – with whom their business connection is I understand close and on-going – could ever have met the late Mrs Fountain except on one occasion, some formal reception in the City.'

I saw Tommy's expression, and told Frewin, 'You can take

252

it from me that Fountain would be astounded.'

'I see . . .' The policeman cleared his throat. 'Mr Johnson – you've been helpful, in your way, but – coming down to brass tacks, now, may I with all respect ask you to stop playing the bloody fool, let me talk to him?'

My turn to be caught wrong-footed. He was chancing his arm, of course, but it made sense: in his shoes I'd have made the same guess, I thought . . . Tommy had moved out of the booth. He was standing with his hands up to his head, as if to support the weight of his brains . . . I extemporized, to Frewin, 'Just thinking over what you just said. Why you'd imagine—'

'Here.' Tommy shouldered in, taking the receiver. 'Chief Inspector. This is Fountain. *Mister*, not captain. Look—'

As I backed out, there was a strong flow of words from the other end. Tommy was blinking as he listened to it: then when it ended he began, 'Yes, I know, you're right, I'm sorry, just didn't want to end up in bloody gaol for something I didn't do . . . Listen – Benedict must be protecting his daughter's reputation – I'm the natural scapegoat, aren't I? I've disappeared – and Martin-Smith happens to be Calderwood's bosom chum. I can tell you that Calderwood – who incidentally is a prime shit . . .'

'So that's it, Tommy. Back to Blighty.'

'Hope I can trust the bugger.'

'Damn sure you can.' We were on our way back to the *Bird*. I'd told him in that message from Göcek that I wouldn't have room for him, but in this emergency I didn't think the long-suffering Lawries would mind being slightly crowded. It would only be for a day or two: the next 24 or 36 hours, I thought, was going to be the crucial period, as far as the rescue of Anne Brennan was concerned.

Ahmet Çevik, we knew, would have been happy to accommodate him in the *Keyiflioğlu*, but the *gulet* was known to the kidnappers now – at least to the one in gaol, who'd been watching it, and maybe to others as well.

However many of them there might be, which we had no way of knowing. There was that one, who'd called himself Schreiber, and there was Raoul. The flail woman would obviously have been hired locally: she and – again – some

253

unknown number of others. Two other points on the subject of Schreiber were (a) he spoke Turkish, would probably have been recruited because of this, and his information on Gill had come from the flail woman; if he'd received it immediately prior to coming to see for himself, see Gill and – and God knows what, but maybe kidnap her as well – it was possible his colleague/colleagues hadn't known what he was doing; and (b) we had no way of knowing at this stage whether his loss of memory was genuine – or if it was, how long it would last.

But the *Keyifliöglu* was, theoretically, known to them, and so were Gill, Tommy and Ahmet – Tommy only as the bearded runner who'd then vanished, but the possibility of his being recognized did exist. What all this boiled down to was that it wouldn't be wise to use Ahmet's ship now, it would be best for him to stay well clear of whatever action might develop in the next day or so, and – most vital of the lot, as I saw it – Gill had to stay out of public view and *never* be left alone.

I went over these points with Tommy as we walked back along the waterfront road – passing the Yacht Club, which was in full blast, belly-dance music and a roar of voices . . . I filled in some essential background, too, Gill's reasons for having believed Anne might be at this end of the Med, and why no publicity – including resort to police, coastguards, etc. – was acceptable.

'What's her father into, then? Star Wars?'

'Could be. Gill doesn't know any detail, and I don't feel any need to know. All we have to do is get her sister out before she ends up dead.'

'Think that could happen?'

'Been known to, hasn't it? And the father's a hard nut, Gill thinks it's quite likely he'd refuse to pay. Most likely couldn't, anyway, even if he was so inclined. What it comes down to is we're the girl's only hope – and I'd be glad of your help, Tommy. So I'm now saying please do *not* go back immediately.'

'Long as I don't get arrested by the Turks meanwhile. Where do we start, and when?'

'Kaya Koy. The deserted village. That'll be my job, and I hope to persuade the Lawries to come along and give me some cover. My face isn't known to the enemy, you see, and obviously the Lawries aren't either, so the three of us could take a taxi out there, rubberneck around and take snaps while I see whatever there is to be seen. Might be signs of occupation somewhere, but anyway I'll get the layout into perspective, then you and I can sneak back after dark. All right?'

'Fine. May be a bit rusty at the creepy-crawlies.'

'Even rusty, we should be better than some scratch bunch of kidnappers.'

'They aren't dim-witted, though, are they? Or someone isn't. I was thinking – snatch the girl in Menorca, ransom demand's sent from the Spanish mainland, payment presumably to be made in the States, and all the time she's being held here in Turkey – what's more, having come here under her own power!'

'There's an original touch to it, all right.'

'And if it hadn't been for the sister – plus you—'

'Yeah, well, let's not count chickens yet . . .'

'How are we off for weaponry?'

'I've the diver's knife on my Scuba gear. And I can provide another knife for you, if you want one. Otherwise we have our agile brains, and two hands each, two feet each. Which, if you remember, have their uses.'

'But no gun – not even a shotgun?'

'Not even that. It'd be more trouble than it's worth. Anywhere around the Med you'd have to declare it on your customs form, and you'd be up to the eyes in red tape from then on. They might even want to escort you out to the three-mile limit when you were departing, before they'd let you have it back. And if you didn't declare it, and a search found it, they'd have you behind bars in no time at all. And if you did have one and you used it on someone, you'd be in such trouble you'd very soon wish you hadn't.'

'I think I know that kind of trouble.'

'Yes. I suppose . . . But I do have a Vèry pistol. Strictly for distress-signal purposes, of course. At close range it'd be something like a blast of napalm. You wouldn't use it without bloody good reason, but it could be a powerful deterrent.'

'Right.'

'Even that has to be declared, and kept locked up . . . But it's irrelevant, Tommy, we can't leave bodies lying around, I've a

255

living to make and I have to come back here, after all.'

'We have to be fairly skilful, then.'

'Aren't we?'

'*Were*, but—'

'Like riding a bicycle. Once you know it, you do it.'

Things weren't exactly silent along the waterfront. Music and voices still wafted on the cooling air, boat people were returning from restaurants or taking late-night strolls. But it was quietening, and four out of every five boats were darkened, lit only by the moon. It had been a new moon last night at Kekova, and now it was thicker, butter-coloured; it would have started the night higher but it didn't have long to last now; as it lowered itself across the bay its beam lay on the still water like a yellow sword-blade.

Nobody was watching the *Keyiflioğlu*. We paused to check this out, then did the same in the immediate vicinity of the *Bird*. Although there was no reason she'd be known to our enemies: who didn't yet know they *were* our enemies. Didn't know me, anyway: not yet.

We boarded her quietly. There was a light burning in the saloon, but the Lawries had retired and there were faint sounds of snoring from that stern cabin. Gill had evidently turned in too. I showed Tommy where things were – like the head, and a bunk he could use in the saloon: he muttered, 'Matt, I want to tell you, I'm so *bloody* grateful—'

I stopped him. For one thing thanks weren't necessary, and for another his recent agonies were the ill wind that had blown him here at just the right time to help Gill and Anne out of theirs. I said something like 'Sleep well', and crept into the fore cabin, to Gill's expectant, vibrant warmth.

She asked me – about half an hour later – both of us so relaxed we mightn't have had a muscle or a bone between us, and as closely entwined as two limp bodies could be, 'What happens tomorrow?'

'Glad you asked. When I said "keep your fingers crossed" – because you didn't want promises—'

'Ones you mightn't be able to keep, I meant.'

'I've thought since – should've told you – we've got a bit more going for us than crossed fingers. You don't know about

256

the outfit I and Tommy worked in, a specialist Royal Marine thing called SBS. But – well, it's *very* specialist—'

'What way?'

'Commando-style functions. Similar to SAS – you've heard of SAS?' A murmur, assentive movement of her head . . . 'Like that, but with the accent on aquatics. But stuff like penetration of hostile territory. And – specialist skills pertaining thereto, you might say . . . OK, neither of us is in anything like the state of fitness we were then, but that may be offset by the opposition being amateurs. The guy who tried to snatch you, Tommy said, was like a sack of jelly-beans – and there's Anne's pansy-looking Raoul, and some old girl with a stick – well, crikey, unless there's some element we don't know about, I think I *could* realistically be quite hopeful.'

She sighed. Her breath on my chest like a blessing, an intimation of love. I told her, 'So tomorrow – daylight for reconnaissance, then the night for getting her out. It's got to be done right away because if we left it any longer they'd have to catch on to the fact we're around. Might have already, I don't know. The one in police custody might have got word out to others, or they may have got to him – anyone's bet, we're as much in the dark about them as they are about us – for instance, the one in gaol doesn't know that I or this boat exist: and that's a big advantage, or it could be . . . But I ought to qualify the optimism by admitting Anne *is* in danger: that's why we couldn't have risked bashing into Kaya Koy tonight, chancing it and maybe blowing it. When we move in tomorrow – today, now – we'll have it planned, know what we're doing, take a lot of care.'

'What'll the rest of us be doing?'

'Don't know. I may move the *Bird*: we could put her closer to that village, go in the back way. Maybe . . . I think I'll suggest to Ahmet that he takes his ship out of Fethiye – to Göcek maybe – so he doesn't get involved, into trouble here. And *your* big job, my darling, will be looking after Anne after we get her. Better be prepared for this, it may be less easy than you'd think. Being kidnapped – *having been* kidnapped – can have savagely traumatic effects on people. She'll need all the love, comfort, and reassurance you can give her.'

'How come you know all this?'

257

'I was involved, once – in the SBS, I had to deal with a terrorist kidnapping.'

'Successful?'

'Yup. My end of it was. And so will this be.'

'OK.' Her head tilted and I felt lips cool and damp on my shoulder. She murmured, 'I'll be ready . . . Sleep now?'

We were breakfasting in the saloon when Ahmet arrived with news of *L'Ecstase*. He'd been ashore early, telephoning various friends whom he'd asked to do some research in Marmaris, Kaş and Antalya – the nearer ports of entry which Raoul might have used – and it was his man in Kaş who'd come up with the info that *L'Ecstase* had cleared from there three days ago, giving her destination as Rhodes; and she'd made her entry at Antalya a week earlier – *ten* days ago – when a Transit Log had been issued to Raoul Sentier, owner and single-handed skipper, with no crew or passengers. This Transit Log had been surrendered at Kaş, of course, when Sentier had cleared to leave Turkish waters.

So in one blow we'd learnt Raoul's other name, and lost him and his boat. And as far as the Turkish authorities were concerned, Anne Brennan didn't exist.

Tommy said, 'Must be another boat. One Schreiber would have been on. Either that or they've lost their transport out of Turkey.'

Ahmet joined us at the table and accepted coffee. Only out of politeness, I guessed, because this was Nescafé and the instant varieties came nowhere near any Turk's idea of coffee.

I said – having given some thought to this development – 'Damn.'

Ted cocked an eyebrow: 'Tell us?'

'Because I agree, there's probably another boat. Not because Raoul's taken off – I'd guess his job would've been to deliver Anne and then fade out. But I think the ones still here would've had their own transport – line of retreat.' Tommy nodded. I went on, 'Trouble is, this other boat could be any one of hundreds. Could be this guy right next door to us, we've no clues at all, have we? We had an identification, knew what we were looking for, now we're back to square one.'

'But,' Gill said, 'we still know Anne's got to be somewhere in or near Kaya Koy.'

She was right. They'd have all pulled out, obviously, if Raoul had taken her with him. We wouldn't have had the attempted kidnapping of Gill yesterday, for instance.

I nodded to her. 'We can assume one, they've got another boat here, and two, Anne's still at Kaya Koy. And as we don't have any way of identifying the boat we may as well forget it, concentrate on those ruins – locating and then extracting Anne. To kick off with, I want to take a look up there this morning – now – and I wondered, Ted – since you have this passion for rubble – whether you and Emma would like to come along. Have a snoop round, take snapshots, look like real tourists? Gill and Tommy can't, you see, they might be recognized: and on my own I'd look a bit suspect, wouldn't I?'

Ahmet suggested, 'If you like, I ask my friend to drive you?'

'Thanks, but I'll pick a taxi at random in the town – we won't start here at the *Bird*, or come back here afterwards. Because the *Bird*'s unknown to them, so far, all Schreiber got to know about was the *Keyifliöglu* – because we advertised . . . What about it, Emma, will you come?'

She said she'd like to. And Ted sighed, muttered that he supposed . . .

I went up on deck with Ahmet. I was worried by this probability of there being another boat, unidentifiable. My thought had been that if we'd found *L'Ecstase* within our reach Tommy and I might have immobilized her, the kidnappers' likely escape route would then have been blocked, and this should have contributed to Anne's safety – on the theory that if you're going to be stuck in someone else's country you wouldn't want a corpse on your hands as well. I thought the danger to Anne might be very real, and immediate, that it was vital that we should get her *out* of those hands as quickly as possible; part of the equation being what Gill had said about her father, that he might well refuse to deal. For all we knew, he might have done so already.

What it came down to was that we were working in the dark, and the only card we held was knowing (if we were right in *this*, even) that Anne was at Kaya Koy. When you've only one card, that's the one to play.

Hoping to God it's a trump.

I told Ahmet, when we were alone together on deck, that I expected to be taking action of some kind after dark tonight, probably at Kaya Koy, and that depending on how things turned out it might come to the notice of the police – there were a couple of villages quite close, for instance, each with their resident pair of *jandarma*, who are equipped with jeeps, automatic weapons and radios – and as he'd identified himself with us fairly publicly it might be wise for him to put some distance between the *Keyiflioğlu* and the scene of possible disturbance, ideally by sunset this evening. Göcek, for instance, was in easy reach, and if he secured at that pier he'd be surrounded by people who'd be able to give him an alibi if one were needed.

He said he'd think about it. And he'd be glad to help, if he could. But why didn't we go to the police anyway? It was a perfectly good question, but it took a bit of answering, and when he left he still looked doubtful. The thing was, I couldn't tell him about Gill's father and the FBI, all that stuff, but I agreed with them now – as Gill had done all along – that any kind of police action now at that village would just about guarantee Anne's death. I should say, her *immediate* death: because another aspect of the scenario I couldn't discuss with Gill was that she'd seen at least one of their faces, and kidnappers' victims are *never* allowed that privilege, not if the intention is to allow them to survive.

I went below, found breakfast finished, Tommy helping Gill to clear up while the Lawries got themselves ready for our excursion.

'Here?'

'Fine . . .'

The driver pulled his battered Opel off the road, rocking on its soft springs. We'd stopped near the patched-up dwelling that had a TV aerial sticking out of it – Gill had mentioned this – so we'd be retracing Gill's route, near enough. If the old woman was around, I'd like to see her, like to know whether she was always around the same area of ruins – where, if that was so, conceivably Anne might be.

Although it was really roasting hot, I was glad to get out of the car, which smelt of the driver's hair oil. His name was Beercan, he'd told us, and Ted commented on this as we started climbing. 'Funny name to give a fellow – eh?'

'Probably spelt BIRKAN.' I pointed ahead, up the track. 'That must be the chapel where Gill was when the old girl appeared. Bones and skulls around somewhere – want to see them?'

'I'm not bothered.' He glanced at Emma, who grimaced, muttered, 'Nice background for happy-hol snap. No *thank* you, Matt.'

'As you like. But I want your pictures, anyway.' I had my Olympus slung round my neck in true tourist style. 'Stand close together about there, would you?'

There might have been eyes on us – there was a virtually unlimited amount of cover, on this hillside, they'd have the place staked out, surely, and we had to look like the real thing. The chapel was behind me now, and I'd seen the litter of old bones – which didn't grab me all that strongly, either . . . 'Hold it . . . Smile, Ted . . .' He bared his teeth, Emma giggled, and I clicked the shutter – 'Right.'

The background in that snap would be the low stone wall right behind them, then a bird's-eye view of an earth-floored enclosure in which about a dozen singularly dirty-looking sheep were huddling in the shade of a makeshift shelter – what looked like hay on a framework of poles.

The old woman's flock, maybe.

'Shall we go on up?'

Ted said grumpily, 'If we have to.'

I'd swept the hillside with my binoculars. They're small – pocket-sized – but very powerful, a legacy of days gone by. Lowering them now, not wanting to be obvious about this. That entire hillside was tiered with the stone walls of roofless houses: then where they petered out – maybe 450, 500 yards from here – where maybe the village had been expanding, houses being tagged on with wider spaces between them – just beyond there, the brownish-green scrubby hillside fell away to provide an area of dead ground – from this viewpoint – then rose again to the summit of an almost conical hill crowned by the other chapel. Gill had mentioned it as being sited more like a lookout post than a place of worship; she'd told me she'd had

261

a thought of climbing up there so as to look down along the coast in the hope of catching a sight of the *Bird of Dawning* when we'd been on our way to Kekova.

She was right, you'd get a terrific southward view from up there. I put my glasses on it for a moment. Picture-postcard stuff: little white church right on the skyline, background of brilliantly blue sky: *very* Mediterranean.

We moved on. Stopping from time to time to use the binos, also to appear to be taking snapshots while actually seeing no need to expose any more film. I was beginning to agree with Ted about rubble – the experience did pall. One's first impression of this mass of silent stone fired the imagination – as Gill had said, you started by thinking of it as it might have been – heard their voices, saw their children playing, heard the tap-tappings of the old ones' sticks: but after a while monotony dulls the vision, one cluster of broken-down houses looks exactly like the last.

And nobody here. No old woman threatening anyone with her flail, no movement anywhere except our own. Only the sheep were proof that people did come here. Sometimes.

I said, eventually, 'Let's go down to the road, then drive to that end.' The eastern end, where habitation had been sparser and bare hillside took over. Ted didn't object: out of sympathy, maybe, because we'd seen nothing of the kind we'd come here to see. We'd been here quite a while, covered a lot of desolation, peered into a hundred former dwellings. Emma climbed down – carefully, backwards – from stonework she'd been perched on in order to look down into a cistern – small entrance at the top which would once have been sealed with a stone lid, narrow neck expanding to a diameter of maybe fifteen feet and extending to a depth of maybe thirty or forty: internally smooth-sided, dry as dust now but formerly part of a water-storage system. Which they'd have needed, in the summers, on this parched hillside.

Emma said, dusting herself off, 'OK, Matt. Wherever you say . . .'

We went down to the car – it reeked of shag-type tobacco now as well as hair-oil – and I asked Beercan to drive on along this valley road to where the houses ended. He shrugged, glancing at me as if he thought I was a glutton for punishment, and got going, lurching slowly over ruts.

It wasn't far. Past fields of healthy-looking tobacco plants, with deep-green trees growing here and there in isolation amongst it all, and the grey panorama of the ruins above. Grey on a background of dirt and scrub. I touched his arm: 'Stop here, would you?'

'*Tamam* . . .'

Ted asked, 'Want us with you?'

'I'd like it . . . But—'

Emma said, 'Come on, you lazy bastard.'

The dip between the wider expanse of hillside and the smaller, conical hill with the chapel on its summit wasn't dead ground from here as it had been from our previous viewpoint. The spacing out of ruins began where the ground fell away; housing density increased again on the rise opposite, then ended abruptly – only bare scrub then, right up to the skyline.

We went up – less steeply than before – about sixty to seventy-five yards. Wider intervals between the wrecks, but otherwise much the same. I wasn't only looking for traces of kidnappers and of Anne Brennan. I was getting the topography into mind, orientating myself, estimating where the moon would rise and where it would set, memorizing contours and salient features. With so much cover, the broken ground and the litter of ruins, moving around at night wouldn't be difficult. Even if we found we *were* a bit rusty in such arts.

The chapel was right up there in front of us now, and from this angle I could see more clearly what had looked like a window – a dark rectangle in the stone wall that looked almost white in the sun's glare: and – I noticed this with surprise, having seen nothing of it before – something projecting from the top of it.

I focussed the binos; wondering, More TV aerials?

It could have been a broomstick, seen with the naked eye, but it was a rough pole, the kind they'd used for making that sunshade for the sheep. The binos were powerful enough to show its irregularities, that it wasn't all that straight. Sticking out at an angle of about 45 degrees from the vertical . . . And it wasn't a window, it was an entrance. From where I'd been looking at it before, a rise in the ground close to the chapel had obscured the lower part of it, but I could see now it extended to the ground, was in fact a doorway, and the pole jutted from the top of it. Maybe wedged between stones just above it.

It could have been there to hang a flag on. Could have: but there wouldn't have been much point. Except to kids, maybe . . . But stuck out like that it would have full exposure to the south, to the vast spread of Mediterranean at the hill's foot on the other side. In which case . . .

'Look, I'm going up a bit higher. If you can't stand the prospect—'

'Of course we can stand it, silly.'

Ted nodded. I think he'd noticed that I thought I might be on to something. Unfortunately I was very well aware that I might *not* be.

There was a building – remains of one – about halfway up (up to the limit of what might be called the built-up area) that looked more substantial than most. It caught the eye: a camera-crazy tourist might well be drawn to it, and from about there I thought I'd get the view I wanted. I told Emma, 'I'd like to take your picture right in front of that large, square-looking building. Make it that far, d'you think?'

She snorted, and took the lead. I reassured Ted, 'Fear not, that's as far as we can go. Too exposed, higher up, I'll save that bit for tonight.'

'Climb up there tonight, will you?'

'Tell you in a minute.' But I wouldn't make the approach from this direction, anyway. *If* there was any approach to be made.

She did have to be *somewhere* on this hillside. Unless all our thinking was haywire.

Emma stood with her back against the wall of this larger ruin, with her arms out horizontally, chin up and eyes squeezed shut, and ordered 'Shoot!' Ted joined her, shaking his head, telling her he'd been in the sun too long. I raised the camera and the glasses too; camera for camouflage, not wanting to be spotted using binos from this position and into that direction.

Not unless children *had* stuck that pole up.

They hadn't.

The streak of light which I caught in the lenses as I focussed them on it wasn't from the pole itself, but from sunlight glinting on what the pole supported. The gleam slanted down in a shallow curve, then curved up again to a bushy-topped tree all by itself on the skyline to the left, maybe a hundred yards from the chapel. Or maybe only fifty yards. Depending on its angle in the horizontal plane, which one couldn't be sure of from here. What I *was* sure of, though, was that that hairline of brilliance was the sun glinting on shiny-coated wire, which couldn't be there for any purpose other than radio reception and/or transmission.

I suppose whoever had put it up hadn't thought of it reflecting sunlight; maybe hadn't thought of anyone having any reason to come snooping, either. Tourists wouldn't bother: they'd have seen all they wanted lower down.

I took the Lawries' photograph. Actually did take one, this time, thinking even at this stage that it might be a moment worth recording. Then, beyond them, a flash of vivid blue — bird, could only have been a roller: I'd been told they nested in these ruins, rollers and also golden orioles . . . I'd never seen one in the wild before, and I'd moved a short way up the slope thinking it might have pitched just over that crest, when I saw the tent.

16

Detective Chief Inspector Ronald Frewin, accompanied by Charles Harrison, rang the bell of the Calderwoods' house in Kensington at about the time Johnson and the Lawries were setting off for Kaya Koy. As British Summer Time is two hours behind local Turkish time it must have seemed very early in the day to a man who'd flown back from New York only the night before.

Frewin apologized to the indignant Mrs Calderwood, but regretted it was absolutely necessary that he should interview her husband there and then, irrespective of jet-lag and the fact he was allegedly in the bath.

They sat down in the morning room, where she left them, Harrison nursing a rather large briefcase and Frewin scanning the columns of *The Times*, and were there about twenty minutes before Calderwood appeared: in dark trousers, striped shirt, silk tie, Cashmere cardigan. A physically impressive man – over six foot, broad-shouldered, thick silver-grey hair, and he obviously kept himself in trim; but he was pale, with dark rings under his eyes and a tense, nervous manner.

Apologies were repeated, and better received than they had been by his wife. He murmured something about realizing they had a job to do: but so had he, and after the transatlantic flight

267

he wasn't feeling at his best . . . 'So let's get it over with. What d'you want to ask me?'

Frewin, who is a small man, has a small, hooked nose like an owl's beak, and small round eyes to match. (Harrison told Tommy, 'Bit like a budgie, tell you the truth.')

He smiled perfunctorily, and began: 'You're acquainted – were acquainted, I should say – with the late Mrs Fountain, sir?'

'Acquainted, yes.'

'And with her husband.'

'I've met him a couple of times. Briefly.'

'You saw Mrs Fountain rather more frequently, I believe.'

'You believe wrongly, then. In fact that's nonsense. Who—'

'Mrs Calderwood has told us—'

'*What?*'

'Mrs Calderwood has told us' – the brown eyes blinked at him – 'that on the evening of Sunday May 24th' – Frewin consulted notes – 'you were on a flight to New York – BA179, takeoff six-thirty p.m. – Mrs Calderwood found this noted in your engagement book, and no doubt you'd confirm that you travelled on that flight?'

'Presumably I did.'

'According to your wife, sir, it was a Concorde flight. In fact the aircraft was a Lockheed Tristar. I suppose she only assumed you'd have been travelling by Concorde – as you invariably do?'

'She – might have made some such assumption.'

'There *are* Concorde departures on Sunday evenings, I understand. A little later, though. I suppose you wanted to – to get away at that time . . . But – are you quite sure you did take that flight? Didn't travel instead on Concorde flight 001 next morning?'

'You told me it's in the book, I thought. I travel a lot, I can't remember every single flight . . .'

'Your umbrella was in the Fountain house that night, sir. That's to say, next morning, it was there.'

'My – umbrella . . .' Frewin's way of abruptly switching subjects – it was the second time he'd done it, in a space of about three minutes – had the effect of keeping Calderwood off-balance. He put a hand to his forehead, shut his eyes: the equivalent of a fighter going into a clinch, needing to steal breathing-space ... Eyes open then, as if something had clicked: 'Heavens – *that*'s where it was. *That* old gamp ... Fountain had it, eh? I lost it *weeks* before ...'

'Where did you lose it, sir?'

'Until this moment, I'd no idea. But it has sentimental value, you see – my father's, the initials were for Gerald Calderwood ... So Fountain had it – I suppose some day when I'd been to see old Benedict—'

'I didn't say Captain Fountain had it, sir. I said it was in his house on the morning after Mrs Fountain died of a broken neck. She'd been entertaining a male visitor that evening, Mr Calderwood, a visitor with whom she'd shared champagne – he'd brought the champagne with him, we believe – and caviar.'

'Really ...'

'Would you have any objection to giving us your finger-prints, sir?'

Frewin had moved one hand, indicating Harrison's brief-case, which contained the equipment. Calderwood's eyes went to it, returned to the Chief Inspector's ... 'Why should you want my—'

'Standard reason, sir – "to eliminate from our enquiries". I'm sure you'd like to be eliminated from this lot?'

'Didn't even know I was – involved in them. Or how I *could* be. Apart from merely *knowing* the Fountains—'

Harrison said quietly to his chief, 'The right hand's all I need.' Frewin nodded, and looked back at Calderwood, who'd stopped short in mid-protest ... 'You see, sir, the umbrella was – we feel certain – left in the Fountains' house by the man whom Mrs Fountain entertained that evening. That *night*, I should say.'

'Well, if I'd left the thing in old Benedict's offices – the odds are that Fountain himself—'

'When Captain Fountain arrived home that night – rather late – we've reason to believe his wife was already dead. And he entered through the garage – having driven into it, sat in the vehicle for – well, for some little while – and—'

'Why would he have done that?'

'He was hoping his wife would go to bed so he wouldn't

have to talk to her, sir, is *his* explanation.'

'*His?*' Calderwood looked stunned. 'Are you telling me Fountain's turned up?'

'If I might keep to the point, sir . . . Your umbrella was still quite damp next morning. On account of being a bit of an antique – you'll agree, they wouldn't make 'em with that fabric now, not in these days of synthetics, eh? So having been out in the rain – did rain quite a bit that night—'

'What if Mrs Fountain had gone out with it – seeing her visitor to his car, or opening the garage for her husband – whatever—'

'In her négligé?'

Calderwood was sweating. A sheen of damp on his nose and forehead. Doing nothing about it, Harrison had realized – having seen instances of this before – because he was hoping it might not be noticeable, didn't want to draw attention to it. He'd begun asking about Tommy Fountain: had they found him – *caught* him? Frewin raised a forefinger: 'On the subject of your umbrella, sir – from its gold collar-band we have one thumb-print.' He glanced at Harrison. 'Thumb, right hand?' Harrison nodded, and Frewin demonstrated: 'Must have held it rather like this.' Using his ballpoint – downwards, with the thumb along its length . . . 'Possibly when putting it in the stand. Obviously, as you mislaid it so long ago, this is only a formality, but you'll appreciate we do have to check.'

Calderwood muttered, 'It seems – somewhat – er – demeaning . . .'

'But quite painless, sir.' Frewin smiled with his lips. 'And not much of an audience to worry about, only the two of us . . . One outstanding problem we'll still be left with, though, is this Concorde flight. British Airways records have it that you were on the Monday morning plane, the BA 001. Could you – explain this? My point is, you must have spent the night – well, *somewhere*. And not here . . . Mrs Calderwood, for instance, is convinced you flew to America that night. So – this may be a delicate matter, one isn't blind to the – er – facts of life, and the information wouldn't – well, we'd keep it strictly between ourselves. As long as confirmation is available, of course . . . Would you like to think about it?'

'No.' The sweating was more obvious now. 'I can't see any

point – if you have this fingerprint which will – your word – eliminate me in any case?'

'I rather doubt it will, sir.'

'What?'

'And I will require – in fact I'd like *now*, please – details of your movements that night . . .' He glanced at Harrison. 'Charles?'

'Yes.' Harrison moved to open the briefcase. Thinking – he confessed afterwards – that Frewin was rather chancing his arm, that with the sudden change of tone – accusation, virtually – he should have cautioned him at this stage . . . He murmured, 'Need the loan of your right hand, sir, please.' The locks flew up. 'Won't take more than a few seconds, and as the Chief Inspector said, entirely—'

'Look.' Calderwood leant forward, clasped his hands together. As if to guard them . . . 'She fell. Tripped. She was trying to stop me leaving. That's my crime, I was trying to *leave*, I – we'd had a row – all right, I'd been seeing her a great deal, we were – lovers, but there'd been no – no commitment, on my part, and she – well, that night she told me she and her husband were splitting up, she expected – well, she'd some-how convinced herself that I'd leave my wife and—'

'You're saying it was an accident?'

'Yes – she grabbed at me, then – there was a bottle – champagne bottle, she slipped on it—'

'Why was it on the floor? Or stairs?'

'On the top landing . . . Well' – he lifted his hands, help-lessly, a gesture of despair – 'I told you, we'd had a row. Rather – squalid, really, I'd never seen her like that before, I was leaving – she was screaming mad, not making sense at all, really *impossible* – she threw it – *at* me, from behind. Actually it hit my shoulder. Then she came rushing after me and – sort of stumbled, the impetus carried her forward, and – there you are.'

He was leaning forward, hands covering his face; breathing hard, noisily – as if he couldn't get enough air into his lungs, Harrison said when he described this scene.

'And you – decided to clear out . . . Are you sure she was dead when you left her?'

'Of *course* I'm sure!'

'You just walked out.'

'I – cleaned up, first ... I – couldn't believe it. Simply couldn't *believe* it. I mean, that it had happened, that I was *there* and—'

'You said – cleaned up?'

'Wiped things – glasses, bottles—'

'Oh, for prints ... Including the bottle on the stairs – which you *left* on the stairs?'

'I thought if it was left there people would guess at – well, at what *did* happen – that she was drunk and accidentally—'

'But you forgot the umbrella.'

Calderwood didn't answer. And Frewin cautioned him, then. But Harrison, giving Tommy his account of this interview – on earlier detail of the investigation he'd been reticent, giving only sketchy explanations, but on this he'd talked freely, had obviously been intrigued by his diminutive chief's handling of it – confided that there'd been no fingerprint on the gold collar-ring of the brolly. That had been – he'd quoted Frewin – 'a little disinformation calculated to jog the memory'.

Emma wanted to look at some slippers she'd seen in a shop window, and Ted needed to cash a cheque, so from where we paid off the taxi I walked back to the *Bird* on my own. Thinking that if we did find Anne and extract her tonight the joy as far as I was concerned would be short-lived. Gill would be nursing an invalid; she'd have to fly back to America with her, then stay at least to see her through the worst of it.

Gill called, 'Matt!'

She was in the midships cockpit. I'd rigged the awning before breakfast and nobody could see her there without walking up the gangplank first – as I was doing now, pushing the flap aside ... 'Hi. All well? Tommy around?'

'Down below,' Tommy's voice called. 'Matt – heard the news?'

I looked back at Gill, and she told me, 'Ahmet's had news of *L'Ecstase*. Didn't leave for Rhodes after all – she's someplace close, some island—'

'Gemiler Island.' Tommy, in the hatchway. 'Friend of his telephoned from Ölü Deniz, got a message to him – another *gulet* skipper, he'd been intending to anchor at Gemiler but

272

went on to Ölü Deniz so he could call in – not wanting to use his radio, for obvious reasons.'

I was looking at him but not really focussing: thinking this might be good news in some ways, but also made things urgent. Maybe *very* urgent ... I said, 'Gemiler Adasi's just round the headland there.'

'I know. Ahmet showed me, on your chart.'

I moved towards the hatch, ushering Gill ahead of me. Seeing that chart in my mind's eye. Gemiler Island's about a dozen miles from Fethiye – out of the gulf, turn left, all the way round the headland and then into the bay. The channel between the island and the mainland coast is only about 200 yards wide, but there's good sheltered anchoring close to the island, with a stern line out to a tree or to a bit of the ruins that adorn the shore; the whole of that little island is smothered in ruins. Alternatively there's a small cove on the mainland, roughly opposite the western end: and if you landed at that point – well, it was where I'd thought of moving the *Bird* to, and I was thinking about it again, quite hard, at this moment.

Raoul might have come back to take his friends out of Turkey – with or without Anne. Officially, having cleared for Rhodes, he had no business to be in Turkish waters: although the odds were he'd get away with it if he wasn't staying long. The coastguard couldn't be everywhere, couldn't check every single boat.

And having cleared, if his intention was to pick up passengers at some fairly quiet spot – like that one – there'd be very little to stop him.

In fact there'd be nothing – except us.

'Here.' Tommy had the chart out – Turkish Admiralty chart 313. He pointed. 'There, Ahmet said.'

'Right. The anchorage is here, boats line up with their sterns to the island – along this bit of coast. Deep water out in the middle, ruins just under the surface near the edge.'

'Ahmet said *there*.'

'Ah – that's the alternative. I was thinking of it as a berth for us, as it happens. There's a restaurant on the beach there, in an olive grove. And you see, if you climbed up the line of this stream – stream bed only, at this time of year – up this slot between the hills, then yomp half a mile north-east – see where you're at?'

273

Gill squawked, 'Kaya Koy!'

'Right. And obviously why *L'Ecstase* is there. Which proves a point – if we needed proof . . . But actually there's a better place to start from.' I pointed it out to them. 'Here. There's a small beach at the head of this cove. Not much of an anchorage, not for *The Bird* anyway. My idea was – *is*, I think – anchor on this north side of Gemiler, and then it's only about five minutes in the inflatable out of the channel and around to this landing place. Then to get to Kaya Koy we'd yomp up here – *here*, Tommy. You and me, tonight.'

From that side, if the moon was up as we climbed we'd have the chapel as a leading-mark on the skyline. But I'd take a compass course from the chart anyway, so we could do without the moon if it wasn't there when we needed it.

Gill was holding my arm. 'You haven't said anything yet about your trip this morning, Matt. Did you – do any good?'

I slid the arm round her. 'Answer's affirmative – I hope . . .'

I told them about the radio aerial: and got a stream of questions, then, like could they be in touch from up there with the French boat where she was lying now – answer no, they couldn't, but they could have been when she was farther out, well off the coast: and for that matter they could be in touch – given the right equipment – with just about any place in the world. They could be in communication, for instance, with Spain or the USA.

'But not with that boat just a couple of miles from them?'

'Blanked off.' I pointed it out on the chart. 'Land-mass right between them . . . But they don't need a radio link, do they? They can drop in on each other and chat whenever they want to . . . Anyway – a more interesting find, spin-off from that one, is there's a tent, down-slope of the chapel and in a dip so you don't see it from the road either. I happened to be in a spot where I had a view of it – just a corner, until I climbed up on some rubble -- ordinary little green tent, two-man, could be, about thirty yards from the chapel. They wouldn't have Anne there, obviously, but—'

I checked the time. Distracted by a sense of urgency. The sooner we moved, the better. I wanted to be where I could see *L'Ecstase* and not lose sight of her. And then—

Then, we'd see . . . It was going to take a bit of working out.

Although I was already getting some ideas of how we might set about it. The way plans do form: starting with an overall view of location and objective, establishing the parameters. Then – starting any minute now – would come the in-filling of detail: all of it depending, of course, on that French yacht's movements.

And the practicalities, the nuts and bolts. Ideas often look brilliant until you get down to detail and the snags reveal themselves. In this case there were going to be a handful of alternatives, and one would settle – eventually – for the one with fewest snags. As I saw it then, the problems mostly concerned the *Bird of Dawning*, where I'd put her while we made our landing. I had a fair notion of what to do about *L'Ecstase* – as long as she stayed where she was now – and the beach I'd pointed out to them was surely the best choice of landing place; but the *Bird* – well, locations she might be left in would be (a) Gemiler, (b) Ölü Deniz, (c) at a pinch, in the outer approaches to the cove where we'd be landing, (d) possibly but even less likely another small inlet farther south.

I checked this on the chart, and the only possibility was a bay called Ködürümsü. Lousy anchorage, open to west and north-west, so if the Meltemi got up – well, forget Ködürümsü. No question of leaving the *Bird*, and Gill as her temporary skipper, in a hole like that.

The *Bird* might stay offshore, maybe. Patrolling up and down a line between two headlands that had lights on them – Iblis and Kötü, no navigational hazards anywhere near . . . Gill was perfectly capable of handling her. But there'd be some danger of coastguard interference: if coastguard radar picked up a yacht behaving in such an eccentric way . . .

There weren't any other anchorages worth considering. I didn't like Gemiler as a prospect because it was close to the scene of action, and if we did find Anne and brought her out – well, that was where we'd been, where maybe there'd have been some violent disturbances ashore, and we'd be bringing Anne into Fethiye as evidence that *we*'d done all that. And the same applied to Ölü Deniz – particularly in the light of the plans I had for *L'Ecstase*.

Ölü Deniz is a very touristic place, more so than anywhere else on this stretch of coast. It's an inland lagoon with a narrow

275

entrance from the sea, but yachts aren't allowed in there now, have to anchor outside near the entrance. There's a fairly large beach that gets to be as crowded as Margate or Blackpool: easy road access from Fethiye is, I suppose, largely responsible for this.

Birth of an idea. That beach. Its eastern end, where there was a PTT and a small shop or two: quite well removed from the anchorage. And that road to Fethiye . . .

Tommy was saying something, but I cut in: 'Look – sorry – I'm going along to have a word with Ahmet. Be a few minutes. If Ted and Emma come back before I do, hang on to them so we can shove off straight away.' I saw the question looming, and confirmed, 'To Gemiler. We'll anchor off the island – for a while, anyway. Marvellous swimming place, the customers always love it.'

A policeman – the civil variety, blue-clad – was just leaving the *Keyifliöglu*, joining two others who were waiting for him on the quayside, as I came hurrying. As a matter of principle I stopped hurrying, let them move away before I boarded the *gulet* and found Ahmet on the point of coming in search of me. I got as far as thanking him for getting us the news of *L'Ecstase* being at Gemiler Adasi, when he cut in with – 'The German who was in prison – that policeman came here to tell me—'

'Haven't let him out, have they?'

'Not *let* him . . . They move him to the hospital' – Ahmet touched his own black hair – 'for his head, you know – and from the hospital, although there was a guard—'

'Escaped?'

A nod . . . 'I think for Gill now you should be very watchful, Matt – could be he tries once more?'

Less serious from that angle, I thought – because Gill would be safe in the *Bird* and we'd be pulling out of here very shortly – than on account of Raoul and whoever was using that tent – at Kaya Koy – unless the tent was Schreiber's, unless he and Raoul were the only foreigners in that team – because now Raoul and any others would hear about Gill, the look-alike girl and the two guys who'd intervened to save her. I didn't think the news could have got out before this, because surely they'd have evacuated; and *L'Ecstase* wouldn't be in Turkish waters now.

Might have come back because of what happened to Schreiber – radio call, and back to evacuate *now*?

Ahmet saw me frowning, guessed I was angry with his police for having allowed Schreiber to escape. And I suppose I was: would have been, if there'd been time for getting angry . . . He said, 'We have a saying – if you go to the mountains with your uncle, take your own bread and cheese.'

'Meaning don't trust your uncle. The police . . .'

He blinked a few times. It was a sign of stress. 'Trust only yourself, I think.'

'Sound principle, all right . . . But listen – I'm taking my boat to Gemiler now. Right away. You don't have to know it, but that's where I'll be.'

'I think you should tell the *Sahil Gijvenlik*, Matt. About the French boat.'

'I can't.' (*Sahil Gijvenlik* meant the coastguard.) 'Fact is, there's good reason to believe Gill's sister would be killed if they saw uniforms around. That's why we have to do it on our own – *not* trust uncle . . . You moving to Göcek?'

He'd decided against it. He had only a couple of days before his German charterers would be arriving, he had work to do on the *gulet* which he could do best here in Fethiye. There'd be no risk of trouble for him: the *Keyiflioğlu* would be here all night, and he and Mustapha would be on board her; there'd be plenty of witnesses to this, maybe even – he pointed along the quayside – police witnesses.

His decision to stay here fitted the idea I'd had. And if anything was to be done about it, the only time was *now*. I asked him, 'That friend of yours who has the taxi, the one who took Gill to Kaya Koy—'

'His name is Ali.'

'Would he be prepared to work all night? If he was well paid for it? And then keep his mouth shut – would you trust him?'

We talked for a few minutes more, I explained what I wanted and he said he thought he might be able to set it up. It might not be possible to get in touch with Ali very quickly, though.

'I'll leave it with you, then. See you, Ahmet – and meanwhile, thanks for all you've done already. We'd have been lost without you.'

277

The Lawries were on board, when I got back to the *Bird*; within a few minutes I'd cast off the stern line and was hauling her up to her anchor.

From Fethiye to Gemiler Adasi is actually rather more than a dozen miles, more like fifteen; although as the crow flies – as distinct from *The Bird* – it would have been less than five. That crow, incidentally, would have flapped right over the top of Kaya Koy on its way south.

But anyway my *Bird* made it in nearer two hours than three. Once we were out of Fethiye Bay a healthy breath of the Meltemi gave us a pleasantly fast passage around the Sahin and Iblis headlands, a passage as comfortable as it was swift; we had lunch on the way, and when bodies weren't stuffing themselves they were spread out to the tanning sun.

Gill and Emma were a deep bronze by this time, and Emma had accused Ted of looking like a Tamil Tiger.

The contrast – to my mind – was striking. Sunbathing, lolling around: and Anne Brennan to be found and rescued tonight, *L'Ecstase* maybe already gone . . . I was wishing this bird *could* fly.

When we'd cleared Iblis Burnu I turned her east, to pass along the south coast of that rocky peninsula, then a couple of miles farther on a sharp swing to the north-north-west – genoa furled at this point and mainsail down, diesel taking over – put us on the last stretch, a run of only about a mile to the point just offshore where we'd enter the narrow Gemiler channel from the west.

'Someone take the wheel.'

Tommy offered. Gill was with Emma up forward, still basking. Tommy took over, I pointed out the entrance to the channel, warned him that there were rocks around the island's western tip, and went below to get a small but very high-powered telescope – another relic of times past.

In a few minutes, as we turned into the channel – turning east, to starboard – we'd have the mainland cove in which *L'Ecstase* had been lying at anchor close on our left.

'Throttle down, Tommy. Couple of knots'll do us.'

I didn't want to rush past, I wanted as good a look as I could get. If she was still here.

278

We'd have a view of her from where I intended to moor, but this was the closest we'd come to her. Closest for some while, anyway: until after sunset, probably. I'd been working things out a bit more clearly, on the way round, reached a few slightly less tentative conclusions.

What I was dreading was that *L'Ecstase* wouldn't be here now.

Using binos to start with, for their wider field of view. Only the outer approaches to the cove were visible from here; it would open itself to us as we got into the Gemiler channel. Minutes to go, yet. Tommy remembering those rocks, keeping the *Bird* middled between the island's western end and the protruding mainland point which was the western enclosure of that cove.

Cove beginning to open itself up to view . . .

L'Ecstase was at anchor, swinging. Not moored as several other boats were – two or three yachts, a *gulet* and some day-trip caiques from Fethiye, all tucked inside on the left with stern lines out to shore – but out in the middle, on her own. Recognizable from those snaps, although from this distance with binoculars the scruffiness of her paintwork didn't show up as clearly.

Switching from binos to telescope . . . 'Gill, want to see the boat Anne was in?'

She came running, snatched up the glasses. I asked the Lawries to lie down again – or look the other way. People do look at other boats – nothing more natural, when they're arriving in an anchorage, but it might be a bit much to have five people all staring fixedly at that one rather scruffy-looking yacht.

Swimming-ladder port quarter. Lying the way she was, that was fine – out of sight from shore and from the other boats in there. And she'd stay that way, this wind wasn't likely to change: not that there was much of it, although a couple of windsurfers were making the best of it . . . *L'Ecstase*'s mainsail was furled lumpily on the boom; the 'scope I was using was sharp enough to pick out the thin line parcelling the sail-cover.

And now Raoul – clearly recognizable. Standing, in conversation with a shorter, thickset guy with a balding head and a

279

clipped black beard. I'd know *him* again too, now. He was sitting, smoking a cigar. It was possible, of course, that he wasn't one of 'them', could be visiting from one of the other boats, but I guessed Raoul wouldn't be keen to have visitors, in present circumstances. The Algerian was standing with one arm up, hand grasping the port-side shroud. A pose rather similar to those in Anne's snapshots: maybe waiting for the bearded guy to take his photograph.

'See Wonderboy, Gill?'

'Sure do.' Holding her breath, to keep the glasses steady. Then a murmur: 'Oh Jesus, what I'd like to do to *you*, you shit . . .'

I thought, *I'll do it for you. Tonight.*

And I had the picture well enough. From the ladder to the cockpit, main hatch, and maybe a hatch I couldn't see from here over the engine-space right aft. There was room enough there, anyway. The ports in the sides of the coachroof told me near enough what her internal lay-out would be: and there was an anchor-winch on the foredeck.

It was good to have this sight of her in daylight; it would be dark when I boarded her. As long as she did stay here that long.

If they got under way, I decided, I'd radio the *Sahil Gijvenlik*. No matter how much Gill might protest. There'd be nothing to lose, by then. The odds were that when they left they wouldn't have Anne on board; there'd be no other way of stopping them, and if she *was* on board they wouldn't harm her when they knew they were about to be boarded.

But they *wouldn't* take her with them, I thought. She'd be left at Kaya Koy: either in the flail-woman's keeping, or dead. More likely the latter. Again, the sense of contrast hit me: blue sky, and placid, sheltered water, general air of idleness and pleasure-seeking, and with it the thought of – well, the *fact* of kidnap, which in itself is an act of brutality, and a clear potential for murder.

By this time we were well into the channel and approaching the anchorage close to the north shore of the island. I'd be dropping the hook in something like 25 metres of water: the channel was deep in its centre, steeply shelving into shallows where the ruins were both submerged and awash all along this coastline.

I folded the telescope, took over the wheel from Tommy, told him, 'Gill's handled the anchor before, you might take the stern line. Watch out for sea urchins when you land.'

I didn't want him lamed, at this stage.

There'd have been room for us at the end of the line of moored boats, but in order to be less obvious – in case Raoul was sensitive about being stared at – I parked the *Bird* in a comfortably wide gap between the Stars and Stripes on a 65-foot Nicholson and the ubiquitous Turkish scarlet on a 16-metre *gulet*. Even if Raoul was that sensitive, and had seen us studying him – he and the beard had turned to look when we'd been passing – he couldn't retain any suspicions of us now, and from the foredeck we could still keep an eye on him. One watchkeeper permanently on the bow: Gill, Tommy and I could take turns at it.

And please God we'd have all day to sit it out. I wondered where that bastard Schreiber was: whether maybe he hadn't got through to them yet. There were quite a few things one couldn't know about – until they jumped up and hit one.

Emma asked, 'What now, Matt?'

'Enjoy a lazy day, that's what. What you came for. We have to give you folk a *little* value for your money. Swim, sunbathe, browse around those ruins if you like.'

'What about the French boat?'

'We'll watch her. Hoping she doesn't move.'

'Then what?'

'Well. Tommy and I will be going up to Kaya Koy. Wouldn't be very clever if while we were on our way up' – I pointed – 'thataway, we'll be landing in the inflatable, around the other side of that point – if they happened to come down to their boat *this* way – right here – and buggered off.'

'So you're saying—'

'Saying I have to make sure it can't happen.'

Tommy told her, 'He means – I think – that we'll immobilize *L'Ecstase.*'

'We'll talk about it. But first, a couple of *easy* jobs – number one being to get our esteemed charterers settled.'

It involved no more than folding the swimming-ladder down, and rigging the awning. This was essential because the temperature was now into the low nineties, they'd need some

281

respite from that furnace in the sky, as well as leaping overboard to cool off from time to time. In fact all five of us had a swim then; and even Ted found he didn't object to ruins that you could stand on under water, look down on while you paddled slowly over them.

Gill took the first watch on the foredeck. In dark glasses and a floppy sunhat and with instructions to keep the lowest of profiles, vanish altogether if the French showed any interest in this direction. They were still on deck, those two, lounging in the stern. At one point the bearded guy dived in and took a swim, but Raoul might have been keeping his curly hair dry.

My first task involved the inflatable. I wanted to put it through its paces, make sure it wouldn't let us down tonight, and also to make a recce of the beach where we'd be landing. So I topped-up the tank, checked over the Yamaha, then embarked Tommy and roared away, no doubt spoiling a few siestas.

It took about two minutes to cut a broad white swathe eastward out of the channel, then around the bulge of mainland left-handed into the approaches to the cove that has this little beach at its top end. Distance maybe three-quarters of a mile: and no problems with the outboard, which had started on the first pull. I'd brought glasses with me, but didn't need them to spot the chapel stuck right up there on the ridge – slightly west of where I'd expected it to be. Something like half a mile inland and 1200 feet above sea-level. I slowed the motor as we swept into the outer part of the cove, made a wide circle at slow speed, keeping clear of a windsurfer while checking visually on the route we'd take from that beach. Shingle beach, not sand. We'd have to slant left, I saw: to have climbed directly toward the chapel would have meant a really tough climb, very sheer over the section immediately below the chapel: when they'd put it there, that cliff-like approach would have spelt security, no doubt. But slanting to the left at an angle of about thirty degrees to the direct line of sight would make the approach much easier: I thought we might even find a path, up that way.

I didn't use the glasses. It wasn't necessary, and someone might have been up there with *his* glasses. Not that we'd be all that noticeable: there were several other boats around – one

282

fishing, and a power-boat anchored with swimmers in the water around it. But for the same reason I didn't do any explaining of the scene to Tommy – we'd have had to yell, because even at low revs the Yamaha's noisy when you're right beside it, and our voices would have been audible from miles away.

(Oddly enough, an approaching outboard's not loud from any distance. If you stand on a beach with one powering directly at you, it's surprising how close it can come before the racket's really noticeable. I speak from experience acquired in a bygone age.)

The next thing was to decide where to park the inflatable when we landed. I didn't want to leave it in the open on that beach: and these cliffs had a lot of small caves in them, if we could find one close enough that could be the answer. And we did – in fact there'd have been a choice of them, but this was just about tailor-made for the job. For one thing, as we puttered in towards it we lost our view of the chapel: so any watcher up there would have lost his view of us, reciprocally. The cave was easily big enough to accommodate the boat, had a couple of feet of sea over its rock floor, and extended round to the left, just inside the entrance, with some irregular rock formations to which the painter could be secured. We drifted right in: I'd cut the engine, used a paddle, used it again to check the depths inside.

We could talk, now. And to anyone watching us, we were just messing about in a boat. Summer playtime. Others doing the same, all over.

The inflatable would be invisible in here, at night. Even in daylight you'd need to come close to the cliff-face to see it. We'd have a swim of about 200 yards to the beach.

Tommy asked, 'Swim back with Anne afterwards?'

'One swims, brings the boat in, other one waits with her on the beach. Unless she's in better nick than I'd expect.'

He nodded. 'That's it, then. Looks good, Matt.'

'Well. Touch wood . . . Only thing is' – at this stage I hadn't told him very much, I'd needed to check this topography first to ensure the plan was viable – 'we won't be coming here from Gemiler. Slightly longer trip – about two miles.' I pointed with the paddle, in the course of punting us out of the cave – 'from

283

Ölü Deniz, to be precise. Listen – see if you can pick any holes in this . . .'

I explained it, while the inflatable drifted out into the bright, hot sun again. In that shallow cave it had felt quite cold. Tommy heard me out, then nodded.

'Fine, in principle, but two queries. I *think* only two . . . First, why Ölü Deniz?'

'Because it's there. I mean it's close. And we need an alternative anchorage to Gemiler – if *that*'s what you're thinking. If we stayed around there, anyone ashore with his eyes open would see where I'd put her – achieving fuck-all and leaving Gill and the Lawries in some danger . . . Also, that Deniz place gets crowded, won't be long before someone boards to see what's the matter with this Frog just stuck there – or reports to the coastguard – so we get a breather before the shit hits the fan but not so long that the buggers starve or die of thirst, whatever. Right?'

'Check . . . Second query – why d'you have to do it solo?'

'Because I have Scuba gear and you don't.'

'Wouldn't need it. Only about – what, six hundred yards?'

'Another reason is I need you to be ready to start off in the inflatable, leaving not from the *Bird* but from the other side of the island. Paddle away from the *Bird* maybe when I start my swim.'

'Gill be OK on her own, you reckon?'

'Sure she will. There's no reason they'd single out the *Bird* as opposition. They shouldn't know anything about her.'

'OK . . . But look, if I parked the inflatable round the other side, then I could back you up and—'

'Unnecessary complication. I won't need any help with those two, Tommy.'

As it turned out, I was only going to have to deal with one of them. When we got back to the *Bird*, topped up the Yamaha's tank again and then had a swim, I took over the foredeck watch from Gill. I brought my Scuba gear up on to the bow with me, to check the regulator and the demand-valve, and so on. I'd done a full routine on all the gear after my last dive, but it had been lying idle for some time and I'd sooner double-check than drown. I put it all ready in the fore cabin, then, with the swimfins and accessories such as wrist-compass, depthgauge, knife, underwater torch. On an afterthought I added a few metres of nylon cord.

Gill had been swimming meanwhile with the Lawries, exploring the water's-edge ruins and taking a long time over it, trying to work out what this and that time-worn, tide-worn pattern of stonework might have been. She came up to the foredeck, letting the sun dry her lovely body in its two little wisps of peacock-blue bikini ... 'Those ruins are really intriguing, Matt.'

'I know. There's a tunnel, too – if you climb up on the ridge there – a stone tunnel leading down to the sea, the other side. The story is some chieftain built it so his wife or daughter, whichever, could get down to bathe without having the *hoi polloi* see her looking anything like you're looking now.'

'Load of shit if I ever heard one.' She squatted beside me. 'Going to tell me what tonight's programme is, some time?'

'Yup. Couldn't have before, there were a few uncertainties. But here it is – and para one is you'll have the *Bird* and the Lawries to look after while Tommy and I are chasing our tails hither and thither. *And*, if by some mischance I'm not back with you by say 0600, you'd better up-anchor and go back to Fethiye. I know you could handle that all right. Not that it'll happen, but—'

'While you'll be doing what, exactly?'

'Well, hang on – if things did go wrong and you had to take her back on your own, I'd suggest one, call on Ahmet for any immediate help you want, and two, telephone your ambassador in Ankara, tell him what's been going on and ask him to put his oar in. That could shortcut a lot of fuss and bother. OK?'

She nodded. 'But as you said, it won't happen. Tell me what *will* be happening.'

'Sure. I'll get the chart.'

It was as I stood up to go and fetch it that I saw movement on the French boat. It was the bearded guy departing – hauling a dinghy up to the ladder, climbing down into it and then pulling for the shore, leaving Raoul in sole occupation – as it turned out, because the other one didn't come back – leaving him to me.

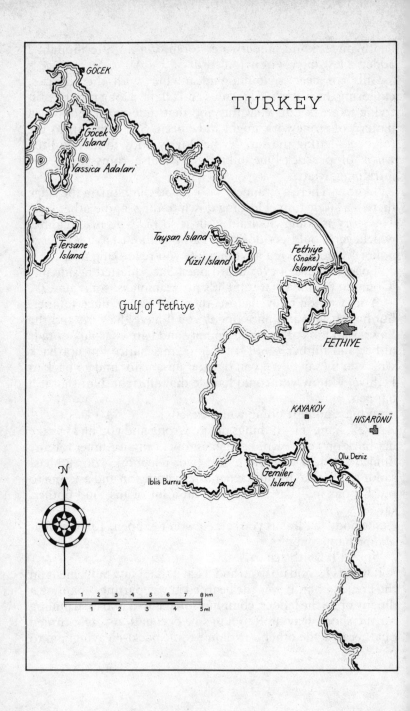

17

As the day faded, the sky a bright apricot that slowly ripened, dolphins came rolling into the channel, lazily showing themselves then tantalizingly vanishing, showing up again after a minute or two in some entirely different quarter so that you had to keep looking in all directions to catch the next appearance. Turks on the *gulet* near us were whistling at them, encouraging them to show themselves and come closer; I remembered someone – may have been Abidin Kurt – telling me about the friendly feelings that Turkish seamen have for dolphins: even fishermen, to whom the animals are competition, whistle and call to them like old friends whenever they're around.

L'Ecstase was still here, and Raoul was still alone on board. The yacht had a white riding-light at her masthead and a glow of inside illumination yellowish in her cabin ports.

We'd had supper early, finishing by about eight, and it was shortly after that that the dolphins had first appeared. I was with Gill and Tommy now on the *Bird*'s bow and the Lawries were perched on the forward part of the raised coachroof, all of us watching the live display and the deepening apricot glow: Tommy and I watching the French boat too.

Then the animals had gone. At least, hadn't shown themselves in the last five minutes. Ten to nine . . . Clink of ice in

Emma's glass behind me: she and Ted were the only bar customers this evening. The colour had begun to fade, its reflection in the sea's surface softening, and where it was shadowed by land the water was turning black. Lights on shore – over around the little restaurant – and on the boats here and over the way became the decorative element now, taking over as natural light drained away.

Tommy murmured, 'You'd think that with that Kraut on the loose there'd have been signs of a flap.'

You'd think . . .

Meaning *guess*. One *knew* so little. They mightn't attach great importance to the fact there'd been this girl who resembled the one they'd kidnapped and who'd been trying to find her, using that portrait. Raoul knew Anne had a sister; if he'd heard Schreiber's story he'd have no doubt who was on the trail. But he might *not* have heard it. Schreiber had only got away from the hospital that day, might be in hiding, might not have been able to move out of Fethiye.

Alternatively, maybe they had to wait for orders, might not be free to move without them. One disadvantage, maybe, of such a worldwide operation.

So many maybes, mights and ifs – speculation, areas of blindness, unknowns that might prejudice success but could only be played off the cuff. I thought we probably had the edge on them in that they wouldn't be expecting intrusion up there among the ruins, but I could be wrong, couldn't be sure they weren't waiting for us.

By 9.15 it was dark, and Tommy was in the inflatable, ready to start paddling eastward out of the channel as soon as he saw me start. In the boat with him he had my jeans, sweater and trainers, a towel, three life-jackets and some chocolate and biscuits and a thermos of tea laced with Spanish brandy; he also had his own back-pack containing everything he'd got with him in Turkey, including all his cash and travellers' cheques, passport and return air ticket from Istanbul to Zurich. One other item too: a plastic shopping-bag in which Gill had packed some clothes she thought Anne might need.

Tempting fate, maybe. I truly dreaded the thought of maybe having to bring it back unused.

I went over the stern, down the swimming-ladder, finned up to the *Bird*'s forefoot, surfaced to give Tommy a thumbs-up sign and then got going on a true course of 290 degrees by wrist-compass, swimming at a depth of 10 feet on the gauge. I'd taken this course from the chart, having first fixed the boat's position accurately by shore bearings – fixed, to be precise, the position of her stem, my starting-point.

Gill's whisper lingered in my ears: 'Come back in one piece, Matt, please.'

It lingered in the back of my mind that success tonight would deprive me of Gill, at least for some time. I thought as I finned, *Winner take nothing* . . .

But I hadn't won yet.

In the mouth of the cove on the other side I came up for a cautious check: slowly up, breaking surface gently and spotting the dark silhouette of *L'Ecstase* about thirty yards ahead. Lights still visible from inside, and nothing moving on deck.

No dinghy on its way out, either, no other boat on the move.

Two minutes later, having quietly paddled right around the boat – hearing music, seeing no human occupant – I rested with one hand on Raoul's swimming-ladder. Wondering whether the fact he'd left it rigged might mean he was expecting visitors.

If he was, they'd have their work cut out to find him. *Their* turn to do some wondering.

Ladders like this one, hooked over the gunwale at the top and resting against the boat's hull – usually with struts protruding at right-angles to the ladder near its lower end to allow for the hull's curve inward – are awkward to climb silently, tend to thump against the hull – which makes a hell of a noise, for anyone inside. To become slightly less clumsy I ducked under to remove my fins, pushed them gently over the gunwale above my head before taking the matter any farther. Then – slowly, very cautiously . . . Feet on the lowest rung, weight on the arms, slowly lifting, slow enough not to make the suction sound that comes with a quicker exit from the water, or the noise water makes sluicing from an emerging body, or a creak of the ladder against the timber hull.

Then I was on *L'Ecstase*'s stern. Crouching, shedding gear as near silently as possible. Hearing the music louder now –

French pop, mostly sobs and grunts – from inside.

Engine access was at the after end of the cockpit, a hatch set at an angle of 45 degrees – against which a relaxed helmsman could lean, I supposed. A ring in the lower edge for lifting. Taking note of these features while moving forward, sloth-like, to the main hatch, entrance to Raoul's boudoir.

Music stopped abruptly. A Frenchwoman embarked on a stream of nasal, machinegun-like patter. I could see Raoul's head. The top of it, a smallish dome of curly black wool. The hatch was double-doored, like mine in *The Bird*, except *The Bird*'s is mahogany and this was varnished boxwood. Had been varnished, in need of attention now. One of its halves was open – which was how I could see down into the cabin – latched back, the other half was shut but not fastened. I moved one hand to the closed half, eased it back quietly, and launched myself in.

Raoul was sitting at his cabin table, about five feet below me and two or three feet from the foot of the ladder, so it wasn't difficult to land on top of him, and the first he knew of there being any foreign body in his boat was when my weight hit him. He was slammed down across the table, the chair crashed over and some plates of cheese and stuff went flying. I had a hand over his mouth pulling his head back sort of around my shoulder, with the dual purposes of enforcing silence and ensuring immobility.

He wasn't trying to resist, wasn't struggling at all. If there'd been two of them, this lad wouldn't have counted, a back-hander would have kept him quiet while one dealt with the other guy. His eyes, trying to get a sight of me, had rolled up in their sockets: I've seen a frightened horse look like that. All whites, and that loony look . . . I shifted back, twisting to the right, removing him from the table and letting him drop – about three and a half feet – to the cabin sole, then thumping down on my knees on top of him. Still no fight in him . . . I kept one hand on the back of his neck while with the other I unwound the length of halyard which I'd brought coiled around my waist.

He began to talk, then, asking me in jerky, breathless French who I was and what I wanted. There was no reason to enlighten him, or let him know which language I spoke;

especially as my French isn't up to much and he'd have picked up the English accent at once if he'd had even half an ear. I had his hands pulled together behind his back now, putting a good strong lashing on the wrists. Then sheet from his bunk: I could just reach it, a quarter-bunk on the starboard side, and the pillow-case looked as if it might come in handy. Sheet first, though: while he was telling me that he had a lot of money on board, American dollars, and that I could have it all, I dragged some of the sheet down, put a knee on it and used my diver's knife, hacking a strip out to make a gag, two or three turns of it round his head and between his teeth and enough left over to knot at the back of his neck.

Then the pillow-case over his head, and I lashed his ankles together, connecting them to the tied wrists with enough tension on the cord to make movement difficult, and the spare end of the cord went round his neck to hold the pillow-case in place.

The cabin sole was as good a place as any for him. I left him there, went up into the cockpit, located the engine controls and after a period of trial-and-error got the diesel started. Throttle right beside the wheel: gear-lever starboard side of the binnacle. I left the gear in neutral, diesel chugging at minimal revs, went forward, brought the anchor warp to the winch, found a ratchet-handle nearby and fitted it, uncleated the warp and took a couple of turns around the winch, began to pump the ratchet. It wasn't a self-tailing winch, like those I have on the *Bird*: you had to pump with one hand and keep tension on the rope with the other. It was an awkward way of doing a very simple job, and when *L'Ecstase* was over her anchor I found it easier to haul in hand-over-hand.

All so easy. *Too* easy – so far, and it bothered me. When things go this smoothly – well, nothing runs to plan for ever. OK, so we'd barely started, but I'd sooner have had a few problems cropping up now than big ones later. Biggest of all being the hideous possibility of Anne Brennan being already dead: or of their killing her before we could get to her. Then not only her death, but the effect it would have on Gill . . .

Navigation lights: switches would be either in the cockpit or down below, at the navstation if this old craft had one. I didn't want to have to ask Raoul – although I'm sure he'd have told me, like a shot — and luckily they weren't hard to find. I switched them on, and went back up. Honey-coloured eyes on the *Bird* would be watching anxiously for the red and the green: I turned the yacht the long way round, to starboard, all the way around so she'd see the green, then both together when I was bow-on to her, then as *L'Ecstase* steadied on course to get out round this end of the island she'd be seeing only the red, for several minutes. I'd told her that when she saw this succession of lights she could be sure all was well, and relax.

Not that she would: not really until we got back into Fethiye and she was reunited with kid sister.

Please God.

Noisy diesel, Raoul had. And if there was an autopilot its controls were well hidden. No matter: there were only a few miles to go and I could see enough of Raoul's trussed form from here to know he was continuing to accept his fate resignedly.

By this time tomorrow or the day after he might not be feeling so good about it. But a few days' even quite acute discomfort wasn't really much punishment for him, I thought, compared with the ordeal and humiliation he'd inflicted on kid sister. Although with any luck — not *his* — he might get a long spell in a Turkish slammer, which by all accounts might not be exactly *grande luxe*. It depended on how all this turned out, what the Turks made of it when they found him. As long as they didn't find *me* anywhere near him, and we got Anne out of this alive and well, I didn't much care. Freeing Anne was the object of the operation; punishment of criminals, in Turkish territory, was a matter for the Turks.

L'Ecstase was chugging along at about four knots, I reckoned, judging by the flow of water along her side. I'd rounded the end of Gemiler now, was steering south-east and keeping an eye out for Tommy in the inflatable, although it might be another half-mile — say eight minutes — before we met. He'd have started the outboard after passing round the eastern end of Gemiler Adasi, far enough from the anchorage to be barely noticeable. None of this would matter unless there was a police investigation — of me, of the *Bird* — after the event; but if there was, I didn't want the nearby *gulet*'s crew telling them

I'd sent away the inflatable after dark. With luck, they wouldn't even have noticed Tommy paddling away – the Yank had gone, by the way, we had no neighbour that side now – and when the boat returned – touch wood – in the early hours of the morning, there'd still be just one man in it, and he'd have been on a fishing trip.

Ahmet's proverb about not trusting your uncle – one thing we did have to put all our faith in was the outboard. Outboards are tricky articles, have a tendency to let one down: but everything hung on this one's continuing to work. One had no back-up – except paddles, which would be far too slow – and if it failed, we'd have lost out, and so would Anne. I'd had experience of such let-downs, in the past – although not, admittedly, with a Yamaha, and with this particular motor I'd had no problems.

Yet.

Ten minutes after deciding I ought to see him in about eight, I saw Tommy's torch flash two longs – M for Matt, meaning he'd spotted my lights – and I aimed mine at him, gave him a single long flash, a T for Tommy, signifying come on, come aboard. I cut the revs, put the engine in neutral, shone the torch on the ladder on the quarter and waited about a minute before hearing the outboard, then seeing the swirl of white as he came swinging in alongside.

No speech. We'd agreed this. No English language for Raoul to hear. I took my own parcel of gear from him, then the boat's painter, and while he was climbing aboard I led it aft and tethered it there. Then back to the controls: Tommy was taking a gander at Raoul while I got *L'Ecstase* moving again, on course for Ölü Deniz. When he was ready to take over I let him have the wheel while I got dressed.

There's a small wooded island on the port hand as one approaches the entrance to the Ölü Deniz lagoon, and it's beyond this, inside it, that boats moor – in the usual way, an anchor out ahead and a stern-line to shore.

There was plenty of room, thank heaven. This place does get very crowded. In fact mostly by day, I suppose, day visitors taking a brief look; not many yachtsmen or even *gulet* parties would get much pleasure from spending nights here. Music

293

from a hotel or beach-bar was louder than you'd want even before *L'Ecstase* had turned in around the island: it occurred to me that Raoul would have plenty to listen to while he waited for discovery and release.

Tommy took the stern-line ashore in the inflatable, secured it to a tree. I hove in the slack and made it fast, and had the anchor warp adjusted and cleated by the time he was back on board – leaving the inflatable at the ladder, ready for our departure. Nobody had taken much notice of our arrival. One face had appeared on a *tirhandil* next inshore of us, watched for a minute or two and then gone below, but on a yacht to starboard there'd been no movement. Probably trying to get to sleep, fingers in their ears against the thumping music.

I'd had something in mind: said close to Tommy's ear, 'Hang on a minute. May be some stuff of Anne's below.'

American dollars, Raoul had offered me. They'd be Anne's, I guessed, and she might like to have them back.

The forward cabin seemed most likely. I stepped over Raoul, and went into it, found two bunks with drawers under them, one narrow clothes-hanging cupboard. Raoul's gear only, nothing feminine. Same in the bunk drawers. He'd have got rid of stuff that might incriminate him, obviously, in case of a customs or coastguard search.

Looking round: then back to the hanging-cupboard: there was a rolled duvet in the bottom, could have had other gear under it. But it didn't.

Back into the saloon, or main cabin. Chart-table with an upper slot for charts, three drawers under that.

Ship's papers – in French. Clearance from Kaş. Some reference books – harbour plans, leaflets of maintenance instructions, a cruising handbook – French again. Next drawer: personal documents, some letters – all in French – a wallet containing Turkish lira and French francs, credit cards . . .

Right at the back, Anne's handbag.

US passport: dollar cheques and dollar notes: credit cards, letters, odds and ends.

Putting the stuff back in the bag and zipping it, glancing down at Raoul: conscious of a strong, personal loathing . . . This stuff in my hands was like a part of Anne herself: could

294

even be the nearest we'd get to her. Thanks to this craven, merciless little shit . . .

Well: maybe the Turks wouldn't be *too* nice to him.

I'd turned away: swung back then, with an afterthought – that those papers of his, letters and suchlike – might contain a name, a telephone number – *something* – in Madrid, Los Angeles, wherever, and the FBI might like to browse. I pulled the drawer out, scooped the contents together into one handful – leaving his wallet, which had only cash and credit cards in it – went up into the cockpit and shut the double doors. Tommy asked quietly, 'OK?' and I pointed at the ladder.

We cast off – paddling, not wanting to use the motor yet. I'd stuffed the papers into the bottom of the bag that held Anne's clothes – Gill could take them back to the States with her, if she thought it worthwhile – and put Anne's handbag in there too. My Scuba gear was loose in the bottom of the boat, as was an old pair of fins for Tommy's use. Under paddle-power we slid out through the narrow gap between the island and the mainland point, got well out on the other side before starting the outboard. Then at the first pull it roared into life and we were on our way.

It felt like a long swim from the cave to the beach. And we'd barely started yet.

The moon was starting with us. Rising out of the inland mountains in the south-east, the three-night-old crescent had quite a bit of sky to cross, so would be with us for several hours, unlike its recent rather brief appearances. The Meltemi breeze was from the west, and cool on wet bodies and damp clothes – we'd made the swim towing our gear on inflated life-jackets.

You couldn't see the chapel, from this beach. The sheerness of the hillside above us hid it. We'd see it from the flank, about halfway up, I guessed. I'd described the topography and the lay-out of the ruins, sketching it for Tommy's benefit on the back of a chart, on the *Bird*'s foredeck this afternoon. In fact with this moon now he'd hardly have needed that briefing; from up on the ridge we'd have it all spread out and open to us.

Except that a good bit of the reverse slope would be in shadow, for a while.

As we climbed – it was a track, of sorts – the hillside steepened on the left, became less so on the right. At the halfway stage the chapel was in view; we left the goat-track – if that's what it was – and headed towards the ridge. Five minutes' hard slog, and we were there – *almost* there – with the moonlit skyline just ahead and the chapel also floodlit to our right. I signalled to Tommy, crouched low and ran over the crest, skidded down into comparative darkness. He joined me, and we moved to our right, looking for that tent.

They surely wouldn't sit around in that cold stone chapel – not at night, unless they were waiting for their radio receiver to start uttering. There *might* be someone in there, but the tent was the more obvious place to find them.

Skyline to the right, above us, edged with moonglow: I crept up closer to it, stopped again with both the chapel and the tent in sight.

There was a light burning in the tent.

Tommy, closing up into contact and whispering-distance, thrust something towards me: 'Mask . . .'

I'd forgotten this. His suggestion, earlier in the day, and he'd said he'd see to it – triangles of material cut from an old dark-coloured shirt of mine, to cover our faces up to the eyes. Small precaution, might avert future problems.

The light in the tent, greenish through its wall, was probably one of those Camping-Gaz things. The chapel was moonlit from the south, the entrance a black slab. There'd be no one in there, for sure. I could see the projecting pole, but moonlight didn't do for the wire what sunlight had. The point of interest here being that if they'd been in the process of evacuating, they'd have dismantled that aerial: for the time being one had to accept the evidence of the pole still being there.

So now – the tent. I'd looked round at Tommy, about to propose a move towards it: but he held up a finger, touched his ear . . . Eyes on the tent: and ears better than mine, evidently. But then I caught it too: a murmur of low voices, a muttering on the breeze: then, almost startlingly loud, a man's chuckle.

Cheerful, deep-voiced chuckle, out of the preceding quiet. And as if that laugh had taken the lid off, another voice rose – tone of protest, higher-pitched and insistent until a quieter answer stopped it, probably telling it to shut up . . . The language was German: and the last one had been the voice of the guy who'd chuckled. Restraint seemed to have ended, there was a continuing exchange now – one voice urgent and the other calm, controlling. I touched Tommy's shoulder: we'd waited long enough, might as well move in on them now; aware of feeling as I hadn't in years – this sense of an objective and a fixed intention, everything else peripheral but to be made use of – moonlight, the shape of the ground, the wind and the scents it carried . . .

Jarring sound, then: made one jump: a double-take categorized it as electronic bleeping. Because in such surroundings it was so unexpected. There was sudden movement in the tent, and one voice raised sharply, the upheaval resolving itself into the tent-flaps opening – fall-out of light across the scrubby slope, then an emerging body. The squeaky bleating hadn't lasted; on its heels the higher-pitched of the two voices had exclaimed – in German – something like 'There, at last!' and the flat-toned answer might have been 'All right, all right . . .'

That one had backed out of the tent, in the flood of gaz-light that came with him. He was short, thickset, bearded, and we'd seen him before – on board *L'Ecstase* with Raoul. The tent flaps were shut again, and he was a dark, stocky figure climbing towards the chapel.

Some monitor in the tent must have been triggered by a call on the radio. And – no time like the present . . .

I signed to Tommy: chapel. His head turned, eyes questioning: I whispered, 'However you like. We'll use the other guy.' The one *I'd* handle now, the guy in the tent. Tommy crawled away upslope and I began traversing downward. Gill's 'small gorilla' momentarily moonlit before vanishing into the black oblong of the chapel's entrance, and torchlight flickered in there. I heard the bleeper again from the tent, very briefly, and guessed the man in there had switched on for a moment, ensuring the radio demand was still there, then switched off again, reassured.

But he was the one to use, for our purposes – purpose, singular, namely locating Anne Brennan – because by the sound of him he was already rattled.

Near the tent – near enough – I stopped and waited for sounds of action from above.

Not a long wait. And I only heard anything at all because I was listening for it, the guy didn't get any chance to yell. I was on the move then, pushing into the tent. Schreiber – seated, jerking round, unmistakably matching Gill's description of him – had a diver's knife at his throat and his right arm clamped, doubled, reversed against the joint: the prick of the knife deterred movement with the other. I warned, 'Quiet. I'll kill you if I have to.'

It was a pity we were going to have to talk to him, let him know we were British. If he survived, the Turks might sweat it out of him, or he might volunteer the information, but this couldn't be helped. Anyway, if everything else went as planned there'd be no proof, and we weren't the only Brits in Turkey.

I knew Schreiber spoke English: he'd spoken some to Gill. He was in shock now, his eyes bulging, and he looked as if even before this someone had been unkind to him. Either in the slammer, or maybe Tommy's bouncing him on the road, but his face had suffered recent damage.

He didn't like the look of me, either. Masks *are* frightening. 'Schreiber . . .'

His mouth gaped open: surprise on top of fright. Tommy said behind me, 'Other one's dead. Want this?'

Wire – probably the flex from the radio in the chapel to this monitor. The other guy would *not* be dead, of course, but the statement had had its desired effect: Schreiber had quivered as from an electric shock, and he wasn't just scared now, he was in terror. I muttered 'Wrists – behind him', and while Tommy applied a tight lashing with the flex I held my knife where he could focus on its eight-inch blade – razor-sharp on one side, serrated on the other, carbon-steel a quarter-inch thick. He was sweating, shaking – and from the smell – well . . .

A bird book lay open at an illustration of a golden oriole. There was also a camera with a zoom lens, and binoculars. Bird-watching would have been their cover, evidently . . . The radio monitor was a plastic box with a light that would flash when it bleeped. Tommy said, 'I put the set out of action. Smart job, East German.'

'You from the East, Schreiber?'

He nodded.

'You'll lead us to the American girl, now.'

298

He swallowed. Began to shake his head. Then felt the point of the knife against his windpipe, heard me telling him he was no use to us otherwise, that if he wanted to live he'd take us to wherever she was, and give us no trouble along the way. Eyes bulging at me, watering, his face really an awful mess, and his breathing quickening into sobs. I felt sure he'd been softened-up for us, somewhere or other: that, or the moral fibre was non-existent.

There were two hold-alls in the tent. Tommy frisked through them. Passports – air tickets – money . . . I told him as he glanced up questioningly, 'Leave it all.' For the *jandarma* to find, tomorrow

No weapons, anyway.

I used the rest of the wire that Tommy had brought, doubled and noosed as a choke-lead, round the German's neck. Glancing around then, wondering if there was anything else we should do before embarking on the next stage . . . The gaz-light, for instance. I decided, best leave it burning, leave all external appearances as they had been. And push on: nothing having blown up in our faces – *yet* . . .

Tommy glanced at me, having made his own inspection. 'All set?'

I jerked Schreiber to his feet, got him moving.

The stink of sheep suggested that we were approaching the area where Gill had met the flail woman. An association of ideas which in fact proved wrong.

Moonlight on Kaya Koy created a fantasia in black and white, cubes and rectangles piled and ranked, as repetitious and confusing as one of those really maddening jigsaw puzzles. We'd come down bare hillside to the upper level of the ruins at that end of the village, then through the dip and up into the central part, stark and desolate, blackly shadowed between the moonlit sepulchres that had once been homes. But we weren't heading for the sheep-pen near the chapel: instead, for somewhere lower, closer to the road. A moment earlier I'd had a long-range glimpse of that chapel, the one where the bones lay around; it had been ahead of us then, but now we'd turned downhill.

Schreiber clumsy – stumbling, panting . . .

Ahead – then to the right – a shoulder-high wall had a drop of at least a hundred feet on its other side. I'd seen it from below, before this – there was an open, level area that might once have been the village square or market-place, with a stone facing to a section of almost vertical hillside behind it. It was between us and the chapel and that sheep-pen now: we were roughly in the centre of the area of ruins. The stink of sheep was stronger: there had to be a second flock a lot closer to us than the other.

Schreiber shambled on. I had his wire lead in one hand, knife in the other so any time he looked round he could see the gleam of steel. Tommy kept with us more or less but on his own, making good use of the terrain and shadows: if some watcher spotted me and the German, he wouldn't know we had an escort.

Leaving that steep fall of ground behind us on the right; it was all downhill now, between broken walls and heaps of rubble, house-fronts with window-holes like empty eye-sockets . . .

Schreiber stopped. I moved up beside him, shortening the lead by looping it around that hand. 'Well?'

He pointed. 'Is here.'

'With sheep?'

A nod: and a glance at the knife . . .

'In *with* the sheep?'

Motions with both hands now. Like swimming, breaststroke – parting not water, though, but the flock, passing through them. Then he outlined a doorway – a low one, one hand horizontal to indicate the top of it: a curved top, an arch . . . 'Some rocks – for filling – for blocking up . . .'

Through a lot of sheep, an entrance they'd walled up?

'Who guards her?'

The sheep would, of course, with their constant noise, and the fact that while tourists might walk anywhere around these ruins they'd hardly invade a filthy, stinking sheep-pen . . . Schreiber said, 'One man is guard. The old woman – she has two son.'

'Name Selma?'

A nod . . . 'Two son, of Selma.'

'Grown men?'

'Grown – sure. Only one, on guard.'

'Where?'

His hand moved, vaguely circular motion. 'Where – he can see. The sheep, that place . . .'

'Seeing us now, maybe?'

A shrug. 'Maybe.'

Tommy closed in, a tall ghost detaching itself like a shadow from other shadows, appearing from behind the circular top of another of those water-storage cisterns, like the one Emma Lawrie had found so interesting. Keeping a distance now but near enough to hear me telling Schreiber, 'When we get close, call him. Just him, I don't want all of them . . . Tommy, push on ahead, take care of him when he shows – OK?'

Tommy slid by, ghost-like. In contrast to Schreiber lurching clumsily ahead of me . . . In and out of the shadows of walls and bits of houses, a tower here that might have been a grain store. Stones scattered from the German's feet, rattled down the slope . . .

He'd stopped again.

We were in shadow here, from a high wall on the left. A little farther down there'd be no such cover: moonlight poured across the track there, over a low barrier of stones piled to complete an enclosure.

Despite that flood of light, Tommy wasn't visible.

'Sheep-pen?'

Schreiber nodded. His breathing like a bellows – squeaky, a whimper in it . . . I prodded him with the knife's haft: 'Go on.'

Half a minute later, I saw him. Seeing over that rough wall around the yard to a higher level, ruins of a house on an elevated site, the dark mass of a rock outcrop. I'd seen a crouched figure separate itself from one area of shadow and melt into another.

A jerk on the wire rein stopped Schreiber. Obviously that Turk had seen us. Probably heard, then seen . . .

'Call to him, tell him come down here.'

At least Anne had to be alive. Or there'd have been no guard.

Schreiber croaked, 'Yilmaz? Ersin?'

It showed again, then: from shadow into moonlight, peasant-like figure hunched, peering down towards us. A gabble of Turkish: Schreiber answered . . . There was a makeshift gate in the wall – branches, scraps of timber – down on the left. Ersin – Schreiber had used that name again – was coming down, stepping from rock to rock: moonlight shone on steel, some weapon.

Tommy'd be there – somewhere . . .

I pushed Schreiber forward again. He was at the gate when Ersin landed in the yard and Tommy, timing it perfectly, vaulted the wall from the track, right beside him.

And missed his footing, fell . . .

The Turk had swung round – to a dark thickening of shadow that rose in front of him: his arm swinging up with the machete – glinting arc of silver – checked, was doubled back to an audible *crack* as the shoulder dislocated, ringing clang of the dropped weapon clattering on rock, then three solid, thudding impacts of Tommy's knee and fists. A moment later, his quiet 'OK'.

No other sound or movement. We waited – listening, watching shadows and skylines. Sheep-stink, Schreiber's gasping breaths.

Nothing else.

'Right. Where is she?'

The sheep began to shift around nervously as he led us towards them – Tommy with me now – and then as it took root in their feeble brains that they weren't alone it was all panic, animals barrelling in all directions, bleating and jostling, cannoning off the walls.

Schreiber put his hand on the end wall, rough stone . . .

'Here.'

'Watch him, Tommy.' Suddenly, I hadn't finished with Schreiber. If he and his friends had been keeping a human being in this filth, walled up . . .

I put my face to one of the gaps. To a reek of putrefaction, out of cold, dank emptiness. If the RSPCA found some brute keeping a dog in a place like this, they'd prosecute.

'Anne? Anne Brennan? We've come to take you out of this. Your sister Gill—'

A squawk, with an element of hiss in it. The kind of sound a cat might make: and I was wishing to God we could have had Gill with us, at this stage . . . Waiting a moment, then trying again: 'Anne – Anne, it's OK now, we've come to take you out of this filthy place – taking you to Gill – all right, Anne?'

Gill's voice, then, out of the dark hole – sharp and thin, definitely a sound of Gill – in fright, distress, suspicion, still uncannily the same: 'What – where *is* Gill, who—'

'I'm Matt Johnson, skipper of the yacht *Bird of Dawning*. Gill's on board – I brought her here from Menorca, looking for you. And my chum here's name is Tommy. Anne, you're safe now, d'you hear?'

Silence . . . Then in a sudden gush, tone of panic: 'I – I have no clothes, none at all, I mean I'm – look, they – they—'

Sobbing, hysteria, drowned it. This could have been Gill: in my mind, Gill and Anne as one . . . I begged, 'Listen. We've brought clothes for you, Gill packed some, they're in the boat and for now you can have my shirt – no, Tommy's, he's tall, cover you better. I'll push it through – starting to pull stones out now – OK?'

I made Schreiber start on it. They were heavy blocks, each a couple of feet across, Anne certainly couldn't have moved them. I backed out of earshot of the German, reminded Tommy where that old cistern was, the place we'd stopped, only minutes ago . . . 'I saw one like it this morning. Maybe thirty feet deep, smooth sides. If you take that Turk and drop him in it, he won't get out until they haul him out with ropes.'

'Good thinking, Matt.' He was pulling his shirt off. He muttered, 'Christ, that poor kid . . .'

I went back to her. Thinking briefly of the cistern with its vertical, smooth-sided walls, that it might do for Schreiber too – when I'd finished with him. Which I hadn't, yet . . .

He'd got the second lump of stone out. I pushed him out of my way. 'Anne, here comes the shirt. Bit damp, I'm afraid.'

'What isn't, around here . . .'

The Brennans bred true, I thought. Father might be a shit, and mother heaven knew what, but you could say that for them. Gill could have made that comment: and kid sister, making it, had sounded darned near normal. She'd pulled the shirt out of my hand, and I'd got a grip on another of the stones. That Gill-like voice again: 'What did you say your name is?' I told her, and she said, 'I have to warn you, Matt, I'm – foul . . . I mean, literally, I'm – Jesus, I'm – *horrible* . . .'

Gush of crying: frantic, an impression it was shaking her

303

apart. I grabbed Schreiber, flung him at the wall, growled 'Work!' And told Anne, 'Listen, Anne, listen now – it's the pigs who put you in there who are horrible. Not you, not in a million years. They'll be paying for it, don't worry.'

Schreiber would. Schreiber could foot the whole bill, in a minute, soon as I had time for him . . .

'Anne, there's a whole lot of quite warm, clean sea just down the hill, you can have a bathe before you put on the clothes Gill sent.'

Another stone came out: Schreiber staggering aside with it, dropping it, lurching back . . . I might have been able to get her out through the gap we had now, but I didn't want to while he was still here, didn't want to inflict the sight of him on her. Playing for time, I explained, 'Tell you the programme, Anne. When we get down to the boat – half an hour to get to it – well, first you have your bathe, and put Gill's clothes on. There's a hot drink, chocolate and stuff in the boat. Then – thirty minutes by road – car – followed by – well, a hot shower if you want it, and a proper meal and a comfortable bed with clean sheets, and Gill will be with you in the morning – early, I'll be fetching her while you're asleep . . . How's that sound?'

'Like' – her voice quavered, but she controlled it – 'a load of bull. But I'll buy it.'

'You really *are* like your sister . . .'

'What's that mean?'

'Means – well, I thought Gill was a one-off, but there are two of you . . .' I heard her laugh. Actually *laugh*, for Christ's sake, in that hellhole. There'd be a reaction, there'd have to be, no one could be that superhuman . . . Tommy came into the pen, then, and I told her, 'Tommy'll take over here now, Anne. He'll pull out a couple more stones, then you'll be able to climb through. He's a nice guy, you can trust him . . . I've got a small job to do, I'll be back in a few minutes, OK?'

She said, 'Hurry back, please': and she'd begun to cry again. I wished to God I'd been able to bring Gill with us: but Tommy began chatting her up in calm, soothing tones as he set to work on the wall.

Schreiber, now . . .

I jerked him round, sent him stumbling ahead of me towards the gate.

18

We were paddling; I'd stopped the outboard. And the moon had left us, dropping behind the mountains to the north-east; there was a glow in that quarter of the sky still, but here the sea was only a dark mirror for the stars, the land a haze of black with a flickering edging of phosphorescence where the sea licked along the long, shallow curve of the Ölü Deniz beach.

The eastern end of the beach, this was. From the cove where we'd embarked (with Anne bathed, dressed, fed with all the chocolate and biscuits and warmed with the laced tea) I'd driven the inflatable straight out to sea then slanted east for two miles – passing about that same distance south of the Ölü Deniz anchorage, so Raoul in his pillow-case and the *jandarma* in their smart villa on the beachfront wouldn't have heard even a faint mutter of the Yamaha – and then with the north–south stretch of coast in sight ahead I'd turned to port, to run up on this course we were on now. Aiming to land them not on the beach but close to it, tucking the boat inside a small promontory which the chart showed and which I could see now. Tommy, in the bow, had pointed with his paddle, and we'd adjusted our course, to get in there. So slowly the sea might have been treacle.

Anne was beside me in the stern. Silent now, at times shivering, and a few times small sounds from her: reactions to her own thoughts, fears, recent horrors. In due course, no doubt, Gill would hear it all. What part the flail woman had played, for instance. We'd seen nothing of her, or of the other son, although with the sheep scattered and bleating all over the place, and Schreiber's final scream echoing and reverberating through the ruins, I'd thought we would, and while Tommy had carried Anne down to the cove I'd hung back, acting as rearguard, in case they did come after us.

Checking the time again. 0135. These two would be ashore in a few minutes, and Tommy would then have a yomp over sand for several hundred yards, then find his way to the road inland of the built-up area behind the beach – the PTT building, etc. – and the car with Ahmet's pal Ali should be there from 0200 to 0205. If they didn't make it, they'd have an hour to wait: which might be dangerous, on account of the *jandarma*.

Jandarma who one hoped would not have been alerted by any of the night's events. Because those guys aren't diplomats or psychologists or necessarily well disposed towards strangers who move around – or hang around – in darkness. They're regular soldiers, and as I believe I've mentioned they're stationed usually in pairs in every village throughout the vast expanse of Turkey; they're hard-faced, trained to be so. A Turk once explained to me, 'You don't keep order by smiling at people.'

With some kinds of people, I suppose you don't. But I wouldn't have wanted Anne, in her present state, to be subjected to *jandarma* interrogation.

'Stand by, Tommy . . .'

Gliding in. Tommy looking round to see Anne was ready, and putting his gear where he could reach it. He had only the one bag to carry, he'd transferred the papers from *L'Ecstase* to it, would have to remember to leave them – with Anne – at the *Keyiflioğlu*, when he got her there. He'd be handing her over into Ahmet's care, then continuing in the car to the hotel at Göcek. From there on he hoped his friends the Çerçis would ship him up to Istanbul.

He was kneeling on the blister in the bow, using his paddle to test the depth of water. Anne poised to move forward . . . I said, 'I'll say goodbye for the moment, Anne. See you some

306

time tomorrow. But you'll see Gill before that. I want to tell you, I think you're marvellous.'

'No, I'm a *fool*. I – I'm more grateful to you than I can say, but – I feel so *stupid*, and—'

'Very far from stupid. Believe me ... You'll have bad moments, but – try not to dwell on things, just keep in mind it's over – and then talk to Gill, let her help.'

'You're – incredible, Matt—'

Mutual admiration society ... I called, 'Good luck, Tommy.'

'See you. In London – somewhere ...'

He went over the bow, in thigh-deep, reached in over the side then to lift Anne out and carry her to the beach. Back again then for his gear ... 'Matt, you saved my life, I won't forget it.'

'Go on. Fuck off. Be quick, now.'

They weren't visible for long. By the time I'd swung the boat around they were a shifting blur in the dark: then not even that much. And she was in Tommy's hands now, out of mine.

I'd arranged with Ahmet that he'd ask Ali to be here at 0100, 0200, 0300 and 0400, each time for just five minutes. The reason for such short stays was the proximity of the *jandarma*. Their house wasn't more than 500 metres from this end of the beach road. I'd suggested to start with that Ali might park himself there around midnight and just wait – as long as it took – but that way he'd almost certainly have been picked up and questioned. They might even have waited with him, to see what came. Whereas a taxi which might have dropped campers in the woods where the Fethiye road came down by the villages of Hisarönü and Yeniköy might reasonably run on down to this end to turn, maybe hoping to pick up late wanderers; there were a lot of holiday people in tents and cabins in the area.

Ahmet had prefixed his suggestions with yet another of his proverbs: 'Don't roll up your trousers before you get to the river.' I'd then said OK, let him stay at home and wait for a phone call. There *is* a call-box outside the PTT office. But (a) Tommy would have needed tokens, which you have to buy from the desk in the office – which would be shut – and (b) as in other countries, public telephones tend to be out of order

307

when you need them most urgently.

I paddled south, with no intention of starting the motor before I was a mile or so clear. Leaving the beach I was picturing the two of them struggling through soft sand, and Ali behind the wheel of his car watching nervously for *jandarma*.

Soft snoring from the stern cabin. Gill with half an ear to it as she very quietly made herself a mug of coffee. Wearing jeans and sweater: she'd been on deck most of the night.

The *Bird of Dawning* and the big *gulet* that lay near her had this Gemiler anchorage to themselves. And there was obviously no one awake on that Turkish boat. All dead quiet, as peaceful as it had been all night. She'd been up there listening, hour after hour – expecting she didn't know what, but maybe shots, screams, explosions . . .

Now it was past three. Three-twenty – she checked again . . . Matt and Tommy had left, going their separate ways, before nine-thirty, and she'd seen the French yacht move off with its navigation lights burning soon after ten. Matt's estimate for completing that stage of the operation had been ten-thirty, and she'd assumed that the following stages would have been similarly ahead of schedule. He'd told her that he'd allowed for landing Anne and Tommy on the Ölü Deniz beach at any hour from 1 a.m. onward: two and a half hours ago, that would have been.

So by now, *surely* . . .

She'd given up smoking several years ago, but if there'd been a cigarette on board this *Bird* she'd have been sucking in smoke, by now.

Couldn't even pace up and down, for fear of disturbing the Lawries.

She padded up on to the *Bird*'s bow. Bare feet cold on decks wet with seadew. Standing – one hand on the forestay, the furled genoa: fingers of the other drumming on her thigh in the fast tempo of anxiety.

Should have slept: or tried to. Fat hope, though . . .

There'd been a moon for a while, but it hadn't lasted long, had lowered itself behind the high ground that shut off virtually all the northern and eastern sky. Only the stars shed a small amount of light, their reflections more or less static in the

308

still water here inside the channel but quivery at a distance, out beyond the end of the island where she was looking most of the time.

As if looking could produce results, make anything happen faster.

Matt might have been *too* confident. Or not as confident as he'd seemed, might have been putting that on for her benefit. She'd wondered: trusting him, believing him, but still scared – for Anne, him, herself, and hoping he wouldn't see *how* scared.

Black patch, moving . . .

Don't believe it. The darkness, and the deeper shadow from the island were confusing, imagination compounded the illusions . . .

But that was the way he *would* come. Or *they* would – if things had gone wrong, if there'd been a change of plan: meaning failure, in which case Anne—

Holding her breath. Up on her toes, grasping the forestay, straining her eyes: she heard her own whisper – 'Oh God, *please* . . .'

Flicker of whiteness. Salt water scattering from a paddle.

It *was*. It actually *was*!

She had one hand up, waving unseen in the dark: her mouth shaping to scream his name – she shut it, coming to her senses just in time . . . Letting go of the stay, hurrying down the side deck into the stern, to the swimming-ladder . . . She leant with the top rail of the pushpit pressing against her thighs, watching the beetle-like black shape approaching. One guy in it – only one – and the regular dipping of the paddle was easy to see now.

'Matt?'

'Hi. Catch this, will you?'

Tossing her the boat's painter: its end looped itself on the rail and she snatched at it, led it around the stanchion and in over the top of the ladder, hauled him in close and cleated it. Reaching to help: 'Matt, are you OK, did you—'

'Everything's fine . . . Give me some room, would you?'

Then he was on the stern, she was in his arms, and he was telling her 'Kid sister's in good shape, considering what she's been through. In fact she's fantastic . . . Hey, no crying, this is

309

good news – Gill, my darling—'

'Where was she, how did you find her?'

'She was in – you know, one of those ruins. Bottom part of what was a house once, I suppose. Only one way in, and they'd walled it up with heavy stones, leaving gaps they could push food through. Not that they could've given her much, poor kid.'

'*Bastards!*'

'Right. She was very cold, hungry, scared rigid. Well, who wouldn't be. But let me tell you, your kid sister has real guts, she really got herself together in no time at all. Ate all the stuff we brought, drank most of the tea—'

'Was she glad of the chance of clothes?'

'She most certainly was. That was a stroke of genius. But honestly, that girl's a wonder . . .'

I'd decided not to mention that she'd been naked when we'd found her. Anne could tell her, if she wanted to: when she was ready to. She *would* want to, of course: and should, too – infinitely better than keeping it locked up, like some hidden, personal shame.

Which it would be, for a long time. Maybe years, maybe for ever.

'Did you see that old woman?'

'No. Can't say I was looking for her.'

'Anne mention her?'

'No. But we weren't asking any questions, the main thing was to make Anne feel secure with us, hold her together until you can be with her – that's what she needs.'

'So can we go now?'

'Soon as it's light, sure. Don't worry, she's OK meanwhile, I explained—'

'Why not go *now*?'

I explained: this whole scheme had been aimed at me, Tommy and the *Bird* seeming to have nothing to do with Anne's escape from her kidnappers. And yachts don't rush from place to place in the middle of the night for no reason. On the face of it, *we* didn't have a reason. We'd move at first light: it was a rational time to weigh anchor, even a traditional time, natural to a seaman's way of thinking. Then in Fethiye of

310

course we'd get the news: Anne would have been brought along to the *Keyiflіöglu* by a fisherman: she'd been stumbling down the road from Kaya Koy, a farmer had given her a lift in his truck, then this fisherman who like many others had been shown the photo and knew that Ahmet Çevik had been asking around about some missing Yank girl, had found her lost and in tears and delivered her to the *gulet*. None of these kind people would be identifiable, and Anne's story was to be as vague as possible: there'd been fighting among her kidnappers, she'd managed to push some stones out and escape, then found the road and stumbled towards the aura of light in the sky over Fethiye.

'She can realistically not have much memory . . . The less the better. But then – what I said before. When you've spent a little time with her, put her mind at rest, made her feel safe – telephone your embassy in Ankara. Tell 'em what's been going on, and who your father is, the likely form of ransom, and the FBI, all that. My bet is they'll have you and Anne out of Turkey in no time at all.'

'I hope you're right.'

'Will you call your father too?'

'Only to spit in his eye.' She grabbed hold of me, suddenly: 'Matt, I still can't *believe* this! That she's – that you actually did—'

I kissed her: partly to stop the flow. Stroking her: murmuring sweet nothings. Like calming a horse . . . Then: 'About calling your father – you must, you know, and as soon as you can. To let him know the heat's off, no question of any ransom now.'

'Yeah. I guess . . .' In the light seeping up through the hatch I could see the dark smudges of tension and sleeplessness under her eyes. She asked me – we were keeping our voices low, on account of the Lawries down there asleep – 'What did you have to do, Matt? I mean – fight anyone?'

'We had to – subdue a couple of guys. Three actually. Four if you include Raoul. Incidentally, I took Anne's passport and dollars and stuff from that yacht . . . One of the three was the German who attacked you – East German, name of Schreiber.'

'Did you – kill anyone?'

'Didn't have to. Fortunately. Just incapacitated them. Some

311

got tied up and some got dropped down a hole. They deserve to be dead, and at one stage I was – tempted . . .' I took a breath . . . 'Forget it, now. As far as you know, nothing happened tonight. Except I went fishing . . . Kid sister's escape's going to be a smashing surprise for you – OK?'

She nodded. Then: '*Couldn't* we move to Fethiye now?'

'We'd only draw attention to ourselves. Much better not do that. We'll move at first light. Have breakfast, then move.'

'What time's first light?'

'Officially around five, I suppose. But there's no sun here, over those mountains, until about seven, earliest.'

'We can move at five, though?'

'OK. Fethiye before eight, that means. Bet you she'll be still asleep. Bet? Thousand lira?'

'I love you, Matt. Funny thing' – talking fast, suddenly, an outpouring of thoughts saved up during the hours of waiting, maybe – 'I used to think I loved a guy who in fact was absolutely fucking worthless. Now I love you, who in total contrast, Matt my darling' – excitement taking over again: like a loose switch making contact on and off – 'honest to God, I *don't* believe it, I keep pinching myself but I *know* I'm going to wake up and—'

'Hush.' I put a finger on her lips: she'd been getting louder and louder, and I didn't want the Lawries woken . . . 'Let's go down? Fore hatch?'

She murmured later, a damp breath in my ear, 'Remember me saying you acted *old*? How you seemed so fucking *cautious*?'

Shift of mental gear: then the truth: 'I was scared witless.'

'Yeah.' Her sniff was derisive. '*I* bet . . .'

But it was true, I had been – in the intervals when there'd been time to recognize it. Not of personal danger, but of the risk of triggering Anne's murder. We could have done so, easily. Then Gill would have spent the rest of her life as one of the world's walking wounded – because of *me*. The kind of situation I'd steered clear of, in recent years – the 'caution' she'd felt contempt for, an attitude based on the simple truth that if you aren't involved in any lasting way you're less likely to do anyone any lasting harm.

We breakfasted at five. Had to tell the Lawries some of it, of

312

course: Ted would have accepted the bare statement that all was well, no problems: and they could have heard the good news of Anne's escape when we got to Fethiye. But Emma wanted more than that. I let Gill tell her, only interrupting to correct the odd flight of fancy.

Then Gill attended to the weighing of the *Bird*'s anchor for the last time, and we nosed out of the Gemiler channel westbound, in a pearly light with the hills in various shades of mauve over black underpinning: rocks at sea level black, darkness lingering in the land's shadow; we were well out, halfway to Fethiye, before the sun spilled up out of the mountains like a flood of molten lava.

I'd come near to killing Schreiber. At the time it had felt – necessary, *right*. With even a physical need, a kind of ache in the hands and muscles matching the almost irresistible compulsion.

Almost. In fact I think I didn't so much resist it as find I couldn't do it. Maybe if the confrontation had taken place down there in the sheep-pen, in sight and smell of the hole they'd kept her in, I'd have killed him. I don't know. I'm glad I didn't – apart from any other consideration, it wouldn't have been worth the trouble it might have caused me. I don't believe this was in my thinking at the crucial moment: I truly don't remember, I have only this mental picture of Schreiber cringing – doubtless knowing murder when he saw it, and seeing it staring him in the face.

Maybe that was what did it: maybe the word *murder* came to mind, at the sight and sound of his abject terror. Anyway, I gave him an option. He was going into this cistern in one of two ways. I'd knock him senseless and drop him in, or he could make it easier for himself – climb in, hang by his arms from the rim before he dropped.

He found it difficult to make the choice. But I moved towards him, and he made it quickly. Only he couldn't hold his weight on his arms, or his hands slipped, or something. He went straight down, letting out a night-splitting scream as he disappeared into the hole – which luckily must have contained most of the sound of it – and the next sound was the crash as he hit the bottom. No doubt at all, there'd have been some bones broken.

*   *   *

We motored in past Fethiye Adasi just after eight-thirty: the gulf was as smooth as a lake, blazing blue . . . And the story's told now, really – except for tag-ends, scraps. One of them – great news at the time, calling for yet more blessings on the heads of my extraordinarily obliging passengers – was that the Lawries had decided not to return via Malta. They'd as soon, Ted said, end their charter in Athens. It would cost him something, by way of changed air bookings, but this didn't bother him, and we'd get in a few extra days' cruising – real cruising, the kind they'd come for. We'd start northward – they could shop for carpets at the hotel at Göcek, take that trip up the Dalyan river, and we might visit Bodrum: then Rhodes, and from there island-hop across the Aegean. As my next charter was to start in Athens, nothing could have suited me better.

Except I wouldn't have Gill with me.

Everything else turned out pretty well as expected. Gill made her phone call to the US embassy, they checked with Washington, and within hours the Turkish police, who'd been pressing to interrogate Anne, dropped any such intention. Gill was told that the provincial governor had stepped in, on orders from Ankara. Also, in another telephone call, she gathered that Anne would be required to make formal depositions in Washington, under recent legislation about crimes committed against US citizens abroad being punishable under US law and in the USA. The likelihood being that alleged kidnappers – two East Germans and an Algerian now in police custody, one of them under armed police guard in hospital – would be extradited to America, the Turks having intimated that they'd be only too glad to get rid of them.

Rumours abounded: one heard, for instance, that several badly damaged bodies had been found in a cistern in the deserted village, and another in some French yacht. The police major, a rather smart, hawkish-looking guy with the impressive name of Erol Buldanlioğlu, the one who'd been waiting to question Anne – Gill had held him off, until they'd dropped the idea anyway, protesting she wasn't fit for such further ordeal – Major Buldanlioğlu visited me on board the *Bird of Dawning* on the second morning, accepted a cup of coffee and asked me whether during our night at Gemiler Adasi I or my passengers

314

had heard any kind of commotion from the direction of Kaya Koy.

I hadn't, of course. Nor had my passengers; and they confirmed this. I pointed out that there were some very solid hills between that anchorage and the deserted village; one could hardly have expected to hear anything.

'You spent all the night fishing, I understand.'

'*Went* fishing. Didn't catch any.'

'Perhaps you were using the wrong kinds of equipment.'

'Tackle . . . Well, maybe. To be honest, it's the first time I've tried it, in these waters. If I show you the gear I used, maybe you'd advise me – if you're an expert, major?'

'Expert – ah – seeker of truth, Mr Johnson. Not fishing.' The hawk eyes weren't unfriendly, only very shrewd. 'You must be a man of much patience – to stay out all night while catching nothing. Are you certain you caught nothing of any kind?'

'Not even a cold.' I glanced at the Lawries. 'But I'd promised these people fresh fish for breakfast, you see, and I hate to disappoint my customers.'

Ted offered, 'He's a bloody fine sailor, any road.'

The major nodded. 'You have friends also here in Turkey, Mr Johnson, who speak well of you.' The stare was unwavering. 'But you would be wise not to take further advantage – excuse my poor use of English – I should say, not to spoil the welcome you receive here.'

I think I looked puzzled. The ingenuous, clean-living sailor could hardly have surmised that he was being told to keep his nose clean from here on in. Talk became general, then, chit-chat with the Lawries, who were suitably – and genuinely – complimentary on their impressions of Turkey on this first visit.

There'd been nothing as yet in any of the three- to four-day-old UK newspapers about any development in the Fountain murder inquiry. Tommy might have been back in England by about this time – or maybe not yet, but anyway I knew I'd hear from him in due course. He'd promised to write full and detailed reports, and send any news cuttings, in care of poste restante here in Marmaris, and I'd have that to look forward to – I hoped, with fingers crossed and, as Gill phrased it, 'knocking on wood' – when I got back here with my next lot of charterers.

One point of interest, and for the record – about the flail-woman. Anne told Gill she wasn't the ogress we'd imagined her to be. She'd used that flail as a deterrent to keep her sons away from the cell in the sheep-pen. It had been the bearded German's decision to take Anne's clothes from her; he'd been in charge of this end of the operation, and stripping kidnap victims is a fairly standard gambit, aimed primarily at the destruction of morale. The old woman had done it, on his orders, but angrily and reluctantly – as much as anything, Anne guessed, from knowing the effect it would have on her simple-minded, earthy 'boys'; and she'd driven them off several times, when they'd been trying to see through gaps in the walled-up doorway.

It was amazing, I thought, and to Anne's enormous credit, that she'd come out of it sane. Equally, it sickened me to think that at some future date the people who'd inflicted such things on her would be walking around free, still passing themselves off as human beings.

I saw Major Buldanlıöğlu a second time – at the airport, Dalaman, where I'd gone to see Gill and Anne off to Istanbul, the first stage of their flight home to the States. When he'd visited me on the boat he'd been in plain clothes, but this time he was in uniform and he'd come to say goodbye to them formally, representing the local police chief or maybe the governor, I don't remember. He made Anne a brief but charming speech, regretting the barbarous treatment she'd received on Turkish territory, and expressing the hope that she'd return one day in happier circumstances.

Then he nodded to me. 'Mr Johnson. You are sailing from Fethiye this evening, I believe. Your business here all finished, eh?'

'I'll be back – in three weeks or so. My business is charter-cruising, major.'

'Of course. I would – how d'you say? – stick to it, if I were you.'

'I hope to.' Maybe he wasn't sure I'd got the message, last time. I added, 'This is the best cruising area in the Mediter-ranean.'

'How nice to hear so.' He smiled as he saluted: hard-eyed behind the smile. I'd been warned – again – and I was reminded of Charles Harrison. Police forces of the world uniting, beady eyes on Johnson. Only the FBI – I'd gathered – approved of Johnson, who'd saved them from having to leave Anne Brennan to be murdered. Gill had guessed right: whatever it was the kidnappers had been demanding, they weren't to have been given it.

Buldanlïöglu had gone; I turned back to Gill. Anne drifting away: there was a minuscule duty-free counter and she'd said in the taxi she might take a bottle of *raki* home for her father. Gill had commented, 'Quart of strychnine might be neater.'

Gill, the original of the species . . . Eye to eye, kissing-range, and anonymous in the crowd. But I had only a limited share of her attention now; most of it was focussed on Anne, who was going to need all of big sister's support for – well, I suppose for as long as it took. To me the symptoms weren't obvious – Anne hiding most of it under her shell, of course – but Gill had told me she cried a lot and had terrifying dreams, also that she was still fixated on Raoul: knowing the brutal facts but still clinging to her earlier concept of him, memories of Raoul the tender lover.

Easier on herself that way, I suppose. Clinging to that image as protection against the knowledge of having been so completely suckered, so devastatingly humiliated.

I held Gill's hands. There were things that might have been said: but we could read them in each other's eyes, none of them needed *saying*.

So – in keeping with the surroundings – an attempt at small-talk . . .

'You'll miss the Fourth.'

'Oh.' A shrug. This was the third – third of July – and she'd be in London tonight, in the air again tomorrow. 'I suppose . . .'

'Gill, darling – please come back—'

I'd been going to say, in a dimly joking sort of way, 'please come back before the *next* Fourth of July': but she broke in, hissing, 'Of *course* I'll bloody well—'

Anne – rejoining us, brittly flippant – 'Don't you dare get mad with this guy. He's my hero . . .'

317

'Gill—'

She glanced back, frowning . . . 'Gill, darling – this winter, if I could set up some charters in the Caribbean, say November to February—'

'Think you *could*?'

'Damn sure, if you could—'

'Look.' That impatient jerk of her head. 'Just wire me. Wire me where and when. OK?'

Ten minutes later, watching them walk out to the aircraft, at least I had that straw to clutch at.